Follow the trail of breadcrumbs . . .

"Vanishments," Sir Hanson read. "Mysterious vanishments within the Dark Woods, cause unknown, sorcery suspected." He shook his head. "But that's impossible. Who'd go *into* the Dark Woods these days? Everyone *knows* that they're rife with witches who'd turn a child into gingerbread and gobble him up before you can blink. And since the construction of the Dark Woods Bypass, there's no need to risk traveling through this unholy place. Only a fool would do so."

Once more, Sir Hanson's head filled with the king's indignant voice giving him his assignment: *We're not talking about a bunch of children or village idiots here, Hanson; we're talking about some of the most cunning, ruthless, successful merchants in my realm! These were not stupid men, and yet, they were all last observed going into the Dark Woods and not coming out again.*

Men? Sir Hanson had echoed. *But in the old tales, isn't it always children who—*

His Majesty cared not a festering fig for the old tales. *Do you think I'd be wasting any of my manpower if this was about* children? *Children do not pay taxes, or see fit to remember their beloved king with appropriately lavish gifts at Yuletide. To the fuming pits with the children: These are* real *people who've vanished, and I want to know the reason why!*

—from "Crumbs" by Esther M. Friesner

FANTASY GONE WRONG

EDITED BY
Martin H. Greenberg
and Brittiany A. Koren

DAW BOOKS, INC.
DONALD A. WOLLHEIM, FOUNDER
375 Hudson Street, New York, NY 10014
ELIZABETH R. WOLLHEIM
SHEILA E. GILBERT
PUBLISHERS
www.dawbooks.com

First Printing, September 2006
1 2 3 4 5 6 7 8 9

DAW TRADEMARK REGISTERED
U.S. PAT. OFF. AND FOREIGN COUNTRIES
—MARCA REGISTRADA.
HECHO EN U.S.A.

PRINTED IN THE U.S.A.

ACKNOWLEDGMENTS

For Robert J. Ambrose,
When my reality wasn't always what I expected,
And my fantasies were far from coming true,
You were there to listen.
Thanks, Dad, for always knowing.

—B.A.K.

CONTENTS

INTRODUCTION

Brittiany A. Koren

Late one evening, my husband and I were talking, bouncing ideas off one another about our future and looking back to see if our lives had turned out to be the way we had tried to plan it. Not quite, but we decided we were content in our amusement, as we quietly tucked our three children into bed after numerous drinks of water, teeth brushing, and finding the correct stuffed animals. Again, all was still in the house. A peaceful time for reflection. It was a night like most, still I'll remember it the rest of my life. It was also the night the wheels began turning for this anthology.

Why was there such a fascination with humorous fantasy that was making more headway into the theaters? My personal favorites were movies like *Shrek* and *Ella Enchanted* that I had enjoyed many times, watching along with my kids. But still, what was so interesting about stories that went wrong? They weren't the typical epic fantasy, but still had all the context of one.

Well, I decided, so many times there is an expectancy of where our lives should be and where it's going to end up. As in most stories there is a path, if you will, that we should be on. However, that path isn't always the right one we need to have under our feet, although, sometimes it still leads us to where we need to go even if it makes getting there a little more bumpy.

The stories herein are just that. It's slapstick humor with all the elements of a good fantasy: dragons, elves, knights in shining armor, quests, and the occasional talking magical creature.

I asked sixteen wonderful authors to write stories about a fantasy with a little humor (after all, everyone needs to laugh) and an irony to the story that was far from being foreseen, stories where the paths were far from the expected. And I'm very pleased with the results. From Mickey Zucker Reichert's "Battle of Wits" where the battle is more in the mind than on the field, to Lisanne Norman's story about how gaming can sometimes be more lifelike than reality in "Is This Real Enough" to Brian Stableford's "The Poisoned Chalice" where an elf wonders if his quest will ever end. All the stories are rich with prose that will make you laugh and make you wonder how your own life has taken that different path. And how you've survived to become the wiser, or at least enjoyed the scenery along the way. I greatly enjoyed reading these tales and I want to thank these outstanding authors for sharing their talents and showing us their version of fantasy gone wrong.

THE POISONED CHALICE

Brian Stableford

Brian Stableford hopes to publish his hundredth book before the end of 2006. Titles that are helping him through the nineties include *Kiss the Goat: A Twenty-First Century Ghost Story* from Prime Press, translations of various volumes in Paul Feval's pioneering crime fiction series featuring the Habits Noirs—beginning with *Salem Street*—from Black Coat Press, and a definitive reference book, *Science Fact and Fiction*, from Routledge.

WORLD'S EDGE 4 MILES said the relevant arm of the signpost. At least, that's what it said now. The 4 replaced a scratched-out 5, which had replaced a scratched-out 6, and so on to 10. There had been other numbers before that, but someone had repainted the sign some years ago to make way for a new set.

The signpost's only other surviving arm was set at right angles to the first. Since the repainting the hamlet to which it pointed the way had apparently changed its name to

Brinkville. The arm pointing in the direction from which Umsonofer had come had been broken off.

The elf lowered his backpack to the ground and sat down on it. His long journey was almost over. He was very tired. It was nearly sundown, and he'd been walking since noon. There was a stream beside the road, making its leisurely way to the Big Drop, and he knelt down with cupped hands to take a drink. He intended to go on, by starlight if necessary, until he reached his destination. There would be time enough to start looking for somewhere to sleep, and perhaps get a bite to eat, on the way back.

When he stood up and turned around, though, he found that he was hemmed in by three stout dwarfs. He was a foot taller than any one of them, but his girth measurement was a good yard less. Had he had time to draw his poniard, he'd have had a substantial advantage in reach, but they were crowding him and their two-headed axes were already in their hands.

"This is a really bad idea, lads," he said.

"No it's not," said the oldest of the dwarfs. "Since you're on your way to die, you won't be needing any of your luggage, so the charitable thing to do is to drop your pack and your dagger, and take off your clothes. It's a balmy evening, so you won't get cold before you jump— and if you do, it'll give you an incentive to run to meet your fate."

"I'm not a jumper," Umsonofer told them. "I have to throw something off the edge, but then I'm coming back. You can rob me on the way home, if you want to."

"No need to lie about it, old son," said the dwarf. "We don't mind suicide around here—it's our chief source of income these days. Don't get many elves, mind—but then, you don't look much of an elf. A touch of the human in your family tree, I shouldn't wonder."

The insult was gratuitous. Umsonofer's family had been pure elf for at least fifty generations. On the other hand, fifty generations wasn't that much, by elvish standards, even though it extended to a past more remote than the Seven Magic Wars, the Troll Rebellion, the Invasion of the Giant Moths, and the Great Moon Disaster. There was, of course, no proof that the Ers of any previous era had ever erred in that uniquely perverted fashion, but such appearances tended to persist, like stains that would never wash out. Now that humans were finally extinct, people would probably forget, in time, what "a touch of human" might look like—but the world might have dwindled to a mere boulder by then.

The elf had met dwarfish bandits before, in lands where the Rule of Law was a great deal more secure than it was hereabouts, and he knew what the best tactic was for dealing with a situation like this. He picked up his pack, leaped over the stream with a single mighty bound, and took off at a run. Dwarfs' legs were even shorter than their bodies; they couldn't run to save their lives. That, presumably, was why they were so stubborn and tough in armed self-defense.

The land on the other side of the stream had been cultivated within the last ten years, but it had lain fallow long enough to accumulate the usual litter of scrub, including some rather nasty brambles. It wasn't the ideal ground for sprinting—but it was, alas, entirely suitable for setting an ambush. There were two more dwarfs crouching in the bushes, and they had a trip rope. Umsonofer hadn't taken twelve paces before he was brought crashing to the ground with a bone-jarring thump.

He had been holding on to the pack with iron determination, but the impact jarred him so badly that he lost his grip. When he was eventually able to sit up again, he had been disarmed and the dwarfs had already ripped his pack apart, immediately identifying the most interesting and mysterious object within. They had dropped the rest of his meager possessions in order to study the magical seal on the black leather bag, although one of the five was hanging back, standing over him in a calculatedly menacing attitude.

"Have to take it to the village," one of the dwarfs was saying. "Need the sorceress to get into that."

"Then we'll have to split the take twenty ways instead of five," another complained. "And the old woman will want at least double."

"Best to torture the elf here until he opens it for us," opined a third.

"I don't know the spellkey!" Umsonofer was quick to protest. "And if I did . . . opening that bag would cause the death of everyone present."

"Sure," said the oldest dwarf. "I never heard *that* one before. He really might not know the spellkey, though— and if we apply gentle persuasion out here, his screams will likely attract more than the lads from the village. Best take him home, just in case. Smack him over the head would you, Potbelly."

"You don't under—" Umsonofer began, before the double-headed axe descended upon him.

Umsonofer woke soaking wet, with a terrible headache. Someone had thrown water over him to bring him around. He rapidly figured out that he had been hit with the flat of the axe rather than the edge, but he wasn't sure whether he ought to be grateful for that. He opened his eyes to find himself propped up in a sitting position, with a roof over his head and a fire near his feet. It was difficult to see much else because of all the dwarfs crowding around him. Dwarfs had a less generous sense of personal space than elves, presumably because their flesh was so ambitious in extending from its vertical axis.

There were three females present, but it wasn't hard to identify the sorceress. She had only one eye, only one tooth, and the craziest eyes Umsonofer had ever seen. Sorcery was a costly business; the power it gave its practitioners to defy cause and effect tended to be debited from their health and welfare in other ways.

The sorceress didn't beat about the bush. "I can't open this, darling," she said. "Not without the spellkey—or something to set me on the right track. Shaggyback here says you don't know it—which is a pity, if true, because it's going to take a long time to feed you to the fire feet first."

"Did he also tell you that opening the bag would kill you all?" Umsonofer asked her. "Your hairy friend thought it was just a ploy, but he didn't have the time or the wit to think it through. You know magic, though, and you've been trying to break into the bag for hours. Why do you think I was on my way to throw it over the edge of the world, if it's something valuable? What do *you* think it might be?"

The crazy eyes narrowed. "Why don't you tell us what's in it?" the crone said finally. "Who knows—we might believe you."

"It's a weapon left over from the Magic Wars," Umsonofer said, knowing that they weren't going to believe him, even though it was the truth. "Forged by the last surviving coven of human magicians—the Brotherhood of the Unseeing Eye—when they knew that defeat and extinction were inevitable. It was their last bid to take all the other races with them: a doomsday weapon. They called it the Poisoned Chalice."

"Never heard of it," the sorceress retorted—but there was an extra glimmer of light in her mad eye. She *had* heard of the Brotherhood of the Unseeing Eye, and understood the kind of lust that might lead the magically ambitious to sacrifice both their eyes instead of the more usual one.

"Few people have heard of it because few who've encountered it have survived to tell the tale," Umsonofer told her, "but you might have felt its existence, in your wildest dreams."

"When you live in Brinkville, darling," the seeress told him darkly, "you can always feel the world dissolving under you, even when you're wide awake and haven't touched a potion in a fortnight."

"Believe it or not," Umsonofer said, "it's not much better a thousand miles closer to the center—not since the seventh war ended, in fact. Our sorcerers reckon that we might just turn the corner, if we can get rid of *that* for good and all. Why else would I have come all this way?"

"To jump," the oldest male dwarf put in. "Just like everybody else who comes this way."

"If I wanted to jump," Umsonofer pointed out, "I'd have given you the pack, and my clothes too. I tried to run away—doesn't that suggest that I had no desire to die?"

"Start feeding him to the fire," suggested a voice from the crowd. "If he hasn't coughed up the spellkey by the time we reach his knees, we can slit his throat and cook the rest of him properly. There's not much meat on him, but he'll see us through to the weekend."

"You know better than that, Mother," Umsonofer said to the sorceress, who certainly didn't look as if she hadn't touched a potion for a fortnight, or slept peacefully for the best part of a year. "You've felt this moment creeping up on you for weeks. If you can just remember your dreams, and interpret them correctly. . . ."

"Shut up!" said the old female, with such vituperation

that Umsonofer knew he'd hit a raw nerve. Unfortunately, he also knew that it wasn't always a good idea to hit nerves as raw as that, especially when they belonged to people as corrupted by long exercise of the Black Arts as the dwarf sorceress seemed to be.

"I'll make up my own mind," she said, "when I see what's in the bag. Tell me the spellkey—or as much of it as you know."

"What's in the bag," Umsonofer told her, "is a chalice—a drinking cup. It seems to be made of gold, and studded with precious gems, but that's just glamor. The same glamor will fill you with a raging thirst, and you'll try to drain the cup, but the cup doesn't drain. No matter how fast you drink, there's always more liquid inside. It's said that it tastes exceedingly sweet, but I wouldn't know. What I do know is that when your thirst is slaked, you drift off into sleep, and never wake up."

"It's just a tale," said Shaggyback.

"It might not be," the old woman said. "Better let me look before anyone else—I can see through any glamor. It won't hurt me."

"Yes it will," the elf said insistently. "Nothing with intelligence can resist the sight of it."

"Better let Hammertoes take the first look, then," said someone in the crowd—at which point a scuffle broke out.

"Stop that!" Shaggyback commanded. "He's lying. Somebody had to put it *in* the bag. If it was put in, it can be taken out. Right, Mother?" He obviously hadn't taken the hint about the Brotherhood of the Unseeing Eye.

"It could be direly dangerous," the sorceress opined gravely. "I'd need at least a forty percent share of the sale price—not for myself, you understand, but to keep my potion stocks up to strength, for the sake of the common good."

While the haggling went on, Umsonofer had time to think. He could see only one way out of his predicament that would leave his feet intact for the walk to the end of the world, so when the dwarfs had settled their dispute, he told the sorceress what the spellkey was. Then he shut his eyes, and waited.

Fortunately, having such a tremendous advantage of numbers, the dwarfs hadn't bothered to tie their prisoner up. More than once, in similar situations, Umsonofer had had to work himself free before he could even begin groping around for the chalice.

The game of seek-and-find had never been unduly difficult, because no one had ever contrived to hide the doomsday device, or even release it in such a way that it fell into a deep hole or rolled into an inconveniently narrow gap. Even so, it was never pleasant rummaging among so many dead bodies—and it wasn't just the chalice he had to find. He also had to find the bag in which to secure it. Even though he was only four miles away, he could hardly walk to the edge of the world with his eyes tightly shut—not, at least, if he hoped to come back safely from the brink.

It took him ten minutes to locate the chalice, and another thirty to find the bag, put the chalice inside, and recite the spellkey to seal it again.

By the time he opened his eyes again the only source of light was the red glow of the fire's dwindling embers; the last of the candles the dwarfs had lit before proceeding to their fatal orgy had flickered out. Fortunately his long experience as a groper in the dark had taught Umsonofer to take such difficulties in his ample stride. He located more candles easily enough, and there was enough heat left in the embers to set one aglow. He had been anxious, when the dwarfs had begun to discuss cooking and eating him, that there might not be a crumb to eat in the house, but he found some bread and salted meat, and even a few potatoes—but he wasn't about to start cooking in the midst of twenty reeking corpses when he was only four miles short of his goal.

There had been a certain amount of fighting over the chalice, as there always was, but once the dwarfs had all had a chance to slake their uncanny thirst, the party had lost its zip. They had all had time to lie down and make themselves comfortable before passing away. The expressions on their faces were by no means blissful; their dreams had turned to nightmares before the end. Umsonofer was glad to close the door behind him.

He had brought a candle out with him, mounted in a ray, but its light was very feeble. The clouds weren't supposed to drift beyond the world's limit, but the clouds presently in the sky had either lost their bearings or didn't know the rule; the few stars visible through the gaps shed too little light to help him comfortably on his way. The building in which he'd been confined had been the hamlet's communal blockhouse, but the shadows of several other sleeping huts were discernible in the gloom, as were two big barns and a couple of empty pigsties. He could have bedded himself down for the night easily enough, but he wasn't sure that the chalice had killed every dwarf in the neighborhood. Besides, there might be worse things than bandit dwarfs around—things that could scent dead meat from miles away, once the breeze had carried it that far.

In any case, his head was hurting too much to let him sleep.

Umsonofer started walking as soon as he had figured out which way the edge of the world must lie. He used his left hand to protect the flame of his candle from the wind, and resisted the temptation to move so quickly that he would be in danger of tripping. He had to make every effort to avoid breaking his neck and leaving the chalice to be picked up by some greedy ghoul or inquisitive ogre, who might carry it back in toward the center. Eventually he found the bank of the stream he had jumped earlier, and followed its course toward the Big Drop.

"Why me?" he asked himself, talking aloud in order to have the company of his voice. "Why, of all the elves in all the world, did I have to end up with this lousy job?"

The questions were rhetorical—which was perhaps as well, given that Umsonofer was no philosopher. The simple answer was that somebody had to do it who knew how to keep his eyes tightly shut and his wits about him. When it came to not peeping, Umsonofer was a real champion; it wasn't a talent that was useful for much else, but in this particular context it was invaluable—and Ladamesansmerci, the greatest elvish sorceress in the world, had spotted it. If only she hadn't been 666 years old, the gratitude she'd expressed when he'd agreed to take on the mission would have been a good deal easier to bear.

In daylight, even in his present wretched state, Umsonofer would have covered the four miles to the world's edge in an hour. In the dark it took more than two. He never lost his footing, though, and—even more importantly—he managed to see the edge before accidentally stepping over it. His candle sputtered out immediately thereafter, but that didn't matter. Although there were clouds massing in the sky behind him, the sky above the empty space that stretched away from the world's rim was much clearer, and the sky directly in front of him was full of stars.

Although he had an elf's height, and had come to a stop no more than ten elvish paces from the world's edge, Umsonofer couldn't see whether the stars extended downward to form a vast sphere around the floating world—as orthodox opinion had it—or whether their realm came to a stop somewhere beneath the horizontal, giving way to a bottomless pit of darkness, as some minority believers asserted. He couldn't tell, either, whether the world was a flat disk like a dinner plate or the flat top of an infinitely deep column. The temptation to take a look over the edge was easily resistible for an elf with his talent for not peeking.

He took the bag containing the chalice out of his pack, and hurled it with all his might. It was a good throw; the bag sailed over the rim of the world and fell out of sight. Perhaps it would fall forever, and perhaps not. Umsonofer didn't care about that, just as long as it never came back. In spite of his headache he felt a surge of relief and a sense of triumph as he turned on his heel to head back to civilization.

Alas, the ground gave way beneath his feet as the edge of the world suffered yet another landslip, and he found himself falling, along with a slowly disintegrating mass of stony soil and tangled vegetable matter.

At first he was lost in confusion, and the shadow of the world seemed to fill half the sky, but once Umsonofer had been falling for an hour or so—by which time panic had faded into numb acceptance of his destiny—he was able to determine a few mildly intriguing facts.

The world was definitely not the flat top of a cylindrical column; it was a disk, albeit one that was much flatter on top than underneath, its nether surface being curved and exceedingly lumpy. Nor was the disk supported on any other structure or entity; it floated free, buoyed up against the force that had gripped Umsonofer by some mysterious counterforce. All this he could see by the light of the sun, which now seemed horizontal to his own position as it painstakingly made its way around the bottom of the world prior to rising again in the east.

The stars did not form a perfect sphere around the world—or if they did, there was something else between the nether surface of the world and the downward stars, something that was considerably broader than the world. It looked like a vast glowing mist, although he could not tell from his present height whether it glowed by its own light or merely reflected the light of the sun.

As the world continued to dwindle in the sky, until it was no more than a coin-size black circle eclipsing a mere dozen stars, Umsonofer realized how tiny and insignificant a creature he was, and how small the world was by comparison with the universe that contained it. Although he had never been a philosopher, the idea that there might be more worlds than one, scattered upon the face of infinity like seeds on a freshly plowed field, seemed slightly more relevant, as well as more likely, than it ever had before.

"Well," he said philosophically, "I guess I'll die a wiser elf than I've lived."

The stars were growing dimmer, though, because Umsonofer's view was compromised by the slowly spreading detritus of the landslip. When he had started to fall, the ground that had given way had all been beneath him; but as the huge clod came apart, some of the particles were rising up around him—or, to be strictly accurate, appeared to do so because they were falling at a slightly lower speed than he was. He was gradually enveloped by a haze in which particles of dust mingled with what he first took for rain, although he eventually realized that it must be water from the stream he had followed to the world's edge—which, Umsonofer realized now, had probably been a stupid thing to do.

If he fell far enough—and he had, as yet, no particular

reason to think that he might not fall forever—the debris falling with him might eventually become dense enough to blind him and choke him. In the meantime, he could probably obtain enough water to avoid dying of thirst, although hunger might be a different matter.

"Well," the elf said, trying desperately to find a bright side to his predicament, "at least I got rid of the human doomsday weapon. Elfkind is safe—along with dwarf-kind, trollkind, and all the rest—until the world falls apart completely. Which won't be for tens of thousand of years, at the present rate of attrition. I'm a hero."

He still had some bread and salted meat in his pocket, so he was able to make a meal while he fell—and then, as his headache eased sufficiently, he was able to go to sleep.

His dreams were pleasant enough—at least, that was the impression he had before he forgot them completely.

As he emerged by degrees from sleep—without opening his eyes—Umsonofer's first impression was that he must still be falling through empty space, but he found out quickly enough that he was lying on something solid, which felt like compacted earth. Evidently, Umsonofer thought—conscientiously applying his newfound wisdom—the philosophers who favored the idea that bodies falling in empty space did so with a constant and relatively gentle velocity were not the crazy dreamers that almost everyone assumed.

He opened his eyes, but it was pitch-dark.

"Hello?" he croaked. He had not intended to croak, but it took him some little while to moisten his mouth enough to call out more loudly. "Is anyone there?"

There was a meager trickle of light as a feeble lantern was unshielded. "Shh!" said a voice. "The little ones are trying to sleep."

By the wan light of the lantern, Umsonofer saw a face looming out of the darkness a few feet from his own. He had never seen a human face before, except in cautionary works of art, but he had no difficulty recognizing this one for what it was—an adolescent human female—and he cried out in horror.

"It's all right," a slightly peevish voice informed him. "You're not in the afterworld, condemned to eternal torment for the genocidal crimes of your vile species. You're in the Web, where all the world's jumpers end up—in a burrow actually, a quarter of a mile or so from where the lump that came down with you ended up. Might make a nice burrow itself, that one, although we probably won't need another for a long time to come, unless you're the first of a whole crowd. The scavengers are picking over it at present—not much in the way of edible tubers, they reckon, but plenty of nice fat worms, and they'll be able to fill their bottles and skins from the waterfall while they're over that way."

Umsonofer's eyes had adjusted to the light well enough to show him that they were in some sort of cave, thirty feet in diameter at its widest, with tunnel entrances at either end. Apart from the human adolescent there were half a dozen sleeping children lying to either side of him. He felt a pang of relief as he realized that they weren't all human. One was an elf; three were dwarfs.

"Don't get many elf jumpers in these parts," the human said. "Little Mindarofurk will be pleased to meet you, and so will Landameofurkh. I'm Isabel, by the way."

"I'm not a jumper," Umsnofer said dully. "I fell."

"You'd be surprised how many say that," Isabel told him. "It's okay to change your mind on the way down; practically everybody does. Something to do with getting the world's problems in perspective as you watch it shrink to insignificance, according to the oldster elves. I was born down here, of course, like all human folk for a dozen generations. And no, we're not at war with elves and dwarfs. Down here, we all work together—have to, because of the spiders. If you loathe humans as much as some of your kind, you're welcome to try your luck with the spiders, but I wouldn't recommend it."

"Giants, are they?" Umsonofer asked.

"Oh yes—but that's not the half of it. Spiders can only eat liquid food, so if they catch you they truss your arms and legs up in swathes of silk and feed you all sorts of things to fatten you up, until they shoot you full of poison that dissolves your insides, so they can suck you slowly dry. They're seriously nasty—and clever too. Hang on—here's the oldsters coming back in a hurry. They've probably got one on their tail."

As she completed the last sentence more humans began to wriggle out of both tunnel entrances, in company with dwarfs. The sole elf came last of all, making up a party of nine. All the newcomers were dragging sacks made of some kind of silk, heavy with miscellaneous plunder.

It was the elf who came to speak to Umsonofer. "I'm Landameofurkh," she said. "Has Isabel told you where you are?"

Umsonofer introduced himself. "Some kind of spider-web beneath the world," he said. "More specifically, in a burrow excavated in one of the larger lumps of earth that's recently fallen off our world's edge."

"Right," said Landameofurkh. "How are you feeling? Still want to die, or are you ready to take a second stab at life?"

"I never did want to die," Umsonofer told her. "I just came to the edge of the world to throw something off and got caught by a land. . . . " The *slip* stuck in his throat as he saw, over Landameofurkh's shoulder, one of the humans take the bag containing the poisoned chalice out of his silken sack.

"Feels like a cup," the human announced, palpating the chalice inside its container. "Can't get the bag open, though. Some kind of elvish spellseal on it. Bag might be as useful as whatever's inside, if we can get the trick of it. How about it, Landameofurkh?"

It occurred to Umsonofer that the sensible thing to do was to keep quiet, and not let on that he knew anything about the mysterious bag—but Landameofurkh had seen the expression on his face, and he had already told her too much.

"That's what you threw off the edge?" the elf said to him. "Why?"

"It's a weapon," he said, tersely. "Something too dangerous to look at. Fatal, in fact."

"That's silly," said the human who was holding the bag. "Who could possibly make a weapon that was fatal to anyone who looked at it?" He was presumably descended from humans who had jumped before the last of the Magic Wars; he'd never heard of the Brotherhood of the Unseeing Eye.

"A blind man," Umsonofer told him tersely. "Or a whole company of blind men."

"Is that *man* in the broad sense, or the narrow sense?" the human asked, although he must have known that when an elf said "man" he invariably meant "human."

"Don't try to open it," Umsonofer said. "If you have any sorcerers down here, don't take it to them. Just let it be. In fact, if there's a bottom side to this Webworld, just let me take it down there and drop it again."

"Human manufacture," said the human softly, glancing sideways at the three other adult members of his species who were present, and then at Isabel. "Not so dangerous then, considering how the Wars eventually worked out. Are you disappointed to discover that it's only the humans on the flying island who were exterminated?"

"That's not fair, Kasimir," Landameofurkh objected. "Down here, we all work together. The only enemy we have is the spiders.

"Absolutely," Kasimir said. "And the only weapons we have are sticks and stones and a few blunt knives. So if *this* one will work on spiders, it might be useful, no matter how dangerous it is to elves, dwarfs, and the like."

"Humans too," Umsonofer was quick to say, realizing the direction in which Kasimir's thoughts were heading. "Humans made it, that's true—but not until all hope of winning the war was lost. It wasn't intended to turn the tide—it was intended to drag the other races down along with humans. *Anyone* who looks at it falls victim to it— anyone with the intelligence to be deluded by its glamor. It wouldn't work against a spider, though, no matter how big."

Kasimir thought about it for a moment before saying: "You can't know that. You can't know that it kills humans, if you elves didn't find it until the last human in the world was already dead—and you can't know that it won't kill the spiders down here, since we know far better than you how smart they are. But Landameofurkh's right—down here, we all work together, so I don't want you or anyone else endangered. We can test both questions at the same time, if you'll tell me the spellkey. Three spiders chased us away from the fresh fall and they're prowling around outside right now. One of us—one of us humans, that is—can take the bag to the burrow entrance, and open it there. If it kills the spiders, but not the man, we'll finally have the means to turn the tide in this long losing battle of ours. If it kills the spiders *and* the man, someone with his eyes tight shut will have to put it back in the bag, and we'll have to make careful plans for its future use. If it kills the man but not the spiders, then I'll agree with you that it's useless, and we'll drop it off the bottom of the world—but we have to try. We got a lot more jumpers in the old days than we do nowadays, and we've been dying faster than our kids are born for twenty years and more."

Umsonofer told his new allies that it wasn't as simple as that, but they wouldn't believe him. They argued for a long time, but Kasimir was implacable. He was determined to try the experiment, even if he had to keep his eyes shut while he did so; like most humans, he had been born a philosopher.

If Kasimir had been an elf, or even a dwarf, Umsonofer would have tried harder to talk him out of it, but Umsonofer's own feelings were more mixed now than they had ever been before. Isabel might think that it was elfkind that was unutterably vile and worthy of eternal torment, but elfkind didn't see things that way at all, and Umsonofer had been carrying the human doomsday weapon in his pack for far too long. He even contrived, in the end, to tell himself that the glamor might not work down here, in a society that plainly had no use for gold and precious gems.

"All right," Umsonofer said finally. "You can take it to the burrow entrance and try it on the spiders—but I'll be right behind you in the tunnel. If it doesn't work, the chalice is going straight back into the bag until I can figure out a way of getting rid of it for good. And if you value your life, you'll keep your eyes shut—no peeking."

When the time came, Umsonofer crept along the tunnel in Kasimir's wake, until the human stopped. The tunnel was just about wide enough for Umsonofer to squeeze past the human to recover the cup, if things went as badly awry as he expected—and once he had got it back into the bag, he would have time to take stock of the situation before deciding what to do next.

He whispered the spellkey, to make sure that no one but Kasimir would obtain the deadly information—and then he closed his eyes, as he had done so many times before.

When the human went limp, and his sphincter muscles relaxed, Umsonofer felt a curious shiver pass along his own body, which was not entirely composed of fatalistic sadness. There was something in him that was not displeased to have proof that the human doomsday weapon really did work on humans too. He squeezed past the corpse and began groping about for the chalice of death and its protective container.

Neither of them was anywhere to be felt.

Umsonofer moved farther and farther forward, unable to judge how far he had emerged from the burrow's entrance, or what kind of menace might be lurking there.

He knew he had overreached, though, when he was roughly seized at the shoulders by a pair of massive jaws, as strong and precise as magic-tempered bronze, which dragged his lower body from its protective hole like an ill-fitting cork from a bottle. He felt something akin to a broad needle stab him in the back of the neck.

Umsonofer woke to find his arms and legs trussed up tight—not bound together but separately glued to rope-like strands that stretched him out like a letter *X*. He remembered what Isabel had said about the spiders fattening their victims up before liquefying their insides, and wondered how long the business of food-preparation would last.

He wondered, too, whether it might be best not to open his eyes, given that he had no idea where the chalice was, but decided in the end that he had little enough to lose.

He had not expected the spiders to be quite as abominable as they were. They were as big as elephants, with much longer and hairier legs. They were black as night, and there was something in the way they moved, so smoothly and silently, that flooded his consciousness with pure fear. Their heads seemed surprisingly *sticky*, their tentacular palps—each as big and flexible as the limbs of a giant octopus—glistening with what might have been saliva. Their multitudinous eyes glowed crimson.

Hung up as he was, above the upper plane of the web, on a dendritic frame of some kind, Umsonofer could see at least forty spiders at various distances. Only two of them were studying him at close range, but that was more than enough. He had been unlucky enough in the course of his life to encounter half a dozen ghouls, three ogres, two chimeras, and a mad dog, not to mention various would-be assassins of the dwarf and goblin species, but he had always been able to turn on his heel and run like hell, ultimately outdistancing his adversaries. He had never seen anything half as awful as one of these spiders, and had never experienced such utter helplessness.

By way of distraction, the elf wondered whether the web was a sort of world, floating like his own in the ether, or whether it was the bottom layer of all existence, stretching like an aerialist's safety net from one end of the universe to the other, set to catch the detritus of a whole host of slowly disintegrating worlds. There had to be some such bottom layer, he supposed, given that the worlds *were* disintegrating, and that streams and rivers would be ceaselessly carrying their water away even if the solid ground were more secure than it was. Was the water recycled somehow? Perhaps it was pumped up the walls of the universe so that it might fall again as rain onto the world or worlds. Perhaps, on the other hand, there was an infinite number of layers to the universe, through which everything was ceaselessly falling, periodically molded into worlds and set afloat by creatures with kinder habits than the Web's top predators.

In spite of his best efforts, though, Umsonofer could not bring himself to care. He was a philosopher now, by choice as well as necessity, but the consolations of philosophy still seemed very meager.

In the end, he looked the nearest spider in its many eyes, and said: "I could do with something to drink. If you're going to fatten me up, you'd best not let me die of thirst before you start, or there'll be nothing left of me but a shriveled husk by the time you want to drink me."

He hadn't expected the spider to understand elvish speech, but it seemed to take heed of what he'd said. It actually turned away, as if to search for something—and then it went toward something that was lying on the ground twenty elvish paces from the frame on which it had strung up its victim.

Umsonofer recognized the bag containing the poisoned chalice. It was still bulging.

He realized then what must have happened back at the burrow. After reciting the spellkey, Kasimir had been unable to resist the temptation to peek inside the bag before taking the chalice out. He had seen it—but he had been so enthusiastic to lift it to his lips to drink he had lifted the bag with it. When it had fallen from his grasp, the open bag must have enveloped it again, rendering it invisible . . . but not inaccessible.

A spider had picked it up—and one of its companions had then picked Umsonofer up. The spiders had not yet caught sight of the doomsday weapon—but now, as his captor cast about for something in which to bring him a little liquid to quench his thirst, Umsonofer was finally about to confront it himself.

"Oh well," the elf murmured, unable to suppress a wry smile, "at least it'll be quick, if I do get to drink from it."

He didn't. As soon as the spider's inquisitive palps had tumbled the chalice from its packaging, the monster paused as if hypnotized, and every one of its myriad vermilion eyes seemed to be staring madly. Umsonofer realized, as magical appetite surged through him like an internal tide, that he might yet have a deal of suffering still to do, given that his chances of slaking that murderous thirst now seemed very small indeed.

The spiders, on the other hand, had every opportunity to slake *their* thirst. As connoisseurs of liquid food, they obviously found the inexhaustible nectar of the cup to be exceedingly tasteful. The spider that had released the cup drank deep, and was then shunted aside by another. Then there were twenty struggling to get to the weirdly glowing object—and after that, Umsonofer lost count.

He also lost sight of the chalice, which gave him some slight relief from his own inexpressible torment.

For obvious reasons, Umsonofer had never witnessed one of the brawls that followed the periodic unveiling of his dubious prize, but his ears had always assured him that they were relatively unviolent affairs, presumably because elves, dwarfs, and the like had thirsts appropriate to the size of their stomachs, and were not long delayed in slaking them. The spiders were huge, and had thirsts to match; the delay involved in waiting for each drinker to finish became intolerable to its impatient rivals with astonishing rapidity, and the spiders were predators, lacking the refined discretion characteristic of omnivores. Newcomers arrived on the scene at a faster rate than poisoned spiders died, and the struggles of the swarm grew increasingly agitated.

It was not a situation that could endure for long, though. Something had to give—and what gave was the delicately spun but ancient web. Overladen with creatures that were normally wary of overmuch congregation, a whole section of it gave way, and fell away just as the stream-weakened land at the edge of Umsonofer's world had fallen away.

The chalice fell too, without the hapless elf ever catching sight of it again. The dendritic structure to which he was attached was left on the lip of the hole.

When the elf finally felt better, he looked downward with some interest. There were no stars to be seen in the depths of the hole, but there was something down there like a soft white mist, stretching as far as the eye could see in every direction. Another web, perhaps? Or authentic cloud? Who could tell, without actually jumping down? And who was likely to do that, unless and until desperation drove them to it?

"The chance would be a fine thing," Umsonofer muttered glumly, wishing that he had a drink of perfectly ordinary water.

They did not come to find him for at least twenty-four hours, but they did come in the end, wondering at the scarcity of spiders—and the consequent abundance of recoverable loot—for many miles around. They found him barely alive, but not so barely that he could not be revived and cut free, and assisted to tell his story.

Eventually the entire party gathered around the rim of the hole to look down into the vast abyss that had swallowed up so many of their enemies. It was a moment made for philosophy.

"They'll be back, of course," said Landameofurkh sadly. "They'll breed, and occupy the territory again, and we'll be right back where we were, struggling to survive."

"But a breathing space is a breathing space," Isabel observed. "We'll be able to tell our grandchildren about this, so they'll know that the spiders *can* be defeated, provided that there are heroes brave enough to try."

It was a very human thing to say, but Umsonofer found himself nodding his head. "And we'll have reinforcements in the meantime," he said. "As long as the world keeps falling apart, there'll be jumpers—and as long as they have far enough to fall, they'll always change their minds on the way down. And fallers too, of course . . . but I hope I'm the last of my kind of hero. I'd hate to think of it raining poisoned chalices for the next ten thousand years."

"I don't understand about that," Isabel said, furrowing her horrid brow as only a human could. "How did it keep filling up again? Where did all the poison come from?"

"I'm the kind of person who can always resist the temptation to peek," Umsonofer told her, "so I'm not really equipped for philosophy—but I've seen a lot more of the universe than most philosophers have. One thing it's not short of is ingenious ways to kill people—and yes, I do mean *people* in the broad sense, not in the narrow one. The old world's just a crumbling flying island, and we live on the shore of infinity now. If we have to go farther down, in the end, we might as well all go down together."

BATTLE OF WITS

Mickey Zucker Reichert

Mickey Zucker Reichert is a pediatrician, dog trainer, animal wrangler, alligator wrestler, coach, parent, and all-around nice person (most of the time) as well as the author of more than fifty short stories and more than twenty novels, including (but not limited to) the Bifrost Guardians pentology, two trilogies about the Renshai, the Books of Barakhai series, *The Legend of* and *The Return of Nightfall, The Unknown Soldier, A Time to Die, Flightless Falcon,* and *Spirit Fox* (with Jennifer Wingert). She shares a forty-acre farm with a stunning husband, three perfect children, seven dogs, eight parrots, way too many cats, four horses, eleven goats, thirteen geese, three snakes (that we know of), a dozen chickens, three lizards, two peacocks, three guinea pigs, two hundred fifteen total gallons of fish tank (fish included), two hermit crabs, a llama, a guanaco, and a duck. Loneliness is so underrated!

WIND TWISTED, HOWLING, THROUGH the crags of the Pellorth Mountains, bearing the smoke, sparks, and embers of Kymystro's dragon breath. As brilliant and scarlet as the depths of fire, he perched on the tallest peak, horny head raised, leathery orange wings splayed in victory. Filled with the unfettered joy of triumph, he spat a fiery torrent at the stars while six terrified centaur children cowered with their mother in the cave behind him. For the next several days, he would feast on the father, who lay helpless in a deep ravine. A foreleg broken in defense of his younglings assured the father could not escape his fate. Now in possession of the centaurs' vast treasure, Kymystro intended to remain until his confined supply of food became depleted. From the summit, Kymystro saw all; Kymystro ruled the world.

The unicorn Masikah awakened with a stabbing headache caused, at least in part, by the singed wren pecking incessantly at her forelock.

"Unicorn! Unicorn, wake up!" the wren twittered. "Wake up!" Disheveled feathers stuck out in every direction, making her look more like a soft porcupine than a bird.

Masikah leaped to her hooves, her snowy coat shimmering in the moonlight. "What's wrong? What's . . . ?" Her nose crinkled in disgust. "Bird, you reek!"

The wren became more agitated, if possible. "It's a dragon, Masikah! He's taken Treasure Peak."

"Treasure Peak?" Masikah's slender legs beat a worried tattoo against the forest floor. "What about the centaurs?"

"Captured." The wren let out a low moan of concern that emerged more like a whistle. "The dragon plans to eat them."

Now fully awake, Masikah shook her head, rearranging her silken mane. The horn weighed heavy on her forehead, like the leaden crown of an aging king. "How do you know what the dragon plans?"

"He said so." The bird landed on Masikah's back, folding wings blackened by soot and ash. "He shouted it at the heavens. He's declared himself king of the entire world."

Irritation shot through Masikah to join the growing vat of anxiety. "King of the world, he claims. We'll just see about that." She spread her silvery wings. The wren flew off to rest as Masikah leaped into the air and—

Hold it right there, Mickey!

Shock froze my fingers to my Gateway keyboard. "Are you talking to me?"

You described me as a unicorn. Unicorns can't fly. They don't have wings, silvery or otherwise. Masikah gave me a withering look through one huge blue eye.

"Sometimes they do." I nervously defended myself from the character I had created. "I've seen toys—"

Toys, feh. Masikah shook the length of her body with a noise like a tarp snapping in a hurricane, and her wings dropped off in the dirt. *What, Barbie toys? Sissy animé?* She snorted. *Why is it that every plaything for little girls has to have those cutesy, lacy little wings?* Masikah pawed the ground, kicking up divots. *Even the girls themselves have to have wings. It's not enough to be a princess anymore.* Her tone turned mocking. *They have to be a* fairy *princess. With glittery pink butterfly wings, no less. Ugh.* She made retching noises. *Makes me want to puke.*

I reattached the wings with a stroke of my keyboard, growing seriously irritated myself. "First, I have a four-year-old daughter. She loves fairy princess costumes. Wore one to preschool today . . ."

Argh. Puke, puke, puke! Masikah spat with each repetition.

". . . second, and more important, there's a cruel oaf of a dragon on Treasure Peak holding a family of centaurs hostage."

Masikah looked at me expectantly, then spoke slowly, as if to someone exceptionally stupid. *Yeeeeesss . . . and what does that have to do with me?*

A^itr58nbm's90-&*vzx2. (I slammed my hands down on all the keys at once.) "You have to save them. And you can't make it to the mountaintop without wings."

Masikah sprang into the air, ditched the wings, then stamped all four hooves simultaneously. *Unicorns . . . don't . . . have . . . wings. Pegasus has wings.*

I had had enough. Characters don't just refuse to do things, to be things, to defy their author's description. I had a fantasy to tell, and it had gone terribly, terribly wrong. "So you're a . . . pegacorn, all right?"

A pegacorn? Masikah turned her back to me, crossing her forelegs daintily. *That's not even a word!*

"It is too!"

Oh, yeah? Then how come it's got that wavy red underline on your screen? It's clearly not in your spell checker.

"My spell checker?" I couldn't believe this was happening. I'd been writing novels for over twenty years now and never gotten a word of backtalk from any of my characters. "How . . ." I started and stopped. "What . . . ?" Utterly incoherent, I finally sputtered out, "How are you even talking to me?"

Masikah smiled an impish, flat-toothed smile. *Your brilliant and detailed writing brought me to life.*

Flattered, I grinned back at her. "Really?"

No. Not really, you incompetent moron. You never heard of sarcasm? You don't even know the difference between a unicorn and Pegasus. She muttered beneath her breath. *A unicorn with wings, please. Don't you know even basic anatomy?*

"Actually," I started. "I'm a—"

Doctor. Yeah, yeah, I know. I read it in your bio. She

pranced wildly, smashing the detached wings into the ground. *If you'd put down the histology text once in a while and pulled out rudimentary mythology 101, you'd know what a unicorn is.*

Now it was my turn to mumble. "Apparently, it's a vastly irritating creature that needs a good lesson in how to treat its creator."

What?

"Never mind." I pulled at my lip, then returned to my keyboard. "All right, Masikah. Let's just say you're the product of a Pegasus mother and a unicorn father."

It's not a Pegasus, don't you know? There's only one Pegasus. And he's hung like a horse, so he'd make a piss-poor mother.

Too worried about the centaur family to argue, I only rolled my eyes. "Fine. The Pegasus is your father. And a unicorn—"

—just happened to be roaming through the forest— Masikah heavily emphasized the last word. *Which is where unicorns live, you know. Spirits of the woodlands and all that.*

"Yes, okay—"

When a great, winged shape hurtled out of the sky casting a massive shadow over the treetops.

I went with it. It seemed easier than fighting.

Instead of assuming him a dragon come to kill her and her ilk, she nursed the many and varied stab wounds he suffered crashing through the heavy canopy of trees.

Rather than address the absurdity, I finished the story. "They fell in love, married, lived happily ever after."

And I'm their gruesome Frankenstein's Monster of a love child.

"That would be you."

Thus, a pegacorn.

"Or a unisus. You pick."

"Hmmm." Masikah did not fight when I, once again, added the wings. She tested them, unfolding first one and inspecting it from end to tip, then the other. *How am I supposed to groom these? Blood feathers, shafts, and all that stuff made for beaks?*

I didn't answer. Those sorts of details, like dealing with menstrual cycles, bathroom breaks, and lice, don't belong in most "once upon a time" fantasies.

Masikah continued to examine the wings, flapping experimentally. *You'll have to change your earlier description, you know. You said I was a unicorn.*

"The editor will fix it," I promised. "Let her earn her share of the royalties."

Masikah continued to check out her new appendages.

I sighed, relieved to have solved the current crisis and unconcerned about the need to convince her. After all, I was getting paid by the word. I continued: Masikah leaped into the air and sped toward Treasure Mountain. Her silvery wings cut the air like—

No.

My wrists drooped to the Kensington pad behind the keyboard, the one supposed to prevent carpal tunnel syndrome but mostly used as a paw rest by whichever cat chose to oversee a particular story. "What is it now?"

I'm not going to Treasure Mountain.

"Why not?"

There's a dragon there. A fearsome one. Named Kymystro, if I recall.

I'd named the thing myself but had already forgotten if Masikah had it right. So much time, and so many words, had passed. I scanned back up the screen to the first paragraph while Masikah tapped a hoof impatiently. There it was: Kymystro. "Yes, of course there's a dragon on the mountain. That's what I need you for."

You need me to die? But I'm the world's only pegacorn!

Tired of arguing, feeling a bit wicked, I leaned toward the screen. "Pegasus . . . is very prolific."

Masikah had an equally fast answer. *But unicorns only cycle once a century.*

I weighed my options. I could make Pegasus a prolific *adulterer;* but, thinking of my four-year-old daughter, I chose the lesser of evils. "You're the oldest of twelve siblings. You're two thousand years old."

I am?

"You are."

But I don't feel a day over seventeen hundred.

"Now fly! Fly to Treasure Mountain and save that centaur family."

Masikah flapped a wing in my general direction. *Let one of my younger brothers do it.*

I had to leave my computer to find the big bottle of ibuprofen. While I was gone, my blue and gold macaw clambered off her cage to methodically pluck off and shatter the insert and down arrow key covers. Masikah left muddy hoofprints on the screen.

"Your brothers," I said through gritted teeth while waiting for the ibuprofen to kick in, "are indisposed saving other needy woodland and mountain creatures." Anticipating another loophole, I added, "Your sisters, too."

Oh, dear. Masikah raised a careful hoof to her mouth. *There are a lot of fantasy stories needing pegacorns, aren't there?*

"Yes," I said with all the sincerity I could muster. "And I need you for this one." I started again: Masikah leaped into the air, silvery wings cutting the air like—

Nah, I don't think so.

I felt a ball of fire rising into my throat. My acid reflux had returned, probably hastened by the handful of ibuprofen

I had taken. "What do you mean, you don't think so? The centaurs need you. Kymystro might be eating the father at this very moment!"

He's not. Masikah sounded certain.

How can you possibly know that?

Masikah breathed on one of her pearly white hooves, then polished it with a wing. *Because you're here arguing with me, not writing a dramatic death scene complete with terrified, wailing half-human children.*

I sighed, cracked my knuckles, and began anew: The sun tipped over the mountains, dragging bands of multi-colored light in widening rainbow rings. Kymystro folded his leathern wings and stepped down from the zenith, striding toward the ravine where Father Centaur lay, exhausted from his struggles. His shattered leg refused to hold him, yet he had fought long past surrender. He could hear the cries of his children in the distance, screaming for him in a panic that goaded him to keep trying long after the battle was lost.

Masikah winced. *That's awful. But we're in a fantasy story, right? These things always work out happily.*

The father pawed at the cliffs, pain spearing his injured leg so fiercely his vision disappeared. He grunted in agony, felt blood run from his splintered hooves.

Tears filled Masikah's huge, blue eyes. *His leg needs healing.*

I smiled despite the grimness of the scene I was creating. I was winning. "He needs the touch of a unicorn horn."

Or a doctor, Mickey.

"I'm a pediatrician, not an orthopedic surgeon/veterinarian. It would take a miracle to fix that smashed leg. He needs the magic of a unicorn horn."

Yes. Masikah considered for several moments. *Too bad I'm a pegacorn.*

My story came crashing down again. I had nearly cornered her, but the moment was lost. "Pegacorn horns work the same way."

Who says?

"I do. And I *made* you."

I thought Pegasus and a unicorn made me.

I had had more than enough. This creature I invented reminded me too much of my twelve-year-old son, a true pre-adolescent who invoked arguments so one-sidedly twisted he could turn a lawyer honest. "Look, Masikah. You're going to Treasure Mountain. And that's final."

No.

"Yes."

No.

"Yes!"

No!

Visions of my eight-year-old now. I balled my hands to fists, though I found nothing to punch in the world I had created. Badly. Very badly. As a parent, I knew I had only one recourse. "Then I'm taking away your pretty wings."

Go ahead. I didn't want them anyway.

Masikah spoke the truth. I needed her to wear those wings more than she did.

". . . and replacing them with filthy bat wings." The shimmering feathers disintegrated. In their place appeared tarry wings swarming with irregular, lumpy warts better suited to Kymystro.

Masikah made a strangled noise but still refused to move.

"And that shiny white coat . . ."

Yes? Masikah's voice held a meekness I had never heard before.

"Dank purple."

Purple?! Masikah studied herself, traumatized as her coat turned a dingy shade of violet and I added green spots for an uglier effect.

Masikah screamed. *I look like Barney!*

I was on a roll. Masikah's teeth crooked in several directions, rotting in her gums. Her flowing tail coalesced into a stubby wad of skin with a few donkey hairs sticking from it like a paintbrush. Her mane looked as if a child had hacked at it with a pair of rusty scissors, and the massive friendly blue eyes grew bloodshot and frantic.

All right! You win! she proclaimed, returning the story to my control.

Masikah leaped into the air, her grubby wings slapping air like awkward paddles. Charged with worry for the centaur's family, she sped to Treasure Mountain just in time to find the dragon, Kymystro, descending on a deep ravine, talons spread wide, mouth twisted in a sharp toothy grimace. "Stop," she shouted in a burst of rot-toothed, fetid breath.

"Unicorn?" The dragon poised mid-dive to stare at Masikah. "Where did . . . ? How . . . ? What in deepest, darkest hell happened to you?"

"She did," Masikah said, jabbing a hoof toward the computer screen, where I prepared to type the final, bloody showdown. "And I'm the heroine." Her red eyes narrowed, and her voice emerged as thick and vile as a demon's. *"You should see what she has in store for you!"*

Kymystro's eyes went round as dinner plates. With a sudden burst of wing beats, he rose from the mountaintop and flew toward the sun, never to be seen in one of my stories again. I sat, stunned, the great battle taking up half the space in my brain now indefinitely postponed. My mind seized. My fingers stilled on the keyboard, not knowing what to write. The desperation; the frantic action; verbs like *crashed* and *flailed* and *spasmed* no longer had a place on this peaceful mountain, where the only sound was the moaning of a wounded centaur.

Masikah touched him with her horn, and I watched as

health flowed back into his body. His lungs filled with steady breath, his dragging leg straightened, his pelt returned to a rich, dark chestnut. A moment later, he scuttled wildly from his rescuer. "What the hell are you?"

"I'm a unicorn," Masikah said gently, her musical voice a grim parody to the ugliness of her being. "At least, I was." She looked at me. *And now, I put my life in jeopardy to save another. I performed a heroic action despite my reticence and rescued the lives of eight centaurs. The rules of writing decree that I get rewarded.* Masikah looked at me with those hideous crimson eyes, but still managed to get across her need and desperation. *Don't they?*

I let her sweat. It was only fair; she had done the same to me. "It's not truly heroism if I have to force you."

Masikah studied her hooves. *I guess I deserved that.* She gave a horsey shrug. *And I suppose I can live with being . . . whatever it is I am.* Bending a knee to make a climbing step, she assisted the centaur from his prison, then flew to the lip beside him.

"My family," the centaur whispered.

"Let's find them," Masikah gently replied, her voice a sudden croak, her body slimy green, and her legs long and amphibious. She hopped along beside the centaur as he watched her newest transformation with wild, uncertain eyes.

But by the time Masikah reached the cave mouth, she had, once again, become the unicorn described in the second paragraph of this story. She kicked up her heels and raised her flowing tail, a clear horsey version of the all-too-human "moon."

I didn't tie her to railroad tracks. Kids, it seems, have softened me.

THE HERO OF KILLORGLIN

Fiona Patton

Fiona Patton was born in Calgary, Alberta, and grew up in the United States. In 1975 she returned to Canada and now lives on seventy-five acres of rural scrubland with her partner, one teeny chihuahua that has more winter coats than she does, five male cats, and a ferocious little female fire-cat that rules the roost with an iron paw.

THE LATE SUMMER BREEZE whispered across the hills and loughs of County Kerry. It wove through the tree-sheltered valleys where placid herds of brown-and-white cattle grazed beside cream-colored sheep and dun-colored roe deer and feathered across the reeds and grasses of the many low-lying bogs and marshlands. On a shallow rise overlooking a pool of still, clear water, Brae Diardin of the Ulaidh Fianna lay beneath the sweeping branches of a single hawthorn tree, her tunic flung carelessly to one side, and the faintest outline of a white hound with red ears shimmering in the sunlight above her pale skin and bright copper hair. Reaching out with one bare toe, she gave her dog, Balo, a scratch under his graying muzzle, echoing his grunt of contentment with one of her own.

The two of them had come south three days ago after the Fianna had repelled an attack by their ancient enemies, the Fomair, off the coast of Ulster. They and Brae's three siblings had figured prominently in that battle and so, in reward, they'd been sent to the quiet ring fort of Staigue on the west coast of Munster to enjoy the last of the hot summer days while the rest of Fionn mac Cumhail's legendary warriors chased down the few remaining Fomair that had eluded them in Donegal.

"Which is just fine with us, isn't it, boy?" Brae said fondly, moving her foot to scratch the hound under his worn leather collar. "You're getting far too old to go hunting giants and goblins these days, aren't you?"

Balo's ears perked up at her words, but he laid his head back down almost at once and she reached over to inspect his right forepaw, feeling the slight swelling around the ankle joint beneath her fingers. At almost twenty-five years old and one of the fabled faery-hounds of the Aes Sidhe, Brae was in her prime and could expect to live far longer than the earthly members of the Fianna, but Balo was a mortal hound and nearing ten. The battle against the Fomair and the subsequent journey south had left him stiff and lame. Soon they would have only one journey left: to her mother's home in Anglesey where Balo would spend his final days before her hearth, warm and safe.

But warm and safe without Brae.

A single cloud passed across the sun, bringing the faintest hint of autumn on the breeze, and she shivered. She couldn't imagine a time without Balo by her side, racing through the oak and rowan trees that sheltered the royal palace at Tara, or bounding through the surf at Ferriter's Cove, or along the sandy strand at Ardmore.

They'd been together in wartime and peacetime for most of Balo's life; ever since Brae's Aunt Tamair had dropped the squirming ten-week-old bundle of brindle energy into her arms after she'd been accepted into the Fianna at age fifteen. At eight months, he'd followed her to battle when invaders from the north had landed at Broadhaven, and a year later he'd saved her life at Lough Gill when the bluff had given way under her feet while fighting a trow. They'd hunted for deer and rabbits in the dappled woods of Powerscourt and salmon in the deep waters of the Shannon River. They'd stood together against the enemies of Ulaidh from Maulin Head to Schull and traveled the otherworldly paths under the sea to Ynys-Witrin in southern Logres. Always together.

With a sigh, Brae draped one arm across the hound's warm flank and he turned to swipe at her face with his tongue.

"You still have a couple more months of hunting in you, don't you, boy?" she asked, resting her face against his. Balo's tail began to thump against the grass in response to the worried tone in her voice and she nodded in resignation. "But only just," she admitted. "So, we'd better make it count, eh?" Shaking off the somber mood, she smiled down at him. "So that means no more excitement, all right?" she said, reaching down to take his muzzle in her cupped hands. "No more giants, sea serpents, northerners, monsters, or otherworldly hound packs. We'll go to Anglesey in the fall; that'll give your paws a chance to heal, but in the meantime, Munster's at peace and the Fianna are on guard. There shouldn't be any reason why we can't spend the rest of this summer lying back and doing nothing. Agreed?"

She touched her forehead to his to seal the bargain but as she straightened, the wind brought a sudden, unfamiliar scent wafting down to them. Balo gave a woof of warning, there was a snap of branches above their heads, and looking up, they saw a small red and white creature staring down at them through the leaves of the hawthorn tree.

"It's a cat."

The next day, lying with her head pillowed on Balo's flank, Brae gave her older sister, Isien, a sleepy-eyed look in response to her indignant statement. The four siblings had spent the morning hunting with their dogs and now all eight lay sprawled under the hawthorn tree with the boneless grace that only well-fed hounds, mortal or Sidhe, could master. Giving a great yawn, Brae shook her head.

"No," she corrected lazily, "it's a *fire*-cat."

"No, it's a *cat*-cat," Isien insisted, flicking her own copper-colored hair from her eyes. "What's it doing here?"

Brae craned her neck to see the creature wrap its over-size white paws about Balo's muzzle and begin washing his face. It bit down on his lip and Balo shook his head, sending cat tumbling into a bed of cowslips.

"Being too cute to be believed?" she hazarded.

"And taking its life in its . . . claws," Cullen, the youngest sibling, observed. Cocking his head to one side, he watched as the cat flung itself at the old hound once again, scaling his shoulder like a brightly painted woodpecker.

"Balo won't hurt it," Brae answered carelessly.

"But where did it come from?" Isien persisted.

Brae pointed wordlessly up into the hawthorn branches.

"Why?"

"I have no idea."

*   *   *

After it had received Brae and Balo's full attention, the red and white creature had scaled swiftly down the tree trunk headfirst, digging its tiny claws into the bark to keep its balance and, once standing in the meadow grass, had revealed itself to be a small, half-grown calico cat with wild multicolored fur sticking out in all directions and a disconcertingly intelligent expression in its wide golden eyes. It had immediately attached itself to Balo, following him and Brae back to Staigue and, despite Brae's best efforts to lock it out of her room, had somehow managed to be found sleeping beside the hound in his nest of old blankets by Brae's bedroll the next morning. It had eaten half the dog's breakfast, then disappeared, only to reappear once more after the morning's hunt.

Now Isien's twin brother, Tierney, glanced over from where he and his own hound lay in a tangle of copper hair and brindle fur. "How'd you know it's a fire-cat?" he asked. "Instead of just a plain old moggy?"

"Because it's not plain," Brae answered, lacing her fingers behind her head and closing her eyes. "It's *fire*-colored."

Tierney considered her answer, then gave a satisfied nod, but Isien snorted, unconvinced.

"It has *white* feet," she pointed out.

"Ash," Brae answered.

"And black markings."

"Soot."

Reaching over, Cullen chucked the cat under the chin and it immediately spun about to sink its tiny teeth into his hand.

"Ow! It's a wild little monster, whatever it is," he observed, sucking at the double row of punctures along the base of his thumb.

"That also makes it a fire-cat," Brae stated.

"No," Isien retorted, "that still makes it a *cat*-cat."

"It could be a Sidhe cat," Tierney offered. "It has got red ears. And Cnu Deireoil says single hawthorn trees are entrances to Sidhe Raths. So are the bottoms of deep, secretive pools." He made a grand gesture at the sparkling water below them, then pulled his hand back hastily as the cat took a swipe at it.

"No mortal cat nor Sidhe-cat either would *ever* exit through a pool of water," Isien pointed out.

"But they are found in trees," Tierney answered.

"Says who?"

"Brae."

Her sister opened one eye with a triumphant expression and Isien shrugged.

"That may be, but it still doesn't explain what it's doing here. And why . . ." She frowned. "It seems to be so taken with Balo," she added as the cat settled down against the hound's chest and began to knead on his right forepaw, its ruddy pelt gleaming in the noon sun.

"Maybe we should ask him." Tierney said.

Cullen frowned in confusion. "Ask who, Balo?"

"No, whelp, Cnu Deireoil," his brother answered in disgust.

Cullen flushed as red as his own hair. "Oh. I knew that." Pulling at his hound's ears, he put on a careless expression. "I heard that cats were familiars for druids," he said.

"Balo isn't a druid," Brae pointed out.

"Maybe he was a druid and he was cursed and turned into a dog."

"I got him when he was just weaned. I don't think the druid could have been that young."

"Maybe his father was the druid and he angered a powerful being like a demon or a wizard and it turned his son into a dog," Cullen persisted eagerly, warming to his subject. "Or maybe even the cat was a Druid and got cursed and turned into a . . . well, into a cat, instead and it's come to us for our help to break the spell. Just like that hag needed Fionn's help to turn into a beauty, you know?"

"What hag?" Brae asked.

Cullen flushed again. "Just . . . just a hag I heard a story about once."

"The whelp likes older women," Tierney said with a grin. Cullen turned on him with a snarl, but his older brother just laughed at him.

"Stop it or I'll dunk you both," Isien said sternly. "Balo is a dog and that cat is a cat. It probably just wandered away from one farm or another." She watched as it began to knead against Balo's side and shook her head. "Mind you, it's a very confused cat," she added.

"I still think we need to ask Cnu Deireoil about it," Tierney said thoughtfully. "There just might be something in what the whelp says. And if it has come to us for aid," he continued, ignoring the suspicious glance Cullen shot him. "We have to help it. It's what we do. So we'll need to know how."

"Fine," Brae answered with a yawn. "We'll ask and we'll help, but later. Right now I'm bored, I'm hot, and I want to go swimming."

Standing, she shed her tunic and her human seeming in the same fluid motion, spun about, and made for the pool at a dead run. Cullen gave a whoop of pleasure and gave chase a heartbeat later, his hound at his heels. Tierney and Isien shared a superior glance before they and their own dogs followed. They caught up with their younger siblings at the pool's edge, then as one, four gleaming white faery-hounds with blazing red ears and three brindle hounds dove into the inviting waters below.

Stretched out on the hillside, Balo and the cat watched them go with equally indulgent expressions.

"It's a fire-cat."

Dusk found them gathered in Staigue's cool stone refectory hall, attacking half a dozen trenchers piled high with meat while their hounds dug into four wooden bowls of bones and ends at their feet. Beside them, Cnu Deireoil, Sidhe Bard of the Fianna, strummed quietly on his harp and considered Brae's words. When she punctuated her statement with a large flagon of beer, he pushed a lock of golden hair from his face and, after taking a long swallow, glanced down at the cat who was currently shoving her head between Balo and his supper.

The Bard pursed his lips. "Possibly," he allowed. "But fire-cats are very rare. They're usually seen only in the far north. It's said that they're the messengers of Danu, able to travel from realm to realm in the blink of an eye. But it's also said that the Goddess sends them only into the land of mortals at great need, for although they may be very courageous, they're also fickle and easily distracted, much like their mortal counterparts. Ow."

The Bard reached down to disengage the cat's claws from his ankle. "I spoke only the truth, little Cnu Cath," he admonished. "I'm sorry if you find my words offensive, but there they are, nonetheless."

The cat regarded him with a steady golden glare, then rolled onto its back with a coy expression.

"It seems to understand you," Cullen noted. "It's showing its belly in submission."

The Bard gave a loud snort as the cat smiled slyly. "Is it now?" he asked. "Lay your hand on its belly then if you think that's the case."

Cullen immediately stuck his hand out, then gave a

yelp of pain and surprise as it was suddenly enveloped by a ring of teeth and claws.

The cat jumped back in bristling indignation as Cullen jerked his hand away and the Bard snickered.

"Cats show their bellies so that all five sets of weapons in their arsenal may be brought to bear at the same time," he lectured. "You see, a cat knows when and how to fight to the best advantage. There's great wisdom to be gained in following their example."

Cullen watched as the cat returned its attention to Balo's supper, pulling a piece of tripe right out from between his teeth. The dog woofed at it but did little else as the cat dragged its prize under the table.

"It doesn't seem like great wisdom to follow that example," he pointed out. "If Balo wasn't so gentle he'd have eaten the little moggy."

"And you don't think it knew that?"

Cullen just shrugged. "Maybe."

"Maybe nothing. Cats are excellent judges of character."

"But do you really think it's a *Sidhe* cat," Isien asked, bringing them back to the question at hand. "A messenger from Danu?"

Cnu Deireoil shrugged. "All we can do is wait and see," he answered in a noncommittal tone. "If it does have a message for us, it will reveal it in its own good time. In the meantime, I suggest you treat it as an honored guest with all the traditional hospitality that involves."

"But we don't know anything about how to be hospitable to cats," Brae protested weakly. "We're faery-*hounds.*"

"So learn. How hard can it be?"

Glancing down at the cat who was now crouched over its piece of tripe, growling low in its throat and lashing its tail back and forth, Brae swallowed involuntarily.

"I'm thinking it might be pretty hard," she answered.

The cat favored her with one sly glance before returning to its meal as the Bard gave another snicker.

Days passed and summer slowly handed over its dominion to autumn. The trees changed their green mantels for those of gold and red and bronze and the air grew heavy with the spicy odors of fallen leaves and ripened grains. At Staigue, the fire-cat settled into a comfortable routine of stealing Balo's meat and grooming his paws, while the old hound suffered its ministrations and its thieving without protest. Each afternoon, both cat and dog accompanied Brae to the hawthorn tree, sitting together while she stared up into its branches, wondering if tomorrow would be the day they would have to begin their journey to Anglesey; and wondering too, just what she was supposed to tell her mother about Balo's new companion. And each night, as they fell asleep in the dog's nest of blankets, she decided to wait just one more day for some sign that the fire-cat was indeed a messenger from Danu or some otherworldly creature come to them for aid.

The equinox came and went and the days grew shorter and the nights colder. As the small pack of Fianna and their hounds went out into the woodlands to hunt the season's deer, Balo began to tire. He grew loathe to leave the warmth of Staigue's main hearth, and one morning, the fire-cat took a piece out of Brae's hand for even suggesting that he accompany them. That day Brae hunted without him by her side for the first time in nine years, and that night she took his graying muzzle between her cupped hands, and laid her forehead against his. "That's it then," she told him gently. "We leave tomorrow."

*   *   *

The snowstorm that hit the region late that night took them all by surprise. Brae awoke the next morning to the howling winds and dark cold of a winter's day and the ominous silence of an empty room. Both hound and fire-cat were gone.

"Brae, you can not go out in this weather!"

"Watch me."

"You'll be buried under a mountain of snow!"

"I don't care."

"Brae . . ." Isien attempted to catch hold of her younger sister as she pulled on a pair of fur-lined boots, but Brea shook her off with a warning growl.

"Balo's my hound, my responsibility. I have to find him."

"He's probably gone out to die with some dignity," Tierney said, but closed his mouth with a snap as Brae rounded on him.

"I don't care what he's gone off to do," she snarled. Grabbing a pair of rabbit skin gloves, she stuffed them into her belt, before reaching for her weapons. "I should have taken him to Anglesey a long time ago," she added quietly.

"Maybe," Isien agreed, "but you couldn't have known. It hasn't snowed before Samhain in Munster for three decades."

"I should have known anyway. I should have smelled it coming. I didn't. I missed it."

"We all missed it," Cullen attempted.

"I missed it," Brae repeated. "That's all that matters."

Her three siblings argued with her all the way down the stone passageway that protected Staigue's main keep, but on reaching the heavy oak gatehouse doors they were suddenly confronted by a small figure dressed from head to toe in multicolored furs and covered in a foot and a half of snow. It shook off the white mantle with a disgusted gesture, before dropping its hood to reveal a young girl's pale, scowling face beneath a wild shock of red and brown hair. Stomping forward she stood, fists on hips, to stare up at Brae from a pair of furious golden eyes.

"What have you done with my dog!" she demanded.

News of the strange girl's arrival swept through the fort, and by the time the chaos caused by her words and Brae's response had cleared, most of the residents of Staigue were crowded into the refectory hall. Standing dripping on the flagstones, the girl cast a haughty glance across the room until she caught sight of a man hurrying forward, his golden hair gleaming in the torchlight. His deep, respectful bow did little to soften her expression.

"I am Cnu Deireoil, Bard of the Fianna," he said formally.

Pulling off a pair of large white mittens, the girl eyed him critically before inclining her head with a regal gesture. "Caoit of the Ferrishyn Sidhe," she replied. "Your name and deeds are known to us, Little Nut of the Daoine Sidhe." She turned to regard Brae with a baleful stare. "As are those of the Sidhe-hound children of Diardin," she added in a voice that suggested she remained unimpressed by whatever she might have heard.

Cnu Deireoil nodded before anyone else could speak. "And how may we aid you this day, Caoit of the Ferrishyn Sidhe?" he asked politely.

"I have been sent by the Goddess Danu to aid the people of Killorglin, kindred to the Tuatha de Danann," she replied, ignoring both Tierney and Cullen as they mouthed *I told you so* at their sisters. "They have been beset by a giant weasel the size of a bullock that has been ravaging their cattle and carrying off full-grown cows in its jaws. Any crops that have not been shredded by its passage have been either despoiled or consumed by an army of vermin that run before it." She punctuated her words with a savage grimace, showing a mouthful of pointy white teeth in response to the thought of an army of vermin. "The people fear that come winter they will starve," she continued. "Which they likely will," she noted almost as an aside. "And so they prayed to Danu, and she has sent me to summon a hero to defeat this terrible scourge and thus save them. From the weasel anyway," she added. "How they defeat starvation is their own problem."

Cnu Deireoil bowed again. "We will send messengers out to Fionn mac Cumhail as soon as the weather clears," he promised but Caoit gave a disdainful sniff.

"I've not come to summon Demne son of Muirne of the Fianna," she replied coldly, "but the great warrior-hound Balo of the Cwn Ulaidh Fianna." Before anyone in the hall could react to her words she whirled on Brae, her teeth bared. "And you let him go out into that"—she stabbed one finger at the snow-blocked window—"all on his own!"

Brae snarled back at her at once. "I didn't let him go anywhere!" she shouted in reply.

"Yes, you did! We had it all arranged, he and I! We were to leave in three days! That would have given him enough time—with my help, by the way—to gather his strength and assuage his guilt about leaving you behind so you wouldn't get killed! But oh no, that would have been too easy! Now he's run off on our quest alone *without me* because you had to go and tell him you were taking him into retirement on the eve of a snowstorm! Stupid mutt!"

Both faery-cat and faery-hound took a single threatening step toward one another, but before they could come any closer, Cnu Deireoil stepped swiftly between them.

"I think we should offer our guest a warm cup of . . . milk," he said smoothly. "Before tempers get the better of hospitality."

"I have to find Balo," Brae growled back at him.

"And you will, but the storm has increased in its ferocity, young one," the Bard said gently. "No one's going anywhere just yet."

The storm abated by noon, the sun breaking through the clouds to reveal a vast ocean of white fields without a paw print to be seen. Throwing open the gatehouse door, Brae stared out at the figure of the hawthorn tree standing stark and alone on its distant rise, her expression grim.

"You're sure he's making for Killorglin?" she asked stiffly.

Beside her, Caoit gave another disdainful sniff. "Straight and true, north across the Reeks, no doubt," she answered.

"The snow should cushion the journey, anyway," Tierney said, glancing past his sister's shoulder.

Isien shook her head. "It'll make it harder to track him though," she noted.

"I'll track him," Brae answered darkly. "I'll track him to Falias and back if I have too."

"So it's a good thing we aren't going that far, right, Brae?" Cullen asked with an attempt at a reassuring smile. "Because Killorglin's so much closer we should catch up to Balo in no time, and he'll be fine, right?"

As Brae strode wordlessly into the snow with Caoit at her heels, Tierney gave his younger brother's shoulder a comforting squeeze. "Yeah, whelp," he answered. "He'll be fine."

Turning to shoo their own three hounds back into the keep, Isien closed the gatehouse door before bringing up the rear with a worried frown.

"So, why Balo?"

The five of them had been traveling most of the afternoon, following an ancient hunting path that ran due north. No one had spoken since leaving Staigue and finally Isien had given a snort of impatience. Now Caoit gave her a rolling-eyed grimace in response to her question.

"Why not Balo?" she retorted.

"He's a dog."

"So? The Sidhe have their own tales of quests and heroes, you know. They don't have to be your tales."

"Certainly, but tales of other Sidhe."

"Of you lot, you mean? Please. It's easy to accomplish great deeds when you have supernatural abilities. Much harder when you don't."

"Point taken but . . ."

"But what?"

"But he's still just a *dog*."

"So?" Whirling about, Caoit caught the older woman in a golden-eyed glare. "Did Balo of the Cwn Ulaidh Fianna not travel to Ynys-Witrin in far away Logres to ask for the aid of the legendary Cwn Annwn and their master this very summer past?" she demanded.

"There was a little more to it than that," Cullen said hotly. "I went with—"

Caoit made an imperious gesture, cutting him off in mid protest "And did he not stand against the army of Dolar Durba, son of the King of the Sea, the traditional enemy of the Fianna and the Tuatha de Danann both and almost single-handedly slay a giant the size of a yew tree in that selfsame battle?"

"He did have *some* help," Isien said coldly. "From the warrior bands of Fionn mac Cumhail."

Caoit gave a dismissive snort. "Before the hearths of mortals the stories of the Fianna are told as the stories of Fionn no matter how many others may have played their part in his victories. So it is with the Sidhe. No matter how many others may have played their part, Balo of the Cwn Ulaidh Fianna is *still a great hero*." Fixing a wrinkle in her hood with a snap, she returned her attention to the path.

Ahead of them, even Brae had to smile a little at her indignation.

They picked up Balo's trail on the edge of the Kerry Reeks just as the moon was rising. A light rain had begun to fall, and Brae peered anxiously through the misting darkness but the hound was nowhere in sight.

"Who'd have thought he could move so fast," Tierney said, shaking his head in wonder. "He's a ten-year-old dog."

"The ministrations of the fire-cats of the Ferrishyn Sidhe are not to be treated lightly," Caoit replied in a sanctimonious tone.

Tierney just blinked at her. "Huh?"

Caoit snorted. "Me lick dog, me make dog stronger," she snapped.

"Oh. Hey, I have a sore foot—"

"No."

"But—"

"We all have sore feet," Isien interrupted. "We should rest for a bit."

Brae shook her head. "Not yet."

"Brae—"

"Not yet. I'm not losing his trail in this rain."

"His trail leads to Killorglin," Caoit answered. "You won't lose it."

"I don't care. I'm not stopping yet." Turning, she plunged into the Reeks and after a moment, the others followed with equally resigned expressions.

They finally convinced Brae to stop around midnight after Caoit stepped into a bog. Ears ringing from her blistering scream, Tierney and Cullen carried her to a dry bit of land where she could pull off her boot with a disgusted gesture. As one, the four Fianna, including Brae who was more tired than she wanted to admit, flopped down beside her.

"I hate the Reeks," Caoit growled.

"So how'd you figure on reaching Killorglin originally," Brae asked.

"*My* plan was to go northeast to Lough Leane and follow the river on dry land."

"That why Balo left you behind?" Cullen asked tactlessly.

Caoit's eyes narrowed. "Likely," she snarled, shaking out one sopping mitten. "I may have made some mention in passing about not caring much for snow or rain or *bogs*. Dogs, they take everything so pissing literally."

"On that note"—Cullen rose—"I'll be back in a moment." He disappeared into the darkness.

"Don't fall into a bog," Isien called after him.

"I won't, Mama."

They set out at dawn the next morning, doing their best to keep to the patches of thick saxifrage that marked the higher, slightly dryer ground, but after three hours of slogging through marshlands and frozen weeds, Cullen gave an explosive sigh.

"So, Caoit," he said suddenly, "there's something I've always wondered."

The girl raised a ruddy eyebrow at him, but gestured

that he continue while the others glanced at him suspiciously. Noting the twinkle in his eyes, Brae held her breath.

"Is there really a Goddess that drives a chariot pulled by cats," he asked, his whole expression one of purely innocent curiosity.

Caoit's golden eyes narrowed. "There's something *I've* always wondered," she asked instead, her voice dripping with false sweetness. "Do the faery-hounds of the Fianna really roll in manure like their mortal counterparts?"

Without waiting for an answer, she leaped across a thin, winding stream, clambered onto the opposite bank, and disappeared through a pair of saplings on the other side.

Cullen glanced over at Tierney. "I guess she didn't really want an answer," he observed mildly.

Tierney just shrugged. "Cats," he noted, "have no sense of humor."

They reached the western edge of the Reeks without further hazardous conversation by noon the next day. A high outcropping of rocks afforded them a view of the entire countryside from the Bay of Dingle to the shores of Lough Leane and they peered down at the village of Killorglin lying at the very mouth of the bay.

"Seems peaceful enough," Tierney noted.

Brae shook her head, gesturing wordlessly to the east and the miles of ravaged fields crawling with rodents and littered with the bloated corpses of cattle and sheep.

Isien turned to Caoit. "I don't see—" she began, and then froze as a rank, musty odor came to them on a trail of blood and decay. As one, the five of them looked down to see the giant weasel slink out from a cave far below them. Brae gaped at it.

The creature was huge, twice again the size of the biggest bullock she'd ever seen. It's pelt was coarse and caked with filth and dried offal, and its powerful furred legs ended in claws as wide and wicked as curved swords. It's great mouth slavered with blood-filled foam and, as they watched, it caught up the half-eaten body of a sheep, flung it into the air in a spray of rot, and swallowed it in one bite.

Cullen gave an involuntary curse. "Just how did you figure the two of you were going to handle that ... thing?" he demanded in an incredulous voice.

Caoit flexed her fingers inside her mittens as if she were unsheathing her claws. "Balo was to slay the weasel and I the vermin," she answered coldly.

"I don't see Balo." Tierney noted.

"There he is." Isien pointed to a tiny figure creeping through the underbrush upwind toward the creature, which thankfully remained unaware of his presence. So far.

Brae shot Caoit an angry glance before throwing one leg over the edge of the outcropping. "Come on," she growled, "let's get down there before he gets himself killed."

"I'll meet up with you later," Caoit answered, giving them a wide-eyed look in response to four questioning expressions. "The weasel is your adversary," she explained impatiently. "The vermin is mine." She disappeared back the way they had come and Cullen shook his head.

"What was it about cats knowing when and how to fight to the best advantage?" he asked.

"I don't know," Tierney said, "but I wish we really did have the wisdom to follow her example."

"Just shut up and get down here," Brae growled. She scaled the rocks as quickly and as quietly as she could.

Once at the bottom, she drew her sword and, just as Balo broke from the underbrush to charge the creature, she drew her sword.

"Diord Fionn!"

Screaming the Fianna's ancient battle cry, she lunged forward.

They fought the creature for a day and a night, drawing on their otherworldly blood to give them strength. Beside them, Balo fought like a demon, howling and snarling and tearing at it from every angle; never wavering though his fur grew grayer and grayer as the battle continued.

Early on, the villagers had rallied to their aid, but it wasn't until nearly dawn the next day that the weasel showed any signs of flagging. Twisting and spinning about with lightning speed, it did its share of killing and soon more than the bodies of sheep and cattle littered the ground. But finally Brae risked a slice from one slashing claw that might have opened up her belly to slice through a back hamstring in one blow. The creature screamed in both pain and rage, and stumbling back on three legs, it turned to flee only to come face to face with Balo's snarling, blood-covered visage. The old hound hurled itself forward in one last, exhausted attack, latching on to the weasel's throat with a scream of his own. The creature fell backward, jerked its head from side to side in a desperate attempt to get free and the Fianna closed in from all sides. Finally Balo bit down and a great spurt of blood sprayed out from between his jaws. The weasel stiffened, then fell, to lie still on the bloody ground, but only when Brae staggered up to him to catch him in her arms did Balo finally release his grip.

*   *   *

Sunrise found them lying, bloodied and spent, on the beachhead just past Killorglin. The villagers brought them clean water, bandages, and food, then retired to deal with the weasel's corpse. As the smell of burning flesh wafted past them, Cullen, Tierney, and Isien attacked the plates of meat and bread in weary glee, but Brae just sat with Balo's head cradled in her lap, stroking his muzzle with a worried expression. The old hound had taken a dozen injuries in a dozen places and, after cleaning them as best she could, she shook her head at him in exasperation.

"Foolish animal," she chided fondly. "Did you honestly think you could take on a monster that size without help?"

As Balo's tail thumped against the ground, he turned his head to lick her wrist, and she scratched him gently behind one battered ear.

"Yes, of course, I forgive you, just don't do it again, all right? Who do you think you are, Bran and Sceolan both?"

A shadow passed over them and Brae looked up to see Caoit, her face and hair smeared with blood and tiny bits of fur, her eyes wide and wild, standing over them.

"He thinks he's Balo of the Cwn Ulaidh Fianna," she answered with a smile. "The hero of Killorglin."

"Yes, I imagine he does." Brae took his muzzle gently in her cupped hands. "And I suppose he is, but he's also Balo, the old hound of Brae Diardin and he's going to Anglesey to live out the rest of his life in warmth and safety before he gets himself killed running off on any more ridiculous quests."

A breath of cold air blew in off the bay and Caoit looked up, her eyes returning to their usual golden brilliance. "There is one more quest that he might set out on, you know," she said, crouching down beside them. "A quest worthy of such a mighty warrior as he." When Brae looked up, she gestured at a small coracle pulled up on the pebble-strewn shore nearby. "Far across the sea," she began in a quiet singsong voice that Brae suddenly recognized from her mother's cottage long ago. "There lies a magical land where Gods and their hounds hunt for deer and rabbits in dappled woodlands and fish for salmon in deep running rivers. They race through groves of oak and rowan trees and bound through surf along sandy strands: the magical land of everlasting youth."

Brae blinked. "Balo could go to Tir na n'Og?"

Caoit blinked back at her. "Why not?" she demanded. "Are not the greatest of all heroes granted the gift of eternal life? And hasn't Balo proved himself to be just that? He could run and play on the shining shores as one of Danu's own hunting pack, warm and safe and young forever. But only if you let him, only if you release him." She stood. "You have a little time to think about it," she said. "The tide can wait a bit and I"—she shook a piece of rodent brains off her hand with a disgusted expression—"have to bathe."

An hour later, Brae laid Balo very gently into the coracle, her eyes brimming over with tears. As he settled onto a soft woolen blanket in the bottom, she reached down and undid his old leather collar.

"I'll miss you more than anything," she said thickly, taking his gray muzzle in her hands. "But maybe if I can manage to be as brave and as loyal as you, I might join you there one day. Who knows."

She straightened as Caoit, clean and sleekly groomed, flowed into the boat beside him. "Maybe," the girl allowed in a generous tone. "If anyone can do it I suppose a faery-hound can."

Looking out at the tide, Brae nodded. "Well, I guess

this is good-bye then, boy. It's going to seem awfully lonely from now on hunting without a brindle hound by my side."

Brae stepped back, but as Balo began to whine, she moved forward again. Caoit rolled her eyes.

"Yes, of course I was going to tell her. Dogs, honestly!" She turned, an expression of annoyance in her golden eyes.

"You really don't think he'd let you fumble about on your own, do you? In the spring return to Glencolumbkille in Donegal. In a whitewashed cottage overlooking the site of Balo's great victory over Dolar Durba's giant you will find a brindle whelp ready to join the Cwn Ulaidh Fianna and hunt by Brae Diardin's side." As the coracle began to back slowly into the rising water, she cocked her head to one side. "You can name it Balo if you like, I suppose," she said. "But it's going to be a female."

"I could name it Caoit then," Brae offered.

The girl growled low in her throat. "Give a cat's name to a dog if you dare," she warned, "but don't be surprised to find yourself overwhelmed with vermin next year. We don't take such insults lightly."

"Cats have no sense of humor."

"Dogs have no sense of danger."

As the coracle moved farther out into the bay, Caoit shrugged out of her clothes, and suddenly the red and white creature from the hawthorn tree stared out across the waves. Beside her, a brindle hound, both young and strong, barked out his promise to see Brae again someday and then the coracle slowly disappeared, taking the fire-cat, Caoit of the Ferrishyn Sidhe, and the mortal hound, Balo of the Cwn Ulaidh Fianna, Hero of Killorglin, to Tir na n'Og.

GOBLIN LULLABY

Jim C. Hines

Jim C. Hines made his first pro fiction sale in 1998 with a story called "Blade of the Bunny," that seems to have set the tone for his writing career. His work has since appeared in over twenty-five magazines and anthologies. His fantasy novel *GoblinQuest* will be published by DAW in November 2006, with a sequel, *Goblin Hero,* to follow in 2007. He is currently hard at work on a third book in the series. Jim lives in Michigan with his wife and two children. He would like to dedicate "Goblin Lullaby" to his four-month-old son Jamie, whose presence was . . . inspirational, to say the least.

> *Lay your head down and close your eyes.*
> *Make no sound as you rest,*
> *for the faintest snores or cries*
> *bring tunnel cats to chew your flesh.*

From the goblin lullaby "Sleep in Silence"

THE DRUMS STARTED AGAIN just as Grell was setting the last
of the newborns in the oversize wooden crib at the back of
the nursery cave. She clenched her teeth as she watched
the baby goblin's blue face wrinkle in protest. With one
hand, she readied a sugar-knot, a bit of hard honey candy
knotted in cloth. The instant the drooling mouth opened,
she jammed the sugar-knot inside.

The swaddled goblin baby started and opened her
eyes, but the sugar-knot worked. Instead of screaming,
she began to suck herself back to sleep . . . even as the
other fourteen newborns crammed into the crib stirred
and fussed. Fifteen if you counted the runt Jig, currently
harnessed in a makeshift sling against Grell's chest. Normally the goblins would have left him on the surface to
die, but another nursery worker named Kralk had bet
Grell a month of diaper cleaning that Jig wouldn't survive long enough to see the next full moon. The pale,
wrinkled baby hadn't left Grell's sight since.

"Stupid war drums," Grell muttered. "Might as well
send a messenger to the enemy, screaming 'Ready your
weapons, because another swarm of goblins is preparing
to charge in like idiots!'" She crossed the nursery, gathering more sugar-knots from the shelves and shoving
them into the pockets on either side of her heavily stained
apron. Lanterns on the floor gave off green light and
filled the obsidian-walled cave with the scent of fer-
mented plant oils and distilled mushrooms. Grell always
added mushrooms to the mix. On most nights, the sour
smell seemed to help the babies sleep, but not tonight.

Kralk, the only other so-called adult in the nursery
cave, gave a lazy shrug. Ill-fitting metal plates rang softly
on her forearms. Piecemeal armor also protected her legs
from the overeager attacks of the goblins who were old
enough to walk. "The warriors say it gives them strength
and brings fear to their enemies."

"These are the same warriors who end up bleeding all over the mountain every time another band of adventurers comes a-questing?" Grell snapped. She jabbed the end of her cane into Kralk's shoulder. "Go take care of the older ones before they get all excited. Braf is getting his adult fangs, and he's chewing everything that moves." Last night she had caught Braf gnawing one leg of the crib. Only a well-placed whack with Grell's cane had stopped him from chewing all the way through.

Grell began shoving sugar-knots into the mouths of the other babies. She caught herself moving with the rhythm of the war drum, which only annoyed her further.

Three days the goblins had been fighting this latest group of adventurers. Three days of crying babies and cranky toddlers. Three days without a decent night's sleep. Her eyes were gritty, her joints ached, and the next time she caught Kralk sitting on that bucket sucking candy from the children's sugar-knots, Grell was going to ram her cane down her throat.

No . . . Grell had a better idea. Shoving the rest of the sugar-knots into her pocket, she turned away from the crib and headed for the door out of the nursery. The low wooden door was the heaviest, sturdiest door in the goblin lair, not out of concern for the safety of the children, but to muffle the sounds from the nursery.

"Where are you going?" Kralk shouted, loud enough to startle the few babies who had stopped crying.

"To shut those fools up," Grell said, snatching one of the lanterns. She wrapped an extra blanket over her shoulder, tying the ends around Jig's sling. She took a well-patched sack and brushed the cobwebs from the strap. Into this she shoved a few rags, a fresh skin of milk, and a teething stick. She shifted her cane to her other hand as she slipped the strap over one shoulder, adjusting Jig's sling to balance it out. The pain in her lower back made her grimace.

"Why don't you leave Jig here?" Kralk called.

Grell spat. "And wipe your share of arses for a month when I come back and find him 'mysteriously' dead? No thanks." She slammed her cane against the rock, rousing the babies into even louder crying fits. The delightful sound of Kralk's curses followed her as she slipped into the tunnel to the main lair.

Nobody challenged Grell as she made her way through the lair and out of the mountain. She could move quietly when she wanted, and most of the warriors were busy getting themselves slaughtered. When she reached the crumbling overhang where the goblin lair opened to the rest of the world, she extinguished the lantern and hid it behind a small bush. The sun was starting to rise, turning the skies pink and making her eyes water.

She tightened the blanket around herself and Jig. The runt didn't even produce enough heat to help her ward off the chill of the morning air. His rheumy yellow eyes were wrinkled shut against the sun, but aside from the sucking of his sugar-knot, he didn't make a sound. "Smart baby," Grell muttered. "You're better company than Kralk, I'll give you that much."

The wind whipped through stunted pine trees, sprinkling them both with brown needles. Jig sneezed, spitting his sugar-knot onto his stomach and spraying Grell with a mist of spit and other unsavory things. Jamming the knot back into Jig's mouth, Grell headed downhill toward the source of the drumbeat.

The drummer was easy enough to find, standing at the back of a rocky ledge as he watched the battle below. Grell waited amidst the trees to make sure he was alone, then slipped a knife from her belt. She set her cane on the rock. All it would take was one quick blow . . . either to the drum or the drummer, she hadn't decided yet. She glanced down to make sure Jig was still content, then limped quietly into the open.

When she was almost within range, three things happened. An arrow hissed through the air . . . and through the drum, and then through the goblin. A tall, lithe figure dropped from the trees beside the clearing, a new arrow already nocked in his longbow. And baby Jig spat his sugar-knot into the dirt and began to cry.

Grell reacted without thinking: she lifted Jig from his sling, positioning him between herself and the archer.

"Drop the knife."

In the suddenness of the attack, she had forgotten about the knife. It was a miracle she hadn't stuck the baby. Keeping a firm grip on Jig, she loosened her fingers and let the knife clatter to the rock.

More shouts rose from the fight below. The archer whirled, fired, and drew another arrow, all before Grell could even think about shoving him off the outcropping. The wooden scales of his breastplate rattled slightly. The naked wood appeared flimsy to Grell's eye, but no goblin lived to be her age without learning a few things. That was elvish armor, magically hardened to be tougher and lighter than steel. Elves had a real fetish when it came to trees and wood.

"You'd bring your child to the field of battle?" he asked.

Grell lowered the wailing, struggling infant back into her sling. Jig was too puny to stop an arrow anyway. "He's not mine," she said. That was right . . . most surface-dwellers kept and raised the children they bore. The system seemed terribly inefficient to Grell.

"I've never seen a goblin infant," said the elf, stepping closer.

"You thought goblins sprang fully formed from the rocks for you to slaughter?" She jammed a knuckle into

Jig's mouth for him to suck. His baby fangs were just beginning to pierce the gums, but the pain in her finger was better than listening to him cry.

"We slaughtered nobody." The voice came from below the outcropping. The elf relaxed his bow and knelt, hauling his companion up onto the ledge. "You goblins attacked us. We defended ourselves."

Grell stepped to the edge and studied the woods below. Goblin blood turned the earth a gruesome shade of blue. Elves wove through the trees, making no noise save the twang of bowstrings and the ripping sound of blades tearing through goblin armor and flesh. "Defended yourselves? Next time, why don't you defend yourselves over in the hobgoblin tunnels rather than sneaking onto our land to do it?"

The archer caught his companion by the arm. "She's an old woman, Jonathan. With a child."

"She's a goblin, Rindar." But he relaxed slightly. He was bulkier than his companion, and the mane of red hair meant he was no elf. Red stubble dotted his chin, though he was too young to grow a proper beard. He wore a heavy mail shirt, with a green tabard depicting a white dragon coiled around a tree. "If we let her live, she'll lead another attack against us."

Grell kicked the corpse of the goblin drummer. "If you let me live, I'll go back to the nursery and get some sleep."

"I won't risk letting you go free," said Jonathan. "Not until my quest is complete."

Grell rolled her eyes. "What is it about you humans and your quests? Last month it was that knight who wanted to hunt a dragon. Before that it was the wizard and those little fellows. But no matter how important these stupid quests are supposed to be, you all have time to stop and kill goblins along the way."

Jonathan glared. "You're lucky honor prevents me from slaying women or children, goblin."

Grell would have to remember that. Next time they should send an all-female group to ambush the adventurers.

"We will be away from your mountain soon enough," Jonathan went on. "Once we have rescued the stone witch, we can use her power to help overthrow my uncle Wendel, and I shall take my rightful—"

"The stone witch?" Grell asked. Jig was beginning to fuss again. She bounced him against her chest, but he kept kicking and clawing. Why did baby claws have to be so blasted sharp? She caught one tiny hand and began biting off the tips of the black nails as Jig squirmed.

Jonathan drew his sword, adjusting his grip until the moonlight glinted off the blade. "This sword belonged to her lover, the great knight Gregor Williamson. " For a magical artifact, it was an unimpressive thing. Plain, single-edged steel, with a leather-wrapped hilt. The crossguard was hammered brass. "It is the key to resisting the curse laid upon the witch by her traitorous brother, the Warlock of Silverdale. Many years I searched for this blade, while living in the deepest woods with the elves."

Grell spat a bit of claw onto the rock. "Many years?" She was no expert on humans, but she guessed the prince's age to be no more than fourteen or fifteen.

Jonathan's face darkened, but he kept talking. "Even after all these centuries, the edge remains magically sharp, an artifact of great power. With this blade, I will free my—"

At that point, baby Jig interrupted Jonathan's lecture. With a noise that could have come from a goblin twice his size, Jig filled his diaper.

"Disgusting," Jonathan said, backing away.

"What do you feed him?" asked the elf, Rindar. His

nose wrinkled, but he seemed less horrified than his human companion.

"Milk diluted with the blood of whatever we happened to kill that day," Grell said. She set Jig on the ground and untied the knots holding his diaper in place. Moving with the efficiency of many years, she wiped him clean, knotted a replacement diaper between his kicking legs, and carried the soiled diaper to the edge of the ledge. Holding it by one corner, she flung the worst of the contents down the mountainside, narrowly missing one of the elven warriors. She bundled the diaper into a ball and crammed it back into her sack. Kralk could wash it when she returned.

Jonathan was still staring in horror. He pointed his sword at Grell. "On your hand—"

Grell glanced down, then wiped her soiled hand on her apron. Drool dripped down Jig's chin as he grinned at her, showing tiny white fangs on the blue nubs of his gums.

"If I take you to the witch's tomb, will you go away?" Grell asked.

They stared. "You know where the witch is imprisoned?" asked the elf.

Grell pointed to the goblin corpses below. "So did any one of them, if you'd bothered to ask." She dumped Jig back into the sling and adjusted the straps. She wasn't looking forward to this hike. Her back and shoulders already hurt, and her knee popped with every step she took. "Hand me my cane. Unless your noble quest requires you to wipe out another patrol of goblins first?"

Silver minnows darted away from Grell's cane as she waded up a shallow stream. Algae and other plant guck made the footing treacherous. Mud swirled from the rock with each step. She hadn't hiked to the witch's tomb in years. Had the way always been so steep?

"Jonathan will be a great ruler," said Rindar, walking

alongside. Jonathan followed a few steps behind, sword in hand as he searched the mountainside for more goblins to defend himself against. The other elves brought up the rear, silent as ghosts.

Like his pointy-eared companions, Rindar showed no trace of discomfort or fatigue. Stupid elves.

"I've done my best to teach him wisdom and peace," Rindar added, "though he still struggles with his passions. His uncle Wendel ordered him executed when he was barely older than the child you carry. Jonathan was the rightful heir to the throne, the only obstacle to Wendel's power. Only fate saved him. My cousin was at the palace that day, serving as ambassador to the humans. He overheard, and conspired to save Jonathan. When Wendel's servant came to take the child, my cousin spirited him away to the south, where we—"

"Why didn't Wendel just cut the boy's throat?" Grell asked. "Why trust a servant to do it?"

"What?" Rindar blinked, giving Grell a moment of satisfaction. How many goblins could say they had shaken the composure of an elf?

Before Grell could answer, Rindar stopped in midstep. One hand seized Grell's arm, halting her motion. He raised his other hand, fingers balled in a fist.

Grell's ears perked. She heard it too. The clatter of pebbles farther up the mountain, and a faint whispering.

"What is it, Rindar?" asked Jonathan. Those puny round ears really were as useless as they looked.

"Ambush," whispered the elf.

"The goblin has led us into a trap." Jonathan advanced toward Grell, sword raised, but Rindar shook his head.

"*Think*, your majesty. Goblins are not known for such carefully laid ambushes. I warned you when you found that sword that there was danger in wielding it. The magic in that blade—"

"—can be traced by anyone with the proper skill and power," Jonathan finished, sounding annoyed. "Yes, I know."

"How far to the tomb of the stone witch?" asked Rindar.

"Not far." Grell's legs were killing her. The cold water had soaked her sandals and numbed her feet.

"They will have trouble pinpointing our location," Rindar said. "We should still be able to rescue the stone witch before Wendel's scouts discover us, so long as we move swiftly and silently."

Jig hiccuped in his sleep, bouncing his head against Grell's chest. His eyes blinked open. Grell fished for a sugar-knot, but she wasn't fast enough. Hungry and cold, Jig opened his mouth and wailed.

Horns began to blow. She heard men running and shouting through the trees. She flattened her ears. First the drums, now horns. Couldn't anyone fight a *quiet* battle?

"Lead them away," Rindar snapped. Instantly, the other elves leaped from the stream, racing between the trees on either side. Rindar grabbed Jonathan by the arm. "We are outnumbered. We must get to the witch."

The elves had already drawn their bows, firing at targets they could only hear as they disappeared into the woods. Show-offs.

"Come," said Rindar.

Grell finally dug a sugar-knot from her sack. It was covered in dirt and fuzz, but most goblins ate worse things on a daily basis. She would have to stop and feed Jig soon, but hopefully this would keep him quiet until they reached the tomb. Or until Wendel's army killed them.

Grell put both hands on her cane, resting as much of her weight as she could without snapping the wood.

"There," she said. "That jagged crack, behind the fallen pine tree."

She followed them to the entrance. The pine tree was twice as thick as a goblin. (And many goblins could be thick indeed.) She stooped, squeezing through the space where generations of goblins had broken away the smaller branches. Inside, the sunlight dimmed, giving way to a pink glow from the far side of the cave. Insects littered the floor, unmoving and seemingly dead. A young deer lay beyond, its nose almost touching a scattered pile of berries.

Jonathan swung his sword at the fallen tree. The enchanted blade sheared through the branches like they were nothing but smoke.

"The witch is there," said Grell, pointing to the rear of the cave. A line of boulders blocked the body from view. More than one goblin had tried to see what lay hidden there, but the curse on the witch was too powerful. A single step inside the cave was safe enough. A second left you feeling as though you hadn't slept in days. A third step, and all the war drums in the world would fail to rouse you.

Grell yawned. Exhausted as she was, the fate of the stone witch was highly tempting.

"Do you remember the incantation I taught you?" Rindar asked.

"I remember," said Jonathan, clutching his sword.

Rindar squeezed Jonathan's arm, a proud smile momentarily melting that frigid elvish face. "This is your moment. The goblin and I can go no farther." He pointed at the deer. "Without the sword, we'll suffer the same fate as that poor creature." He peered more closely at the deer, and his forehead wrinkled. "Those berries are fresh. Someone else has been here."

"They were thrown in," said Grell. Jig was getting

fussy, and it smelled like he had filled his diaper again. She sat down, groaning as she dropped her sack and pulled Jig out of his sling.

"Why?" asked Jonathan.

"Because deer like berries." He still looked confused. This was the future leader of the humans? "The deer come into the cave. The curse makes them sleep. The goblins come around every few days and use ropes and poles to drag the deer out. The animals are usually groggy when they wake up, so there's time to cut their throats."

Rindar's left eye twitched. Grell couldn't tell if he was angry or trying not to laugh. "A curse left by one of the mightiest warlocks ever to roam this world, and you goblins use it . . . to hunt deer?"

"Deer, rabbits, squirrels. Sometimes wolves or coyotes will sneak in to eat the other animals. Once a family of bears tried to hibernate here for the winter. Those were good days." She shook a bladder of milk and snake blood, mixing it all together while Jig fussed.

Removing the stopper, she jammed the end between his lips. The curved neck of the bladder let her shove small, measured swallows into his mouth.

Another horn blew. Jig jumped, and bloody milk dribbled down his chin and chest. He coughed the rest into Grell's face for good measure.

"They're getting closer," said Rindar. He drew his sword and slipped out of the cave. "Be quick, your majesty." Without a sound, he disappeared.

Jig whimpered, and Grell poked the end of the bladder back into his mouth. Jonathan had his sword in both hands, and was taking slow, measured steps toward the rear of the cave.

"A lifetime I've waited for this moment," he whispered. "A lifetime I've borne the injustices of my uncle, exiled to the elven woods, unable even to speak with other humans, for fear I would be discovered. But no longer. Finally I will return to the northlands and claim the throne for my own." He stopped, glancing at the light coming through the entrance, then at the sword in his hands. When he spoke again, it was in a voice so soft another human probably wouldn't have heard. "And I will leave the only home I've ever known."

Jig choked and coughed. Grell yanked the skin away and sat him up, where he proceeded to spit up. "You barely drank anything," Grell snapped, wiping the warm, damp mess from her leg. "How can that stunted little body produce so much more than it takes in?"

Jonathan took a deep breath and kept walking. Pink light cast weird shadows over his face as he stepped past the rocks. "Rindar never told me she would be so beautiful."

Grell snorted. "Don't you listen to your own bards? Name one song where the hero rescues an ugly maiden."

"Shut up, goblin."

Grell shrugged and turned her attention back to Jig who, from the smell of it, had taken Grell's words as a personal challenge to prove exactly how much more his little body could expel. She waited to make sure he was finished, then set him down with his head resting on her leg. Holding the skin of milk in one hand, she used her other to untie the leaking diaper, wipe the worst of the mess, and wad the whole thing into a squishy ball.

Outside, she could hear the elves and humans fighting in the distance. The occasional close scream let her track Rindar's progress as he led the rest away from the cave.

With one last look at the entrance, Jonathan raised the sword. "Rise, milady. I hold the sword of Gregor Williamson. By the love and power bound within this ancient steel, I command you to awaken." The light at the rear of the cave grew brighter, turning the color of human blood.

.

The horns blew again. Grell's shoulders tensed. "How much longer?" she asked.

"Soon," said Jonathan. "Soon I will begin to avenge the injustices of—"

"And then you'll be gone?" Grell asked.

"You know nothing of war, goblin." Jonathan took a step back, breathing hard. Sweat dripped down his face. Apparently breaking ancient curses was hard work. "The elves are too few to stand against Wendel here. We will retreat to the safety of the elven forest. The stone witch will need time to regain her full powers. We will strike again and again, sapping my uncle's strength, until we—"

"The elven forest?" Grell repeated. "That's south of here, right?"

"That's right. We will—"

"And this Wendel fellow. His lands are north of here?"

Jonathan nodded impatiently. "As the witch's strength grows, Wendel's will wane, and—"

"And we'll be stuck in the middle of your stupid war," Grell finished. The goblin chief would certainly send patrols out to ambush both sides. Goblins had a long, proud tradition of looting battlefields and defeating enemies who were too battered to fight back. And the whole time, the goblins would beat those thrice-damned drums, the humans would blow their horns, and they would all be screaming and shouting, because none of them would have the decency to die quietly.

"You have something to say to me, goblin?" Jonathan pointed his sword at her. "Speak, if you must."

"Do you *want* Wendel's throne?" Grell snapped.

Jonathan stared. "My father's blood pounds through my veins like fire, screaming for justice. My mother's dying screams echo in my dreams, demanding—"

"Do you *want* it?" she repeated. Jonathan's jaw

clenched, but he said nothing. Grell rolled her eyes. "Go home, boy."

"You know nothing of justice or honor, goblin." Jonathan closed his eyes and raised his sword again.

"I know children," Grell said. "Go home. Let the rest of us get some sleep."

Jonathan spun, his face dark. "Be careful how you address me, or I'll remember you serve no further use."

"I thought honorable men didn't kill women and children," Grell said.

"You're a goblin. You'd turn on me in the end anyway, and I'd be forced to cut you down." Jonathan began to move around from the witch's stone grave, sword held high.

He had taken only a single step when Grell grabbed the wadded diaper and hurled it at him.

The prince moved with the reflexes of an elf-trained warrior, instinctively moving to block the missile with his sword . . . his enchanted sword, with the supernaturally sharp edge. The blade sliced clean through the diaper, spraying its contents all over his neck, chest, and arms.

Grell had never seen such an expression of horror and disgust. For several heartbeats, Jonathan stood frozen. Then he was screaming and ripping the tabard from his body. The sword clattered to the ground as he tried desperately to get the tabard over his head while avoiding the soiled spots.

He didn't have time to realize his mistake. With the tabard still raised partially over his face, Jonathan toppled to the ground, asleep.

"What a shame," Grell said. The body of the would-be prince had fallen behind the rocks. "Waste of a good meal."

Grell found Rindar in hand-to-hand combat with two human scouts. For some reason, Rindar had gone back to using his bow and arrow, while the humans thrust at him with short swords. Rindar twisted and leaped, avoiding lunge after lunge until one of the humans stumbled. Quicker than Grell could see, Rindar drew and fired. The arrow ripped through both men, who collapsed to the ground.

Elves were such show-offs. Grell hobbled closer, slapping the rocks with her cane so he would be sure to hear.

"What happened?" Rindar asked. "Is Jonathan—"

"He got halfway through his incantation and dropped his sword."

The sound that escaped Rindar's open mouth was somewhere between a sob and a cough. "How?"

Grell shrugged. "I was busy with an oozing diaper at the time. Maybe the warlock placed a second curse to trap any would-be rescuers. Maybe his hands were sweaty and he lost his grip. Maybe he just didn't want to be king. How should I know?"

Rindar's face went still, losing what little color it had. "Jonathan . . . the sword . . . can we retrieve it?"

"He was standing behind the tomb when he fell." She leaned on her cane, using her other hand to bounce Jig in his sling.

Rindar slipped his bow over one shoulder. He looked like he was about to fall down. "I shouldn't have left him," he whispered.

"You said he was the last heir to that throne, right?" Grell asked.

Rindar nodded.

"So his uncle would be the legitimate ruler now."

Another slow, stunned nod.

"Which means there's really no reason to keep up all this fighting?"

Rindar moved slowly, like a man underwater. He removed a silver chain from around his neck. A long, gold whistle hung at the end of the chain. The high, piercing sound was more than enough to start Jig crying again.

"I failed him," Rindar whispered.

Grell was already making her way back to the cave, flattening her ears against Jig's crying. If that fool elf kept standing there all forlorn, he would be an easy target for Wendel and his human soldiers. As for Grell, there was no way she was going to hike back to the lair with humans and elves racing about the mountain. Goblins too, once they scrounged another drum. She could wait until tomorrow, when the elves had retreated and things settled down.

Inside the witch's cave, she emptied out her sack and set the still-wailing Jig inside. She stifled a yawn as she looped the strap over the end of her cane. With both hands, she lifted the sack farther into the cave until Jig's cries died down.

With that, she gathered the fallen branches from outside the cave and lay them down beside her. She bundled a clean rag beneath her head and closed her eyes. The sticks would prevent her from rolling into the cave and falling under the enchantment. Rocks dug into her back, and the pink light from the back was a bit distracting, not to mention the pine-scented breeze blowing in the entrance.

But for the first time in days, neither horns nor drums nor wailing children interrupted her rest.

CRUMBS

Esther M. Friesner

Nebula Award—winner Esther Friesner is the author of thirty-one novels and over one hundred short stories, in addition to being the editor of seven popular anthologies. Her works have been published in the United States, the United Kingdom, Japan, Germany, Russia, France, and Italy. She is also a published poet, a playwright, and once wrote an advice column, "Ask Auntie Esther." Her articles on fiction writing have appeared in *Writer's Market* and Writer's Digest Books.

Besides winning two Nebula Awards in succession for Best Short Story (1995 and 1996), she was a Nebula finalist three times and a Hugo finalist once. She received the Skylark Award from NESFA and the award for Most Promising New Fantasy Writer of 1986 from *Romantic Times*.

Her latest publications include a short story collection, *Death and the Librarian and Other Stories* from Thorndike Press, *Turn the Other Chick* from Baen

Books, fifth in the popular "Chicks in Chainmail" series that she created and edits, and the paperback edition of *E.Godz*, also from Baen, which she co-wrote with Robert Asprin. She is currently working on three YA novels as well as continuing to write and publish short fiction.

Educated at Vassar College, she went on to receive her M.A. and Ph.D. from Yale University, where she taught Spanish for a number of years. She lives in Connecticut with her husband, two all-grown-up children, two rambunctious cats, and a fluctuating population of hamsters.

SIR HANSON THE HAWK-eyed rode his mount to the edge of the Dark Woods, peered into their sinister shadows, and pondered the next step of the quest he was about to undertake in the name of his sovereign, Good King Donald. As the boldest, bravest, and third-handsomest knight ever to couch lance in the service of his king, there could be only one thought going through his mind at such a solemn moment, namely:

"Why do *I* always get the squirrel-butt jobs?"

It was a rhetorical question whose answer he knew well: The boldest, bravest, and third-handsomest knight in the realm was also the poorest, having come of nouveau only relatively riche peasant stock. Being a knight was a costly business. Horses didn't grow on trees. And while Good King Donald was quite good, he applied most of said goodness to himself.

Oh, he was open-handed to others when it suited him, but it only suited him to demonstrate generosity to those knights whose quests brought home the bacon. (Also the gold, the jewels, and the damsels whose doting parents were wealthy enough to shower largesse upon the warrior who'd saved their Little Pumpkin from becoming dragon chow.) This was not favoritism, but pure reciprocity: All knights were compelled to tender the spoils of their adventurings to the king, who in turn restored to them a fair share of said tribute. ("Fair" being based on the king's conviction that his loyal knights were most likely holding back a good ten percent of their gross booty.)

The system worked. That is to say, it worked for Good King Donald and for those knights who came into his employ from wealthier families. Along with sword, shield, lance, and banner, each affluent applicant for a position in the king's chivalric entourage likewise packed "A small, most unworthy gift for Your Majesty, in gratitude for Your Majesty's most unlooked-for favor in accepting my humble self into your service."

It *did* sound ever so much more romantic than: "Hey, King! Here's your bribe!"

The gift-of-unworthiness was not obligatory, by any means. Neither was His Majesty required to hand out the really *tasty* quests—the quests where the gold and jewels and truly hot damsels practically fell into your lap—to any knight whose family circumstances prohibited him from bringing that gift with him when he first joined the team.

Funny, the way it always just *happened* to work out, though.

Thus, as he lingered at the border of the Dark Woods, Sir Hanson the Hawk-eyed well might have been pausing to regain his balance, for his career as a knight had been the most vicious of whirligigs: No choice assignments without a plump gift to the king, no way of obtaining a plump enough gift for the king without a choice assignment. Sir Hanson the Hawk-eyed could have changed his name to Sir Hanson the Knightly-scutwork-until-you-die without violating any truth-in-advertising laws.

The quest to which he was presently assigned was a case in point. It was a simple Missing Persons affair, and while the Persons thus Missing were important enough, none involved were princess-level important.

"Maybe it's a dragon that's responsible," Sir Hanson muttered as he leaned slightly forward upon the pommel of his saddle. "There aren't supposed to be any dragons in the Dark Woods, just trolls and goblins and giants and flesh-eating witches, but you never can tell with dragons: They pretty much turn up wherever they like. Who's going to tell them not to? And where there's dragons, there's hoards of gold. It can't be helped." He ended on an optimistic note that rang somewhat tinny, even to his own ears.

He consulted the scrap of parchment in his hand one more time. Sir Hanson had requested that the palace scribe write down the particulars of the case, being a firm believer in the Rule of the Six P's, viz.: *Prior Planning Prevents Poorly Prepared Paladins*.

"Vanishments," Sir Hanson read. "Mysterious vanishments within the Dark Woods, cause unknown, sorcery suspected." He shook his head. "But that's impossible. Who'd go *into* the Dark Woods these days? Everyone *knows* that they're rife with witches who'd turn a child into gingerbread and gobble him up before you can blink. And since the construction of the Dark Woods Bypass, there's no need to risk traveling through this unholy place. Only a fool would do so."

Once more, Sir Hanson's head filled with the king's indignant voice giving him his assignment: *We're not talking about a bunch of children or village idiots here, Hanson; we're talking about some of the most cunning, ruthless, successful merchants in my realm! These were not stupid men, and yet, they were all last observed going into the Dark Woods and not coming out again.*

Men? Sir Hanson had echoed. *But in the old tales, isn't it always children who—*

His Majesty cared not a festering fig for the old tales. *Do you think I'd be wasting any of my manpower if this was about* children? *Children do not pay taxes, or see fit to remember their beloved king with appropriately lavish gifts at Yuletide. To the fuming pits with the children: These are* real *people who've vanished, and I want to know the reason why.*

It was interviews like that that sometimes made Sir Hanson the Hawk-eyed pause to wonder just what, exactly, Good King Donald was good *for.*

Sir Hanson took up the reins, and urged his steed forward. "On, Barbelindo!" he cried, lifting his chin and striking a heroic pose.

The horse just stood there and, very slowly and with supreme contempt, turned to look at him. In spite of the grandiloquent name Sir Hanson had bestowed upon his mount, they both knew the truth: Barbelindo the Bold was really Bessie, a stolid, serviceable stopgap steed from his father's modest stable. Instead of a proper knight's horse—a fiery stallion with coat of midnight and eyes of flame—all Sir Hanson could afford was Bessie, a mare with coat of oatmeal, eyes of hazelnut, and an expression that made him swear she was always laughing at him.

Covert equine insubordination aside, she was obedient enough. Her one non-negotiable point, however, was her name. And so, muttering angrily under his breath, Sir Hanson managed to grit out a terse, "Giddup, Bessie," before the beast would consent to carry him on to adventure 'neath the Dark Woods' drear and dreadful boughs.

They rode down a forest path that was not entirely unfamiliar to him, even though he had never traveled its tree-shadowed twists and turns himself before now. The

Dark Woods and its reputed perils were old hat to Sir Hanson, who had grown up bored halfway out of his skull by tales of this selfsame place of dangers dire and dolorous, whenever Auntie Gretel came to visit. It never failed: the conversation with her brother Hansel always slewed back to their childhood adventures with the Dark Woods, the breadcrumb trail, and the witch they'd so cleverly slaughtered.

"Ah, there was gold aplenty in that gingerbread house!" Auntie Gretel cackled. "God knows how the crone came to have it."

"Who cares how she got it?" her brother Hansel responded. "What matters is we did. Gold's a good dog: It knows its proper master!"

"True, dear brother, true." This was invariably the point where Auntie Gretel sighed happily and twirled the fat strand of pearls around her neck.

Unfortunately this was invariably also the point where young Hanson let loose a cavernous yawn. (Family histories are wasted on the young.) That yawn made young Hanson's father cuff his ear and deliver a lecture about how the witch's purloined riches became the foundation of the family's modest fortune.

"Aye, and the reason why a poor woodchopper's son like me will become the father of a belted knight some day!" he concluded, clouting young Hanson in the other ear for good measure.

Sir Hanson's mother was just as weary as her son of hearing the old, old story. She took pains to confide a few salient details that Dad and Auntie Gretel left out, details she'd learned once upon a time *in vino veritas*, when her husband had turned truthful in his cups.

"Abandoned by their parents in the Dark Woods?" she said with a sarcastic lift of one eyebrow. "Did you never *meet* your grandparents? Your Grandpa Hansel-the-Elder would sooner chop off his own arm for the stewpot! Your pa and auntie ran off into the Dark Woods on purpose, by themselves, because they'd heard about the witch's gold and decided it'd be great sport to rob her. That whole bit about the witch caging your pa to fatten him up while making your auntie keep house for her, that's trash and moonshine. Gretel's such a slob, she wouldn't know which end of a broom to hold if you shoved it up her—er, never mind.

"You see, the witch was a keen cardsharp—loved gambling to the point where she couldn't think straight when the gaming fever was on her. Gretel challenged her to a long sit-down over the devil's pasteboards—hand after hand of Trim the Brisket, Five Yellow Dogs, Seeking Aubrey's Ankle, and Camelot Hold 'Em—and by the time the sun went down, she'd won most of the old woman's gold."

"And the witch let her go home with her winnings?" young Hanson inquired of his mother.

Her laughter shook cobwebs from the ceiling corners. "After she caught on that Gretel'd marked the cards? Fat chance! But while Gretel was separating the witch from her treasure, your pa'd been rummaging through the old besom's books until he found one full of simple spells.

"The witch was just about to mount her broomstick and fly after those treacherous brats when your pa launched an incantation that brought the gingerbread cottage tumbling down on the crone's skull. She was crushed beneath an avalanche of stale cake and candy pieces, your pa and auntie took to their heels with her gold in a little casket between 'em, and that, dear heart o' mine, is what *really* happened."

"Oh," said young Hanson, who rather liked the family history account better.

Now he rode along the way his pa and aunt had trodden so long ago. It did not take him long to notice that something was not quite right about the path through the Dark Woods.

"A troll-haunted woodland road with *fresh* wagon ruts? And so many?" He blinked at the evidence of his eyes. True, merchants had vanished 'neath the not-so-jolly greenwood shade, but Sir Hanson was expecting to find hoofprints of horse or donkey, something proper to a lone wayfarer who'd taken a wrong turn into the forest and was waylaid by crone or creature. When a merchant went into the Dark Woods with a wagon heavily laden enough to leave ruts this deep, it meant he'd gone in with property and purpose.

Sir Hanson had just reached this conclusion when his musings were shattered by a loud, ungodly bawling. It came from under an abandoned wagon dead center on the forest path. He dismounted and peered into the shadows beneath the cart, expecting to encounter a banshee, at the very least. Instead he found a weeping child.

It didn't take much parley to persuade the tyke—a dirty-faced, towheaded boy who looked barely nine years old—to come out and accept an apple. As the lad crunched into the rosy fruit with the grace of a starving dog, Sir Hanson tried to question him, thus:

"Boy, how did you come to be here?"

"Mumf vavver tol' mezoo wait here furrim 'til heecumback f'me," the boy replied, cheeks bulging like a chipmunk's. Then he swallowed and repeated: "My father told me to wait here for him until he comes back for me."

"Your father left you here?" Sir Hanson had a bad feeling about this. The whole thing smacked of mid-woodland child abandonment, something with which he was more than a little familiar.

On the other hand, there was still the matter of the

wagon. People abandoned children far more readily than
they gave up all claim to a fine vehicle like this one.
Come to think of it, though the cart was here, where were
the beasts to pull it? The roadway bore ample, pungent
evidence that the cart had been brought this far by the
labor of oxen, yet oxen there were none. It was all most
puzzling.

"Lad, did you father happen to mention where he was
going and why he took the oxen with him but left you behind?" Sir Hanson handed the boy a piece of bread and a
small chunk of cheese to grease the wheels of conversation.

The boy was not quite so desperate for food after the
apple, so he munched the bread and cheese in smaller
bites while replying: "Oh, he had to take the oxen.
They're all he had to offer up after the last time. But kids
ain't allowed to go into the candy house. My father said
that she turns away anyone who tries to bring one in,
'cause it's no fit place for children."

"Whereas the Dark Woods is quite the *ideal* place to
leave a child alone." Sir Hanson's mouth tightened. "The
candy house, you say? Odd. That sounds very much like
the place where my father and auntie once met a woodland witch."

"A witch, that's right!" The boy bobbed his head happily, licking crumbs from his lips. "That's her, the one my
father's gone to see; a witch top to toe, he says."

Sir Hanson liked what he was hearing less and less.
His hands began to twitch, as though they dreamed their
own dextrous dreams of what they would do to this
child's father once the formal introductions were over.
"Boy, which way did your father go?" he asked.

"Down this path," the boy said, pointing in the direction
made obvious by the wagon ruts. Then he paused, a worried
look in his eyes. "Are you going to leave me, too?"

For answer, Sir Hanson picked up the boy and plunked

him down astraddle Bessie's rump, then remounted. "I am called Sir Hanson the Hawk-eyed. Let's find this errant father of yours, lad," he said with a backward glance.

"Bardric," the boy said.

"All right, your father Bardric. I'm sure we can—"

"My father's name is Wulfram the goldsmith," the boy cut in. "*My* name is Bardric. Or were you going to call me 'lad' and 'boy' and 'hey, you' all the time?"

As Sir Hanson and his newfound companion trotted on down the road, they passed more and more abandoned carts. The graveyard of derelict vehicles presented a more chilling tableau than any set piece of gnarled and sinister trees, their bare branches like black claws, their lightning-blasted limbs home to birds of ill- or somewhat-under-the-weather omen.

"This likes me not," said Sir Hanson. Bessie stopped dead in her tracks, turned, and gave him one of those equine *Oh, please!* looks such as she always dispensed whenever he assumed the mantle of pretentious parlance so dear to his blue-blooded paladin peers. "What I mean to say"—Sir Hanson gave the sarcastic steed a killing look—"is this smells funny."

"No, it doesn't," Bardric said, his nose twitching like a squirrel's. "It smells like gingerbread."

Indeed it did, and after navigating her way through an especially nasty bottleneck of forsaken carts, Bessie brought Sir Hanson and the boy out of the Dark Woods and into a bright clearing whose centerpiece was a wonderful cottage made all of gingerbread and decorated with lashings of sweetmeats and candy.

"Wow!" Sir Hanson exclaimed in astonishment. Unluckily, Bessie took "Wow!" for "Whoa!" and pulled up short. The surprise of this sudden stop sent the unready knight toppling from the saddle, landing flat on his back on the ground.

The ground was lumpy. The ground was talkative.

"Hey! Get offa me, you big clod! I'm workin' here!"

Sir Hanson rolled himself over quickly and pushed himself up on his forearms, then stared in astonishment at the wee goblin who'd broken his fall. The creature wore a crisp peppermint-striped tunic emblazoned with an embroidered badge bearing the name *Drogo*. Beneath it was a brass pin with the words *Employee of the Month*.

Sir Hanson stood up and bowed to the goblin. "My apologies, good monsterling. It was an accident."

"Yeah, that's what they all say." The goblin clambered to his feet and brushed loam off his livery. "'Specially the cheapskates what leave their carts parked back in the woods so's they won't hafta tip a poor, honest, hard-workin' goblin." He spat to emphasize his contempt for such niggardly highpockets. "So you want I should take care of the horse or you wanna stand there yapping all day? No skin off my scales, either way." Then he glanced up and caught sight of the boy, still holding on to Bessie's back. A cloud crossed Drogo's grotesque visage. "Hey, wassa matter, you don't know the regs? No kids allowed!"

Sir Hanson calmly drew his sword and leveled it at the goblin's wrinkled throat. "That, sir, is no child. That is Malagendron, the most puissant wizard in seven kingdoms. He has taken a fancy to view the world through a child's eyes, and who am I to argue with a sorcerer who has the capability to summon up a legion of fiends at the drop of a hat? Goblin-eating fiends," he clarified.

Drogo gave "Malagendron" a dubious look, but between Sir Hanson's persuasive steel-edged argument and the cardinal rule of You-never-can-tell-with-wizards, he decided to err on the side of cowardice.

"Oooookay, buddy, he's a wizard, have it your way."

He cut a brief bow to "Malagendron," then turned back to Sir Hanson and said, "So you want valet parking or not?"

"Wow," said Bardric, his eyes growing wide and wider as he took in the scene that burst upon his senses the instant he and Sir Hanson passed through the gingerbread cottage's door. "This is— It doesn't make sense that— It's impossible for—" He gave up trying to put his astonishment into words and merely whistled, low and long.

Sir Hanson agreed with him on all counts, including that whistle. "This is beyond belief. How can a simple woodland cottage hold a hall like this, clearly at least three stories high and the length of ten such huts? How could it contain so many people making so much noise, yet we heard not one hint of this commotion on *that* side of the door?" He made a sweeping gesture, wishing to indicate the humble pastry portal.

The door was gone, and in its place there stood a woman of surpassing allure, clad in a gown of rich carmine velvet. She must have paid a pretty penny for it, though a shrewd consumer would point out that she'd been short-changed as far as upper body coverage. The neckline swooped so low that for all intents she wore a skirt with sleeves.

Sir Hanson's dramatic gesture wound up lodged warmly between her bared bosoms. He gasped and jerked back his hand, blushing. The woman gave him a smile that dripped piquant knowledge.

"Have we met?" she purred, fingers playing idly with her thick black curls.

"Er, no," Sir Hanson managed to say. "I'm new."

"Wouldn't you rather be used?"

"I beg your pardon?"

The lady laughed. "Never mind. Welcome, good sir knight. I am Bezique the enchantress. Your pleasure is my sole concern, however—" She cast a sidelong look at Bardric. The boy was gazing rapturously at her cleavage with the single-mindedness of a cat regarding an unattended anchovy. "Hmm. I was about to say that we do not permit children on the premises, but given the way this one's staring—"

"He's not a child, he's a wizard, and we're only staying long enough to find his father," a flustered Sir Hanson blurted.

Bezique lifted one shapely eyebrow. "Do tell. Very well, then. Welcome, O mighty wizard." She curtsied low before Bardric, who almost choked on his own tongue as a result of the view. "What name do men employ who speak of thee?"

Poor Bardric uttered a series of hormone-hampered squeaks and gurgles before managing to gasp: "'S Murgedandron—Rhododendron—Didjamindron—*Bob!*"

"Oh, ho, ho, my powerful wizard, you jest with the lady," Sir Hanson cried in haste, slapping Bardric on the back. Grinning stiffly at Bezique he added: "This is *Malagendron*, just as we told that likely little goblin out there who parked my horse Bess—Barbelindo."

"I see." The enchantress laid a finger to her soft lips. "And who are you, apart from being the third-handsomest knight I've ever seen?"

"I am called Sir Hanson the Hawk-eyed," he replied.

"Sir Hanson . . ." Bezique looked pensive. "There's something about you that reminds me of— No matter: You didn't come here to chat with me, much as I'd like that. The games await, and I'm certain that Lady Luck perches on your shoulder, eager to show you that you're her special darling. What would you prefer to play, good sir?"

"Er, what do you offer?" Sir Hanson hedged.

"Wouldn't *you* like to know?" The lady's throaty laugh

made the ruby necklace resting on her bosoms bounce, which sent poor Bardric rocketing into puberty on the spot.

Shortly thereafter, her hands resting on her guests' shoulders, Bezique guided the newcomers on a grand tour of the gingerbread cottage's many attractions.

"Now over there you have the card tables—your choice of Dragon's Grandma, Sixty-two Ogres, Over-Under-Up-Me-Jerkin, and of course everyone's favorite, The Dwarf's Drawers. And *there* we have the dicing tables, if you fancy a game of Fewmets instead. You'll notice that our older customers prefer the one-armed brigands, over by the far wall—"

"Oooh! I wanna try that!" Bardric tugged on Bezique's arm and pointed to where many men were gathered around a long table with a large wheel in the center. "It looks like fun!"

As the boy spoke, the ogre in charge of the game gave the wheel a forceful spin, then reached into the cage at his elbow, plucked out a hamster, and tossed it onto the reeling wheel. The little creature's cry was midway between terror and delight as it went whirling and bouncing around and around before falling into one of the many numbered hollows on the wheel's perimeter.

"My apologies, great Malagendron," Bezique said smoothly. "The Great Wheel is off-limits to wizards. All of our equipment is proof against any magical attempts at cheating, but the hamsters themselves are susceptible to sorcerous influence." She steered them away, toward a different part of the hall.

The heady reek of ale and stronger waters made Sir Hanson's head spin as Bezique conducted him and Bardric up to the bar. The tapster, a troll of dour aspect, leaned one warty elbow on the sleek mahogany countertop and rumbled, "What'll it be?"

"Give these men whatever they like, Thrombo," Bezique said.

"Oh no, I couldn't possibly—" Sir Hanson began.

"Shurrup'n drink!" the troll roared, slamming down a monstrously huge tankard. "The first one's always free."

With the cool assurance of one who knows nothing of alcohol, but has heard it being ordered just so, time after time, by the grown-ups in his life, young Bardric rapped out: "I'll have a Wyvern's Revenge, straight up, with a twist, and don't bruise the gin."

"You'll do no such thing!"

A big-bellied, broad-shouldered man came charging up to the bar, grabbed Bardric by the back of his tunic, and hoisted him off his feet. "What are you doing *here* when I told you to stay *there*? And who told you that you could drink, scamp?" he bawled in the boy's face while Bardric kicked wildly and impotently. "At your age? Your mother would have my skin if she found out that—*Argh!*"

The man's tirade was brought to an unexpected halt by Sir Hanson's brawny hand closing on the back of *his* tunic and jerking him backward so hard that he dropped Bardric. "And what part of your pathetic anatomy do you think that good woman would have if she found out you deserted the lad *there*, in the middle of the Dark Woods?" The knight gave his captive a brusque shake to emphasize his point, then let him go.

The man staggered a few steps off, turned, and assumed an air of wounded dignity. "How dare you, sirrah!" he huffed. "Do you know who I am?"

"Apart from a bad father?" Sir Hanson replied. "You're Wulfram the goldsmith, and a 'special' friend of Good King Donald's, unless I miss my guess."

"That's *Master* Wulfram to you, O Sir Paltry of Penniless," the goldsmith thundered. "And how do you know of the favor our beloved king has given me?"

"Because, *Master* Wulfram," Sir Hanson said coldly, "I am the one whom our beloved king saddled with the quest of finding out what became of you and a dozen or so more of His Majesty's most generous 'friends.'" He cast a look over the varied delights of the enchanted cottage, recognizing more than a few of the missing merchants at the bar and the gaming tables. "Now I know."

"By my broomstick!" Bezique exclaimed, staring at Sir Hanson. "And now I know where I've seen such a prissy, self-righteous face before! You've a father named Hansel, perchance? And an Aunt Gretel, too?"

Sir Hanson gave the enchantress a somewhat baffled look. "Even so, m'lady. How did you—?" It came to him. "You're *that* witch?" He gave her a closer look. "I must say, you've aged well, for a dead crone."

Bezique slapped his face with dispassionate competence. "So hale, so handsome, so hearty, and yet—so hamheaded. Pity. Did you ever stop to think that I might have had a *mother*? Or that I'd consult my crystal to conjure up a vision of her doom?"

"Very resourceful of you m'lady," Sir Hanson said. "And much as I apologize for my father and aunt having killed your mother"—(Here he drew his sword.)—"I'd appreciate it if you didn't force me to do the same to you."

He did not hold the sword like a man who means business, for he acted most reluctantly. Though he found Bezique both charming and attractive, he had his knightly duty to perform.

"I am sent here to return these men to the bosoms of their loving families," he declared. "Clearly your spells are both the vile lure and the unsavory bond keeping them tethered here. On peril of your life, release them from your toils, O sorceress!"

Bezique, the troll barkeep, Master Wulfram, and every

other merchant and employee in the general vicinity stared at Sir Hanson for about three heartbeats. Then they all burst out laughing.

Only little Bardric refrained from shaming his rescuer with such raucous mockery. The boy gazed up at the knight, gently touched his swordarm, and said: "There's no spells to break, Sir Hanson. They come here 'cause they *want* to."

"Have *you* fallen under some enchantment while I wasn't looking?" Sir Hanson demanded of the lad. "What power on earth would compel sensible, prosperous men to dare the heart of the Dark Woods, abandoning carts, kine, and kids en route? What power if not the blackest magic?"

"Well, I don't know about anyone else here," Master Wulfram spoke up. "But I had to come back and try to break even. If the wife finds out I lost all my gold and trade-goods again, *plus* another pair of oxen, she'll kill me."

Sir Hanson's mouth hung open like a dropped drawbridge. "You all came here because you *wanted* to?"

"Who wouldn't?" one of the other merchants spoke up. "There's gold to be won by easier means than our daily toil."

"The one-armed brigand I played this morning just spewed out five hundred silver pieces!" another man announced, to loud cheers. Neither he nor his audience considered the fact that he'd fed the machine over five *thousand* of those same bits of silver.

"The hamsters love me!" a third merchant shouted from his place beside the Great Wheel.

Bezique laid her graceful hands upon Sir Hanson's arm and gently coaxed him to resheath his sword, then steered the stunned knight to a small table in the most intimate corner of the bar. A buxom wood sprite clad in a pair of maple-seed pasties and a whisper of ivy-trimmed panties set two glasses and a pitcher of something green between them before flying off again.

"You see, after Mother died—" Bezique began.

"I can't beg your forgiveness for that enough, m'lady," Sir Hanson broke in. "I vow upon my honor as a knight, I will make full restitution for every coin my father and aunt stole from her!"

Bezique waved away his impassioned offer. "Water under the troll-infested bridge," she said. "Mother knew the risks of the profession. It was her own fault for letting her gambling addiction get the better of her." She absent-mindedly dug two huge chunks of spicy cake out of the wall beside her and passed him one. "Here. On the house."

Between bites of gingerbread, she continued: "Some years after Mother died, I took over this location. The other woodland witches were very helpful when it came to reconstructing the old place. Did you know that with gingerbread cottages you need permits from the Building Inspector *and* a reputable baker? But alas, soon after that, your *dear* King Donald built that blasted Dark Woods Bypass."

"I understand your feelings, m'lady, but understand ours," Sir Hanson said. "The Dark Woods teems with anthropophagous perils. A worthy king must look to the welfare of his subjects."

Bezique sipped her drink languidly. "And building a road that charges ruinous tolls that go straight into the Royal Treasury is *so* magnanimous," she drawled.

As little as he personally cared for Good King Donald, Sir Hanson felt impelled by his oath of knighthood to defend his sovereign. "All good citizens of this realm must stand ready to make sacrifices in the name of security," he intoned. "If the king had not built the Dark Woods

Bypass, toll road or no, the child-devouring witches would have already won."

Bezique laughed. "Do you believe *everything* you're told? Eat children? Gah! Do you have any idea how hard they are to *clean*? To say nothing of the calories, or choosing the proper wine. And don't you *dare* mention Chianti!"

"You can't mean to say you exist on gingerbread," Sir Hanson protested.

"We almost existed on nothing, thanks to your precious king," Bezique shot back. "Do you know how badly his stupid toll road impacted the local economy? When you call something a bypass, simple folk presume it's shielding them from something they *should* pass by! No more moony swains and lasses came to see us for love potions, no more harried husbands sought cures for their wives' peevish fits, nor peeved wives sought something to make their less-than-lusty mates a bit more *manly*, if you follow me."

Sir Hanson wore the look of one who has awakened from a bad dream into a substandard reality. "Is that all you did?" he asked. "Sell potions to the peasants?"

"Peasants?" Bezique showed her teeth in a feral grin. "Just ask Good Queen Ivana why it took her ten years to produce the crown prince, and then only after she made a trip into the Dark Woods."

Sir Hanson slumped back in his chair. "I'm dead," he announced.

Bezique stood up, leaned across the table in a most scenic manner, took his face in both her hands, and gave him a long, deep kiss. He responded eagerly, and when at last she broke their embrace she observed, "You don't kiss like a corpse. Why claim kinship?"

"Because my mission hither was to bring back the errant merchants. It doesn't look like they'll come willingly, and I can't force all of them. Good King Donald has little use for knights who fail him."

"Bother Good King Donald. Stay here, sir knight, and serve us."

" 'Us?' "

The enchantress spread her arms wide, indicating the flash and glitter of the vast gambling den. "Does this *look* like a one-witch operation? We woodland sorceresses formed a corporation, once we realized what Good King Donald had done to us. We reasoned that if the public no longer had any *need* to enter the Dark Woods, perhaps we should make them *want* to do so."

Sir Hanson shook his head sadly. "Fair lady, I'd gladly stay here and turn my sword to your service, but if I return a failure, King Donald will imprison me for a false knight, and force my father to ruin himself with my ransom. And if I don't return at all, Good King Donald will declare me a traitor and confiscate my father's property to the last crumb."

"We could fake your death," Bezique suggested. "I'd really like to take you on as my new chief of security. In fact, I'd really just like to take you on." She licked her lips.

Sir Hanson shook his head. "As I would like to serve you, in all ways possible, and in one or two that might not be possible but that it would be a lot of fun to try anyway. However, if I'm reported dead, it would break my parents' hearts, and then there's Good King Donald's death-tax to be paid, and—and—and—" He sighed. "And even if I could evade all those consequences, I wouldn't have long to enjoy my new life here. Mark me, the king will order knight after knight into the Dark Woods until he finally learns about the riches gathered here, and then he'll send an army here to take 'em from you. That man loves gold like a pig loves slop, and there's only so much that witchery can do to ward off cold steel."

"Do you sense a *unifying theme* to the woes confronting you and me and all this kingdom?" the enchantress asked grimly. "Have you never thought how . . . *pleasant* things might be, were we rid of such rapacious royalty?"

"*Kill* him?" Sir Hanson was aghast. No matter his personal feelings about Good King Donald, he was still an honorable knight. As such, he could not countenance the summary snuffing of his liege lord, and he said so. "Besides, the regal wretch has always got at least fifty guards protecting his miserable royal hide at all times," he concluded.

Bezique leaned across the table and traced titillating patterns on Sir Hanson's dampening palms. "Oh, I wasn't going to suggest that *we* kill him," she said.

"A trail of crumbs, is it?" Good King Donald lowered his voice until it was barely audible and darted his eyes to left and right, vigilant against prying eyes. He and Sir Hanson were barricaded together in a secret chamber in the topmost turret of the castle, but the king wasn't taking any chances. He'd commanded his guards to leave him alone with the man, (following the ceremonial weapons-removal-and-strip-search, of course). The news this knight had brought back from his quest more than made up for the fact that he'd failed to fetch the missing merchants.

"Aye, crumbs," said Sir Hanson, reaching into the little pouch at his belt. "Like these I first showed you." He sprinkled a pinch of gold bits across the tabletop.

The king's eyes lit up like bonfires into which he flung all caution. "You left a whole *trail* of them behind you?"

Sir Hanson nodded solemnly. "Not all the way to the castle, nor even all the way to the edge of the Dark Woods, lest uninvited eyes catch sight of them and deprive you, my king, of a treasure trove that's yours by right. No birds will gobble crumbs like these; the route back to the dragon's cavern will remain well-blazed. There was such plentiful store of gold in that cave that I could safely squander as much as I needed to mark the path."

"And you say that the dragon in whose cavern you found this fortune is—?"

"The cave is filled with dragon bones, Sire," Sir Hanson replied. "And so much gold that even if you were to take your fifty stout guardsmen with you, there'd be more than enough for all of them to have a share."

"Share . . ." The king repeated the word as though it were coined in some foreign tongue. He pursed his lips in thought, then asked: "Is gold very heavy, good Sir Hanson the Hawk-eyed?"

"Heavy enough, but not so heavy that one man, alone and unassisted, couldn't carry off a fortune in his bare hands. And if he took an ox cart with him, the beasts could bear away enough to purchase an empire or two. So if you bring your guards, they would be able to carry—"

"Never mind about my guards," said the king. "Go get me some oxen, good Duke Hanson the *Silent*."

"*He's* the one who jumped to conclusions," said the newly made duke to his sorcerous sweetheart. They were closeted together in her bedchamber, just off the casino floor, whither she'd dragged him the instant he returned to inform her of the success of his errand. "It wasn't as if I lied."

"Of course you didn't," Bezique replied dreamily, doing magical things with her hands.

"The trail *was* well-blazed. He could have followed it out again easily enough."

"Mmmm."

"And the cavern *did* hold just as much gold as I told him. I saw the same vision in your crystal that you did."

"Such a clever boy. Hold still. Stupid armor. Where's my monkey wrench?"

But conscience would not allow Duke Hanson to enjoy Bezique's attentions. He sat up and exclaimed: "And the cave *was* filled with dragon bones, just as I said! Is it *my* fault that there was still a living dragon wrapped around them?"

"Found it!" cried Bezique, brandishing the wrench.

Some time later, a loud whoop rang through the raisin-studded rafters of the gaming hall. At the joyful sound, Master Wulfram looked up glumly from his losing hand of Sixty-two Ogres.

"'Bout time *someone* got lucky in here," he grumbled.

"Shut up and play cards, Pa," said Bardric, raking in the pot.

FELLOW TRAVELER

Donald J. Bingle

Donald J. Bingle is probably best known as the world's top-ranked player of classic role-playing games for more than fifteen years, but he is also a frequent contributor to short story anthologies in the science fiction, fantasy, horror, and comedy genres, including the DAW anthologies *Civil War Fantastic, Historical Hauntings, Sol's Children, Renaissance Faire, All Hell Breaking Loose, Slipstreams,* and *Time Twisters*. He is also the author of *Forced Conversion*, a science fiction novel set in the near future, when everyone can have heaven, any heaven they want, but some people don't want to go. His latest novel, *Greensword*, is a darkly comedic eco-thriller about a group of misfit environmentalists who are about to save the world from global warming, but don't want to get caught doing it. He and his fantastic wife, Linda, also a top-ranked gamer, live in Illinois with three dogs: Smoosh, Makai, and Mauka. Don can be reached at www.orphyte.com/donaldjbingle.

CORBIN HAD ALWAYS SAID that he would rather walk barefoot over broken pottery shards behind a donkey with diarrhea while wearing his scratchy winter greatcoat on the fiercest, most breezeless midsummer afternoon with a squabbling, squirming, and overweight six-year-old under each arm, than travel with barbarians. And he had always gotten a laugh when he said it.

So what had he done?

He had decided to travel with barbarians.

It had seemed like a good idea at the time. He wanted to go from here to there, but there were rumors of brigands and boogens and marauding disobeyers of civil authority and . . . and he had little to no ability to defend himself or, frankly, anything or anyone else.

After all, back when he was known as Corey the Comedian, working bars with a traveling troupe of performers, he had never needed fighting skills and he had never feared the open road. The troupe's manager always hired itinerant warriors to protect the players and their wagons full of costumes, props, and magic items. Consequently, neither he nor any of the various actors, comedians, or attractive and comely dancers and singers had any worries of ambush or other unseemly encounters. Indeed, one of the ways he had convinced his mom to let him go on the open road as a teenager years ago was that he promised always to use protection.

"No worries of ickiness," he had intoned. He'd always had a way with words.

Unfortunately, even though he was well protected in his travels by moonlighting city guards and heroes for hire, he was not quite so well protected from the vagaries and vicissitudes of life. In short, his career had not flourished. He was, he had been forced to admit after constant and rude reminders from his dwindling audiences, a not-particularly-funny comedian. The manager of the troupe had not only noticed this vocational flaw, he had joined in the heckling. Corey could live with that, but when the manager "forgot" to mention once that the troupe was leaving town early the next morning, Corey had taken it as a possible indicator that he was not indispensable to the troupe's performances.

Corey had, of course, wished to stay with the troupe and did his best to help in other ways, but he did not have a good enough memory to transform himself into a teller of epic tales and was insufficiently coordinated to become a juggler. He had tried to sing a time or two, but really wasn't fond enough of vegetables to continue that particular career path. He was useless, even behind the scenes. He couldn't remember what props went where, and nobody liked his cooking, including him.

When you came right down to it, Corey was only part of an itinerant troupe of players because he liked staying up late and hanging around bars. In the end, he was reduced to playing the part of any corpse that was needed in the group's various dramatic performances. Even this was problematic, as he had an unfortunate tendency to squirm uncontrollably when he lay on his back too long. It was in an attempt to improve his corpse portrayals that he discovered his new calling.

He convinced a mage who was riding the same circuit of miserable hamlets and villages as his troupe to teach him a magical spell that allowed him to feign death. Magicians, of course, don't like to give out their secrets, but feigning death is not really one of those "wow" spells that everyone clamored to know. Corey was sufficiently adept or appreciative or, perhaps, annoying that the magician, Magnifico the Magnificent Mage, went on to teach him a few more of the lesser spells.

His change in profession was just in the small, bleeding gash of time, as Corey was fired just a fortnight later . . . or, at least, the troupe moved out to another, undisclosed town under the cover of darkness, without him being informed.

That's how he came to be traveling alone to the west while the troupe and its mercenary guards traveled east . . . or north . . . or south . . . or southeast . . . or north-northeast . . . or some other direction, for all he knew. No one was talking. Even the street urchins and panhandlers had apparently been paid off.

Having been spurned by the troupe, Corey decided to take his magic act on a solo tour of the smallest and least sophisticated hamlets and hovels he could find. His new moniker was Corbinico the Comedic Conjurer. Of course, in a fortnight he had not learned much magic. And in a decade he had not learned much comedy. But he believed that he had learned just enough spells and just the right spells to punctuate his otherwise uneven comedic monologue and amuse an audience of simple folk with simple minds and not enough wealth to waste vegetables as projectiles.

He could make someone hear a whisper. He could make someone sneeze or make them itch in an embarrassing spot. He could give someone a bit of a zap—causing pain, but not really much damage. He could untie simple knots, no matter how tight, without using his hands. And he could feign death.

Not really much of a routine, but he would work that out as he walked. All he had to do was get to the farm country, where the roads were safe and the inhabitants guileless. The immediate problem was that his magical abilities did not provide much in the way of offensive or defensive fighting power and the road west to the farmlands was risky.

That's why he needed protection.

That's why he decided to travel with the barbarians.

He didn't have the money to hire professional, or even semiprofessional, guards. But he figured if he just traveled along with the barbarians, he would be safe. They were known as fierce fighters, especially when attacked from downwind. They were skilled with the various blood-encrusted bladed weapons they carried with them, they were too stupid to retreat, and they generally carried no treasure worth stealing.

That made them the perfect companions for a lone traveler seeking protection, except, of course, for the stench, the lack of intelligent conversation, the inedible trail food, and the lack of any rest stops along the way. (Horses peed while they walked; why should barbarians do any different?)

Oh, and the fact that barbarians hate magic and will kill a magician without a moment's thought should they run across one.

Corey wasn't stupid, just unemployable, so he omitted mentioning that he was a magician when he conversed with his would-be companions about their upcoming travels. It was pretty easy to avoid the topic. The conversation went something like this:

"We go toward setting sun. Go far," said Torg, the largest and smelliest of the breed. Torg had one bright blue eye and one green eye that was clouded over and oozing pus.

"Me go with you," said Corey, stifling a gag. "Be friends. Share food. Be strong,"

Torg looked him over and said something rude to Barack and Kindo, his two lackeys and partners in slime. "You little. No strong. We eat food yours. We be strong. We go toward setting sun."

"Yeah, whatever," said Corey, smiling broadly and nodding like an idiot.

*　　*　　*

It all might have worked out all right, traveling west together, with the brute barbarian beasts not knowing of Corey's magical proclivities, if Corey's troupe hadn't also traveled west . . . and left a squad of professional mercenaries behind to make sure that Corey didn't follow. That might have made for considerable excitement and gratuitous bloodshed, except for the fact that barbarians are so fierce, they don't think they need to set a watch for the night.

Instead, as the dawn rose in the east, Corey, Torg, Barack, and Kindo woke up . . . well, gained consciousness . . . each with a large lump on his head. Each was tied firmly to his own tree trunk, his face turned toward the burning rays of the sun. After the appropriate amount of confusion, swearing, straining ineffectively at their bonds, and finger-pointing (without actually being able to use fingers), a sullen silence set in. The foursome actually might have stayed in such position for some time, but the barbarians let loose with their morning pee and Corey was downwind. Something snapped and he did something incredibly useful and stupid.

He muttered a few magical phrases and the ropes tying them to the trees began to untie themselves.

Each of the constituent members of the barbarian horde (any group of two or more barbarians technically qualifies as a horde, entomologically speaking, though there is some dispute as to whether the term *horde* actually is an abbreviation for the word *horrid*) looked at the ropes, then looked at Corey, then looked at one another, then looked at their weapons piled next to where the campfire had been, then looked at Corey, then smiled (not in a friendly "thanks for the help, good buddy" way, but in a drooling, toothy "I get his intestines" kind of way), then tried to engage in what appeared to be a barbarian variant of rock-paper-scissors, except that they couldn't see each other's hands, so Torg just growled and the others looked down (as if to agree that he not only got the intestines, but the brain as well).

Things didn't look good. The pee-soaked, battle-lusting barbarians certainly didn't look good. And Corey, what with being knocked out and tied to a tree and not having had an opportunity to take care of his morning biological functions, and being so concerned about being sliced in half that he was about to imitate the barbarian peeing-on-oneself practice, he didn't look so good, either. Here he was, about to be killed for being a magician and he was barely even a magician apprentice wannabe, who had cast less than a half-dozen miserable, puny little spells in his entire adult life. It wasn't as if he were a threat to the barbarian horde, or all barbarian hordes, or their women, or, more importantly, their goats. It's not like he was the most powerful mage in all the world. Of course, they didn't know that.

Of course! *They* didn't know that.

Corey extricated himself from his loosening bonds and leaped between the group of three barbarians, still in the midst of stepping out of their now-untied bonds, and their trusty, crusty weapons. He took up an exaggerated fighting/casting stance that he had seen one of the more flamboyant actors use in a performance of *The Veiled Threat of Seven Parts* and, in the deepest voice he could muster, shouted: "I am the greatest magician in all the world. I am Corbin the Conqueror. I have the power of Life and Death in my hands."

Well, that started a lot of barbarian yammering and various slit-eyed looks as the horde either discussed his claim or tried to figure out what the hell he was saying. Finally, Torg pushed Barack forward. The barbarian underling began to edge toward Corbin the Conqueror and the stash of weapons behind him.

"Death will come to you," shouted Corbin, looking sternly at the more tremulously trepidatious than intrepid tribesman before uttering a few arcane phrases. The words "Death, death, death will come to you," whispered in Barack's ear. The barbarian lackey backed off, twisting about like a dog chasing its tail to see who or what had whispered in his ear until he got dizzy and fell down.

Kindo made a minor move next, but yet another muttering by Corbin caused the maneuver to abort, as Kindo grabbed at his suddenly itching privates, even more than he had the night before.

Torg spat at the ground in disgust, then pushed his underlings to either side, and strode forward, as manfully as one can with urine-soaked goat breeches. "You no strong. Torg strong."

"Fair warning," sneered Corbin. "I have the power of Life and Death in my hands." He gazed quickly about the sky and saw a buzzard lazing overhead, no doubt waiting to get in on the leftovers of any violent encounter. Corbin pointed at the bird. "I show you."

With as much showiness and force as he could muster, Corbin gesticulated broadly and shouted magical phrases in basso profundo, ending with his hands and his eyes pointed straight at the innocent scavenger. "Death to you," added the magician, as his minor zap spell sprang from the tips of his stubby fingers heavenward toward the unsuspecting fowl.

The bird screeched in pain and fell from the sky, dead (maybe from the zap or maybe from the fall; Corbin wasn't picky, he was just grateful).

Corbin smirked crookedly and looked Torg straight in the eye (the blue one). "I can do that ten thousand times a day." He waggled his little finger to discharge the static that always clung after a zap spell, sending a minor spark into Torg's snot-encrusted nose. "Do not anger me, puny one. I am the most powerful mage the world has ever known."

The barbarians bought it, muck, slime, and stinker. Their eyes widened, then cast downward. They fell to their knees. They wrung their hands in supplication. They bowed in obeisance. They quivered in fear when they weren't quavering in awe.

The trip went much better after that. They rested when Corey wanted them to rest. They allowed him to walk where he wanted (upwind). They offered him the largest, moldiest portions of what he was sure they believed were fine cheeses. They even bathed, at his direction, in a river rapids they were crossing, scouring away months of grime and replacing their usual stench with the smell of wet goat hair, at least for a while.

Corbin almost thought things would work out until it came time to camp for the night. Oh, the horde was obedient and helpful: stoking the fire; cooking up fish for him that they usually ate raw (without cleaning them first); mounding up dry grass for a mattress; and more. But Corbin saw the gleam in Torg's good eye (he avoided looking at the pus in the bad eye) and realized that the barbarian would come for him in the night (and not in the "gee, we don't have any goats here" way). Suddenly things looked a lot darker, and not just because the sun had set.

Corbin was right. At the darkest hour, Torg came for him. Corbin couldn't see him, of course. There was no moon. But he could smell him. So he did the only thing he could do when faced with a superior fighting foe. He leaped up, screamed like a little girl, tried his best to duck as he heard the swish of a weapon aimed for him, and collapsed to the ground, feigning death.

In case you've never tried it, feigning death is pretty cool . . . especially to the touch. You can hear and see and smell normally, but you appear to be completely dead. No pulse, no apparent breathing, no reaction to stimuli. Skin cold and clammy. Corbin worried a bit that Torg might mutilate his corpse in rage or celebration, but the brute only nudged him a few times with a heavily callused toe with a frighteningly long toenail.

Torg hooted in victory, waking both of the rest of the horde, and jumped up and down a few times. Then he clapped his companions on the head for being inferior to their fearsome leader and everyone went to sleep. Corbin dozed himself.

The horde was just about to decamp the next morning, when Corbin calmly canceled the spell and sat up, refreshed and unharmed. He looked squarely at Torg. "I hold the power of Life as well as Death. The next time someone from your tribe kills me, I will rise again and kill not only you, but all of your women . . . and all of your goats."

And so it was that Corey the Comedian became the God-King of the barbarian horde (I mean the full horde; not just the three guys he had traveled with). Torg became the high priest of the acolytes of Corbin, the Conqueror of Life and Death. Barack and Kindo carried Corbin around in a litter. He was fed the best goat and the best berries and offered the best women the barbarians had to offer. Life was good. And Corbin didn't just take advantage; he was an enlightened leader who instituted wise policies, like cooking fish and peeing in the bushes instead of on oneself.

For quite a few months, it seemed as if it really had been a good idea to travel with barbarians.

And then came the armed legions of the king.

Soon, and apparently for the rest of their lives, the horde was surrounded by ten thousand armored soldiers, a force that had been assembled to rid the kingdom of the pestilent scourge of the barbarians. And everyone in the horde, every man, woman, and goat, looked to Corbin and cried in unison the phrase he had used at the beginning of every speech, every judicial pronouncement, every greeting he had ever made since becoming the God-King of the Horde: "I am Corbin, the Conqueror of Life and Death. I can kill ten thousand times a day. And I can rise from the dead to do it again tomorrow."

You have to admit, it's a good line. But, of course, that's what the horde was looking for him to do. Kill ten thousand times. The king's legion, of course, had no such expectation. Accordingly, the knights bugled their charge, lowered their lances, and came at the tribesmen. The horde didn't even bother to pick up their weapons, such was their faith in Corbin the Conqueror . . . their stupid, misguided faith.

It was going to be a slaughter.

Suddenly traveling with barbarians didn't seem like it had been a good idea after all. So Corbin did the only thing he could do.

He feigned death.

Note to self: feigning death atop an open, wooden tower when the enemy has archers, lots and lots of archers (many of them shooting flaming arrows), not really a good idea.

FOOD FIGHT

Alan Dean Foster

Foster's sometimes humorous, occasionally poignant, but always entertaining short fiction has appeared in all the major SF magazines as well as in original anthologies and several "Best of the Year" compendiums. His published oeuvre includes more than one hundred books. Foster's work to date includes excursions into hard science-fiction, fantasy, horror, detective, western, historical, and contemporary fiction. He has also written numerous nonfiction articles on film, science, and scuba diving, as well as having produced the novel versions of many films, including such well-known productions as Star Wars, the first three *Alien* films, and *Alien Nation*. His novel *Cyber Way* won the Southwest Book Award for Fiction in 1990, the first work of science fiction ever to do so. The Fosters reside in Prescott in a house built of brick salvaged from a turn-of-the-century miners' brothel, along with assorted dogs, cats, fish, several hundred houseplants, visiting javelina, porcupines, eagles, red-tailed hawks, skunks, coyotes, bobcats, and the ensorceled chair of the nefarious Dr. John Dee. He is presently at work on several new novels and media projects.

"MY COFFEE KEEPS INSULTING me."

Dr. Erin Alderfield flicked a glance to her left to make sure the recorder light was still on, scratched unobtrusively at the place on her slim neck where the thin gold necklace she was wearing never seemed to sit quite right, tilted her head downward so she could look over the wire brim of her glasses, and thoughtfully regarded her patient. Seated on the couch across from her, Morton Ropern pushed nervously at the front of his forehead where twenty years earlier he used to have a good deal more hair and waited for the therapist to respond.

It did not take long. "Mr. Ropern, coffee does not talk. Coffee has no body, no organic physicality, and therefore no brain, much less larynx, lungs, and tongue. It is a liquid: nothing more, nothing less, sometimes imbibed chilled, more often hot. It cannot talk."

Far from being dissuaded by this bracing dose of cold realism, Morty Ropern's reply spilled out (so to speak) even faster than before. "And it isn't just the coffee. It's the cream, the sugar, and the bagel I have that usually accompanies it every morning." He hesitated. "For some reason, the onion tends to keep quiet." While still somewhat south of frantic, his expression could at least be said to be verging decidedly on the fretful. "Dr. Alderfield, what I am going to *do*?" The slight but trim forty-year-old looked anxiously around the neat, bookshelf-heavy office. "No matter where I am anymore, food *talks* to me."

Dr. Alderfield checked the recorder again. Usually each day at work was much like another, every patient similar to the one who preceded or followed. Not today. Not this patient. She was beginning to scent the rapidly expanding zygote of an incipient scientific paper.

"Does all food talk to you?" she inquired with admirable solicitude, "or just breakfast?"

"All food, everywhere." Inordinately relieved not to have had his phobia dismissed out of hand (much less with derisive laughter), Ropern worried on. "And not just my food. Other people's food, too. Food in supermarkets, food in convenience stores. Sometimes I just overhear it talking to itself, but more often than not lately it recognizes something in me and addresses itself directly to me."

Perhaps it senses a kindred flakiness, Dr. Alderfield found herself thinking, though she of course said nothing of the kind. "I see." Turning slightly to her right, she nodded in the direction of the wood-grained cabinet that dominated the far wall. "Behind that lower door is a small refrigerator. Inside are various cold drinks, water, and some small snacks." She returned her attention to her patient. "Is any of it, um, communicating with you now?"

Ropern looked in the indicated direction. Somewhat to Alderfield's surprise (and professional delight), the patient did not hesitate. "Mostly it's all chatting among itself. But there's a half-gallon container of orange juice whose drink-by date expired two weeks ago, and it wants me to tell you that it's pissed."

Profession and experience aside, Dr. Alderfield was also human. This response from her patient compelled her to, if not actually bite her tongue, to clamp her lightly glossed lips tightly together and for a moment turn her head away from him. When she had once more sufficiently composed herself, she looked back.

"I didn't realize that food could have, um, feelings."

Ropern's gaze met hers unflinchingly. "It hates waste."

"I see." She sat back in her chair, crossing legs that were shapely from decades of competition track, then city jogging. "How does it feel about being consumed?"

"Fulfilled," the patient responded immediately. He looked away, toward the window that opened out onto the noisy canyon of glass and steel towers. She recognized his expression immediately: it was the look of a patient suddenly wondering what he was doing in her office. "As far as I know, I'm the only one who can hear food talking."

She nodded reassuringly, then asked the question that could not be avoided. "I'm sure that is a condition that can be dealt with, given time and proper therapy. What I need to know now is—do you talk back?"

Guilt and embarrassment vied for control of his facial muscles. In the end, it was a draw. "I try not to, but sometimes I have no choice."

"Really?" It was not the expected response. But then, nothing about this case was expected. "It becomes a compulsion, then?" Mentally she revised the prescription she had already intended to write for him.

"No, not a compulsion." Rising, Ropern began to pace the office. Sensing his nervousness, she let him roam at will. Purposefully the room contained no sharp or edged objects. "For example, yesterday I was walking to work and I passed a guy eating the biggest, greasiest, grossest hamburger you ever saw. A real mess-on-a-bun. I could overhear the ingredients conspiring."

"'Conspiring?'" It was becoming harder and harder for her to maintain her professional aplomb in the face of such continuing, albeit inventive, illogicality.

Ropern, however, was dead serious. "The cheese was whispering to the meat patties and they were both conniving with the sauce. The onions and pickles tried to take a stance against them, but they didn't have a chance."

"I see. A chance to do what?"

"Help the poor slob. The cheese was murmuring, 'We're gonna kill this guy. His cholesterol's gotta be approaching four hundred. Let's push him over the edge.' " Ropern stopped pacing so abruptly that for just an instant Alderfield was alarmed. But his tone and manner were so subdued that she was quickly reassured. This patient's mania was not dangerous, only bizarre.

"Have you ever felt yourself similarly threatened?" she heard herself inquiring.

"Oh sure, plenty of times," Ropern assured her. "Usually by the same kinds of fatty, unhealthy foods. They're pretty transparent in their intentions."

"You're lucky," she told him. "Most people have to resort to reading nutritional charts."

"I don't feel lucky," he replied morosely. "I feel isolated, alone, and put-upon. I can't shut out the racket. Everywhere I go it's food, food, food everywhere, and all of it yammering away like a crowd at a football game." He glanced up sharply again. "A friend suggested I see you, but I really don't think I'm crazy."

"Of course you're not." Her voice was soothing, comforting. Practiced. "You're—perceptive. It's the exact nature of your perception that we have to define, and deal with."

That brought forth the first smile he had shown since checking in with her receptionist. "You're very understanding, Dr. Alderfield. My friend said you were understanding."

She shrugged off the compliment. "It's my job to understand. And to help those people who come to me to understand themselves, the world around them, and how they fit into it." Looking down, she checked her watch. "We can delve further into understanding, but not anymore today. Can you come back Friday, around ten in the morning?"

"I'll make time," he told her. A hand thrust out as he rose and came toward her. She did not flinch. The fingers enveloped one of her hands and shook it gratefully. "I feel better already. I've been carrying this around inside me for so long. Just being able to talk to someone about it is an enormous help." His eyes darting in the direction of the concealed refrigerator, he looked suddenly uneasy again. "I can't talk to food about it, of course."

"Of course," she agreed readily. "Friday, then." She nodded firmly toward the door. "My receptionist, Mary Elizabeth, will give you a reminder card."

He started to exit, paused at the doorway to look back. "You're so accepting. I don't suppose you've ever had any food talk to *you*?"

She smiled. "One time in Zurich I had a peach melba call to me, but that's about the only occasion I can recall."

Wholly overlooking the gentle sarcasm, he nodded knowingly. "Desserts are the worst. They have this bad habit of always shouting." Then he was out the door and gone.

What a refreshing, and fascinating, change of pace, she thought as she walked over to the refrigerator to get something to drink. A patient who wasn't in love with his mother, didn't want to murder his boss, was confident in his chosen sexuality, and presented no immediate apparent danger to himself or to anyone else. On the other hand, his was the most purely wacky mania she had encountered in fifteen years as a practicing professional. As she plucked a glass off the shelf and opened the door to the small fridge, she was already composing the first paragraphs of the paper she intended to write.

Cold shock coursed down her front from chest to feet
as the bottom fell out of the container and a quart of orange juice spilled down her suit to run down her legs.
Looking down in dismay, she could only stare as the
sticky liquid began to pool up in her expensive shoes.

After finishing the day at the firm where he worked
shuffling sales statistics for a major retailer, Morton
Ropern decided to take the long route back to his apartment, detouring by way of the harbor walk. Usually he
avoided it because of all the cafés and tourist shops sell-
ing seafood and such, but it was too nice an evening to
terminate prematurely, and he felt strengthened by his
session with the new therapist.

He found that for the first time in a long while he was
able to ignore the mutterings of the cooked crabs that
whispered darkly from atop hillocks of preserving ice.
Clam chowder simmered expectantly, waiting for hungry
imbibers. Cotton candy leered at passing visitors, while
rows of fudge commented stolidly from within their win-
dow-mounted trays. Such food stalls and displays were
always a problem for him, though nothing was worse
than the occasional unavoidable visits he had to make to
the supermarket. To most folk, buying food was a necessary chore. For him, it was akin to temporarily imprisoning a sympathetic eight-year-old in an animal shelter.

"Buy me!" the cans of soup would scream at him as he
hurried past. He wasn't a big fan of soup, but he in-
evitably found himself shuttling one or two cans into his
shopping cart just to shut them up. "Bread—man can't
live without bread!" he would hear as he tried to make his
way through the bakery section. "Eat us and the bullies at
the beach won't kick sand in your face!" the steaks and
chops chorused accusingly. The cacophony, the pleading,
the endless demands were unrelenting and deafening. It

was all he could do to escape with a basket containing the minimal necessities.

He didn't even dare to try and shop the imported foods aisle.

Restaurants were mildly less stressful. There was less competition for his attention and the food was invariably more refined. Not only the menu, but the dialogue. He had once managed to carry on a very civilized tête-à-tête with a plate of oysters Rockefeller before the last of them found its way down his gullet. Butter set on the table tended to leave him alone, reserving its banter exclusively for the accompanying bread rolls, while the respective components of a properly prepared main course vied for consumption and his attention with the utmost politeness.

"You first," the main course would invariably declaim to the vegetables.

"No, no, you first—you're the entrée," the assortment of squash, beans, and carrots would counter.

"Don't be silly—you'll get cold," the steak or fish or chicken would reply.

"Don't argue—I'll go." Leave it to a phlegmatic side dish of potato or rice to behave more sensibly than anything else on the table.

"You're all going," Morty Ropern would tell them. At least their incessant demanding chatter helped him to eat sensibly, compelling him to vary his intake without favoring one dish over another.

All this and more he explained to the attentive Dr. Alderfield that Friday morning and on subsequent visits. She remained neither judgmental nor accusative, gently bringing him back to the subject at hand when he threatened to wander, prodding him for details when it appeared as if he were going to hold back. With each successive session he felt better and better. She noticed the change, too, until at the end of one visit she finally felt it was time to challenge him with the next step.

"Are you doing anything tomorrow night?"

"What?" His eyes widened slightly.

"Tomorrow night. Are you doing anything? Do you have any plans?"

"Plans, no, I—I thought I might take in a movie."

"Good." She made sure the recorder was off. "Then it's a date."

"A date?" He looked bemused. "Is that kosher? I mean, a therapist going out with one of their patients? I thought . . ."

"You've seen too many television shows. This is not a specifically social occasion: it's all part of your therapy. A movie will be nice—after we've had dinner."

"Din—oh no." He rose from the couch. "I couldn't. I mean, it would be—"

She interrupted him gently. "What? Frightening? Amusing? You're doing much better, Morty. You're not obsessing about culinary conversation anymore. Each time you come in, you end up talking more and more about other things. About aspects of your daily existence that don't involve gossiping food." She smiled encouragingly. "About the rest of life. I think it's time to take the next step." She implemented a deliberately exaggerated pout. "Or is it just that you don't want to be seen with me?"

"Oh no," he said quickly. "I mean, I find you quite attractive—for a therapist. Hell, that didn't come out right." A grin partially compensated for the faux pas. "I'd be delighted to go out with you. To a concert, to the seaside—even to a movie. But dinner. . . ." Concern creased his face as he slowly shook his head. "I don't know."

"I do," she told him confidently. "You'll see. Another step forward in your progress. Tomorrow night then."

Rising, she ushered him toward the door. "We can meet at the snack bar downstairs and then go to a real restaurant. You like French?"

He nodded. "Most of the time. Not when it starts trying to convince me to start smoking again. There's nothing more annoying than a know-it-all main course."

He had high hopes, and dressed accordingly. It had been a while since he had been out on a serious date. Even though he expected it to be as much session as date, there was no denying the somewhat steely attractiveness of Dr. Alderfield and his anticipation at spending the evening with her. If only the food would cooperate. Perhaps she was more right than he suspected. Perhaps the only ones talking at their table would be the two of them.

No such luck.

It started, naturally enough, with the appetizers. Escargot he didn't mind. The sautéed snails usually kept their somewhat snooty chatter to themselves. But the garlic sauce that accompanied them was sputtering right from the start. Aware that she was watching him intently, he did his best to ignore the insults and queries the food kept flinging his way. He succeeded in disregarding the comments of the steaming snails as well as the frequent admonitions and repeated tut-tutting of the Caesar salad that followed.

The main course, however, defeated him.

He had chosen the blandest entrée on the menu; a simple, straightforwardly prepared coq au vin. Unless embellished, wine sauce rarely uttered more than a mumble, and any chicken dish tended to be sufficiently boring to ignore. But Erin (he could hardly spend the entire evening calling her "Dr. Alderfield," they both had decided) had ordered a fantastic veal smitane. When you put veal, mushrooms, and sour cream together, the result was bound to be a conversational as well as gastronomical free-for-all.

Even so, he did not lose control until she started to bring a particular forkful of the main dish toward her mouth.

"Don't eat that," he heard himself saying, much to his horror.

She paused. The evening had gone better than expected, validating her somewhat unorthodox invitation (unorthodox phobias required unorthodox therapies, she had decided). There had been no indication from her patient that the food that had been brought to their table and subsequently devoured by the both of them had voiced so much as a casual greeting. Until now.

Fork halfway to mouth she looked over at him, hesitated, and slowly lowered it back to her plate. "I beg your pardon, Morty? Why not?"

"It's mostly cartilage, with a bit of bone in the center. It'll go down, but it won't sit well." His eyes dropped, embarrassment reflected in his expression as well as his voice. "It—told me so."

She eyed the fork that was now resting on her plate. It looked like any other mouthful sliced from the entrée. "It told you so?"

He swallowed hard. "It's started complaining as soon as you made the cut. It's potentially upsetting, and it's been complaining about it. Loudly."

Loudly. "Morty, food makes the person who's *eating* it upset. It doesn't upset itself."

He looked miserable. "You've eaten the good half," he told her. "The rest is undercooked."

Her characteristic self-control shaken, she found that she was growing angry. She firmly believed they had made a great deal of progress, and now he was just being—silly. Not a medically accurate description, perhaps, but an appropriate one. Sitting up straight, she brought the linen napkin to her mouth, dabbed delicately at her lips, and eyed him evenly. Sometimes therapy, especially in the field, required a directness that might be frowned upon if delivered in the office.

Deliberately, she raised the fork, bit off the bite-size piece it held, chewed, and swallowed. Ropern looked quietly stricken.

She smiled back at him. "It's fine," she told him. After studying her plate, she cut another slice, divided it, and proceeded to down both halves. The sour cream-based sauce was delicious. She told him so.

"Well?" she prompted him. "What is my dinner saying now?"

"Nothing," he replied quietly. "But the peas and onions are lamenting the situation, while the au gratin is remaining determinedly neutral. Potatoes usually do."

She took a sip of the wine they had chosen. The only noise it made was as it slid refreshingly down her throat. "We've done a great deal of work together, Morton . . . Morty. Let's focus on the progress we've made. The last thing we want is regression." She eyed him sternly. "Food does not talk. Not my food, not your food. It doesn't tell you when it's safe or gone bad, it doesn't call out to you from greengrocer's stands, it doesn't fill your head with the kinds of inane inconsequentialities that allow the truly disturbed to set aside the real world in favor of some comforting imaginary one." Reaching across the table, she took his right hand in both of hers. Another bit of atypical therapy, but one she felt was vitally necessary at that moment.

"Does it?" she challenged him, her eyes locking onto his.

He paused. For longer than she would have wished. Just when she was starting to lose hope and thinking they might have to start all over again, from the beginning, a smile creased his face. It grew wider with every passing second.

"I—I guess not," he murmured. "Not if *you* say so."

Breakthrough. Not perfect and entire, but she would take it. Starting next week, they would build on it. Letting go of his hand, she sat back in her chair and took another sip of wine. Knife and fork dug into the remnants of her meal with gusto. She found she was looking forward to the after-dinner movie.

They let him ride with her in the back of the ambulance. He stayed with her all the way to the hospital. The appalled restaurant management not only comped the meal, including the wine, but paid for the transportation to the emergency room. They let him accompany her therein, too, and afterward to the private room where she spent a restless, uneasy, stomach-churning night. Despite her intense discomfort, it was a night of revelations and further progress—though not of a kind she had anticipated.

Not long thereafter, friends were surprised to see them together on increasingly frequent occasions. They were even more surprised when she invited him to move in with her. No one was more startled at this than Morton Ropern himself. Not so much because of the invitation she smilingly proffered, but because he eagerly accepted.

"I don't see it," her best friend Miriam told her when they met for lunch the following week. "I mean, he has a good job and he's decent-enough looking and he isn't gay and he hasn't been married before, but really, Erin, he's no great catch."

Dr. Erin Alderfield munched on her salad. She looked, if not quite radiant, eminently content. "Morty has his special points. It's just that they're not all visible."

"Oh so?" The other woman was far from convinced.

"Like what?" Seated at one of the café's sidewalk tables, she indicated the flow of humanity rushing to and fro nearby. "Tell me one thing I don't see that makes him such a special catch."

Erin looked up from her salad. "You should eat more fruit," she told her friend. "Good for the both of you." A secret smile caused her lips to part. "You could say that Morty's very good at foreign languages."

"For instance?" Miriam prodded her.

The look in her friend's eyes was distant, and glittering. "He can speak chocolate."

MOONLIGHTING

Devon Monk

Devon Monk lives in Oregon with her husband, two sons, and one dog. Her fiction has appeared in *Rotten Relations, Maiden, Matron, Crone,* and *Year's Best Fantasy #2* anthologies and in magazines such as *Amazing Stories, Realms of Fantasy, Black Gate, Talebones, Cicada,* and *Lady Churchill's Rosebud Wristlet*. In addition to writing short fiction, she is currently working on several novels.

THIMBLE JACK CREPT OUT of the broom closet and surveyed the tidy stone kitchen. Watery beams of moonlight flowed through the windows and pooled in the sink, giving Thimble plenty of light to work by. Pixies were creatures of the night, and did their best work when the sun had gone to the soft side of dreaming. He put his hands on his naked hips and strolled around the kitchen looking for dirt. Floors nicely swept, stove turned off for the night, and a small bowl of water left out for him. Everything perfectly in place, everything perfectly clean.

Thimble frowned. The mistress of the house was a compulsive housekeeper. He hadn't had any real work to do for months.

Thimble stretched his dragonfly wings and flitted into the tidy living room, dining room, and small den. All clean. Thimble scowled. He'd been replaced by vacuum cleaners, spray bottles, and scrubbing bubbles! With nothing to clean and no one to punish for being lazy, he was doomed to a life of tedium, with nothing but a bowl of water for his trouble. He was going to go crazy as an ogre.

Wait! The child slept upstairs in the nursery. Surely there would be a misplaced toy, an unstacked book. Thimble felt the heat of wicked hope warm his pixie bones. If he were lucky, he might even have time to tie the child's hair in knots for not picking up her toys. Joy!

Fast as snow melt beneath a unicorn hoof, Thimble danced up the stairs, his bare feet making the sound of distant bells.

He didn't bother looking in the parents' bedroom—the woman didn't even allow a wrinkle in a raisin. But the little girl's room would be gold.

He shoved at the door and walked into the nursery. A single open window at the far side of the room poured silver moonlight across the floor, bookcase, toy chest, and bed.

Thimble pulled at his ears in frustration. Nothing was out of place. Not good. Not good. He flitted to the girl's bed, his wings clicking softly. Maybe she had smuggled a cookie under the covers, forgotten to brush her hair, wash her face—something naughty, anything at all.

He landed on the freshly laundered linens and strode up to inspect her face.

"Dolly!" she screeched.

Thimble jumped and quick-footed it backward. He tripped over her pile of extra pillows.

"Go to sleep," he whispered. It had been decades since he'd been spotted by a human and even longer than that since any creature had spoken to him. He was getting slow, losing his edge. This too-clean house was dulling his pixie reflexes. He pushed up to his feet, and gathered a fistful of magic, ready to send her sleeping if he had to.

The little girl frowned and pulled her dolly out from beneath her covers. She looked at the doll, looked at him, and held the doll out for him. "Dolly," she said again.

Thimble shuddered. It was one of those stiff plastic, yellow-haired, painted-faced things. They gave him the creeps.

"Yes, yes. Lovely. Go to sleep now."

"All gone." The girl tugged the pink ruffled dress and shoes off the doll, wadded them up in her sweaty fist, and shoved them at him. "You."

Clothes! The one thing pixies longed for above all others. But these weren't the clothes he'd spent three hundred years dreaming about: a nice set of trousers, soft jacket, and maybe a jaunty hat. This was a cheap sparkly dress and strappy purple heels. He refused to take them. He would not wear them. He wouldn't be caught dead looking like a fairy tarted up on a twenty-year bender.

But there were rules about clothes. Pixie rules. Rules Thimble could not break. One: take the clothes. Two: put them on. Three: dance and taunt. Four: leave the house forever.

The girl made a grab for him, which he lithely side stepped. She stuck out her lower lip and glared. "You!" She dumped the clothes at his feet.

By the wands, she was not going to back down. Maybe it was time to knock the little whelp out. Thimble drew back a palmful of magic.

"Mommy, Mommy!" the girl yelled.

Thimble heard a deep click as the light turned on in the

parents' bedroom. This would be bad—very bad. If he used his magic to put her to sleep, he wouldn't have time to turn invisible before her parents arrived. But if he went invisible instead, he would be breaking rule number one: take the clothes.

"Hush, now, hush," Thimble said. "See? I have the dress." He picked it up and reluctantly wiggled into it. The dress was a sleeveless number and had a stiff, scratchy skirt that itched his nether regions. The shoes were no better—they pinched and rubbed and made his ankles feel like they were made out of marbles. He took a couple steps and had to throw out his arms and wings to keep from falling flat.

The little girl clapped her hands and smiled.

Having clothes was horrible. But they *were* clothes, and they were *his* clothes. He laughed and pointed at the girl—as good a taunt as he could manage without falling off the high heels and breaking his neck.

He hated these clothes! He loved these clothes! He wanted to hide under a hill so no one could see him! He wanted to dance with joy! The clash of emotions that filled him was staggering. But no matter what he wanted, the only thing he could do was follow rule number four: leave the house. Forever. No more cleaning. No more teasing. No more of anything that Thimble loved. He definitely hated these clothes.

Thimble took to the air. The dress had an opening in the back that his wings fit through, which was good. He didn't think he'd make it very far on heels alone.

"Wait," the little girl said.

But Thimble could not wait. Just as the girl's mother opened the door, he dove into moonlight and flew out the window. The little girl cried, but he did not look back.

A knot of sorrow settled in Thimble's chest as he flew over the land. Being out of the house seemed as strange to him as going to work in the cottage had three hundred years ago. He felt uprooted, alone, and the dress was riding up his rear.

He took a deep breath. He had made a new life for himself three hundred years ago, he could do so again. All he needed was a new house to clean. That thought brought a smile to his lips. Surely not all humans were as fastidious as his last mistress. There had to be humans who still left acorns on their windowsills and bowls of water by the door, inviting pixies into the house. And he knew how to find out: check the pixie stick.

Thimble flew to the magic lands of his childhood and straight into the forest where the pixie stick stood. He angled down and landed neatly next to the stick. The magic stick rang with a sweet constant bell tone, and a shaft of moonlight always found a way through the tree branches to illuminate the oldest pixie artifact. Here every wish in the world could be heard, sorted, and distributed to the creature who could best grant them. Magical notes would cling to the stick until a pixie pulled it off. But there was not a single note on the stick. That couldn't be right. Thimble put his hands behind his back and took a couple steps. His heels sunk in the moss. He lurched and fell.

He hated shoes! He pulled the shoes off and rubbed at his blistered feet, trying to think of a rule that didn't include shoes. Ah, yes. Shoes weren't clothing, they were accessories. He was sure of it. And the rules did not state that pixies must accessorize their new clothes. Thimble threw both shoes into the surrounding brush, and grinned when the plastic hit mud.

Now he could find that new house. He stood, brushed off his dress, and walked around the pixie stick again. Empty. Not a wish or a hope or a request visible. No wonder it was so quiet here. There were no wishes left. With nothing to clean, and no one to tease, he would be crazy as an ogre.

Thimble scowled and kicked the stick. The stick rang like a gong and a single scrap of paper fluttered down and landed in front of Thimble's feet.

Thimble laughed. Thimble danced a quick jig, which wasn't easy in a skirt. Thimble picked up the paper and read the address. He had a wish, a house, a home!

The address wasn't hard to find. Even though it had been three hundred years since Thimble lived in the places of magic, he still knew his way around. Sure the trees had grown, fallen, and grown again, and mountains had studded their feet with new human towns. He had grown up here, and would know his way as well today as in another three hundred years.

Still when he reached the house, he was confused. The place was right—set deep within a forest and tucked up against an imposing rock wall, with a small, spring-fed creek burbling by. But the house did not resemble any of the human houses he had ever seen. This place was made of trees torn out by their roots, packed with mud and clumps of moss and weeds.

Thimble looked at the address written in indelible magic on the note, then looked above the door. It was the right place. Someone inside that house had wished for help keeping the house. Thimble could do that.

He strode up to the door. There were no inviting acorns on the windowsill, which was no surprise since there were no windows. But he couldn't sense a bowl of water by the door either. He brushed away his worry with a short laugh. He'd pinch the owner black and blue until he or she remembered to put the bowl of water out for him every night. He'd clean and tcase and make mischief like no human had ever seen. His heart pounded beetle-quick with excitement, his palms sweated magic. His thighs itched, but that was from the dress. Yes, this was going to work out just fine.

Thimble straightened the straps of his dress. He gave his leg a good scratch, then knocked on the door.

The heavy footsteps of something big, much bigger than a human, so big the ground shook and shale trickled like dry bones down the cliffside, answered his knock. Maybe this was a bad idea.

The door groaned on rusted hinges and swung inward.

A brute of a creature filled the doorway, glowering out over the forest while scratching at his hairy armpit.

This thing was not human. This thing was something Thimble had lived his life avoiding, a dangerous, stupid, pixie-smashing creature. This thing was an ogre.

It was still night, and ogres were creatures of the day. This one yawned, showing rows of pixie-grinding teeth and a curved set of yellowed tusks. Thimble had just woken a sleeping ogre. He held very still. The ogre would never notice him unless he looked down.

The ogre looked down and grunted. "Here for the job?" The ogre's voice rumbled like low thunder and sent more loose rocks tumbling off the cliff.

"I am a pixie," Thimble said. "I will keep the house for you, so long as you leave a bowl of water out for me every night."

The ogre scratched his other arm pit. "Aren't you a little pink for a pixie?"

"Aren't you a little talkative for an ogre?"

The ogre sneered, his thick lip curling back over lumpy teeth.

This was it, Thimble thought. He was going to be smashed into pixie paste and buried in a horrible pink frock.

But instead of smashing and bashing, the ogre grunted a couple times and stepped back into the house.

Thimble swallowed until his heart stopped kicking at his chest. He lifted his chin high and entered the ogre's abode.

He had never seen such a mess in all his years! There was only one room to the house, but it looked like a garbage pit. Broken chairs, cracked dishes, and unrecognizable mounds of things he could only guess at cluttered the misshapen room. The sink in the corner dripped, sending out a trail of mud that smelled like old cabbage across the floor. No living creature in its right mind would want to live here.

The only thing standing was a tattered curtain separating the main room from a cave-like sleeping hollow.

"What do you expect me to do with this?" Thimble asked.

The ogre waved a meaty hand toward the room. "You're the pixie. Take care of it." Then he lumbered into his cave and tugged the curtain into place.

Thimble was left alone with nothing but the broken tuba snores from the ogre. What was he going to do? There wasn't any way he could clean this mess by morning. But the thought of going back to the empty pixie stick, or worse, to a meticulously kept home gave him chills. Better to have something impossible to do than nothing at all. He cracked his knuckles, hiked up his skirt, and got to work.

The morning sun rose over the forest and sent bursts of light and bird song into the mud hut. Thimble yawned and wiped the filthy rag over the last stubborn spot on the wall. He couldn't believe how much he'd gotten done. He'd repaired the table and chairs, mopped the floor, which turned out to be stone, and fixed the sink. He'd washed the dishes, mended the ogre's big smelly socks, and even dusted the two mammoth boots he had found under a pile of dry leaves and sticks.

Not bad for a night's work. No, better than that—it was amazing for a night's work. There wasn't a pixie alive who could have done as much as well. The ogre was sure to be pleased. Thimble would get his water, and maybe after a nice day's sleep, he would feel up to pinching the big beast for making such a mess in the first place.

Thimble's smile turned into a yawn. Later. All he wanted now was sleep. He padded over to the cleanest, driest corner by the door, ready to bed down.

The ogre stirred, snorted, and pulled the ratty curtain aside. The ogre took one look at the room and rubbed his bloodshot eyes. He took a second look at the room and roared.

"What have you done?" The ogre stomped across the clean room until he towered over Thimble.

Thimble was tired. Bone tired. His day had started with a three-year-old girl pushing him around and now this big brute thought he could bully him. Well, Thimble Jack was not a pixie to be intimidated.

"I cleaned your house," Thimble shouted over the ogre's heavy breathing.

"I didn't want you to clean it," the ogre growled. "I wanted it to be worse!"

"Then why did you let a pixie in your house?"

"So you would mess things up."

Thimble pulled at his ears. "We make mischief, not messes, you ignorant clod." And even as the words were out of Thimble's mouth, he knew he had gone too far.

The ogre snarled and spit and raised his fists. But instead of crushing Thimble, the big oaf looked Thimble in the eye and picked up a chair. He smashed it against the tabletop.

"Wait—" Thimble said.

The ogre picked up the other chair and smashed it.

"Don't—"

The ogre clomped over to the wall, and chunks of dirt bigger than Thimble fell to the floor.

"Stop—"

But Thimble's protests seemed only to fuel the ogre's tantrum. He stomped over to the sink and picked up a plate. He threw the plate in the sink and bits of clay shattered onto the floor.

"That's it!" Thimble gathered his magic in both hands and threw it at the ogre.

The ogre reeled like someone had just whacked him across the head, but that wasn't enough to stop the raging brute. He glared at Thimble and picked up a cup.

Thimble flew at the ogre. "If you smash that cup, I will patch it so fast, you won't know what hit you."

The ogre bared his teeth and threw the cup in the sink. Thimble dashed down after it. Just before the mug hit the sink, he threw a handful of magic at it. The cup bounced safely, and landed whole.

The ogre grunted and picked up the bucket in the sink. He heaved it against one wall. Water spilled across the floor.

Thimble flew over the spill. With a flick of his wrist, the water was gone, and so was the dirt beneath it.

The ogre grunted again and kicked the leaf pile around. Thimble sent a breeze to push the leaves back into a pile in the corner.

The ogre grunted several times, a sound strangely like laughter, and picked up the table.

"Oh, for the love of wands, you wouldn't." Thimble braced himself. The table was too big for him to catch when it fell, and it would probably explode into a million messy splinters.

Still holding the table over his head, the ogre stopped, tipped his head to the side and shrugged one shoulder. "Too hard to fix?"

And that's when Thimble noticed it. The ogre wasn't scowling, he was smiling.

"Uh, yes. That's a bit much."

The ogre nodded and put the table back down. He stomped over to the trunk that held his clean folded clothes and looked over his shoulder at Thimble. When Thimble didn't say anything, the ogre cleared his throat.

"Right," Thimble said, more confused than angry. "Don't you dare."

The ogre grunted and busied himself wadding up shirts and breeches and throwing them around the house.

Thimble tried to stay out of the way and do some thinking. The ogre liked making messes, and he liked cleaning. And from the wicked glint in the ogre's eyes, he knew the old boy had other tricks up his sleeve. Staying here would be madness.

But it certainly wouldn't be boring.

Thimble grinned and scratched at the itchy dress. Maybe this wasn't so bad.

"Fine," Thimble said, trying to sound angry. "You mess everything up, but I will clean it. Every night while you sleep, I will wake and make your house fresh as a spring day."

The ogre grunted. "You'll never be able to clean everything before I start wreaking havoc."

"And you'll never be able to ruin everything before I start wreaking order."

They glared at each other, then Thimble nodded. The deal was set.

"Good then, I'm off to sleep. See that you don't keep me awake with your smashing and bashing, or I'll pinch you so hard, you'll be black and blue until your birthday."

The ogre grunted several times. "You don't scare me, Pinkie."

"You don't know me very well, Ugly."

The ogre chuckled again.

Thimble scratched at his thigh and trundled over to the corner by the door.

"See you in the evening," Thimble yawned.

But the ogre followed Thimble to the corner and held his hand out.

"What?" Thimble asked, hoping the big behemoth didn't want him to shake on the deal.

"Give me that ridiculous dress."

"Make me," Thimble said. Bad move. The ogre plucked him up by the wings and stripped the pink frock off him quicker than skinning a grape.

Thimble kicked and bit and pounded on the ogre's hand to no avail.

The ogre put Thimble back down on his feet and patted his head. "When you want it back, you let me know." The ogre pulled a key on a string out from beneath his coarse tunic and unlocked the only cabinet in the house. Thimble saw a flash of gold, a wink of jewels, then the ogre tossed his dress in there and locked the door.

"Monster," Thimble grumbled without much heat.

The ogre shrugged and went about crushing sticks into sawdust.

The truth was, now that he was out of that dress he felt much better. More like his old self. Free to make his own choices and to come or go as he pleased. And even though the ogre was as tempermental as the three-year-old girl, Thimble could handle that so long as there weren't any plastic doll shoes hidden away in the cabinet. Better yet, now he could go back to dreaming about a proper set of clothes, maybe even a jaunty hat. He felt better than he had in years. Thimble curled up, with nothing but dry leaves for a bed, and chuckled, "crazy as an ogre."

The ogre just grunted in reply.

THE ROSE, THE FARMBOY, AND THE GNOME

Phaedra M. Weldon

Phaedra M. Weldon lives and writes in Atlanta, Georgia. Forty hours a week she works as a graphic artist amid a strange but lovable group of people and the rest of her time is spilt among her daughter, husband, cat, puppy, and writing. She began her publishing career in the first Start Trek anthology, *Strange New Worlds.* Her work has been in subsequent Star Trek forums, including a Starfleet Core of Engineers (S.C.E.) novella, "Blackout." Her first original short story, "By the Rules," appeared in *Gateways.* She has since sold "The Light of Ra" to the anthology *Hags, Witches, and Other Bad Girls,* and three Classic BattleTech universe stories, "En Passant," "Personal Best," and "Be Not Afraid of Greatness," all published on the BattleCorps Web site. She also created and is writing the cannon-character-based BattleCorps serial, *The Moral Law.* Currently she is working on a two-book fantasy-noir-mystery for Penguin/Ace.

THE YARD GNOME CACKLED loudly between Jed's ears. *Stupid git. Make a wish—come on—I can turn them all into stone.—*

The headline splashed across the evening edition of the *Goblin Globe* read, "Local Pauper to Wed Princess Penelope." The onionskin newspaper lay in a sprawled, upside-down fan across the worn and termite-ridden wooden floor of Farmboy Jed's one-room shack. Jed could see this clearly from his present position—suspended upside down from his ceiling. His shirt no longer hung over his head and arms, as it had been just recently removed by one of the evening's guests.

He preferred to look at the fortunes of other poor men because if he looked straight ahead, he'd see the floating feet of the Gotti trio, the city's most notorious "debt retriever" gang of fairies.

"Whu-whu-whu-wait!" Jed cried out as the two gorgeous blondes with bobbing breasts (which looked a mite gravity-defying from Jed's new point of view) spread his legs wide, exposing his most valuable assets.

Uncle Gotti's tiny wings were nothing but a gray blur to Jed as the roundish, toothbrush-mustached fairy moved to a better position so Jed could see him. "I'm afraid the time for mercy is over, dear Jed." The fairy's voice was soft, sweet, in a singsong, cavity-forming way. "With interest, and six false promises, I'm afraid your total owed has reached one thousand gold pieces."

One—thousand—gold—

The roar of blood whooshing past Jed's ears deafened him for an instant. He took several deep breaths as he held up (or down, according to perspective) the index finger of his right hand. The Gottis had already taken the left one several months ago. "Uh—excuse me. But did you just say one thousand?"

Uncle Gotti nodded. Jed could hear the tinkle of tiny annoying fairy bells.

"But my debt was only fifty."

"Don't forget our interest. Oh—" Uncle Gotti glanced away from Jed, and he could only imagine that the brutish fairy had looked at his nieces. "You should never have professed your ability to find the shard of some great deity with promises that it would redeem your debt. Oh, really, Jed—and that ridiculous claim that the Elves over in Glenwood Glade held a secret talisman capable of granting magic." He chuckled and held on to the straining belt about his middle. "'Twas the Prince who found the treasures, and you—Farmboy Jed—brought back the ridiculous statue of a gnome."

There were several snorts and a bullhorn laugh. If there was one thing Jed had learned during his brief (very brief) dalliance with a Gotti daughter, it was that beauty truly did run skin deep. Matilda and Mattie—the two buxom blondes who now traced their razor-sharp nails up and down his exposed chest and moving ever closer to his jewels—had voices like grinding metal, and sharp Trenton, New Jersey, accents to boot. And their laughter—

Well, he was sure he could somehow find a nice and willing Wizard who could conjure him in another set of back teeth. That is, if he didn't lose his skin, which was the standard price for debts these days.

"You couldn't even steal a babe from its cradle for the Elves, Jed."

Well, it wasn't like stealing children was a common occurrence nowadays, right? Changelings did not come cheap, and more humans were affording better security systems. Stealing children from cribs had become an all-out specialty skill and not something any upstanding citizen did in today's politically correct climate. Though the pay if one was successful was astronomical.

"But-but the gnome," he tried to protest, though his tongue swelled with the flood of blood to his head. "It has great powers. The Elves said so!"

"And you *trust* Elven magic? How do you know that gnome out there isn't what's left of the last schmuck who tried to steal from them?" Another round of raucous, porcelain-shattering laughter from the girls, and Jed bit down on his remaining teeth. He did not want to lose those as well. He struggled against the magic curse imprisoning his feet, but there was no escaping. Jed was only a man, a simple human, and subject to the laws and whims of magic.

Which just royally stunk.

He was also getting dizzy from the blood pooling at the top of his skull. With a grunt he looked up (or down, whichever way you look at it) and saw the headlines again.

Lucky pauper. Why couldn't *he* have rescued a Princess? Then *he'd* be marrying rich. *He'd* be a Prince. And *he'd* be powerful.

Wait.

Why not?

Princesses get kidnapped all the time, right? It was as daily an occurrence as muggings in the city square. Certainly there's bound to be another one any day now—and then Jed could go and rescue her. They'd marry—and he'd be rich! As a prince, he might even be able to have these criminals (not him of course—he never actually stole the baby, now did he?) thrown in the dungeon and not pay them one gold coin.

He dreamed of stringing them up by their pointy little shoes and plucking their wings off one by one.

Yes!

But wait—would the Gottis give him another chance? No, not with any normal promise of repayment with interest. And they'd never go for another treasure-seeking quest. And as for enlightenment? Too overrated.

It'd have to be something special—something they couldn't take by force. He couldn't think of anything he had that valuable.

Jed wasn't sure if it was delirium brought on by the blood filling his brain or by the thought of being disemboweled by buxom blondes, but he gasped inwardly as his mouth spat out "Wait! Give me a week and if I don't deliver the gold, you can have my—"

He managed to slap his hands over his mouth before he spat out something he'd regret—he couldn't believe he'd been about to offer them that!

The yard gnome's voice rang in his head. *Oh come on . . . you don't really need it now do you?*

Jed kept his jaw firmly clamped down.

"What?" Uncle Gotti was interested.

"Oou—" He pulled at his lower jaw hard, but some invisible force seemed to be attempting to work his mouth for him. He fought it so that his words came out as mere sounds. "Ooy can 'ave my—ahhtttnnj."

Argh! Stop that! Let my tongue go! He railed at his inner conscience. How could it make such a bargain? The mere thought was preposterous. *You can't give them that! Once it's gone, it's gone, and then I'm exiled to the Haunted Forest to be a rotting corpse for all eternity!*

Jed continued to clamp both hands over his mouth as the Gottis stared at him with wide, almost frightened eyes. And who could blame them? He was arguing with himself.

And losing.

"Jed? What is it you'll trade?" Uncle Gotti leaned in closer.

Jed's vision blurred. He really needed to be upright so he could think straight—but that wasn't going to happen till the Gottis let him go.

Oh, just say it. If your plan works, then it won't matter now will it?

And if there is no plan? Dude—you're talking about me giving up my—

Jed's momentary need to argue with the gnome's voice was enough of a distraction for his tongue to free itself. His jaw released his tongue long enough for him to spit out "Soul!"

No! Jed slapped his hands to the sides of his face.

Come on . . . the Elves didn't lie—not really. You could always let me grant you that wish.

Bugger off!

Uncle Gotti clapped his hands. "Ah, Jed. Well done. Well done. I couldn't have asked for a better conclusion to our business today. Darlings . . ." He waved his hand.

Jed felt the binding curse on his ankles release just before he fell on his head. Doh!

"Now," Uncle Gotti was saying, "I have by my watch that it's Sunday evening at five o'clock and a half—"

"Five thirty—" croaked Jed from the floor.

"—so by next Sunday at this time, if you've not produced the amount of one thousand gold pieces, the price becomes your soul. We have a deal?"

Still rubbing his knocked noggin, Jed looked up to see Uncle Gotti's tiny outstretched hand. The fairy's entire palm would fit inside Jed's human-size one. *I could snap it off like a twig,* he thought as he took the fairy's hand in his.

Burrs abruptly sprang up through Uncle Gotti's skin and stuck hard into Jed's. The Farmboy yelled out and pulled his hand away, the inside of his palm covered in tiny dots of blood.

Uncle Gotti gave him a tsk-tsk noise before waggling a finger at him. "Naughty thoughts, Jed. Naughty thoughts. But—" He smiled and his toothbrush mustache bristled out and up. "The deal is in blood, thanks to those thoughts. Matilda. Mattie. Let us enjoy the rest of our evening." He held out his arms as his "nieces" flittered over to him.

I'm not sure those women are really related to him, Jed thought as he watched them fly over his prone body and out through the glassless window.

Nah, ya think? The gnome's tone was more than sarcastic.

Oh, screw you. This is all your fault. Jed grabbed up his shirt from the floor and clasped it around his prickled right hand. His head ached from tasting too much of his blood and he stumbled more than walked to the window. The moon lowered over the kingdom, just as the sun was yanked up and out of sight with a squelch.

Pixies twinkled like glitter in the half darkness. Luckily the gnome was pixie-proof, otherwise the little buggers would all be in his house tearing holes in the wood.

If only I'd replaced it with a fairy-proof yard gnome.

The gnome mooned him.

Jed leaned against the window frame. The wood creaked.

The yard gnome pivoted in the dirt just outside the window. *Where are you gonna find a kidnapped princess? I still think you should let me grant you that wish. I only get to do the one, and if you never make yours, I can't make mine!*

"No." Jed shook his head and then grabbed the window frame with both hands when his vision blurred again. "I might be poor but I'm not stupid (okay—not most of the time). Uncle's right—I don't really trust Elven magic, nor a statue that disappears in the middle of the night."

I do not.

"Do too."

Do not.

"Do Too."

Do not.

But Jed had had enough. "Just zip it. I don't trust you."

And I should trust you? You tried to steal a baby.

"That was—well—I was desperate." Jed frowned. "I'm still desperate."

Make a wish.

Jed eyed the gnome's shadow. "I'm not *that* desperate. I just know if something as freaky as you grants me a wish, it can't be good. Don't be so bothersome." He scowled. "Tomorrow's Monday. There's bound to be some stupid git kidnapped in the paper first headline."

But on Monday morning there was no stupid git listed as being kidnapped. Nor was there one on Tuesday. By Wednesday evening there wasn't even so much as a house invasion.

It was as if the entire kingdom had suddenly put itself on its best behavior.

Wednesday night Jed sat at his single table with a single candle burning to light the single-room shack. He clutched at the nub of his left index finger and stared out at the Pixies as they bashed into the magical shield protecting the house.

Less than four days before the Gottis came back and took his soul.

You desperate enough now? The yard gnome's silhouette became pronounced in the light of the round full moon. The thing hadn't been there a moment ago, gone again and off to do whatever it was yard gnomes do in the moonlight.

"No." Jed folded his arms over his chest. "I'll give it another day. Should be a kidnapping in the morning."

But there wasn't. And none by that afternoon. No evil sorcerer or magician, not even a wicked witch. Where the hell had all the villains gone?

Seemed the gnome knew. *Found out what's up with the lack of serious villainy. It's Villain's Week.*

"Villain's Week?"

Yeah, something the High King instituted about a year ago—gives the villains a week off every year, and gives heroes and the like time to spend with their families. Everyone's at the beach. The gnome pivoted again from his position outside the shack. *Vacation. Kidnappings probably won't resume till next week. Monday morning for sure—they'll be loads of them.*

Vacation? Jed shook his head. "Monday will be too late. I won't have a soul by then."

'Fraid so, Jed old boy. Now are you desperate? Care to make that wish?

"No." Jed paced the shack. "I can't. You'll mess it up somehow."

No I won't. Just try it. Why would I mess this up when my own happiness depends on you?

He narrowed his eyes at the gnome. "How exactly does that work? You keep saying you'll get your wish if I get mine. What kind of wish-giving enchanted thing are you?"

Let's just say I'm one of a kind. The gnome shrugged its ceramic shoulders. The brown cap on his head shifted to the right. *Make a wish, and I'll give you your heart's desire.*

Uh-oh. Jed took a step back. "My heart's desire, huh? I'm not sure you're being vague enough here."

The gnome did a mental shrug. *That's all I can say.*

With a scowl, Jed nodded. "Then I have to phrase this

just right." He cleared his throat. "I wish—uh—I wish to be—no—I wish uh to have—no, no, no."

I wish you'd get your act together. For crying out loud, wish something.

"I wish I was powerful."

There seemed to be a pause in the morning. The birds ceased to chirp. Even the rise of the sun seemed suspended.

Then *Is that it?*

Jed pursed his lips together. He nodded. Then he shrugged. "Yeah . . . that's it."

It's awfully broad.

"Well, I figure if I were powerful, then I could stop the Gottis from taking my soul, see? And I'd no longer be slave to the whims of magical meanness. It stinks being a human in a magical realm. Everyone else has magic. Elves, trolls, wizards, fairies. It's better to be a magical creature."

The gnome looked pensive. *Not sure I can agree with you there. But to each his own. Simply put, you don't want to be a victim anymore.*

With a tap on his chin with the stub of his left finger, Jed nodded. "Yeah, that's it."

Hoo-kay. Your wish is granted.

Instantly there was scream. And then a roar.

"Is that it?" Jed looked around the shack, expecting something to come crashing down at him.

Uh—yeah. You better go get it.

Jed did just that. He ran out of the door, grabbing up the sword he fashioned from tin on Monday evening, and raced down the path. The scream came again, and Jed turned in the direction of the Enchanted Mountains.

An hour later, and nearly out of breath, Jed reached the top of a ledge. A cave mouth yawned open before him. It was dark inside, like the blackness of a tomb that spoke of danger and bravery. Inside lay his destiny—to save a princess and become a Prince.

It felt dangerous. It reeked of doom.

And it smelled like—

Potpourri?

The scream came again from inside the cave mouth. Jed felt bravado fill his chest and he thrust it out as he bellowed. "I'm coming to save you!"

Once inside, the world took on a whole different look.

Chintz draperies of red and gold hung from the cave's walls, woven in and out with pink roses and gold rope with tasseled ends. The floor turned from rock and sand to shiny hardwoods, polished to a slippery finish—which of course with Jed's momentum arrival speed sent Jed sliding forward on his backside to the back of the cave.

Lighted candles glittered from gilded mirrors on every wall and off gold encrusted furniture. The place was a veritable gold mine!

But what caught his attention next was the sight of a fifty-foot dragon towering over him in the back of the cave. Its maw was open, showing very large, very white, and very sharp teeth. It batted about a large, white hanky in its taloned left hand as it—screamed?

No way. Jed scrambled to a standing position and then held out his sword in front of him. So—the dragon was the one screaming?

From what? The hulking monster abruptly did a little dance, banging its enormous taloned feet on the hardwood. Jed was afraid the thing was going to crack the finish if it wasn't careful.

"You there!" the dragon hissed at him. "Kill it!"

"Me?" Jed looked around. Dragons talked? Sure they shot fire, flew in the sky, and sometimes kidnapped maidens. But spoke. "Kill what?"

"That!" it shrieked and pointed to something to the right of Jed.

He turned and nearly toppled over with surprised laughter.

A tiny white mouse with dark shades over its eyes stood on its hind feet. It was making faces at the dragon.

This was nuts.

Jed lowered his sword. "You're afraid of this mouse?" He had to shout a bit to be heard over the dragon's sobs.

The dragon nodded. "Yes! Please! Get rid of it! I'll give you your fondest wish!"

Ah-ha! There it was. Though in the odd packaging of a dragon? Well, who was he to argue with destiny? Jed turned to the mouse.

The mouse whipped around, saw Jed advancing with his sword brandished, squealed once, and then ran off out of the cave mouth. Jed chased after it and saw it launch itself off the ledge.

Oh no. He moved to the side to see if the thing had gone splat on the rocks below. His stomach wasn't as squeamish when he saw it scrambling down the rocks to the valley beyond.

Jed turned and found himself face-to-face with the dragon's head.

"Yow!" He took a step back and found himself tittering on the edge of the ledge. The dragon reached out and scooped him up, turned, and walked them back into the cave mouth.

"Oh, I'm so happy, and so thankful," said the dragon. "My name is Rose. And you are?"

"J-Jed, ma'am." He narrowed his eyes at the dragon. This was a girl? Then he looked at all the gold and pink. Well, maybe so. "I'm happy to be of help."

"Not many knights would venture into the Enchanted Mountains to help an aging dragon, mind you." She set him down beside a small golden couch. The furniture was the size for a human, much too small for a dragon. "Please, have some tea."

"Uh, no thanks." He could smell the tea from the gold-encrusted tea service that appeared magically on the coffee table. His stomach rumbled. When was the last time he'd eaten? "I really need to go—so as for my reward—"

"Oh yes, yes, of course. Your heart's desire, well you'll need to—"

"Ma'am. Miss Rose," Jed waved up at her, still not sure he wasn't going to become a crunchy snack. "Please, I'd be happy with some gold. You have so much of it— maybe two thousand pieces?" He smiled, and thought himself quite clever, doubling the price of his soul's ransom.

But Rose shook her head. "I can give you all the gold you wish, brave knight." She sighed. "But this is dragon's gold, and once it leaves the edges of the Enchanted Mountains, it turns to dust and forgotten dreams."

Jed lowered his shoulders.

Bollocks.

"But perhaps there is something else." Rose spoke up and Jed looked at her. "If you give me a kiss—"

"What?" Jed took a step back and nearly tripped over the couch. "Kiss you?"

"Why yes." Rose looked almost hurt and she leaned in close. Her eyes were the colors of a sunset. The ends of her mouth turned up in a smile. "Then I could give you your heart's desire."

"Uh"—he narrowed his eyes at her—"You're not like . . . a woman turned into a dragon are you? Like if I kiss you, you turn into a rich princess?"

Rose shook her head.

"A rich Prince?" Though the image of a nelly prince

didn't exactly excite Jed in the right way, he did consider the complications for a second. A very brief second.

Rose shook her head again. "Neither. I was born a dragon, and I will die as one. The last of my kind. But I must repay you somehow for your kindness."

Well, he couldn't take the gold, and if he kissed the dragon (ewwwghhhh) she wouldn't turn into a rich princess either. So—what could he ask for a reward?

What can a dragon do?

Fly. Blow smoke and fire.

Terrorize villagers.

And— "Kidnap a princess!"

"Excuse me?" Rose moved back from him.

Jed looked up at her, excitement making his heart pound. "That's it! I need gold to pay off my debt to the Gottis. You can kidnap a princess and she'll reward me with marriage. I'll be rich!"

Rose looked troubled. She put her huge sheet-size handkerchief to her chin. "You want me to kidnap a princess. Well, I know it's been done though the last one to attempt such a fiendish thing ended up stuffed and mounted in Prince Charming's living room." She looked skeptical.

"But I'm not Prince Charming—and I'll only pretend to slay you to rescue the princess."

"Uhm—" She shook her head. "Oh, I don't know. It's such a dirty business."

"Look." Jed slid his tin sword into his string belt. "All you have to do is kidnap a princess. Tie her up and then I'll come rescue her. We're square and I can pay off my debt."

Rose seemed to think this through. "Wouldn't it be better if you just kissed me?"

Ew. No. Jed shook his head. "Please? For my reward?"

With a resigned sigh, Rose agreed. "Sure. When and who?"

Hmm. Good question. There were several princesses in the area, so he'd have to be selective as to whom. In this instance he had a choice, unlike the other schmucks who had to go with what was given.

And if he had to choose a wife, he'd choose the High King's daughter, Princess Vixennia. Beautiful. And rich.

When he told Rose his choice, she looked pinched. "Are you sure? I think her heart's desire lies with another."

"I don't care. Look, you just snatch her up, do your thing, and I'll pretend to wound you. Okay?"

Rose nodded in agreement, and they set the time and place. Midnight tonight. In a cave near the foot of the Haunted Forest.

It all seemed so right.

When Jed arrived home, there was no sign of the yard gnome.

The kidnap went according to Jed's plan. Apparently Princess Vixennia took midnight strolls for clandestine rendezvous with a forbidden love in a brown hat. Rose snatched her up and then carried her back to the cave. There she bound the princess and tossed her in the back of the cave, then sent up the signal (a brief flame flare) to let Jed know she'd done her part of the bargain.

Jed wanted to wait till morning, to let the news of the princess's capture reach the *Goblin Globe*. Had to make sure it was on the front page for posterity.

But when he reached the cave, no one was there.

Wait . . . what?

Jed ran all the way to the back of the cave. He found cut rope and a knotted cloth. Okay, bindings here. But where was the princess?

And where was Rose?

He heard trumpets from the city. Jed's heart sank.

No . . . it can't be. He turned and ran as fast as he could back to the gates. The banners of the king's standard were flying in the breeze. People were lined up along the cypress-planted path.

And there, in the center, was a very unhappy-looking Princess and beside her, atop a white stallion, was a man in shining armor.

Prince Charming.

No! No, no, no! Jed started stamping the ground. But where was Rose? What had he done with Rose? Jed ran up to the nearest peasant. "Ma'am, what happened here?"

"Oh, it was so loverly, sir." The woman had no front teeth, and a huge mole on the end of her nose. "A big scarlet dragon came and took away the Princess—but Prince Charming here—he rescued her ya see, and now they're to be wed—"

"But the dragon," Jed panted. "Where's the dragon?"

"Oh, it's been put into the castle dungeon, it has." She spat on the ground. "Foul creatures. Wanting nothing more than the spoils of kidnapping such a fine lady. The king'll put it death, he will. Mark my words. Evil creatures—don't deserve to live if you ask me." And she bent her head and sent out a cackle that raised the hairs on the back of Jed's neck.

He kicked her cane out from under her. "I didn't."

Rose!

It took a few tight turns and twists, but Jed remembered the old passageways into the dungeons. He'd used them once or twice in his youth, before he'd tried to go on the straight and good path.

Too bad that path had sent him straight back into breaking and entering.

He found Rose in one of the larger cells. She was still too big to fit in properly, so it looked as if she'd been stuffed in, back end first, with her snout sticking out. Large horse-size manacles encircled her wrists and neck, and she was chained to the floor and walls.

She looked miserable.

A group of the king's guards sat in a circle nearby, playing a game or two of Go Fish. Jed moved quietly along the side until he was right up beside Rose's eye.

"Jed?" came Rose's snort.

"Shhhhh!" He nearly had a cow right there at the sound of her voice. He glanced around to the side of the cell opening and made sure the guards hadn't moved.

They looked as if they hadn't heard anything.

"Jed—no one can hear me but you," Rose said in a calming voice.

That's when he realized the voice of the dragon was in his head—just like the voice of the gnome. "Uh—" He turned and faced her eye. "Right. Didn't know that."

She sighed, and a slight bit of black smoke came from her nostrils. "I'm afraid I sort of botched it."

"What happened?"

"Well I fell asleep," she said. "Little miss spoiled was in the back of the cave, twitching and turning, and making all sorts of racket into that gag, so I set up some nice chamomile incense—you know—to soothe things a bit. And well—" Rose focused her eye on Jed. "I sort of fell asleep myself."

"And that's how Prince Charming captured you."

"I'm afraid so. Woke up and I was the one in chains. So—" She blinked at him. "They're going to kill me in the morning. Oh Jed, I'm so sorry."

He leaned against her. "Why are you sorry? I got you into this. Me and my greed." Well, not just greed, bub. "And the need to save my soul. I just wanted to be powerful, you know? To not be stepped on all the time—to be something more."

"Is that it?" Rose's voice sounded incredulous.

"Yeah, that's it."

"Then kiss me."

Jed shook his head. "Ick. I can't do that, Rose."

"Why not? Am I that ugly?"

Jed looked at her. "No—it's just that I'm supposed to get a reward, aren't I? I mean, the gnome said he'd fulfill my heart's desire."

"Then kiss me!"

There was a noise at the end of the hall. He could hear the sound of marching feet. "I think someone's coming. I think it's the guards to kill you."

"Kiss me!"

"NO!"

"It's my last wish!" She looked pleadingly at him.

Well, she *had* tried to help him, though he could tell the poor creature didn't have a violent bone in her body. She was a nice dragon, as far as dragons went, and she hadn't eaten him.

Yet.

"You won't eat me?"

"The Gottis are taking your soul—would it really matter now?"

He gulped. He guessed not. With a backward glance at the hallway and the approaching march of feet, Jed took a deep breath, closed his eyes, and kissed the dragon.

"On the lips, you git."

Oh.

He moved out and repeated his action, and kissed Rose on the lips.

His world pitched forward, and then backward, as he felt his body explode beneath him and then move to fill the space where he stood. He could hear screams in the distance.

What was all the ruckus about?

Abruptly his vision cleared and he was looking down at the guards, who were all looking up at him, their eyes wide and their mouths gaping.

"Handsome! You're so handsome!"

Jed turned to see Rose—only she was looking *up* at him.

Up—at—me?

Oh no!

"Dragon! *Two* dragons!" shouted the guards and they were running here and there along the floor beneath Jed's feet. He drew back on his hind legs—*hind legs!*—and watched them go.

"Darling!" Rose said in a very sexy voice. "Please— can you free me so we can get out of here?"

Jed looked back down at Rose. She was still tethered to the floor and walls. With ease he tore the chains away and broke the manacles, and then he helped pull her out of the cell, her lower half coming out with an audible "pop."

"What happened?" Jed was saying as Rose dusted herself off. He heard the crunch of something brittle and looked down to see he'd stepped on a few guards. Ew. "What did you do to me?"

"You're a dragon!" Rose clapped her hands together. "Oh, I finally got my wish. I've kissed so many toads in my day, and they've all been toads. But I'd never thought to kiss a human." She shook her head. "Who knew?"

"But, but." He looked down at his own blue and green scales. He was also aware of how attractive Rose suddenly was. "I don't want to be a dragon!"

"But the Gottis can't touch you like this," Rose said with a long talon pointing at the dungeon ceiling. "Think about it. No one can touch you—ever again. You're powerful."

He thought about the cave he'd found her in, and about

the gold. It was dragon gold but hey . . . it was still gold. "And I'm rich."

Something stung on his left hip. Jed looked down to see Prince Charming sticking a spear into it. He looked over at Rose. "Will this last? I mean, I won't turn back into a human just yet?"

"No." Rose looked hopeful. "You don't want too, do you?"

Jed looked back down at the Prince and with little more than a belch, set the Prince's robes and hair on fire. The little man went screaming down one of the dungeon tunnels. He looked back over at Rose. "Nah. But let's get back over to my place." He looked down at the still-missing finger of his left hand. "I have a score to settle."

On Monday morning Jed sat beside a simple breakfast of dragon kibble and mulled wine with a copy of the early edition of the *Goblin Globe*. He read aloud to Rose the tragic torching of Farmboy Jed's shack on Harmony Hill, another fiery event just on the heels of the drastic dragon escape of Saturday night. Two dragons, reportedly from the Enchanted Mountains, ravaged the castle grounds during their escape. Princess Vixennia was missing, and Prince Charming had declared an all-out hunt to find the dragons—but only after his hair grew back out.

Rose clapped her hands. "How exciting." Her eyes gleamed a brilliant gold. "Read the *Nosey Nettle* column on page three. It's very interesting."

Jed flipped the oversize onionskin edition and glanced at the headline. "Oh ho! The King's Wizard is perplexed over two yard gnomes reportedly seen appearing and disappearing in the palace gardens." Jed blinked. "A witness claims one of the gnomes resembles Princess Vixennia."

"I told you the princess's heart belonged to another."

He stared at her incredulously. "So the yard gnome

was having an affair with the princess? That's where he was going every night? To see her?"

Rose patted his green-and-blue scaled knee. "That was how I was able to catch the princess. Oh, I love happy endings—even if they are a little out of the norm."

Jed agreed. As for Uncle Gotti and his nieces, Jed glanced up at the ceiling at the new three-globe chandelier, at the tiny lights flittering about each of the globes. Every now and then, with his new super dragon ears, he could hear the Gotti fairies screaming to be set free with promises of fame and fortune.

Oh, please.

A DAY AT THE UNICORN RACES

Christina F. York

Christina F. York is a romance writer who can't resist playing in science fiction and fantasy, and ac-
tion/adventure. She blames it on being a Gemini.
Her short fiction has appeared in the DAW anthologies *Time After Time* and *Hags and Harpies*. Her
latest novel, *Alias: Strategic Reserve*, was published in
March 2006, with another in the works. In addition
to romance novels and Alias tie-ins, she has also
published Star Trek short fiction and novels, the latter in collaboration with writer and husband, J.
Steven York. Chris lives on the Oregon coast, where
she can see the ocean from her office window.

ALPHONSE LISTENED TO THE track announcer calling the end
of the Meadowland Stakes race, as he watched from the
rail. The thunder of hooves shook the ground under his feet
and dust assailed his nose as the racers passed his position.

Fairy Dust was one of his favorites, even though trainers weren't supposed to have favorites.

And Bubbles, the elf jockey, was one of his favorites, too. He probably shouldn't have favorite jockeys, either, but screw that. She looked good in the silks, and he could imagine what she would look like out of them. Hell, he'd even had a preview or two in the changing rooms, even though the women's locker was supposed to be off limits to men.

But Bubbles didn't feature having him in her life, not by a long shot. Not as long as she was a unicorn racer. Just his luck to get all hot and bothered over an elf with a career that didn't leave much room for a love life.

It wasn't like he hadn't tried. He'd done all the polite things, made all the nonthreatening moves he knew.

Both of them.

But she'd been pretty clear. He couldn't find a good answer to "Get your damned hands off of me." She might be little, but dainty wasn't a word that described Bubbles.

Fairy Dust was moving along the rail, challenging for the lead, with only a few seconds left in the race. He seemed to respond to the screaming of the crowd, putting on a last-second burst of speed and moving into a photo finish.

In the infield, the fiddling cat began a tune, providing his regular distraction for the crowd between races.

While the crowd buzzed, waiting for the results, Alphonse slipped through the gate into the paddock, where the mounts were cooling down.

As a trainer, he was one of the few people allowed near the unicorns. Only virgins could ride, but fortunately trainers didn't have to be quite so pure. He'd thought about being a jockey once, but being human reduced his chances, in a career dominated by the lithe elves.

And that whole no-sex thing had been the clincher. Who wanted to voluntarily spend the rest of his life in a constant state of frustration? He had seen firsthand how nasty the jockeys got.

Still, the girls were hot.

Bubbles was still astride Fairy Dust, leaning forward over his neck, stroking his horn, and whispering in his ear.

Alphonse suddenly wished he were a unicorn.

As she stroked the horn, Bubbles stood up slightly in her saddle, leaning forward. The tight silk of her riding pants stretched across her trim bottom.

Was the woman deliberately torturing him?

Bubbles glanced around the paddock, catching sight of Alphonse. Her eyes were bright with the excitement of the race, and a little unfocused, her face flushed. She smiled at Alphonse, and nudged Fairy Dust toward him.

Sliding from the saddle, Bubbles dropped down next to Alphonse. "Did you see the son-of-a-bitch run?" She was buzzing with adrenaline. "Did you *see*?"

Before Alphonse could reply, the finish photo flashed on the tote board. Fairy Dust, muscles straining, had pushed his horn ahead of the number-two finisher by a fraction of an inch.

Bubbles cheered and jumped into Alphonse's arms, wrapping her slender legs around his waist, and kissing him lustily.

For an instant, passion flowed freely.

Then Bubbles broke the kiss and dropped to the ground. Her face clouded, and frustration instantly replaced passion.

"Dammit!" She stomped away. "Don't *do* that to me!"

As she moved off, Alphonse could hear a string of muttered curses. He shook his head.

She *was* trying to torture him.

The jockey's changing room was a miasma of steam and sweat, the clash of a dozen different soap and shampoo scents creating a stomach-churning cloud of olfactory overload.

Bubbles shoved her way to her locker, shouldering past the crowd of elves busily changing silks, shooting dirty looks at anyone who crossed her path.

"Watch out," called a tiny woman wrapped in a towel. "Bubbles is horny. Again!"

"Am not!" Bubbles shot back.

The retort was greeted with a wave of laughter from all over the room.

"You sooo are too," the woman replied. She stopped in front of a locker with the name "Rainbow" stenciled on the front, and pulled out a small silver flask. "Here," she said, and tossed it to Bubbles, "drown your sorrows."

Bubbles tilted her head back and took a long swallow from the flask before tossing it back to Rainbow. "I don't need to drown my sorrows, but I am not about to pass up free gin."

"Honey," Rainbow said, stowing the flask back in her locker, "it may just be time to hang up your silks."

"Bullshit." Bubbles stripped off the garments in question, and tossed them in a basket for cleaning. "Never happen."

"Listen to you, acting all tough," called Sunshine from the next bank of lockers. "Keep this up, you're gonna explode, I swear it."

"You never swear, Sunny. And I am not even going to dignify that with an answer," Bubbles said. She wrapped a rough towel around her, and marched off to the shower.

Maybe a cold shower would just wash away the frustration.

It wasn't that she didn't like Alphonse well enough. Hell, if she weren't a jockey, and he weren't a human, she might even give him a tumble, but it would mean losing her job, and for what?

As Bubbles dressed, Rainbow and Sunshine continued to taunt her. Finally when all three were leaving the locker room, Rainbow threw a friendly arm over Bubbles's shoulder.

"You aren't the only one, you know," she whispered confidentially. "We've all thought about it."

"No shit. Like that's a big surprise."

"No, really," Sunshine said earnestly. "We do think about it. How can you not?"

"But there's nothing we can do about it. Not if we want to keep our jobs. One little tumble, and poof!" Bubbles waved her hands. "Remember Tatiana? She had some scheme that was supposed to fool Angel Heart."

Sunshine's big blue eyes grew wide and a single, perfect tear formed in one corner. "That poor girl! She was in the hospital for months when he threw her!"

Bubbles snorted in disgust. "Well, duh! Thought she could fool a unicorn? Hello! Magical creatures here, not gonna be fooled by some bimbo with a hormone overload."

Rainbow patted Bubbles on the back, as the three women made their way into the now-deserted parking lot. "You try to act like you don't care, but we know better, Bubby. And Alphonse isn't a bad guy, even if he is human. Hey, if I was ready to hang it up, I just might stash my riding boots under his bunk."

Sunshine's mouth turned down at the corners, and she cocked her head to the side. "It's all sad and tragic, you know. There just aren't that many great guys out there, and most of the good ones are taken."

"It's not all that. It isn't love, it's just a little roll in hay. Literally, if Tatiana is any example. And it's way more than a job, anyway," Bubbles shot back. "It's like my entire life. Racing is everything."

Rainbow's ancient Honda, painted in rainbow colors and covered with decals from all the tracks they had visited, sat in the far corner of the lot.

The three women piled in, and Rainbow headed for The Finish Line, the local track hangout.

At a table in the jockey's corner, they had a beer and the conversation picked up where it had left off.

They were nearly shouting over the din in the bar, the blaring jukebox providing a base for the buzz of conversation, punctuated by occasional shrill, alcohol-fueled laughter.

"I say go for it." Rainbow was not going to let it drop.

Bubbles shook her head. "Do I look like I am insane? Even if I am hot for his frame—which I am not, thank you very much—but even if I was, what am I gonna do? Throw away my entire life?"

Sunshine asked dreamily, "I can't think of a better reason." She sighed, a drawn-out, dramatic exhalation. "It must be wonderful."

"Sunny, get a grip! It's not like I'm in love with Al, like we're making lifelong plans here." Bubbles turned to glare at Rainbow. "And I am not hot for him, either."

Rainbow raised a skeptical eyebrow, but she didn't argue.

Across the bar Alphonse watched Bubbles. She hadn't seen him when she came in, and he knew better than to approach a jockey in The Finish Line. The women jockey's corner was strictly off-limits to men, both human and elf.

She was a lost cause. Every time he got close to her, she turned as prickly as a cactus, all sharp points and attitude to spare.

That was the thing about the jockeys. They might be virgins, and the women might be small and dainty. But they weren't all sweetness and light, oh no, not by a long shot. Most of 'em were kind of nasty when you got right down to it.

So why was he still watching Bubbles sip her beer?

Maybe he was the lost cause.

Bubbles paced the floor of her apartment. It was late, but she had a beer buzz, and she didn't want to sleep.

She stomped through the tiny area she laughingly called a living room, sidestepping her broken-down recliner and dodging a basket of unfolded laundry.

She tried not to think about Al, about how it felt when she kissed him. Well, duh! She might be a rider—a virgin—but it didn't' mean she was dead or something. Everything worked just fine, thank you.

And it didn't matter to her whether he was human, elf, or baboon. The consequesces were the same.

She glanced at the kitchen, a wall of counters with a miniature refrigerator, a two-burner cooktop, and a single sink piled with dirty dishes. Not that she needed anything more elaborate. Had to stay at her racing weight, after all.

She yanked open the refrigerator door, wondering if by some miracle she had a beer hidden in there, and glared at the contents. Some wilted salad, a take-out container from Wong Lee's—steamed rice and broccoli—that she couldn't remember ordering. No beer.

Probably a good thing. It would mean an extra hour in the gym, sweating off the calories that came with the cold golden goodness that came in that can. Even a light beer—yuck!—would cost her.

She slammed the refrigerator door, the thought of a beer reminding her of the conversation in The Finish Line. Her parts worked just fine, she just chose not to use some of them. It was a personal decision. Someday she might change her mind, but for now, some things were just more important than sex.

Oh, Sunshine would insist Bubbles was in love with Al, which was so totally not true. Sunshine just read too many romance novels. For her, sex and love were the same thing.

And Rainbow would tell her everybody had to hang it up sometime, that nobody raced forever, and there were other things she could do. But she didn't see Rainbow making any moves in that direction.

What did they know?

She growled, wishing they were here so she could tell them how wrong they were. She was so not ready to quit racing. She loved the excitement of the race, the feeling that she got when she rode a winner. She even enjoyed the feeling of being in Alphonse's arms, and the tinglies that came from kissing him.

But kissing would lead to more, and more would lead to even *more*, and before she knew it, she could be out of racing, and thinking about a second career.

No. Better she didn't even start down that road.

She paced back through the living room, slammed her fist against a lumpy cushion that sat in the recliner, and stomped into the bathroom.

She needed another cold shower.

In the changing room, the jockeys were in the usual state of prerace jitters. Rainbow was standing in front of her locker, fingering her assortment of lucky charms, including the four-leaf clover she had found on a recent picnic.

Rainbow hadn't said much about it, but Bubbles knew it involved a man, and the clover had become a talisman for Rainbow. Judging by the sly smile on her face, there was a girl who was getting ready to hang up her silks.

Not Bubbles.

Bubbles's talisman, if you could call it that, was a battered jockey's cap she had picked up after Angel Heart had thrown Tatiana. Every time she looked at it, she was reminded of Tatiana, who had tried to have it all.

And look where that got her. She slammed the door on the cap, resolve stiffening her spine.

"Take it easy."

Bubbles looked up to find Sunshine looking at her pityingly, her big blue eyes round and solemn.

"What is your problem?" Bubbles growled.

Sunshine just shook her head. Rainbow turned, her face an angry red. "Could you both just keep it down? Some of us have to work today! Just because your boyfriend gives you the best runners, Bubby, doesn't give you the right to screw with the rest of us."

Bubbles sighed with disgust. "He is not my boyfriend. And I get the rides I deserve."

Rainbow waved a hand in dismissal. "Whatever. Just get over your attitude before you get out on the track."

Bubbles turned her back on Rainbow, and caught Sunshine's wide eyes. She hooked a thumb over her shoulder, in Rainbow's direction. "I think we know who's horny today," she muttered.

"Take that back!"

Rainbow was on her in a flash, all elbows and bony fingers, digging into Bubbles' unpadded ribs.

Bubbles went down, with Rainbow astride her, pinning her to the cold concrete floor of the changing room.

"Take it back!"

Bubbles bit her lip and refused to speak. Rainbow was constantly on her ass about Al. It was about time she had a dose of her own medicine.

"I swear, Bubbles, I don't have to take this—"

Rainbow was jerked backward, her words cut off, her face shocked.

Behind her, Bubbles could see Sunshine, tears streaming down her face. "Stop it!" she screamed. "Both of you, just stop it! I can't stand it when you fight."

Bubbles climbed slowly to her feet, brushing off her silks. Though the floor was clean, the gesture gave her a minute to collect herself.

She gave Rainbow a hard look, then turned her attention to Sunny. She had stopped crying, but her nose was red and swollen, and her eyes were puffy.

Bubbles felt instantly contrite for upsetting Sunny, even if Rainbow was acting like a jerk. "Sorry, Sunny. But you have to admit, she was being a bitch."

Rainbow was back on her feet, the color high in her cheeks and her breathing fast. She took a step toward Bubbles, lifting her fists in front of her, then shook her head and backed away.

"Aw, hell!" she said, slapping her locker shut. The clang of metal-on-metal echoed off the bare walls of the room. "You may be right." She turned around to face Bubbles. "But it takes one to know one."

Rainbow stamped away, the sound of her boots clicking against the concrete fading as she disappeared through the door to the paddock.

Sunshine stared after her, her face troubled. "Oh, Bubby," she wailed. "I don't think I've ever seen her that way."

Bubbles sat down on the hard bench in front of her locker. "Neither have I, Sunny. Ever."

Bubbles winced as a thought struck her. "I don't act like that, do I? I mean, you guys are on me all the time, and I was just dishing it back. But I'm not like that."

"Well." Sunshine dropped down onto the bench beside Bubbles and slipped her arm around her friend's narrow shoulders. "You do get a little crabby now and then. Especially when you've been around Al. Not that it's all that bad," she added hastily, as Bubbles tensed. "Not really that bad at all. Just sometimes . . ."

Her voice trailed off, and she drew back. "No, not that bad." She stood quickly, her voice suddenly brisk and unemotional. "I better go make sure Rainbow's okay."

The last race of the day was a big one, and Bubbles was up on Fairy Dust again. The two of them seemed to understand each other, and riding him was usually a pure joy.

But today wasn't one of those days. As they broke from the gate, he surged into the lead, refusing her attempts to slow him down, to set the pace for their run.

Again and again Fairy Dust fought her control. He would not hold back, wouldn't let the other runners tire themselves out. Instead he forced himself faster and faster with each length.

Bubbles could feel him beginning to tire. His stride wasn't as sure, and when another unicorn pulled up on the inside, he hesitated before trying to cut him off.

Bubbles felt a surge of disappointment, then anger, as Foo Foo Fifi went by on her left, Sunshine hunched over his neck, urging him on.

She raised her whip, a tactic she almost never used on Fairy Dust, pushed herself forward, flattening her body against the big animal's neck.

"Run, you son-of-a-bitch!" she shouted, tapping him lightly on the flank with her whip. She didn't need to hit him, never had needed the whip, and she wasn't about to start now.

But she wasn't about to lose, either.

She felt Fairy Dust falter again, then he regained his footing, and his stride steadied.

Then began to pull ahead of the pack, leaving the rest of the racers behind. All except Sunshine and Fifi.

They rounded the last turn, the two racers so close the announcer had fallen momentarily silent. There was no way to say who was in the lead.

The finish line was straight ahead, and neither unicorn was giving an inch.

In the last five lengths, with the rest of the field bearing down on them, Fifi stumbled. He brushed against Fairy Dust, and for one sickening moment, Bubbles thought they were going down.

Instead, Sunshine pulled up on her mount, taking him closer to the rail, and out of the path of Bubbles and Fairy Dust.

It was over in an instant. Fairy Dust flashed across finish line, with Fifi a length behind.

Relief flowed through Bubbles. She had won, despite her ride's erratic behavior.

This was what it was all about.

Bubbles let the reins lie slack against the unicorn's neck. She stood easily in the stirrups, leaning forward to pat her racing partner. They were a good team, even if he was acting peculiar today.

Then Fairy Dust reared, his front feet pawing the air. He snorted once and twisted beneath her.

Bubble's stomach dropped with a sickening wrench, as her feet left the stirrups, and she went flying through the air.

She landed on her back, on the hard-packed dirt of the track, her breath knocked from her lungs, and one leg twisted beneath her.

For one long, agonizing moment, she was afraid to move. Broken bones were a fact of the racing life, and she'd had her share. Still they weren't her idea of a good time.

She stirred, but before she could sit up, the medics were at her side, forcing her back down. They poked and prodded for long minutes, before they would let her move.

She struggled into a sitting position on the hard ground. Waiting behind the medics were her crew: Sunshine, tears welling in her eyes—that girl cried for anything!—and Rainbow.

And beside them was Al. Dear, sweet Al, who had put her up on a mount that damn near killed her.

"What the hell is his problem?" she stormed at Al.

His eyes widened, and he took a small step back, but then he seemed to sort of mentally shake himself and moved up close to her.

"His problem? Nothing much. Except that filly that was in the barn earlier today. Got him all riled up."

Al ran his eyes over her. Her silks were dusty and twisted around from the medic's inspection. Her helmet was askew, hanging over one ear and uncovering a serious case of helmet hair. Her face was covered with a light coat of dust, and there was a bruise already developing on one pale cheek.

"And I know exactly how he feels."

Al held out his hand, and she let him pull her to her feet.

Nothing like a little brush with mortality to make a girl reevaluate her life.

Al's arms went around her, and she lifted up on tiptoe. He kissed her, and all those perfectly working parts began to hum. The tinglies she had felt before intensified.

What the hell. Maybe it *was* time. And afterward she could have *two* beers, if she wanted.

There were always other jobs.

Al watched from the rail as Bubbles prepared for the between-races entertainment.

She may have decided to hang up her silks, but at

least she was still working at the track. And she was still hot.

In the infield Bubbles adjusted the harness and settled herself in the saddle. She waved at Al, a little shiver of pleasure passing through her as she thought about last night.

So this wasn't exactly unicorn racing, but it was still a respectable job.

She smiled at Al. Rainbow and Sunshine stood with him at the rail, grinning.

She braced herself, as the cow's muscles bunched beneath her. The cat raised his fiddle, and Bubbles took a deep breath. She hated the takeoff.

"To the moon!" she whispered.

DRAGONSLAYER:

Being the True and Terrible Tale of a Fearsome Meeting Between a Man and a Monster

Jana Paniccia

Jana Paniccia was born in Windsor, Ontario, and lived in Ottawa, Vancouver, Australia, and Japan before moving to Toronto where she now works for an advisory services firm. In addition to writing, Jana has a keen—some would say insane—interest in other areas of publishing. She is currently co-editing the DAW anthology *Under Cover of Darkness*, with Julie E. Czerneda, and has also done freelance work geared toward the business side of the industry. Jana's short fiction can be found in the anthologies *Children of Magic*, *Women of War*, and *Summoned to Destiny*.

HAMSTER DUGGIN FLICKED A hand outward toward the slice of darkness cutting through the overarching cliff face. "It was 'ere I did it—the dragon's lair!" Even as he spoke, he sized up his adventuresome marks with a cynically measuring eye.

Lord and Lady Orshire, heads of an opal mining family from central Turmalin, hadn't even bothered with the sturdy clothes mentioned on the supply list. *Bodes well for the take if they find it easy to discard their silks at the end of the day.* He would have snorted in derision if he hadn't had their full attention.

Their countryman Lord Kettlebank wasn't nearly as well to do. Why the frail retired councillor kept returning to see the dragon—this was his third, no his fourth, visit—Hamster couldn't guess. But the old man had brought four of his nephews along, so if he wanted to go over the same ground again and again, Hamster wasn't about to persuade him otherwise.

Besides, with all his visits he's donated more to the cause than any of his glitzy neighbors.

Next to the Turmalines waited a pair of foolhardy brothers from Aishail, the prosperous city-state at the mouth of the Blue River. *They'll be the ones to keep an eye on.* On the trek up the mountain from Pebble Pass, the two had managed to climb a wobbly mound of boulders before Hamster had noticed. *Most likely to get killed, sure enough.* One already had a tear in his trousers from trying to jump off the uneven rocks.

A strange scent reminiscent of mint shrouded his last patrons. They were the perfect image of a royal-born Lerei couple, wearing matching blue-green cloaks of a wispy material he was surprised could hold dye. Lord Hanshian and Lady Madashiri.

A youngster no more than five summers old peered out from behind the pale-skinned man. "But, Papa, I thought all dragons live in—"

"What did I say about interrupting?" the man asked, a hint of annoyance in his words.

"But, Papa, you said cousin M—"

Hamster rubbed his temples. *And their son Gushi. My head aches already.*

Having to deal with their child for an entire day only

worsened his stomach; the Lereians' visit already had him on the edge of vomiting from nervous anticipation. They were the first from the far north to seek out his adventure. *The first of many,* he hoped.

With that desire in mind, he smiled at the tousle-headed boy, then waved everyone up. "Now, iffen ya will follow, I'll take ya in. Watch yer step—from here on each step could well be yer last. A dragon's lair ain't no place of safety. Even with 'em dead."

As the twelve travelers clumped uphill behind, Hamster's imagination leaped ahead. *Soon we'll have people from all over the continent coming. If it keeps going at this rate, we can double the charge by next Autumnday.*

Masking his face in seriousness, Hamster led the way with exaggerated slowness, stepping carefully through the jagged cave mouth sure to remind them of the open maw of a large predator. Limestone pillars rose from the ground. Other shards reached down from the ceiling, shining with dimples of green and gold. He moved inward with overstated caution, feeling out the walnuts he had scattered beforehand and cracking them sharply with his boot heels. It was too shadowed for the marks to see what he was doing, and he anted up the tension by offering a quick, "Mind your footing, m'lords, m'ladies. The bones of a hunnert great fools once lie here, and I seem ta have missed a few."

"Akkkk!" Lady Orshire gasped, clambering onto one of the scattered knee-high rocks. "Where?"

Always one allergic to nuts. Hamster shook his head. "You'll see them soon enough in the cavern below, m'lady, iffen ya ain't too fainthearted."

"If these men didn't make it—how did *you* manage it?" one of the Aishails asked.

And the gods smile. Right on cue.

"Well, young sir, you see, two of me mates came up

'ere to build the road ya came in on," Hamster began, offering the tale with the delicacy of spun glass. "It mightn't seem like much to ya now, but back in the day thar was little keeping this wilderness 'n check."

That much of his tale at least was true. All of the hills surrounding the cliffs in which he had found his fortune had once been covered in impenetrable forest. The new road was a beaten trail with brick put down only for dire necessity—to cover waterways and ravines. Perfect for the show. Anything more and the path would be civilized. *Wouldn't want that.*

"One sum'r day, hot as blazes," Hamster continued, "a beast came screamin' from the sky—a seethin' fury o' fangs an' claws that tore int' our site. Now, we'd 'eard the rumors—seen the ruins. Burned-out cottages like the one ya seen outside of Pebble Pass. Coal black and dead of all livin'. A'fore we could run, it killed half our men—sent flames up from our stores. Most ran to'rd the caves screamin' in terror. Holed up in 'em. Not me an' me mates.

"This creature, he was big. Bigger than any o' yer homes, I be bet'n. Fifty, a hunnert feet high—with leathery wings that'd tear the feathers off birds in its wake by its sheer weight."

"And you didn't run? Surely you would have run?" It was the lady from Lerei. She moved toward him, a loud crack sounding as her steps met a random walnut.

Before she could look down, Hamster dashed forward, took her arm, and led her a half dozen feet farther into the cave, certain the others would follow. He didn't stop, even as he answered, "I think we was too afraid t' run, madam. When fear's got ya by the throat, ya do the thing least expected. I led me mates against the dragon—came into this here cave and met its fiery breath with me own obstinacy."

As they passed beyond reach of even the dullest light from the cave mouth, he ducked behind the first of a set of large, misshapen stone columns and came back with an unlit torch. Giving it to one of the Aishails, Hamster retrieved a flint and steel from his belt pouch. At the first shower of sparks, Lady Orshire gasped.

"Shouldn't you have a lamp?" she asked, shifting backward.

"Wouldn't want to trip and break one," Hamster apologized. *And you wouldn't be jumping at a candle lamp, now would you?*

After several misdirected attempts, Hamster sparked the torch to life. He took it back from the Aishail and swept its fiery end toward the now visible columns. "Now these here are the dragon's claws. Eight of 'em in all. Limestone—as ya can see from those lines. Back at the guesthouse, there's some art y'can buy made by Morian Torguth, a famous artist in Pebble Pass. Carvings." *And he sure has come a long way since the back streets of Falushad.*

"An' if ya look close on these walls, ya'll see scoring from our first journey through this tunnel. See those— look like scratches? Tried to track our passage. Mind ya keep up, I tell ya. Me and my mates were lost here fer days before we found the right turn down to the beast's hoard. . . ."

Talking without much chance for a breath, he kept them going for another candle's mark down twisting passages broken up by sporadic high-ceilinged caverns. When they came to a half-caved-in passageway, he insisted on taking Lady Orshire's hand and leading her over the broken rocks—much to her delight. Hamster was certain he'd be the cause of some blushing tales upon her return.

After a climb just hard enough to wind the marks, he

paused to show them a hole deep enough that they
couldn't see the bottom . . .

"Papa, are we there yet?"

. . . And just big enough to eat a small child.

Hamster's face grew red at the kid's more-than-apparent
boredom. *Bloody brat's going to ruin it if I don't fix him
soon.*

With a growing sense of urgency, Hamster stalked
down the tunnels, urging his travelers forward through a
slick, water-damped chamber complete with broken
lanterns and shards of glass. A rusted gauntlet lay deso-
late amid the wreckage. "This here be where some of the
best knights of the realm were brought low. Ya can see
the claw marks gouging the rocks. Those patches o'
brown 're blood. Never sure as they were dragon fodder
or cave creatures. Real fun stuck 'ere at night I tell ya.
The mangled bodies were all I e'er found—no good
leavin' 'em 'ere. Put 'em up right proper down below."

"Papa, can I see?" the young Lereian pleaded, his
brown eyes glowing almost gold as he tugged on his father's belt.

"Tis a sight to chill hearts, dear sir." Hamster pitched
his voice low, knowing it would still echo enough for
all to hear. "It mightn't be right to expose the boy to
such—"

"Papa, I *want* to see!"

"Oh, I'm sure the lad can take it. If an oldster like me
hasn't dropped dead yet, your son should be able to take
it, Hanshian." There was a note of friendliness in Kettlebank's words.

*Don't tell me they know each other—I'd have to chalk
another up for the old-timer.*

Lord Hanshian nodded his agreement. "I don't see
much harm in it."

Refusing to be discouraged by the lack of even a short

argument, Hamster nudged the Lereian in the side. "Good on ya. A sure dragonslayer in training, your young sir." When the Lereian didn't laugh, Hamster offered a mental curse.

Casting the northerner a worried glance, he did the only thing possible—kept talking. Forcing a laugh, he offered a less than pithy, "Least they be long dead. It's been ten years since I struck down the beast."

As he gave them a fictitious history of the caverns, Hamster brought them down a rough spiral tunnel. After what seemed like far too long—with the brat complaining loudly about there having to be a quicker way down, any time was too long—the stale air thickened with steam and their handholds grew precarious from the damp. Moments later, he had the lot of them standing at the edge of a deep pool of odorous water. Flames from his torch caught ripples in the hot spring, giving off an eerie reflection.

With a casual step, he ensured he was standing next to the slightly dishevelled Lady Orshire, who was eyeing the water dubiously. *Walnut lover should drink this right up.*

"As ya no doubt 'ave heard, these waters swell with mystical properties. Heated from the still cooling blood of the great beast lying below, thar known to have a restorative effect on those who drink of 'em. Ya'll heard the tale of young Kaera and Kel the miller? Kaera was an old woman a'fore I brought 'er to these springs, now she and her love are enjoying abiding vigor down in Pebble Pass." He gave Lady Orshire a salacious wink.

"Even now, ever gracious for 'er gift of youth, she's put 'er life to'rd making charms, each containing a flask of these waters. These special charms are available at a reasonable cost at the guesthouse, along with complementary oils from Mount Dajara. Should yer wish it, we may stop for a few candle marks here, upon our return."

"Oh," the Turmalin lady said, gulping down Hamster's offered hook. She reached out for her husband's hand. "I daresay, we must."

Lord Orshire's red face was visible even by torchlight, and his coughing set the pack of nephews to laughing. Even the Aishails joined in.

Past the hot pools, a new tunnel began, one slanting upward for a quarter mark before breaking into random directions. Taking the one with the steep slope down, Hamster pointed out the water seeping down the rocks they passed, and then sidestepped to show them a cavern hung with thousands of tiny rock icicles.

It wasn't another half candle mark before he had them close enough to their destination that his every word would echo into the wide-open chamber below.

"Now, we get to the exciting part, 'at ya all came ta see," he said, keeping his voice loud and resonant, sure to carry. "From here—the dragon's cave ain't a hunnert feet away. Watch 'er step as ye step here. Lots o' traps protect the dragon's hoard a' gold."

"Gold? Papa." Gushi, silent since before the hot pools, tugged on his father's belt again. "That's just a legend!"

"You know you shouldn't disrespect those around you child. Be a good lad. Patience." Lord Hanshian glanced up at Hamster, giving him a less than approving look.

Hamster bit his lip, more than nervous. *Thank gods we're almost there. Once I get them there, it'll be good. I'll make it extra special. No doubts. No cause for doubts. Perfect.*

The others fortunately were already beginning to clump together as if the dragon's death they had come to hear about would take place right before their eyes. It was a scene Hamster was used to seeing. Even the Lereian lady had joined the crowd, her own thin hands gripping Lady Orshire's. He thought there was murmuring . . .

words of comfort he assumed. Ladies were into that—
thinking random foolish talk would ease their fear. *As if
it would.*

As they continued forward, the passage grew steeper,
narrower. He had to hold the torch before him, knowing
those following were getting little more than a glimmer
of it and long, snaking shadows. More than one outcry
sounded as elbows and knees knocked against rough out-
croppings.

"Farshik!" cursed one of the Aishails as his ducked head
smacked an especially sharp rock. The dank passageway
magnified the expletive, making the Aishail wince.

Just ahead, a glimmer of light began to brighten the
path, lessening the jumping shadows from Hamster's
handheld torch. Turning to the dozen adventurers, he
brought his finger to his lips. "Ya must be quiet now. The
dragon's jus' ahead. That light be his chamber, where
death was given to virgins and knights alike. The day I
came in here, I snuck in like a thief—a dagger my only
weapon. Two of me mates had swords. Lot a' good that
did them. Mind your attention. Even in death, this 'ere
dragon has killed."

Sheep. Lots of sheep.

As the tunnel widened, the ceiling abruptly rose six
feet. Hamster tangled his feet on a loose outcropping of
rock and pitched forward, rolling down the steep carved
steps leading into the dragon's den. As he fell, he tossed
the torch away, hearing the splash as it dropped into the
water below.

Lord and Lady Orshire screamed in unison. The boy's
high-pitched voice broke above them with the wail of a
death-cursed ghost. Hamster topped them all as his practiced fall degenerated into an uncontrolled pinwheel and
he tumbled roughly, landing hard on his back at the base
of the stone steps.

"Gasht!" Hamster wheezed out the curse even as he fought back undragonslayerlike tears. His left ankle throbbed with pain but he didn't think it was broken. He lay silent for a moment, staring at the gold-tasseled rope swinging in his face. The barrier rope to keep people from the dragon. As he moved to sit up, a wool-cloaked arm reached down to give him leverage. Kettlebank, Hamster realized. *Not even thinking about the barrier—and he knows what it means. Oh gods.*

"Young man, you need to watch your step—you've tumbled every time I've come." Lord Kettlebank said. "Though this looks to be the worst. You'll need a soak in your own hot pool after this."

Hamster almost choked, not having considered what his tumble would look like on multiple occasions. *I shoulda known better . . . changed it up. I'm get'n too set in my ways.*

With Kettlebank's help, Hamster crossed back to the "safe" side of the barrier—finding himself in the light of the sparkling waterfall he had first seen a decade ago. Its clear mountain water tumbled over the edge of a large break in the cavern's ceiling and gathered into a large pool within. A patch of cobalt blue was plainly visible in the dragon-size rift, rays of bright afternoon sun making it easy to pick out the now-unlit torch floating in the water.

Spot on target!

Forgetting the waterfall, the pain, and the mass of red-gold at his back, he turned back to his patrons, the rest still at the top of the stairs.

"Be careful now, lad. Mind your steps." Kettlebank let go of his arm.

"I'm not hurt," Hamster called upward. "Watch 'er step coming down."

One of my better falls. I don't think I've ever heard panic that well done.

"You sure?" one of the Aishails called.

"'Course. Just a stumble."

One by one the visitors made their way down to stand at Hamster's side, stunned as he once had been by the incredible size and beauty of the cavern. For a moment, none noticed the reason for their arrival.

Too caught by the glass.

Opposite the waterfall stood a sheer face of rock, dotted with glistening glass beads reminiscent of gemstones. He knew from experience the beads sat on thin ridges but to his paying travelers, they would look like the rock itself was encrusted with brilliant diamonds, rubies, sapphires, and emeralds.

"Look at them, Pory," Lady Orshire said to her husband. "There's more here than in the Elector's treasury."

"Or in Arashlin's chest," one of the brothers whispered, speaking of the legendary founding of his country by a pirate living off gold exchanged for a kidnapped princess.

Lady Madashiri gasped, her tears glistening in the ray of sun peeking down through the waterfall's vast opening. Her husband's eyes were almost black, hands clenched into tight fists.

Another one wanting the treasure. That at least was easy to deal with. Hamster laughed, glad to be back on course. "Don't even think about it, m'lord. This treasure's protected by a powerful dragon curse. I seen a fool try once. He ne'er even made back to the surface. Trust me, I'd a' tried long ago if it weren't so deadly."

He bit his lip, wanting to bring the story back to the dragon, the reason they had all come. "As yer can see, I left 'em exactly where he fell." He motioned toward the enormous red-gold dragon lying in the center of the cavern, one luminescent wing half dipped into the waterfall's pool.

"But Papa, dragon's don't leave bod—" This time the boy's voice was impossible to ignore.

The Aishails glanced between the boy and the dragon. "You never did tell us how you killed him," one said, his tone gaining an edge.

Hamster took a deep breath. "Well, you see . . . the dragon attacked us—you can still see here the blackened stone where he caught my two mates." *Gods, I'm losing the accent. Come on. Just a bit more.* He spoke more rapidly. "Dragon's fire burns so's it never fades. Ya can see the black from his breath under yer feet."

Point to the stone. It's fresh black from last week.

"Chunks o' dragon-fired rock can be bought in the guesthouse. A great gift for yer tykes. Maybe ya wants one for yerself?" Hamster asked the brat, trying desperately to win him over.

The kid snorted. "I don't need your raff."

And we wanted northerners? Not a bloody sane one in the lot. If I hear that kid one more time. . . .

"Hey look, Ru. See the way its claws stick up? Bet you I could have one of those off in no time!"

Hamster turned on the Aishail who had spoken, lowering his voice to bear more than a hint of threat. "You don't want to touch the dragon's carcass. Their scales are poison!"

"Oh, sure—how'd you kill him then?" the young man demanded, black hair flying as he ran toward the edge of the stairs and jumped the barrier rope. "Just watch me!"

Hamster dove after, managing to come up with the edge of the boy's shirt despite his still throbbing ankle.

"Hey! All I want to do is see!"

"Fine then—see!" Hamster twisted the Aishail around until his face lined up with the display of bones dug up from the deserted logger cemetery. "Think you're the only fool? Those ones are folk who tried to touch the dragon—you care to join them?"

He shook the young man a bit harder than he should have. "They don't look like much now after the creepers got at them—but when it first happened, their skin broke out in a blotchy red rash that turned pus-filled. Between that and the vomiting, there wasn't much left when they died. I don't want to watch it again."

As Hamster expected, the Aishail went limp when faced with the show of human remains set out artistically on slabs of limestone. *Three torsos. Four heads. Seventeen feet.*

"That's disgusting!" he said, staring a skull in the eye socket.

"I warned you." Dropping his grip, Hamster turned to the others—gathered at the bottom of the steps and about as far away as they could get from the barrier and the dragon beyond. "Come on down—stay back from the rope and nothing'll harm ya."

The dragon's head was facing them straight on, his mouth dangling open just enough that everyone could see his man-long ivory teeth. Timid after Hamster's description of the dead who had dared to touch, they stayed back a decent pace as he guided them around the back of the dragon, pointing out his barbed neck ridges and spikelike claws. As they passed a foreclaw, the dragon's tail crashed down ahead of them, drenching Kettlebank and his nephews.

Lady Orshire shouted. Her husband caught her around the waist and clutched her against his chest. "What the gods have you brought us to, trickster?" he demanded of Hamster.

Bloody Mei! Hamster cursed. He turned hastily, composing an excuse even as he bowed low before the Orshires. "Sometimes the corpse can move. That's what ya get with something so big. Just a twitch, I tell ya. Be safe, lady. No harm can come to ya here."

Kettlebank laughed, breaking the tension. He came up and took Lady Orshire's hand, eyes glistening with delight and good humor. "We didn't drown. The heat will dry us out before the return. Trust me—this'll be the best part. Don't fear."

The best part?

Hamster tried to keep the splintering show together. "Look around, ask questions. You heard me talk about these poor folks—the ones o'er there opposite were the first knights in the cave. I told ya about them at the beginin'" He stretched an arm out to draw their attention to the piecemeal rusted armor bought from a Westland trader for a half-gold. Here and there dry bones were visible, poking out of the appropriate holes. Sheep's bones. He hadn't wanted to pay for more skeletal remains. "Those, sirs and ladies were the ones too lambshanked t' handle the dragon."

After a pause for his own silent snort, he added, "So we'll spend a mark or two here—and when you're all ready, we'll head back to the hot springs."

With that taken care of, Hamster led the Orshires to a rickety bench he had made for the fainthearted. While Lord Orshire comforted his wife, Lord Kettlebank and his nephews drifted off to study the dragon. The Lereians had paused by the waterfall's pool, talking in low voices.

Hamster took the moment to compose himself—walked away from the others and around past Meisherane's left eye. "Tail was a bit much, don't you think?" he muttered.

In response, Mei's eye blinked open and closed, revealing a well of dark brown filled with humor. The dragon had a sense of showmanship even he couldn't beat.

From their first meeting it had all been about showmanship.

*   *   *

He had been standing on the scaffold, wind chilled enough to make him wish they'd get it over with. The gods-cursed herb witch stood next to the mayor of Kejery, gloating still after catching his trick with the ginger-laced red wine cure-all. Soon he'd be warm. Dead, but warm. As the mayor called his name, unseen hands pressed him forward. A man in a black robe brought a noose close.

Hamster fell back as the blast of wind that was Meisherane barreled out of the sky. Claws scraped him up with long bony talons to the screams of panic of the mayor and the executioner. Whisked through the air, view filled with palm-size shiny red scales because he was too afraid to look down, he knew he was going to die. *Least the gallows would have been quick.*

Centuries later, he was dropped to the rough floor of a cavern. His terror-filled eyes lit on the clear mountain waterfall and a wall of brilliant jewels. Too shocked to fear, Hamster faced down the monstrous dragon whose breath could crisp him where he stood.

::I have a proposition for you.:: The dragon's words echoed through Hamster's mind. *::I am Meisherane.::*

"Meisherane!"

The spoken name sparked fear through Hamster's stomach. He rose hastily, every nerve on edge. *No one* knew the dragon's name. *No one.* He was always careful to call Mei "The Dragon" when he spoke to others.

"Meisherane, arise and look at me. Your death is far from the legend your human accomplice has told of."

Hamster shuddered as the Lereian lord's words resonated throughout the cavern with powerful authority. The northerner stood on the rough ground at the base of the dragon's head, wife and child standing at his side. Kettlebank was a mere few steps from them.

The old man nodded sagely to his nephews, ignoring Hamster altogether. "Watch now, you'll see something you'll never see again."

I should have known the old bastard knew more than he let on. Three visits.

One of the Aishails was the first to realize the truth. "Farshik! You lied—"

The expletive burned in Hamster's ears but he ignored it—kept his eyes on the dragon. The named dragon. *Come on, fire the lot of them!*

Meisherane blinked. One of the nephews shouted; the Aishails broke into an argument over whether it was a stunt. Only Kettlebank and the Lereians were unsurprised as Meisherane's head came up off the ground in a neat sweep that took in the entire cavern, then settled near Lord Hanshian.

The Lereian's pale face had turned red. His eyes glowed with a deep omnipresent brown that reminded Hamster of the dragon's own. There was no way to get to safety. No way to retreat back up the tunnel.

Mei knew, he realized. *The tail. He was trying for a diversion.*

"Meisherane, your misdeeds have been noted," Lord Hanshian announced. "We are here to escort you back to Ajagameara. Come now and face your judgment."

"But, Papa, I thought you said I could slay it!" The kid was looking at Hamster.

The back of Hamster's arms grew cold despite the rising heat in the cavern. *The kid's mad.*

"Gushi, we'll talk about killing later. Be silent and you can return the jewels of the Twelve." At his father's words, the little boy looked elated. Puffed his chest out like a lion.

"The jewels of the Twelve?" Hamster whispered.

The Lereians . . . *they are not Lereians* . . . heard him.

The woman's words came sharp and stinging. "You were unlucky to make your pact with this pirate spawn of a dragon, human. He is accused of stealing the entire wealth of our nation for himself."

::Borrowed. I only borrowed them,:: Meisherane broke in, his silent words echoing in Hamster's head.

Lady Madashiri ignored him. "Never has such an incident been known in our history. The proof of his deeds is all around you."

"You mean they're real?" Hamster stuttered, looking up and around at the glowing jewels. He turned on his friend, ignoring the sharp teeth and claws. "You said they were made of glass—the effect of water on limestone. Glass beads of caught sunlight."

::Yes, and you believed me.:: Meisherane's mind voice held a faint note of disbelief. *::Far more pathetic than thinking gingered wine can heal::*

"But. But. If they were real . . ." Hamster's head shook wildly, taking in little of the dragon and less of the watchers. His gaze sharpened on the high walls—the thin ledges holding the gemstones. "You bastard. I wouldn't have had to pander to these lordlings if I had just taken one of those beads!"

::Is that my fault?::

::You can create opportunity of my presence. Light beads become jewels. Bones become testaments to atrocities. I have heard you have a skill for such things,:: Meisherane had said.

That's why Meisherane had wanted to work with him—because Hamster was the best of his kind. He could feed them both and make more besides. *If only I had known, I could've . . . left. Spent years living in wealth.* "I can't believe you lied to me!"

Meisherane turned to face him and let out a hiss that carried steam. *::Even I would not trust the secret of our* *treasure to a human, at least not one striving toward my own genius. Even one who falls so short.::*

Hamster stared up at his partner of ten years—one of the few beings he thought that truly understood him. His face grew warm at the realization he was wrong, far wrong. "Was it all a game then?"

Meisherane hissed. A laugh. *::Ah, in my lifetime, it is more of a single joke than an entire game. You wouldn't be worth that much of my time.::*

Anger grew, burned up through Hamster's chest and out his mouth as if he too could let out steam and fire. "You mean to say this was a joke . . . a joke on my entire life? I can't believe it! Who could do such a thing?"

"A joke such as you have played on the beliefs of each to pass through this chamber," Lord Kettlebank interrupted, from the far side of Meisherane. "Though for my own part, I've enjoyed it, young man. It was a good charade while it lasted. There was a reason I came back more than once. Teaching these young bulls to see behind the facade. It is an important lesson for any who wish to rule . . . or to become traders." The elderly statesman turned to the two from Aishail.

The two exchanged embarrassed glances. "We were looking for a way to bring tokens back to sell off port," one admitted. "Dragon's bones would fetch up well."

At a different time, Hamster would have laughed at their audacity—two men after his own heart. Instead, he cursed. "I don't go causing people harm! As if anyone wants to see reality—I gave them adventure. Just as they asked for. And you—" He stalked toward Meisherane, hands clenching into fists. His cheeks burned with heat. "You—I thought you were my partner!"

He would have given the smug dragon a fistful, but Kettlebank grabbed his arm. The old man couldn't hold him with strength, yet his words caught Hamster solid.

"He's a dragon, boy—nothing you can do to hurt him. Best let him go before this becomes more."

Hamster wilted, let the old lord pull him back. Meisherane remained unmoved. Imperial. As if Hamster's retreat was no surprise.

"Now then, Meisherane. It is time to return." Lady Madashiri said.

::Yes, Gir Madashiri. There is nothing left for me here.:: Hamster knew the derision in the dragon's sending. He had heard it before in his own voice.

He struggled not to curse as a wisp of smoke bellowed from Lady Madashiri's mouth, encompassing her and the other two *not from Lerei* in a fog. A strong twisting wind bashed him against the cavern wall. When the air cleared, three dragons stood where once there was one. *Make that four.* A small arrow-shaped head, pale brown with spindly head ridges, peeped out from beneath the heavyset gold-brown dragon.

There was little to do but stare. They were fearsome beasts. Even the boy was ten times his size. Heart pounding, Hamster almost cried out.

First the lady, her scales a deep bronze, took to the air, breezing past the spray of the waterfall and out into the open sky. Lord Hanshian followed, trailed by his silver-gray son.

::I'll be back for the jewels tonight. I'll be your curse if you're not gone from here by then.:: The little boy's voice was no less high-pitched as a dragon. Deadly nonetheless. Hamster trembled.

Then Meisherane was the only dragon left on the floor of the cavern. The beginning and the end. If he didn't look up, Hamster didn't have to see gold-backed Lord Hanshian resting on the ledge across from the top of the waterfall. Waiting.

Meisherane glanced down and met Hamster's eyes.

::*This has been a fun adventure. But truth be told, you are not as smart as you believe. After all, as your compatriot Kettlebank knows well, dragons do not leave bodies—we burn to ash upon our death.*:: With a flick of his head and a burst of disparaging steam, Meisherane lifted his luminescent wings and sailed upward into the day.

Hamster's eyes stayed focused on the patch of blue visible through the broken eggshell of the ceiling long after the dragons disappeared. *Partners. I should've known.* He let out a long soft sigh.

"Don't you dare." Lady Orshire's shout broke Hamster from his reverie and made him turn. The two Aishails had paused less than a step away—fists taut and white-knuckled. "I won't have you fighting in my presence," she told them.

As the brothers exchanged guilty looks, Hamster shivered in relief. He turned to bow his gratitude, but before he could the lady from Turmalin shook her head in strong disapproval. "How could you be so thoughtless," she demanded. "Taking advantage of people like this. You should be ashamed."

Hamster couldn't respond. There were no words left to save the day. Not for him. *It's done. It's over. Least I had ten years from the gallows.* A shimmering arc of color brought a rainbow out of the waterfall, stealing his attention. Sunlight on water and gemstones—mesmerizing, as it had been on that very first day. *Maybe I could still take one. If we worked together. . . .*

Kettlebank's hand came down on his arm. Tightened. "Don't even think it. I knew about the ashes from the first. I let you go on *only* because you weren't hurting anyone. It was an adventure after all. But there is no more for you here. Don't become what you've warned against." The old man gave a nod toward the display of sheep bones and armour.

"You'd let him go free?" One of the brothers demanded.

"He's lost the one thing he's ever had of value. What more would you do? Kill him? If the dragons didn't, then why should we?" No one seemed to want to answer.

Then Kettlebank's first words hit Hamster. *Ashes.*

Wonder what it'd take to get that much ashes? He wondered. As a bold new plan took shape in his mind's eye, Hamster nodded his agreement to Lord Kettle-bank—let the old man lead him toward the stairs. *First to get out of here. Then to wait out the boy's—the dragon's—return. Then I can start over.*

Plan seeding in his imagination, Hamster offered his current batch of adventurers a rueful smile. "I did say your deposits were not refundable, right?"

THE MURDER OF MR. WOLF

Josepha Sherman

Josepha Sherman is a fantasy novelist, folklorist, and editor, who has written everything from Star Trek novels to biographies of Bill Gates and Jeff Bezos (founder of Amazon.com) to titles such as *Mythology for Storytellers* (from M.E. Sharpe) and *Trickster Tales* (August House). She is also the owner of Sherman Editorial Services (www.ses-ny.com). You can visit her at www.josephasherman.com.

THE NAME'S PEEP. BEAU Peep. Yeah, that's right. Go ahead, make your jokes. Heard them all hundreds of times already.

Want another laugh? My colleague, who's a pretty, sharp-eyed young woman who'd break your arm before you could pull a knife on her, is named Marie Gobeur. That's right: Gobeur. French for sheep. Beau Peep and sheep. And no, I do not herd her. Nothing between us but business.

Well, names aside, we're good at what we do, damned

good. We're detectives for the Crown. Cole Godhebog, Cole the Magnificent, uses the guise of "merry old soul" whenever it pleases him—but there's a sharp intelligence behind that fun-loving facade. And he doesn't like his people killing each other.

Which generally means enter Peep and, oh hell, go with it, Sheep. Okay, it was a nice spring day, and Marie and I had just tied up the last paperwork on the Eater case. You might have read about that one, since the papers love Crimes of Passion. Seems a small-time swindler, Peter "Pumpkin" Eater, had accused his wife of messing around with another man. He decided to cut down on the food bills by keeping Mrs. Eater under lock and key and forgetting to feed her. Fortunately for her, the neighbors noticed they hadn't been seeing her around much, and we were called in. Mr. Eater's now getting prison food, and the former Mrs. Eater is now, rumor has it, shacking up with Tom Piperson.

So there we were, actually without a case for the first time in neither of us could remember how long.

"Hickery Doc's?" Marie suggested.

Why not? We strolled to Hickery Doc's Bar down on the corner. Doc's a retired cop himself and serves cheap beer and the best smoked meats in town, and you can usually find off-duty cops or detectives hanging out there talking shop.

A good crowd was in there today, cops and even a few forensic mages, one of the latter entertaining the crowd with fireworks of colored sparks. Soon Marie was flirting in a what-the-hell sort of way with one of the cops, a wiry young guy named Jack Candlestick who didn't have a real chance with her, and I, ignoring the noise around me, was just about to bite with great relish into one of Doc's overstuffed smoked beef sandwiches when a voice chilly with malice said almost in my ear, "Detective Peep."

Hell. Him. A good day ruined.

Rather than jumping the way he'd expected, I took a big, defiant bite out of the sandwich and chewed, savoring the taste and taking my time. I followed that with a good swig of beer, swallowed, decided against a belch as being over the top, and only then answered, "Yeah."

I didn't have to turn who knew who was there. Only one guy has a voice like that: the Crooked Man. It's not his real name, of course, and he isn't deformed. Physically. But it's a good one for a Crown Security man, for which, of course, read "secret service."

Marie had noticed what was going on, and moved back through the crowd to my side, leaving the suddenly bereft Jack without a backward glance. "Now what?"

There's no love lost between our branch of the legal service and his. We generally handle all the nice, ordinary crimes, like murder. The Crooked Man handles all the cases the Crown officially refuses to acknowledge and involves us when he needs us. You might have read about what the media dubbed "The Jack and Jill Murder/Suicide." What you didn't hear was the whole story, because the young lovers hadn't just been members of the In Crowd, they'd been cousins of the royal family—and no, I'm not going to name names—and they'd also been stoned out of their minds when they took that dive off the hill. Yeah, it had been the Crooked Man's doing that all the story didn't get out.

"You put away the Red Gang," he said with chill relish—only the Crooked Man could have managed that.

"Yeah," I said warily. They'd been a bunch of teenage punks, smalltime hoods who'd been stupid enough to try their inept hands at drug running. As most of them had been legal age, we weren't going to see them around for some time. "And let me guess," I continued. "You're going to tell us we missed someone in the great roundup."

"Little Red."

"Oh come on!" Marie protested. "She's just a kid! A rotten kid, maybe, but definitely not prosecutable as an adult."

"Not in our jurisdiction," I agreed. "She did something wrong, send her to Juvenile."

The Crooked Man smiled thinly, which was not a pretty sight. "Juvenile doesn't handle murder."

The murder scene was pretty messed up, which is, unfortunately, usually the way with crimes in the middle of the forest: Cops get there first, and they're used to cobblestone streets, not to the woods and have little idea how not to trample plants that might have held clues or break branches that might have been already broken by a criminal. They had a white-faced, foul-mouthed Little Red in cuffs by the time Marie and I got there, and a basket lay on its side, spilling out what looked like innocent sausages and bread.

And there lay the body, facedown in the mud. Male, burly, well-dressed—and with the back of his skull bashed in. The mud was mostly made from his blood.

We flashed our badges. Only a few cops caught the names on those badges: You could tell, because they were the ones fighting grins. "Who have we got?" I asked.

"His I.D. says he's a Mr. Ivar Wolf. Wolf Real Estate."

That couldn't be the whole story. Marie and I exchanged a quick glance. The Crooked Man wouldn't have been called in over a real estate agent's death.

Okay, so Mr. Wolf had been more than he'd seemed. Someone, maybe, in the same branch of business as the Crooked Man.

I crouched to examine the body. Nothing outstanding, other than that bashed-in skull. Something not quite blunt had done the job. Like a rock. Spontaneous crime? Spur

of the moment decision? Or was someone being cute and
making it look like a spontaneous crime? That blow certainly would have been enough to do in the unfortunate
Wolf. Whether or not there were any other signs of violence on the body. . . .

I straightened with a sigh. Determining that would be
the work of the forensic magicians. Instead I did my own
hunt for the murder weapon.

Right. Try finding a rock in the forest. Assuming that
the murder weapon had been a rock. Assuming that there
hadn't been someone smart enough to carry it off.

Marie, meanwhile, was doing a good job of matching
up what clear footprints were available against the feet of
the corpse and against those of the cops. Only one possible partial print that didn't match up, but it was so very
partial, thanks to the cops trampling the site as they had,
that it didn't say much else. Other than that it couldn't
have been made by Little Red, either.

Little Red, who was still swearing at the cops. And
whom we now had to question.

Lucky us.

The forensic magicians got there in their usual way: A
great gust of wind that nearly knocked us all over and a
clap of thunder that is, so I've been told, actually nothing
more dramatic than air being displaced by their sudden
arrival. Efficient way to travel, but no thank you, I like
my stomach's contents to stay put. I'd rather stick to standard, safe, nonnauseating walking or riding.

The sudden arrivals were a standard team of three, the
most useful magical number: two men, one tall and
skinny, one short, dark, and stocky, and one woman, plain
but with gorgeous red hair in a long braid down her back.
All three of them were in the standard forensic mage uniform of plain blue tunic and trousers with the royal in-

signia on a breast pocket—a more practical getup than mage robes at a murder scene.

I recognized all three of them; we'd worked before on a few cases. We did the standard "Ken, Ilana, Tom, how's it going?" bit, and then they got down to business. Ilana, the redhead—if you couldn't figure it out by the name— whose specialty is clue preservation, put a stasis spell on the partial footprint so that Marie and I could tote it about without it crumbling. Ken, the tall guy, and Tom, the stocky one, cast glowing spells over and around the body and crime scene in general that gave them the needed data to quickly determined that yes, the blow to the head had killed Wolf and no, there were no other signs of violence. A search spell found no murder weapon either, though all three mages were pretty sure from the mineral feel they got from the fatal wound that it had been a rock. Forensic magicians are strictly Righthand Path, which meant no necromancy, no dead man rising up and naming his killers. I understand that a reanimated corpse doesn't really remember how it died, anyhow, so why risk your soul asking it anything?

Back to square one. As the forensic team carried off the corpse to their lab in another wild rush of wind and clap of thunder, I took a deep breath and tried again with our one suspect. "Come on, Red, admit it. You knew him."

"I told you!" the kid shouted at me. "I never saw him before!"

"Yeah, right. Okay, guys, let's get her back to the stationhouse."

We'd been going at it for an hour by now. I didn't know about Little Red, but I was getting pretty fed up with being stuck in this squad room, with nothing in it but the table, the chairs, and the framed portrait of King Cole. At least the kid had stopped swearing at us by now.

"Yeah, right, and you were taking a stroll in the woods just to look at the pretty flowers," I drawled.

"I went for a walk. That's all."

Marie shook her head. "We saw what was in was the basket. Two sausages, two loaves of bread, a bottle of wine . . . seems like a lot of food for someone just going for a walk. A picnic, maybe. With whom?"

"No one!"

I leaned forward. "Come on, Red. You're already in this up to your pretty red riding hood. Who was it? You were meeting Wolf, weren't you?"

"I told you! I was just taking a walk!"

"With a full basket of goodies."

She turned away from me, pouting. "I was taking it to my grandma."

"Your grandma who's serving five to ten for peddling joy juice? Kind of a long way around to get to Babylon Prison."

No answer to that but a scowl.

Marie's turn, woman to woman. "It was flattering, wasn't it?" she murmured, leaning forward. "A grown man, and after you. Yes, and I bet he said all the right things to you. I bet he made you feel really special."

"Special!" Little Red exploded. "He tried to eat me, that's what!"

The emphasis on *eat* made it pretty clear that whatever Mr. Wolf had been into, it hadn't been cannibalism.

"So you hit him," I said. "Self-defense."

"I didn't hit him!"

"Self-defense, Red. Know what that means?"

"I'm not stupid. Of course I do. But I didn't hit him."

"Then who did?"

"I don't know." But little by little she was looking less like a punk and more like a really scared kid. "H-he was already dead when I got there."

Marie and I exchanged a quick glance. When she'd gotten there? For another meeting? Looked like Little Red hadn't been exactly worried about being eaten if she'd returned for a second course.

Too bad there's no such thing as a truth-telling spell. Ken, the tallest of the three forensic mages, had once told me a horrific tale over a couple of beers of an attempt at a truth-telling spell that had literally melted the suspect's brain.

Instead we had to do it the old-fashioned way, wearing the kid down until I felt that my brain was about to melt. But we finally had the complete and sadly predictable story of a naive girl who wanted desperately to be tough. She had run with a gang as a sort of mascot and then, after we'd pretty much eliminated the gang, had had this fling with an older man as a way of, well, belonging.

"I can't see her being the killer," I said to Marie afterward.

"Neither can I. But she's the only suspect we have."

We could legally hold her for a day. Then, since she was a minor, we had to turn her over to Juvenile or, since we had nothing but the most circumstantial of evidence against her, just let her go. Not much time.

"Okay, let's try this," I said. "What was Wolf really doing for a living?"

Marie nodded. "Good question. Why bring the Crooked Man into this if Wolf was merely a real estate agent?"

I thought about it for a few moments. "Now, here's my take on it: What if our Mr. Wolf, and for the moment forget his taste for underage girls and his real estate cover, was really . . . mmm . . . an inspector?"

"A secret one, you mean?" she asked. "Makes sense."

Yes, it did. If the late Mr. Wolf had actually been a secret buildings inspector hunting corruption and shoddy work, he would have made a few enemies. Maybe even a few deadly enemies.

Well, we spent quite some time talking to the Crooked Man, trying not to think about the clock ticking away on our time to legally hold Little Red. Didn't need the traditional mouse running up it to tell us to get going on this.

Hey, guess what? After wasting much of everyone's time, the Crooked Man finally grudgingly admitted that surprise, surprise, we'd been right and Wolf had, indeed, worked for him. He kept most of the details of that work from us on general principles, being what he was. But after leaving his office, Marie and I put a few facts together, and cross-checked Wolf's real estate client list with police records. Two matches there. And we still did have that magic-preserved partial footprint that might yet net us a match with the murderer.

"All right," I said to Marie, "let's go talk to a few people."

First stop, Dumpty Construction Company. But we were too late on that one: Cops hadn't notified us yet because they weren't ruling it a murder. Again, yet. Mr. Humphrey Dumpty had apparently taken a header off one of his company's walls, which had been high enough to leave the body pretty well scrambled. I saw Marie glance up and up and shudder.

"Looks like he landed feet first," she said.

"Yeah." Not a chance of comparing our partial footprint with what was left of Mr. Dumpty's feet.

Accidents happen—but with the murder of Mr. Wolf so recent we had to wonder if this really had been an accident. In other words: Did he fall, or was he pushed?

A sudden rush of air, a sudden clap of thunder: "Hey, guys," I said. "Busy day."

Tom grunted. "Yeah, right. Let's hear it for slow, boring days."

The three forensic magicians started their work once again. Ken and Tom examined the body, muttering charms together, while Ilana and Marie—Marie being the lightest of us two—levitated up to the top of the wall to look for clues. They were back soon enough, looking frustrated.

"Nothing," Marie said.

"Nothing," Ilana agreed. "Other than pigeons."

But just then I heard Ken exclaim, "Whoa. That's new."

It didn't look like anything new to me, just the same mangled corpse it had been a moment ago, but Ilana and Tom, crouching over the body with Ken, agreed. "Better get this back to the lab." Ilana glanced up at us. "You coming?"

Hell. I made the usual excuses about walking being good for the constitution, riding being the good old-fashioned way to travel, and got nowhere. Even I had to admit we needed to examine the body back in the lab.

The next thing I knew, we were in the lab, solid stone under our feet, and I was throwing up in a bucket that Ilana had hastily and thoughtfully conjured for me. I don't know how the forensic guys do it, but they were already calmly at work without a sign of discomfort. Marie, who has one of those proverbial cast-iron constitutions, was watching their work with a great deal of professional interest.

After a moment, I joined her. Mangled corpses are part of the job and don't bother me—hell, no matter how mangled, they're just empty houses with the tenants gone— but damned if I'll ever get used to teleportation.

"You see?" Ilana said to Ken. "Definitely a K-1."

"I'd say K-2, but a really a cheap one."

She shook her head. "K-1, definitely. See the state of the liver?"

"What's left of it. The damage could have come from the fall."

"Uh, guys?" I asked. "What's a K-1?"

"Protective spell," Tom said shortly, doing something to the corpse that made it suddenly glow a really disgusting hue of gray-green. "The sort of thing anyone can buy in some corner magic store and use without needing any special powers. Only . . . this one isn't quite . . . damn." The glow snapped out of existence. He tried to get it going again, then shook his head: no luck. "You get what you pay for. He was using some bargain-basement version of your basic K-1, and not only didn't it protect him, it managed to scramble itself and his general aura into one big mess."

"So you can't tell if he was murdered?"

"Hell, he's so scrambled I couldn't tell you anything." Ken glanced up at me, wiping a streak of blood—at least I assumed it was only blood—from his face. "Right now all we can be sure about is that it was definitely the fall that killed him."

And we still didn't know if he'd been pushed.

Okay, now we had two cases instead of one.

What followed was how our jobs usually go: Interviewing people who didn't want to be interviewed, had no choice about it, and were not going to make it any easier for us. Marie and I headed back to the construction site and started going down the list of workers.

But at last we could say with certainty that none of the construction workers had seen anything out of the ordinary. They were all pretty well shaken up—seeing your boss go down like that, splat, couldn't have been easy on any of them—but they all swore they'd seen no one up there on the wall with him. No one'd held a grudge against him, at least so they claimed.

Actually, looking at the Dumpty Construction records,

there didn't seem to be much of a reason for grudge-holding. The company was completely above board—since it had done some work for the Crown, it pretty much had to be—and paid its workers good wages. Sure, they'd seen Mr. Wolf around. He'd been there several times but that wasn't surprising as he was involved in the sale of the property.

While we're on the subject, none of the workers matched that partial print, either.

There was a Mrs. Dumpty, and when we went to see her, a couple of days later, it wasn't surprising to find her even more badly shaken up than the workers had been. A painting on one wall of her tastefully decorated living room showed us a pretty, slender, young woman, but the figure we faced had swathed herself in a mourning veil, old style, dripping black jet beads and showing little of the woman underneath, and sobbed her way through the interview. Yes, she'd loved her husband, yes, she'd always been after him to lose some weight, get some exercise, and now, now none of it mattered. Did she know a Mr. Ivar Wolf? Not really, though she thought that her husband had mentioned him a time or two. Since we already knew that Dumpty Construction Company's records were legit, it didn't seem likely that Wolf had had any grounds to threaten or, for that matter, blackmail Dumpty.

We'd given the grieving widow enough trouble. It also was looking like, without any evidence to the contrary, this might really have been death by accident.

Okay, put a hold on the Dumpty case for the moment. On to the second of our two names on the Wolf suspect list: The three Pigg brothers, Arnold, Harold, and Larry. Three plump, pink, well-scrubbed young men, triplets without a doubt. All three unmarried, all three well-to-do. Do-it-yourself types, according to our records, and a quick glance at those records showed that their involvement, or run-in, rather, with Ivar Wolf had been over the houses they'd built for themselves. On the same plot of ground, not surprisingly.

"Mr. Wolf?" Arnold said. "Oh yes, he was here."

"He was the agent who got us this land," Larry added.

"Then he came back," Harold continued, "after we'd built our houses. Said he wanted to see how we were doing."

"Meeting didn't go well?" I prodded.

"Well!" Harold exclaimed. "He said my house was not up to the building code. Not up to the code! Can you imagine?"

"What was wrong?"

"He said there was too much straw in the mix. Too much straw! Can you imagine?"

"And . . .?" Sometimes it seems as though the other half our job, other than interviewing hostile witnesses, is prodding reluctant speakers.

"And he knocked it down!" Harold said indignantly. "Had one of those blasted wind spells: One, two, three, and down! Look at that mess. I still haven't gotten everything to rights."

This time to proper building code standards, I assumed. "Looks like you had some troubles, too," I said to Larry, whose house looked more like a pile of lumber than a home.

"Huh."

"Used the wind spell on you, too, I take it. Guess Mr. Wolf was pretty strict about the legal way to build something."

"Huh."

"But he didn't wreck your house," Marie said to Arnold.

"I used brick. He liked that. Said even the wind spell

couldn't hurt it. But it's a crime what he did to my brothers!"

"Well, he won't be bothering you anymore," I told them all.

They blinked as one. "What do you mean?"

"He's dead," I finished shortly.

The three Piggs reacted in exactly the same way: Surprise, but not much in the way of sorrow. Wouldn't have expected sorrow from them, of course. But was that genuine surprise? Those plump bodies looked soft, but they'd had the strength to build—and rebuild—their houses.

Marie and I exchanged glances. "I have an odd question for you," I told them. "I need to see your feet."

To my surprise, all three brothers drew themselves up in indignation. "I say, something wrong?" I asked.

The three of them nearly drowned each other out with their angry protests: "Don't you know—are you making fun of—"

"All I know," I drawled, "is that we're investigating a murder."

All three gasped. Arnold began, "You can't possibly think that we—"

"I don't think. I'm a detective. Show us your feet, and we'll go away."

The three brothers gave each other reluctant glances. Then Arnold shrugged. "Let's get this over with."

He took off his shoes. So did Harold and Larry. "Oh," said Marie.

All three brothers had the same deformity: Feet that looked almost like, well, pig feet. Considering the brothers' last name, not surprising that they'd be sensitive about the whole issue. And no way that they'd fit our partial print.

Okay, not absolute proof, but proof enough for the

moment. "Sorry to have bothered you," I said, and Marie and I left.

"Now, what?" she asked.

"Now I'm thinking that we're missing something. Something . . . something about Ivar Wolf . . . Little Red . . . yes! Come on, Marie, we're going to pay the Crooked Man another visit."

"You're asking me to defame an agent's name!"

We'd been at this far too long. "We are trying to solve his murder!"

Marie held up a hand. "Now we understand you don't want to dishonor the dead." Her voice was smooth and soothing, almost a purr. "And we don't want to do that, either. But we do want Ivar Wolf to rest in peace. Don't you?"

He stared at her, for the first time since I've known him actually at a loss for words. Marie can be pretty damned convincing when she turns on the Gallic charm. "But . . . you're asking . . ."

"All I want to know is if Mr. Wolf had affairs with other girls, with other young women." Her smile almost sent a shiver running up my spine, and I'm used to her. "You can tell us that. We're not going to tell anyone else."

The Crooked Man didn't stand a chance against her.

As we left his office, Marie, all business once again, said, "We know he had a taste for underage girls or married young women. Where does that get us?"

"Remember a certain painting?"

"In Mr. Dumpty's house! But that doesn't make sense, our partial print's that of a man, and Mrs. Dumpty is a slender young woman!"

"Is she? With all that veiling, who could tell what was underneath?"

We made a brief stop at the forensic magician's lab.

Ken was there, in the process peeling off protective gloves that were covered with something brown and slimy—I didn't care to know just what it was—and I asked him, "That K-1 spell Dumpty used . . . the protection spell that wasn't. Could it have been used as a disguise as well?"

He frowned. "Not normally, no."

"But you guys said it had been scrambled, not easy to read."

Ken nodded thoughtfully. "Go on."

"Could it have been deliberately scrambled, maybe *before* Dumpty took the fall?"

"But . . . oh. To hide who it really was? Geez. Hey, Tom, Ilana, get over here. We've got a body to disinter!"

"You do that," I said. "We have other bodies to catch."

Marie and I caught up with Mrs. Dumpty leaving her house, still swathed in that black mourning veil. "One moment," I called.

"The detectives! I thought you'd already asked all your questions."

"Not quite."

"I've lost my husband! Can't you understand that? Can't you just leave me alone?"

"I'm afraid not, ma'am," I said. "You heard about Cinderella? How that slipper proved who she really was?"

"I . . . don't . . ."

"We have a footprint here. Now, granted, it's only a partial print. But if you'll just step on it, I think we'll see something interesting about—"

I didn't get any further. Mrs. Dumpty turned and ran. But I keep myself pretty fit, and I tackled her. The mourning veil billowed free—

"Well, well, what do you know?" I said. "Look who's here. None other Mr. Dumpty himself. Pretty spry for a dead man, don't you think?"

The picture of pretty young Mrs. Dumpty had given me a clue, although it had taken long enough to percolate through my brain, that, and the fact that the purported widow had been so completely hidden by that damned veil.

Sure enough, Ivar Wolf had been making it with Mrs. Dumpty while her husband was on the construction site. And Mr. D had found out. He might have been overweight, but he was strong from years in the construction business. It had been easy enough for him to follow Wolf into the forest for that never-to-be meeting with Little Red and bash the man over the head. And sure enough, the forensic magicians soon proved that the F-1-bespelled body that had taken the header off the wall had been some unfortunate vagrant left behind the last time the beggars had come to town and so stoned he never felt the shove.

Mrs. D: We found her body in the garden, underneath a nice row of replanted cockleshells. Triple homicide.

It was an open and shut case. And soon after the trial and the guilty verdict, Mr. Dumpty, as they say on the streets, took the drop.

"Humphrey Dumpty sat on a wall," Marie began. "Humphrey Dumpty had a great fall—"

"Marie, you're a better detective than a poet," I said, cutting her off, and took her by the arm. "Come on, let's go get some coffee."

"You paying?"

"This time."

And off we went, Peep and Sheep.

NEW YORKE SNOW

Susan Sizemore

USA Today best-selling author Susan Sizemore writes epic and urban fantasy novels and fantasy short stories, as well as paranormal and historical romance. She lives in the Midwest, knits, collects art glass, and is a fanatical basketball fan. She can be reached at http://susansizemore.com

"I WAS HOPING FOR someone a little more experienced," the man said, looking around the narrow cobbled street furtively, as though he were suddenly guilty about a perfectly normal trade of his money for her body.

"I beg your pardon?" Amali responded politely.

Amali looked around herself from her spot in the shadow of the doorway, wondering what game the customer was playing. Had he seen his wife somewhere up the street? Or was he just mad?

"Perhaps I did not hear you correctly," she added with a smile.

Oh, she could caterwaul with the best of her kind, but

soft words sometimes suited best. At least at the beginning of a transaction. That was what she always told girls she was training up. There was more to learn than how to lie on your back with your skirt hiked up in this trade. She liked to set an example with her own behavior.

The man did not look in her face, but he had no trouble looking at her mostly exposed bosom. "You're attractive, lass, but I've only so much to pay and so much time to spend. I believe in doing the job properly, so I bid you good evening."

He bobbed his head politely and turned away. Amali stared after him, her mouth hanging open a bit. She'd been negotiating her commerce quite skillfully for some time now, and this was the first time she wasn't sure whether she should be offended or not at a man's treatment.

"I'm a doxy!" She finally shouted proudly after him. "What an odd night this is," she added to herself. There was magic in the air. She took a deep breath. Yes, indeed, there was magic filling the streets of Yorke tonight, though she couldn't tell what sort from the scent. "Probably bad for business," she grumbled.

Well, since the street was empty she shrugged her shawl over the low-cut bosom of her gown, and took herself off to Gran Nautha's inn. *No reason to stand about looking hopeful and getting sore feet when there's no men about*, was one of the first bits of advice she gave to her girls, and she might as well take it herself.

The scent of magic twined with the normal acrid aromas of the street until she reached Gran's. Once she opened the door, the smells of boiled cabbage and roasted meat overpowered every other aroma. She stepped into the warmth of the taproom and took a deep, appreciative breath that left her stomach rumbling when she was done.

Some stared at her when she walked in, but she'd

never flinched away from attention. Still she got more looks than she was used to as she moved between the double row of trestle tables to the door that led into the kitchen at the back of the room.

"Big crowd tonight," she said once she was inside the kitchen, with the door closed behind her.

"Aye," Gran answered.

"But not in here," Amali observed as she took a look around the big kitchen. She saw only two servers gathering up trays, and Arno standing behind the carving table chopping roast birds into quarters. Arno was Gran Nautha's man and not one of the inn's staff. The grizzled watchman normally spent his evenings seated at the table in the center of the room, nursing a mug of ale when not on his nightly rounds patrolling the streets.

Gran finished basting a joint roasting over the spit in the huge brick fireplace, then turned to face Amali. Her round face glowed with sweat and there was a harassed air about her. She shook her head. "I'm shorthanded. Two of the serving girls came down with such strong giggle fits I had to lock 'em in the storeroom. What are you looking at? You've seen Amali before. Don't keep customers waiting," she added to the servers, and the girls scurried out.

"It's odd how magic takes some folks," Arno said. "I've been hearing the sound of bells for hours. Gran's got a tingling in her fingers. What are you smelling, girl?"

"Flowers," Amali said. "Or I was until I got a whiff of tonight's cabbage soup."

"Help yourself," Gran said.

"My thanks. Then I'll help with the scullery work."

"No need for that, girl."

Amali fetched herself a crock of soup and some bread and settled at Arno's usual seat. "Business is terrible tonight anyway. I might as well make myself useful." She spooned up half the bowl before asking, "What's going on, do you know?"

"Everybody knows," Arno answered. When she frowned at him, he added, "Except you, it seems. Where have you been?"

"She just got done with a five-day temple retreat," Gran supplied for her. "She's a good girl."

"I am not!" Amali answered indignantly. "Retreats are an inexpensive way of getting a bit of beauty rest. A girl in my profession needs her beauty rest."

Arno cackled. "It's more restful to spend time on your knees than on your back, is it?"

"Just so," Amali agreed. "And bathing in the sacred spring does wonders for my skin." She touched the dark red curls that were her pride and joy. "Vision smoke is good for my hair. Henna has no part in my beauty regime," she added when Gran chuckled.

"Did you have any visions?" Arno asked.

"Seers and priestesses have visions. I had some odd dreams," Amali told him. She was too practical to put any trust in visions, for they were too hard to interpret and had little practical value. "I dreamed about golden spirals and crystal horseshoes and other pretty nonsense. And no one has yet to tell me why there's so much magic polluting the fine streets of Yorke tonight."

"It's the queen mother, of course," Gran answered.

"The evil foreign sorceress," Arno sneered. He looked like he was going to spit, but a stern glance from Gran stopped him from dirtying her spotless kitchen floor. "She's up to no good, and never has been."

Arno was among the many citizens of Yorke that put no trust or faith in the young king's stepmother, though she'd acted as regent for three years now without any undue disaster befalling the kingdom. She was indeed a sorceress, though that was hardly an uncommon aptitude in these parts. It wasn't her use of magic that was despised, but the fact that she was a princess from Cresani whose marriage to the widowed old king had been part of the treaty to end the last war. They'd been wed but two months when the king died, leaving a son still too young to rule. The people of Yorke didn't trust the Cresani witch, but they'd had no say in her ruling them while the king was a lad.

"She won't be regent much longer," Amali observed. "The king's not much of a lad anymore. Doesn't he reach his majority soon?"

"That's what the magic's all about," Gran said. "They've all been invited to celebrate the lad's coming of age."

"They?"

"All the lords and ladies, and their wizards," Arno said. "Not just Yorkeists, but nobles from every nearby land. Gods know what she's plotting to do under the guise of a celebration."

"I've heard nothing about this celebration." Amali rubbed her chin. "Wouldn't a party that grand take years to plan? I was only at the temple for five days. I should have heard gossip even there."

Gran smiled indulgently. "Oh, you think you know everything that happens in our fine rebuilt city of Yorke, and mostly you do. But the foreign witch doesn't need to consult us common folk when she uses her magic to arrange a party."

Amali conceded her point with a nod. "But why all the magic buzzing and whirring around in the city?"

"Wizards showing off for each other and entertaining their masters, most likely," Arno said. "What do they care if they set the rest of us on edge as well?"

"Foreigners don't understand about how sensitive we are," Gran added. "Only a few of them are born with the sight or the smell or all our other senses. I almost feel sorry for them."

"Well, I just hope no child conjures up any monsters in their dreams," Amali said. "You know how dangerous that can be."

"Aye," Gran answered. "Seeing is believing, and believing makes it real, as the old saying goes."

"I'll have to remember to mention that at tonight's meeting." Amali finished her meal and stood up. She glanced at the tub full of dirty crockery on the wash table. "Shall I do dishes?"

The serving girls came back in before Gran could answer, and both of them halted in the middle of the room to stare at Amali. One giggled. One pointed.

"What is the matter with you young and foolish things?" Gran demanded. "Do I have to lock you two up as well?"

"Can't you see?" the giggler asked.

"Is it a joke?" asked the other.

"Where's my dinner?" a man shouted out in the taproom.

"More wine!" shouted another.

Other, less distinct, but ominous rumblings of impatience could be heard beyond the door.

"I'll take care of them," Amali said. She grabbed up a platter of meat from the carving table. "You clean dishes," she ordered the giggler. "You grab a wine jug and come with me," she told the other.

On the way out something sharp nudged her in the back, but when she cast a warning glare over her shoulder she saw that the serving girl was nowhere near her.

When the nudge came again a few minutes later, this time against her hip, she turned around and slapped the man seated nearest her. "Touch me without paying and you'll be very sorry."

Caber the smith rose to his feet. "That's right," he growled. "Mistress Amali's a whore, but she's no tart. If you don't have coin for her—"

"It wasn't me!" The man clutched at his cheek. "There's a beast at her side." He pointed wildly. "That's what did it! A horned beast."

"You're drunk," Caber said.

The other man staggered to his feet. "Aye, but I'm not blind."

"I see it," someone at another table said.

"What is it?" another voice chimed in. "It looks like it's made from pearl and gold."

"You're all drunk," Amali said, growing tired of the debate.

"And it's closing time," Gran announced, stepping out of the kitchen. "Finish up, then get up to your rooms or to your homes, but you can't stay here any longer."

Innkeepers' words were law within their premises, and Gran was known to swing a heavy cudgel. So even though it was early, the customers meekly and quickly made their way out. That is, all but the members of the district council. While the serving girls began to clean up the taproom, the council members gathered around the table nearest the fireplace. Among them were Amali, Gran, and Caber, along with the schoolmaster, the scribe, the healer, a priestess, and the baker.

The city had been devastated by siege during the war three years before When it was rebuilt the inhabitants of the town had decided not to put too much reliance on protection and services from the rulers in the castle. There was nothing formal about the councils that had formed to look after the interests of each district. But the city was working, which it certainly hadn't done during the siege, or in the months after.

"What business do we have tonight?" Gran asked,

once they were all settled and warm cider and sweetcakes had been passed around.

"I've been thinking about the children," Amali spoke up.

Ophi the schoolmaster groaned. "Tell me you're not suggesting we take in more orphans."

Amali frowned at the caustic interruption. "Actually, I was thinking about the magi—"

A banging on the inn door interrupted her this time.

"We're closed!" Gran shouted when the door flew open, crashing against the inn wall "I hate drama," she muttered. "It's hard on the plaster."

An officer in a gold-trimmed scarlet uniform swaggered inside, a hand resting suggestively on his sword hilt. A trio of black-cloaked soldiers wearing the insignia of the queen's guard followed at his back.

"To what do we owe this honor?" Caber asked, rising to his feet. Standing, his was an impressive height indeed.

Amali thought it politic to follow the blacksmith's example no matter how unpopular the queen mother's men were in the city, and also stood. The other council members looked disgruntled, but one by one they rose.

The officer preened at the council's show of respect. "Honor indeed," he said. One by one he gave them a steely look. "I am here to discuss the small matter of a large amount of taxes."

"Taxes?" Gran asked. "What taxes?"

"The queen mother has been asking the same thing, old woman. She's been wondering where the taxes from this district have gotten to."

"We're exempt from taxes," the schoolmaster said. "The rebuilding—"

"You were exempt." The officer cut him off. "Until such time as your dwellings were rebuilt and your businesses reestablished." He gave a significant look around the taproom. "This place is hardly a burned-out hulk."

"It was," Gran said. "No thanks to your employer's soldiers."

"Her Grace was not responsible for the war."

"Yorke didn't start it," Caber spoke up.

"I don't care." The officer then put out a hand and one of the soldiers handed him a parchment roll. The officer dropped the parchment on the table, and stepped back. "I could be arresting you right now for illegal assembly and subversion, but it seemed easier to deliver this district tax assessment while all you so-called district leaders are in one place."

"Assessment!" Gran sputtered.

"Arresting who?" Arno spoke up suddenly from the kitchen doorway. The watchman strode toward the officer. "Lad, have you any idea who you're talking to? Do you know who these people are?"

"Shopkeepers and tradesmen and troublemakers," was the haughty answer. "And tax evaders."

"Heroes," Arno asserted. He pointed at Gran. "Who fed the district when we were nearly starved out? And Amali, why she practically ran this city, and her barely more than a girl at the time."

"Amali?" The officer sneered, and behind him his men snickered. "Oh, yes, I've heard of her."

"From all my satisfied customers, no doubt," Amali spoke up.

Arno was red-faced and looked ready to continue his tirade. Amali was too aware of the officer's sword, and the men who backed him up. She crossed the room and put her hand on Arno's arm.

But the officer's startled cry made her nearly jump out of her skin.

She whirled to face him. "What the—?"

"Unicorn!" he shouted. "It's a unicorn!"

"What's a unicorn?" Arno asked.

"Where?" Caber demanded.

"What kind of vermin is it?" Gran asked. "I won't have vermin in my house."

"No, you old fool!" the officer shouted at Gran. "It's a sacred beast. A holy animal." He looked suspiciously at Amali. "What's it doing here? What's it doing with the likes of you?"

Amali was confused, but she answered calmly. "Don't pay so much attention and the sight will fade." Her tone became singsong, soothing. "You're not from Yorke, are you? You don't understand how our magic works. Calm down, breath deeply, look away, and it will go away."

He continued to stare at whatever invisible being he found so upsetting.

"It's white as snow—whiter. Gold and crystal and white. So pure. Its eyes . . ." He shuddered and put a hand over his face.

"You're not listening. Sergeant, your commander is upset," Amali said to one of the officer's men. "Why don't you see that he gets home safely?"

The sergeant took her advice, and hustled the officer out.

"What was that all about?" Gran asked once they were gone.

"Magic," Amali said, and sighed. "Some people just can't handle their magic."

"Others saw it earlier," Caber said. He rubbed the back of his neck, and peered around with narrow eyes. "What would a unicorn be doing here?"

"But what's—?"

"It's a very rare beast," Caber explained when Arno and Gran asked as one. "It has healing powers, among others. It's attracted—" He glanced sideways at Amali. "To virgins."

Amali gave him an arch look. "Then it's not my fault, is it?" She looked at the rest of the council members. "At least this invisible beast got the guards to leave. Now," she asked, hands on nicely rounded hips, "do we continue the meeting?"

"No," Gran answered immediately. She gingerly fingered the parchment. "I want to read this and think on it. We all need to think a bit before we discuss what to do about"—she made a sour face—"taxes."

"Aye," Caber agreed. And one by one, so did everyone else.

"Can I walk you home?" Caber asked Amali when they were decided.

She didn't feel the need for protection out on the night streets of Yorke, and Caber knew she didn't need it. She knew what he wanted. His wife had died during the siege, and he was lonely. She was tired enough that she wanted to seek her bed to sleep, but she nodded, and let him take her arm and walk with her the short distance to her house.

Once at the door, he said, "Can I?"

She unlocked the door and led him into the front room. A lamp had been left burning on the front table, signaling that the girls were all safely in and snugly sleeping in the room they shared. There were rooms on the second floor used for their trade, but Amali knew how important it was to have a private place to call one's own.

Because Caber was a friend, she said, "We can use my room."

But that was her only concession. She took his coin. But again because of friendship, she put the money into the jar where she kept the girls' education fund. Maggi was trying out for a place with a seamstress, and apprenticeships didn't come cheap. Gods knew the girl showed no promise as a whore, better she was settled into a trade she liked.

Because Caber was such a big man she always preferred being on top when she was with him. They'd barely settled into the act when a sharp pain between her naked shoulder blades sent Amali off her customer and leaping into the air. She came down hard on her backside on the floor.

She saw it then—the unicorn. It was the shape and size of a pony, but delicately made. It was the whitest white she'd ever seen, and gleamed with a faint light of its own. Its hooves were crystal, its spiraling horn of purest gold. The huge eyes that regarded her with a calm sternness were the blue of sapphires, and full of deep wisdom. Enough people had seen it, enough to break open the veil between the mortal world and the magical realm. Now it was real.

It was still real two days later when it followed Amali into Gran's kitchen.

"You don't look like you've slept any," Gran said when she saw Amali.

"I've had plenty of sleep," she answered. "More than enough sleep."

"Well, you look worried."

"You would too, if you were being driven out of business." Amali glared at the creature leaning cozily against her hip. It looked up at her with those big, wise eyes, and she couldn't help but run her fingers through its satiny mane. "Sweet as it is to me, this thing is a terror. First it drove Caber out of my house, now it won't let anyone else come near me. I think it's backward. Maybe the horn caused it some sort of brain injury."

"How can a magical creature be backward?"

"Well, they're only supposed to be attracted to virgins, aren't they? I keep trying to make it understand it's got the wrong woman, but I can't get it to go away. It's driving me crazy. Aren't you, sweetheart?" she added, rubbing her hand up and down the golden horn.

"If you stop petting it, it might go away."

"How can anyone not pet this?"

"Do you want it, or don't you?"

"Oh, I like having it around, but it won't let me work. I like my work. And I wouldn't mind being alone every now and then."

"It *never* leaves your side?"

Amali sighed. "Never."

"Well, I can do something about that."

Gran had been kneading a large pile of dough while they talked. Now she wiped her hands on her apron and came around the worktable. Squarely facing the unicorn, she put her hands on her hips. She and the unicorn looked intently at each other.

"By all the rules of your world and mine, the innkeeper's word is sovereign within her own place," Gran said. "Is that not so?"

The unicorn slowly nodded its head.

"Well, then, get your furry flanks out of my kitchen this instant. Wait for your lady in the taproom. I don't care how fine that coat of yours is, I won't have you shedding it in my bread."

The unicorn tossed its head and stamped its crystal hoof, but it turned, flicked its tail, and walked out of the kitchen.

Gran dusted her hands together. "That ought to give you some peace. Do you want to start taking customers upstairs here?"

Amali hugged her friend, then glanced nervously at the door. "Maybe I could rent a room from you. But that wouldn't strictly be inn business. So it might feel free to charge after any customer I try to take upstairs."

"I never said anything about renting you the room, lass. Though I could use the income if you wanted to pay," Gran added. "What with this tax assessment to worry about."

Amali laughed.

"What's so funny about taxes?"

"Not a thing." She reached into a pocket and pulled out a chamois bag. As she handed it to Gran, she asked, "Do you know what unicorns poop?"

"What?" Gran looked at her suspiciously. "You didn't bring droppings from that creature into my clean kit—"

"Jewels," Amali told her. "When he lifts his tail, jewels come out."

Gran opened the bag and filled her palm with glittering stones. "Gods!"

"And it pisses gold." Gran stared at her, mouth agape, and Amali nodded. "I swear. I think there's enough unicorn droppings there to pay the whole district's taxes, and pay for Maggi's apprenticeship, and organize the fire brigade we need. The council can decide what else."

"Gods, girl, why are you complaining you can't work if the creature's made you rich?"

"Have I ever been one to count on something just being given to me? I've always worked. I earn my way. Besides, I like the sex."

"You could get yourself a good man."

Amali took a step back in surprise. "You know, I never thought of that." She gestured toward the door. "But not as long as I have a unicorn defending my nonexistent virtue."

Gran gave a cackling laugh, but the sound was soon drowned out by crashing and shouting coming from the taproom.

Amali rushed out of the kitchen. The taproom was full of guardsmen surrounding the unicorn. The arrogant officer was back with his men, and they had ropes around the unicorn's neck. The beast's hoofs flailed the air, it swung and stabbed with its horn. But it was not a large creature, and there were many men. The ropes were shining silver threads. Gossamer. Strong enough to bind any magical creature.

Amali rushed forward. "No! Stop! What are you doing?"

The officer didn't bother to answer. He turned on her and brushed her aside like a fly. She flew backward. Her head slammed hard against the wall, and everything went dark.

"You'll be all right, child."

Gran's voice was a comfort, but Amali felt inexplicable grief as she came awake. "What happened?" Hands helped her to sit up and she looked around. For some reason she was lying on the floor in the taproom. "My head hurts."

"Well, of course it does. The doctor came and went and says you'll be fine. You still have a sore knot on your head."

"But how—? The unicorn!" She remembered now. "They took it! Why? Where?"

"The queen mother wanted it."

"But it's mine. At least, it came to me."

"But you don't want it. Weren't you just complaining about how it's ruined your business?"

Amali rubbed the throbbing spot on the back of her head. "Yes, but—"

"Then this is the best thing for you, and for it. Though the queen could've asked nicely instead of sending men to steal the beast away. But politeness is not to be expected from the foreign witch, is it?"

"No, I suppose not," Amali agreed. "But it didn't want to go. It was frightened. I remember." Even troublesome magical creatures shouldn't be forced to do things they didn't want to do.

"You're better off without it," Gran soothed. "Except for the treasure part, that is."

"I don't want treasure."

"That's the bump on your head talking."

"Yes, very likely. But—"

"And it's better off living off in a castle, now isn't it? It's too decorative a thing for our mean streets."

"The streets aren't that mean. We work very hard to keep them that way."

Gran grasped Amali by the shoulders. "Girl, will you listen to me? This is for the best. You'll know that when your head stops hurting."

Maybe she would. She had to admit her thoughts were not at all clear. "I've gotten used to having it around."

"Get yourself a puppy. Or a husband. But don't pine over a lost unicorn. Its appearing to you was a mistake, anyway."

Amali nodded slowly, and was gratified when her head didn't actually fall off, though she was left dizzy. "Yes. Yes, I suppose it was a mistake. The thing will be better off decorating the queen's garden." This was true, but it made her sad. She sighed. "All right, I'll leave it be." What else could she do, anyway?

She let Gran help her to her feet. She swayed on them for a few moments, and the room swung dizzily around her, but everything steadied soon enough.

"I'm going home."

Gran looked dubious. "You could rest upstairs for a while."

Amali gingerly shook her head. "I need to get back to work.

Gran Nautha didn't argue with this logic.

Amali supposed she should have been relieved, yet

she set off down the street with a heavy heart. There was just something about having the unicorn around that was—comforting.

Unicorns were very special creatures, very rare. What were all the things they could do? As she walked along, she ran over all that Caber had told her about the creature. They were symbols of purity, yes. And they could heal. And they were highly prized by kings and nobles who hunted them for—

Amali came to a dead halt in the center of the street. "Oh, my gods!"

All the great nobles were at the castle, being entertained. What did great lords and kings find entertaining? Hunting, of course.

Her heart hammered hard in her chest. "They're going to hunt my unicorn." The knowledge terrified her. And it made her furious. "Oh no—they're not."

She didn't know what she could do, but she wasn't going to stand idly by while a bunch of bored and foolish rich men destroyed something so pure and beautiful for sport. She set off up the long hill to the castle gate with firm purpose, but absolutely no plan whatsoever.

The gatekeeper was a long-time customer of hers, and it was easy enough to convince him that she had noble clients waiting for her inside. Once in the great courtyard she followed her nose. For the unicorn had a distinct, strong scent of rose and iris. Since it was autumn and both flowers were out of season, she had but to find and follow these aromas of spring and summer to find her way to the creature.

She caught the unicorn's scent quickly, and it led her into a vast garden. She actually remembered the garden from when she was a child, and once or twice a year the old king would invite the citizens of Yorke to celebrations inside the castle grounds. Here flagstone paths led across meadows and woods and ornamental flower beds. There were fountains, and streams spanned by delicate bridges. It went on for acre upon acre, and the trees and flowers were riotous with fall color.

Amali was aware of all the great beauty as she passed it, but paid it little mind while she pursued her quest. She did take cover behind a topiary bush the first time she came upon a young woman seated on a bench under a tree. The girl was lovely, dressed in pink and white brocade, with long golden hair framing her perfect features. She had her hands folded demurely in her lap, and her gaze was on the ground. She took no notice when Amali screwed up her courage and tiptoed by.

She came upon several other girls seated still as statues as she followed the scent. They took no mind of her, so she ignored them as well. She had no idea what they might be about, but the games of noble ladies were none of her concern. She could hear hunting horns and shouts every now and then, and the game the noblemen played filled her with dread.

"Where are you, unicorn?" she demanded as she came into a clearing past a stand of aspen trees. She took a deep breath. Yes, the creature was nearby. "Don't you know we have to get out of here?" She took a risk, and shouted, "Unicorn!"

The beast came trotting up behind her and poked its horn into the small of her back.

"Ow." She whirled around and grasped the offending horn. "Why was it I came to rescue you?" Her gaze met the unicorn's, and she smiled. "Because you're sweet, and I'm a fool." She tapped the tip of the beast's golden horn. "And because you want me here for some reason. Isn't that so?" The beast nodded its beautiful head.

"My lady!"

Amali whirled around at the shout, to find a young

man kneeling in the grass near her. "Nobody calls me that!" she told him. The unicorn nudged her toward him. "Hey!"

The young man turned a persuasive smile on her. "But you are my lady."

"I'm anyone's lady for the pri—"

The unicorn nudged her again.

Unicorn bait, she realized. That's what those girls were. "You definitely have the wrong unicorn," she told the young man.

He rose to his feet, all grace and coiled energy. He had the look of a warrior to him. And a king.

"Oh, dear," she murmured.

She wondered if she should bow. More importantly, she wondered when the guards were going to show up and drag her off to some horrible fate.

"This is my unicorn," she stated firmly, figuring she might as well tell the truth and take the consequences. She folded her arms beneath her ample chest and looked defiantly up into eyes as blue as the unicorn's. "It came to me, chose me, and I'm keeping it."

The king kept smiling, and tilted his head as he looked her over. "Of course you are, my lady."

"I'm leaving now," she said, and tried to sidle around the king.

"Oh, you must not go."

She was afraid he'd say something like that. "I don't—"

He took her by the hand. "I don't belong here."

"Of course you do."

This time the voice came from a young woman. The young woman was dark haired and dressed in embroidered gold velvet. She wore a jeweled circlet around her forehead, and was surrounded by courtiers. Guards in black and red stood in the background. This woman, obviously, was the queen mother.

"But you're so young." Amali clapped a hand over her mouth, and felt like a fool. She tried curtsying, to see if that would help any.

"Leave us, please," the queen said. The courtiers and the guards hastily retreated from the clearing. "Not you," the queen added, when Amali began to back away. "Would you please give me a moment alone with your lady?" she politely asked the king.

He bowed, grinned, and waved at Amali, then he was gone.

Amali stood with her hand on the unicorn's head, nervously wondering what would come next.

The king's stepmother walked up to her. "I don't feel very young," she told Amali. "But it was gracious of you to notice. I was sixteen when my husband died. Leaving me—" She made a small, elegant gesture that took in the whole world. "With this."

"The kingdom of Yorke," Amali said.

"It's not much of a kingdom, really. Not in comparison to the rest of the wide world."

Amali bristled. "I like it."

The queen smiled. "Of course you do, that's why you're here." When the unicorn huffed, she added, "One of the reasons. Congratulations, my dear, you are about to live happily ever after."

Amali gave the young woman a narrow-eyed glare. "What do you mean?"

The queen made another of those slight, but significant gestures. "Happily ever after is what you make of it, of course. And it's different for everyone. For example, keep my dear stepson happy in bed and send him off to war when you must, and he'll be the happiest man alive. And he'll adore you for it. He's a charming lad, but not at all complex. For me happily ever after will be knowing that I've fulfilled my obligations to Yorke, and returning to studying sorcery at the Hidden Tower. For you, the rule of Yorke will be the most satis—"

"What are you talking about?" Amali didn't suppose it was wise to abruptly cut off a queen, but she was finding this whole incident quite annoying. "I have a headache," she said. "That's because you stole my unicorn. All I want to do is leave."

The queen never stopped smiling. "You can't leave. This is your home now. You're going to marry my stepson and live happily ever after. By royal decree," she added, and there was steel in her voice, and in her eyes.

Amali gulped. "I really don't understand."

"Sorcery," the queen answered. "Magic. I am a great sorceress, you know."

"So we've heard."

"So speaks the skeptical defender of the citizens of Yorke. And don't try to deny that you are neither, for I know all about you, Amali of the Cobbles District. I'd heard about you even before the spell brought you to my attention."

"Me? Spell? Pardon me?" Amali's head was spinning, and not because of the bump on the back of it.

"I'm very fond of my stepson." She held up a hand, as though she thought Amali was going to protest. "I know stepmothers have a reputation for being wicked, but I was never able to get the hang of it. I took my responsibility to raise him quite seriously. But he has come of age, and I want my own life back. So I decided to find him the perfect bride, the woman who would be perfect for him, and more importantly, the queen Yorke needs. You."

"Me?"

"Yes. So the unicorn has chosen."

Amali looked at the magical beast. "This is your doing?"

It nodded its lovely head and whinnied. The sound held the tone of a wicked chuckle.

"You're serious," Amali said to the queen.

The queen nodded. "I sent the unicorn spell out into the world to find the right woman. The unicorn took shape when it found a woman of purity and beauty. You," she said again.

Amali considered for a moment, then said, "I think you have a defective unicorn."

"Purity of spirit," the queen replied. "Beauty of soul. The unicorn found you. And you found the unicorn when you thought it was in danger. You are the chosen one. Congratulations. I don't suppose you'll want to wear white for the wedding."

"Uh—no," Amali answered, and realized that she'd accepted her fate.

Queen of Yorke. Well, someone had to do it. It might as well be someone who could do a decent job of it. Her Gran Nautha had been right about her finding a good man and settling down. The king would do.

"I prefer wearing scarlet," she told the queen mother.

MEET THE MADFEET

Michael Jasper

Michael Jasper gets by on not enough sleep and too much caffeine in Raleigh, North Carolina, where he lives with his lovely wife, Elizabeth, and their amazing young son, Drew. Michael's fiction has appeared in *Asimov's, Strange Horizons, Interzone, Jigsaw Nation, Aeon,* and *Polyphony,* among many other fine venues. His mixed-genre story collection *Gunning for the Buddha* came out from Prime Books in 2005. His first novel, the paranormal romance *Heart's Revenge,* came out from Five Star Books in June 2006 (under the pseudonym Julia C. Porter). He really doesn't have anything against hobbits. Honest.

EVERYONE WHO LIVES AND breathes in our green land thinks that my predecessor, the Mighty Greybeard, could do no wrong. That includes the accursed little people, those smiling, singing, irritatingly needy little fur-feet.

I tried to stay away from their villages built into the sides of hills and keep out of their business, especially if it entailed a visit to the cramped caves that they call home. Without exception, I found their holes filled with mouse droppings, birds' nests, and blue mold, not to mention the ends of worms and an oozy smell.

Yet the fur-feet kept calling me back, and my fellow wizards claimed to be too busy to respond to their summons. So I went, if only to keep my membership in the Guild active for at least one year more. That was the price I paid for my youth and my vocation: a fledgling wizard must serve the common good, for when he stops, he loses his power. My predecessor, now living a life of repose in the Far Havens, took this fact to heart.

Which explained how I found myself on an early spring day under a glistening white and blue sky, perched on the unforgiving seat of my mule-led cart, venturing into their distant rural villages once again.

I looked down at the piece of parchment pinned to the gray cuff of my sleeve. These directions surely had to be the worst yet; our cartographer had been smoking too much pipeweed again. According to these scribbles, I was to turn left after the stone bridge over Wellwater Springs and continue up the slow incline leading west. I mumbled a quick spell of veracity over the parchment, and the ink glowed a confident baby blue. The directions did not lie.

I felt a tiny shiver run through my bones at the use of Magic. After only three years as a full-fledged Guild member, I thrilled at the way the power felt as it flowed through me. Though I must admit, I still hadn't gotten used to all the energy the Magic required, taking it from me one bite at a time.

I turned off the smooth dirt trail onto the rock-strewn path, and immediately the sky began to fill with rain clouds. The cart's wheels jarred against a boulder, then a hole as big as a small crater. As my mule honked in protest—oh, for an actual *horse*, like the rest of the wizards, I thought, and not for the first time—I realized where we were now heading.

The brown hills. Or I should say, the Brown Hills. I'd never been this far west, nor had I encountered any fur-feet who actually *lived* in this hostile clime. Gone were the fields of wheat and barley hemmed in by quaint rock walls, past me were the alehouses and bakeries on each corner, and behind me were the dancing children and crowded gardens of flowers and vegetables big as your head.

Here, in caves carved out of the petrified mud and crumbling rock of the Brown Hills, lived the Madfoots.

According to the rules of the Guild, every wizard needed to find a specialization, a needy population to whom he or she could provide personalized assistance. Arimea the sorceress had her wood elves and tree sorcery to keep her entertained for decades, if not centuries. Old Raddy had his birds and small animals. And way back when, the dark wizard Malusar had his pet orcs, seven feet tall and built for battle.

Me? I decided to be different. I wanted to be a sort of rogue spirit, a free agent, and not pick favorites. I'd go wherever the Guild sent me, or, even better, I'd travel the land and conquer injustices and right wrongs wherever I went. I could see myself wearing out my leather boots and learning new languages and customs as I traveled across our green land.

That was my dream.

Problem was, the fur-feet picked *me*. With Greybeard gone, they soon found themselves facing mundane squabbles that apparently only a wizard could resolve. Someone stealing your cow's milk? Finding strange shapes in your wheat field? Tired of a fur-foot bullying

you and spilling your ale? Send immediately for Palap-
ateer. Better known as "Greybeard's replacement."

I hoped he was enjoying his ageless retirement, most
likely surrounded by gallons of wine and lovely ladies,
while I toiled on in anonymity and thanklessness for the
Guild.

My only real challenge in almost three years of labor
here in the hilly country of the fur-feet was the recent
rousting of goblins from the western ridges. Now *that*
was enjoyable. The Magic had poured through me like
quicksilver, and many goblins fled from their hiding
spots with singed blue skin and dented skulls. Took me an
entire night and quite a few pints of home brew at the
Dancing Dragon Inn to recover from my exertions.

As the mule and I inched up the jagged hill, accompanied by the constant rumble of thunder, I thought about
using a levitation spell to get us up there faster. But after
recalling my orders from my Guildmaster, I decided to
conserve my energy.

"The little people have need of you once more, Pal,"
Vardamann had told me in his speechifying voice. "They
are being menaced by a vile presence encroaching upon
their domiciles."

"More goblins?" I said, hoping for a challenge worthy
of my skills. Vardamann shook his head. "Trolls?" No.
"Undead warriors?" No again.

I took a deep breath. "Surely not . . . a dragon?"

"See to it, will you, Pal?" Vardamann the Voluminous
said and snapped his fingers with a dry popping sound,
dismissing me.

"I'll *see to it,* Vard," I muttered as more rain clouds
burst over me. "But, my fearless leader, all safe and dry
up in your library, you never said anything about helping
the *Madfoots.*"

As if punishing me for speaking their name, the cart's

back wheel struck a boulder, throwing me face-first toward the mud.

Luckily I had the command for the levitation spell on the tip of my tongue, and I never hit the ground. With a few more words of Magic I continued floating up the mountain.

I'd return for my mule and ruined cart after my work here was complete, which surely wouldn't take long. Dragons these days posed little challenge to wizards like me.

This, I thought as I sat with my knees up to my chin and my cloaks sinking in cold mud, *this* was my punishment for not choosing to work with the faeries of the ageless forest. Or the dwarves of the distant ore-rich mountains. Or the trolls down by the blackened lakes.

My diminutive host was Gammergub, who claimed to be the oldest of the Madfoots. He truly was the ugliest—his skin had an unhealthy blue tinge to it, and his bulgy pointed ears and squinting yellowed eyes were his best features. His back was hunched as a shepherd's crook, and his soiled shirt and short pants were little more than a loincloth.

Gammergub had refused to let me in until I'd shown him a trio of Magic tricks as well as my Guild badge. Still feeling a bit winded from my unexpected levitation spell, I was about to rap my staff against his pointy head, but old Gub finally allowed me into his muddy home.

Now the self-proclaimed Dane of the Madfoots—Mad*feet,* he had insisted—was regaling me about his great-great-grandchildren as he tried to fix tea for me. At least, that was what I thought he was saying; the Madfoot accent was thicker than sludge from the bottom of Lake Mudswallow.

I finally had to grab Gammergub's spindly frame and

lead him to his stool so we could get down to business. The little fellow was heavier and more muscular than he looked—wrestling him into his seat took more energy than I'd expected.

"Tell me about the dragon, Gub," I said, giving him my best attempt at a benevolent smile. "That is why I'm here, isn't it?"

"Ah, yah, yah," Gub said with countless nods. He passed me a chipped mug filled with lukewarm brownish water that gave off a bitter reek. I set it in the mud next to me. "Big dragon. Big, and hungry. Only 'tacks at night, yah, yah. When the sun sets."

I sighed. "It's just now half past noon. Why didn't you tell the Guild this bit of crucial information, so I didn't waste half a day waiting here for the dragon to show itself?"

"Well," Gub said, after a long sip of his tea, "there is some other chores. Need doing 'round here. While we wait, yah, yah. While we wait for the dragon . . ."

I shook my head, listening to the rain pounding against the roof of Gub's cramped hole. The little urchin was already waiting for me at his front door, eager to head out into the driving rain. I got to my feet and bumped my head on the hard rock of the ceiling. I was not looking forward to getting drenched again. I supposed I could use a shielding spell to keep myself dry out there. Couldn't hurt, could it?

"All right," I muttered. "Let's get this over with, Gub."

My first task was to round up over a dozen goats that had slipped out of their pen. I got butted three times before I used a series of binding spells to gather up all the mindless beasts. When I was butted for the fourth time, my concentration slipped, and my shielding charm disappeared. I was now soaked, but the goats were corralled again.

If only I were a rogue wizard, unfettered by the rules and control of the Guild, I thought, and not for the first time. Then I wouldn't be stuck here, herding goats in the rain.

I noticed that the goats seemed panicky whenever Gub came close to any of them. Must have been his smell—usually the fur-feet and animals got along smashingly. Or it could've been due to the way Gub smacked his lips around them.

Feeling a bit out of breath after the goat-binding spells, I could've gone for hot tea and a loaf of bread at that point, even something from Gub's muddy larder. Just a quick rest.

But he was already pulling me off to my next duty. We hiked through the mud farther west, toward what could very well have been the ugliest front yard of any fur-feet I'd ever seen: broken ale bottles littered the dead grass on the other side of a splintered fence. A dead apple tree sat to the right of the muddy path leading up to the half-open front door.

"This thing been haunting ol' Gabgo Madfoot here. Got the old fella shakin' in his suspenders. Yah, yah."

I gave Gub a long look, but he wouldn't meet my gaze. His shoulders drooped further as we stopped outside the entrance to Gabgo's hole. A cold, rancid breeze wafted out the front door.

"So what did Gabgo do to this creature? Is it the ghost of an old enemy? A spook from a friendship gone sour?"

"He did not a thing!" Gub's eyes were suddenly yellow with rage and indignance. "Is just the lot of our poor people. Always taking abuse from foul creatures."

He stopped talking abruptly and looked off to the east, where the hills were rounder and the grassy fields were more plentiful. And the fur-feet living there were fatter and healthier than the few Madfoots—Madfeet—I'd seen today.

"If only we lived in *that* county, not mountains here, yah, yah," he muttered, eyes darkening until they were almost green. "We be shielded from such foul creatures. But no, no, Madfeet stuck in the Brown Hills. No green grass for Madfeet. . . ."

As Gub grumbled, I shook the water from my hood and inched closer to the entrance to Gabgo's hole. I pulled out my crystal of power and ignited it with a word of Magic. Gub stopped talking, and his eyes widened as he gawked at the fist-size gem. The Guild's crystals often had that effect on people.

"Let's just finish this, shall we?" I said. "We can discuss the plight of the Madfoots later."

"Mad*feet*," Gub said absently, still gazing at the crystal.

As soon as I stepped inside, I could hear his bare, hairy feet slapping through the mud as he fled the scene.

Fine, I thought, setting the crystal into its niche at the top of my staff like a Magical torch. I preferred to work alone.

Lit up by the unforgiving light of the crystal, the only redeeming feature of this muddy, crumbling hole was that it contained less garbage than Gammergub's, and its owner appeared to have packed up and moved. Gabgo was long gone.

I searched the entire place, muddying my boots and getting countless cobwebs in my face and loose dirt down my collar. I only cracked my skull twice on the low ceilings and arches. And I could find no evil spirit lurking in any of the corners.

I was about to give up and head back out into the rain when I heard a small tinkling sound, like the clink of rings on cold fingers, or cold chains in the wind.

I drew my sword and held my staff in front of me as I dredged up the words to a spell to ward off the undead.

"Begone," I began in my best deep tone, but the clinking sound of metal continued. It came from below me. I looked down at the rotting burgundy rug under me and tapped my staff on the rug. I was rewarded with a hollow thunk. A trapdoor.

As soon as I ripped the rug away, a black fist covered in dull silver rings punched through the wooden trapdoor I'd just uncovered. Cold air rushed over me, nearly stopping my breath.

"Do not interfere, wizard," hissed a lifeless voice that made my mustache curl up. "These vermin do not belong here. . . ."

"Begone!" I shouted again, and the hand disappeared back through the shattered horizontal door.

After a long moment of silence, I leaned close to the hole. I aimed the light of my staff into the hole, and looked down into the dead black eyes of a barrow-wight.

Cold fear seeped into my heart, and I lost my willpower, gazing into those soulless eyes. The rest of the creature's face was lost in shadow, but the eyes made me feel as helpless as I did on my first day as an apprentice to the mighty Greybeard.

Then I remembered my Guild training, and my confidence returned. No undead creature, even if it was a barrow-wight far from its home, would best me in battle.

I summoned up all my flagging energy, spoke the incantation against the nonliving, and threw open the trapdoor.

A wizard's work, I thought as I jumped down into the unknown, was never done.

I came to in the basement of Gabgo's empty hole, surrounded by half a dozen dull silver rings and a rusted sword that was easily four hundred years old. The ghostly creature had babbled on and on about intruders in these hills, and how they had to be removed, until I'd managed to send him fleeing back to his crypt with my final incantation. Then I'd blacked out.

Desperate for clean air and warmth, I crawled up and out of the hole. I was glad to see the rain had stopped at last. At the gate, Gub stood waiting, arms crossed on his chest.

"Time is a-wasting," he said, then added, "yah, yah."

"You're welcome," I muttered. At some point in my battle with the lost barrow-wight, my staff had gotten broken in two. All I had left was the top half, and luckily my crystal had not come loose from its tip.

"I have bad news," Gub said, still eyeing the crystal as he led me north through the rutted streets of his village. We had less than an hour of sunlight left. "One of our Madfeet children just got carried off, yah, yah. By a giant spider."

I could barely believe my ears. I stopped, wishing my staff were whole so I could lean on it. "I see."

I looked around and saw a flimsy-looking wooden building with the crooked sign proclaiming it the Red Rooster Cellar and Inn. A drink would be nice right about now, even if was a draft of Madfeet ale. I dearly needed to put my feet up and rest.

But Gub was tugging at my arm again, trying to hurry me toward the patch of dark trees north of the village.

"Must hurry, you can save the child. Think it's lovely Marybelle Madfeet, yah, yah. You slay the spider first. *Then* we'll have some ale before you meet with the dragon, yah, yah."

"*Meet* with the dragon," I repeated as we hurried through the empty dirt roads of the village until the ragged Madfeet forest came into sight. "Shall I bring the tea, or will he?"

Gub gave me one last shove, and then I was inside the

forest. At least the rain couldn't get through the thick, vine-encrusted tree limbs above me. I ignited my crystal and drew my dagger. My sword must have been back in Gabgo's basement.

I found the little Madfeet girl about twenty trees into the forest, dangling upside down from a web as thick as my wrist. I used my dagger to cut the child down. She hit the ground with a squeak, and then she was wriggling free of the webs binding her.

Strangely, her arms and legs appeared blue, but surely she hadn't been tied up long enough to slow the blood flow to her limbs. Gub's skin was about the same bluish color, I noted.

Marybelle was tottering off toward the village when the spider dropped toward me, clattering down through the branches clumsily, subtle as an explosion.

This would be easy, I thought, swinging my dagger with relish. I won't even have to waste any Magic on this creature.

And then four other giant spiders dropped down from above, encircling the trees around me with thick, sticky webs.

Gub and I didn't have time to stop at the Red Rooster when I was done with the spiders. As the sun was touching the western horizon, Gub and I left the smoking remains of the forest behind and headed toward the northwest. I could've killed for an ale.

"Didn't have to burn down the whole forest," Gub said. "Nice of you to get rid of the spiders an' all, yah, yah. Never knew there was more than one of 'em. Heh. But we liked them trees there. Came in handy if we ever needed to build a fire."

"Old habits die hard," I said, looking at Gub. Most furfeet adored trees, and wouldn't think of cutting one down. "I've never been good when I'm surrounded. I tend to go with the first really powerful spell I learned. Fireballs."

Gub and I hiked—uphill, of course—to the ridge that overlooked the dragon's distant lair. At the summit, I found myself feeling uncommonly exhausted. Which was ridiculous, of course. I was young and full of energy. Why should a few silly little tasks for the Madfoots— Mad*feet*—have worn me out so?

I certainly hoped the Guildmaster was keeping track of my labors here today. I glanced at my crystal of power, which had gone dark again. I knew Vardamann like to use these crystals to keep his eye on me and the other fledgling wizards.

You'd better be watching, old man, I thought. I doubt even Greybeard would have agreed to do all that I've done today.

Next to me in the fading red light, Gub was looking up, mouth dropping open to reveal teeth yellower than his eyes. From off to the west, I heard a distant hissing sound, barely louder than an exhalation. I blinked and Gub was gone from my side faster than a shadow in a lightning strike. No surprise there.

The dragon was coming, right at sunset, and right on schedule. The hissing sound continued, growing with each passing heartbeat. It was the movement of giant wings, approaching fast.

And here I stood, in the middle of a platform like some sort of sacrificial lamb. I fumbled with my broken half-staff and tried to focus my fatigue-addled brain. I couldn't even ignite my crystal of power.

Now what was the pronunciation for that fireball spell?

Then the sun disappeared, replaced by a flying beast bigger than all the giant spiders of the forest. All I could see were wings that blotted out the night and huge white fangs.

The dragon fell on me, and I knew no more.

I woke in the Far Havens, the otherworld of heroes and wizards after they died. Harps played, the fresh aroma of warm bread filled the air, and soft feathers cradled my old body. My mind was blessedly clear, and the fatigue and aches had been wiped from my limbs. I was at rest, at last. An elven woman in white robes tended to me, and her touch was heavenly.

Then I opened my eyes and saw I was indeed lying on my back, but I was still in the Brown Hills. *Under* them, apparently. I was gagged, robeless, and chained to the floor, with my broken staff sitting perilously close to a small fire in the corner of the cave. The crystal embedded in my staff was glowing a sickly blue color, illuminating piles of jewels, gold and silver coins, and countless other baubles and trinkets.

The woman in white robes was still here, to my surprise. She sat cross-legged next to the fire, cradling her burned right hand. When she saw me, her face hardened in anger.

I blinked and felt a sudden movement around me, as if a tiny tempest had formed in the cave. Another blink of my eyes and I saw the dragon, sitting on its massive haunches in front of me. The woman was gone. I'd run into a shape-shifting dragon.

She was a magnificent creature, delicate wings folded tight against her red-scaled back. Ivory horns jutted from her forehead, and the dragon still favored its injured right forepaw. A trickle of steam escaped her fanged mouth, which looked large enough to snatch up one of the Madfeet goats.

The Madfeet! Traitorous little fur-feet! I'd slay them all.

"Calm yourself, spellweaver," the dragon said in a surprisingly soft voice. "I shall remove your gag if you promise not to try your Magic on me. If you attempt to do so, I will have no choice but to ignite you."

I nodded, and she clawed off my gag.

"So you have your wizard trophy," I said. "Is that why you made this deal with the hair-footed vermin outside?"

I'd never heard a dragon laugh before, and if this was what it sounded like, I didn't want to hear it again. It was so low and insidious it made my beard want to fall off.

"Dragons don't make deals with anyone, luv," she said. "We just allow others to convince themselves they're getting the best of us. Remember, we're *dragons*. Nobody can best us. I say that as a statement of fact, not a boast. I mean, look at your predicament, master wizard."

Long-winded as usual. I preferred the great eagles and their long silences. This conversation could take all night. I'd have to be direct, even if it got me burned to a crisp.

"Could you tell me why you haven't killed me already, ma'am? Don't like the taste of roasted young wizard?"

She seemed to like the direct approach. Either that, or I was mistaking her hungry look for a smile.

"Call me ma'am again and I *will* roast you. I'm Brigga." She heaved a sigh that singed my eyebrows. "I want your crystal," she said. "The cursed thing won't let me touch it."

Everything came clear to me then, as clear as things could get when you are sprawled on your back, naked and chained to the floor, with a dragon hovering over you. I remembered seeing her burned hand while she was still in human form.

She'd tried to steal my crystal. Bad idea.

"Well," I began, "it's not that easy. You see, that crystal is bonded to me by Magic. I'd have to give it to you of my free will, and I'm not sure I could do that. I don't think it's in your best interest."

I had to keep my head clear; I knew she could read my thoughts if she tried hard enough.

"You see," I added, "it's quite powerful."

Brigga's laughter was gone, replaced by a greedy snarl.

"You know nothing of power, human. Give it to me. Now!"

"Let me free first," I said. "I have to actually hand it to you. And you must give me your word that you'll not kill me after I give it to you."

"Sure, sure," she said, snapping the chains one by one that held my arms and legs. "I made the same deal with the goblins."

I was so busy rubbing my sore arms that I almost missed it.

"Did you say . . . *goblins*?"

"Fooled you, didn't we?" Brigga's smile was wide as the entrance to a Madfeet hole as she recalled her trickery. "The goblins dearly want to take over the lands to the east, and they came to me with their plan to bring you here. It was simple to conceal their identity from you with a few words of enchantment. Everyone wins—the goblins get new land, and I get your crystal of power to add to my collection here. And, best of all, I don't have to eat goblin any longer."

If I wasn't already sitting down, I would've fallen over.

"What about the real Madfoots? Madfeets. Mad*feet*. Whoever they are—were." I caught myself. "Not that I really care, of course."

"They're still around here . . . somewhere. My goblin friends chased most of them out of the Hills. Wretched little fur-feet."

I felt a twinge of defensiveness. How dare she talk poorly of the fur-feet? That was *my* specialization.

Brigga arched her long neck down over me until her nostrils were touching my chest. She pushed me across the crowded cave full of glittering jewels and gold, back to where my staff lay.

"Now, enough talking. Hand over the crystal and you can leave here, alive."

In the instant before I reached out my hand to remove the crystal from my ruined staff, I found myself thinking of Gub. Gammergub the goblin. I'd been played by him like a cheap fiddle. Some wizard I was. I didn't deserve to follow in Greybeard's footsteps—I was not cut out for the Guild.

The realization was more painful than a fireball spell.

"Go on," Brigga breathed from behind me. "Quit stalling."

Oh, this was going to hurt, I thought, and then I ripped the crystal from my staff.

But it was going to feel so good, too.

I looked up at Brigga, keeping my thoughts focused on my anger at Gub's betrayal. It wasn't a difficult task at all.

"Are you sure you won't change your mind?"

Brigga held out the paw she'd injured when she'd tried to steal the crystal that bound me to the wizardly world.

"Not a chance," she said, smiling already. "Release it to me, and if I am burned again, you will begin your new life as my personal torch."

"All right," I said. "As you wish."

I could see myself already, walking the unexplored lands to the north, practicing my own brand of Magic and working as a rogue spirit, just like I'd always dreamed about.

"Brigga the Dragon," I said, placing the glowing white

crystal into her paw, "I endow upon you the Crystal of Power."

As my Magical connection to the Guild was broken, a tiny explosion flared inside my head, nearly making me fall.

And then . . . and then I felt like myself again.

Even better than that, I realized. I felt *free*.

"Ah," I said as soon as the crystal was safely in Brigga's paw, "one more thing I forgot to add. You'll need to report in to Vardamann immediately. He likes to greet his newest recruits personally. And you *may* want to use your human form—Vardamann the Voluminous does have a reputation as a dragon-hater."

Brigga sputtered and tried to laugh, but the only sound coming from her was a squeaking sound. Her dragon form was already shrinking back into her smaller, frailer human shape.

"What did you do to me?" she cried out.

"Just gave you what you wanted, Brigga. The crystal is given to all wizards when they join the Guild. That's how they track our actions and make sure we toe the line. It's a source of power, but it's also a means to control us."

"But, but that can't be . . . I'm a dragon!"

"Doesn't mean anything now, my lady. The crystal uses ancient Magic, from long before the time of dragons. I'm afraid being a dragon won't help you much if Vardamann wants to—"

Before I could finish, Brigga's female form shifted and blurred, and she disappeared from her cave with a tiny pop.

"If Vardamann wants to *summon* you, that is." Having been the unhappy recipient of numerous summonings from the Guildmaster, I felt a touch of sympathy for the dragon. Just a touch, though.

I stood there in the middle of Brigga's cave for a few

long moments, just listening to my own breathing and shivering. Somehow I was still alive. I may not have access to all the amenities of the Guild any longer, but who needed all that bureaucracy and politics? I had my spells and my brains. That's all a real wizard needs.

I found my robes outside her chamber, and I left the piles of precious metals and jewels behind. I walked up and out of a side tunnel into a misty, golden dawn outside. The unexplored lands awaited me.

But first, now that I'd recovered my precious energy, I had some goblins to deal with before I left to begin my new life. I owed the fur-feet—the *real* fur-feet—that much. Yah, yah.

FINDER'S KEEPER

Janny Wurts

Through her combined career as an established professional novelist and her background in the trade as a cover artist, Janny Wurts has immersed herself in a lifelong ambition: to create a seamless interface between words and pictures that explore imaginative realms beyond the world we know. She has authored seventeen books, a hardbound collection of short stories, and numerous contributions to fantasy and science fiction anthologies. Novels and stories have been translated worldwide, with most editions in the U.S. and abroad bearing her own jacket and interior art.

THE WIZARD'S RAT WAS missing. At least yesterday Taffire had worn a rat's shape. He did that on days when he meant to cause mischief. Or else when his master dropped items that rolled into the cob-web-choked crannies beneath the tower room's furniture. Usually the runt wyvern looked like a large cat, asleep in the library's sunwashed window seat.

But this morning there was no cat to be found, and no wee, slinking rat trying to pilfer cheese from the pantry.

For an hour the Wizard poked through his things. Toppled books out of cupboards, dumped crocks of quill pens, and riffled through drawers jammed with packets of sea salt and cured toadstools stuffed into bottles. He rattled the shelves with their jars of lizard bones, grumbling and cursing the bother. He had always been a poor housekeeper. The clouds of raised dust left stirred in his wake folded him double with sneezes. He moped for the indignity. The Wizard was *never* accustomed to searching for anything that was lost.

That singular misery was Taffire's job, and now the irritating creature seemed to have misplaced himself.

"Runt wyverns!" the Wizard harrumphed, slit eyes watering.

A fool nuisance, if out of malicious whimsy, Taffire had chosen to hide as a scuttling insect. The Wizard chased down a few suspect silverfish. He clapped three beetles under an upended bowl—they proved innocent— then inspected the foraging ants that dismantled the crumbs on his unwashed plates. For all of his prodding, and through fifteen different spells of unmasking, they kept their six legs and antennae.

None proved to be Taffire.

"Idiot Wyrm!" huffed the Wizard, flopping down in a chair. He eased his narrow feet on a cushion. There he pondered, perplexed, tugging snags from his beard. How did one search for a finder who'd vanished? A dratted problem, since such drake born talent was fed and kept housed to resolve such mistakes in the first place! The Wizard lamented his plight, discontent. His morning tea had gone cold in his cup, with nothing left but to wait till his skinny apprentice woke herself up.

"Broomshanks!" he barked, as the unkempt girl stumbled in, yawning and rubbing puffed eyes. "Taffire's hiding, or stolen, or lost. Before breakfast, your task is to find him!"

"But he could be anywhere, *anything*!" Broomshanks protested, dismayed. Never mind the bad turn, that she and the runt wyvern had never gotten along. She had scars on her ankles. Countless marks left by nips, scalds, and blisters, for each of the times she had carelessly stepped on his tail. "Why not use your mighty spell of 'come hither'?"

The Wizard frowned. "I tried that already. It brought no results." He had spider silk stuck to his cuffs, and sore knees from groping beneath the lion claw legs of the armoires. That, and the strayed brace of dried toads' feet snagged in his hem, left him grumpy. "You can start," he told Broomshanks, "by sweeping and cleaning this tower from top to bottom!"

The apprentice scowled. She *had* let the dirty dishes pile up. Unwashed pots, fusty laundry, and dust mice went flying as she set to work at the wizard's request. No shadowed cranny would be overlooked. Wherever a shape-shifting wyvern might lurk, she'd scour him out, or chase him to light with her dust rag.

And so she would have, had Taffire been hiding, or playing a prank with his usual caprice. In fact, standing guard through the past moonless night, the small wyvern had singed a trespassing imp. The demonly thing had tried to break in with determined intent to steal valuables. Taffire had smoked it out by the bookcase and sent it off squalling, a scorched tail streaming sparks from its flaming rump. His intervention had foiled the malicious invasion, but not without a baleful mishap. The imp had struck back with a spell, as he chased it. When the sun rose, Taffire did not cast a shadow: every beautiful, glittering scale, claw, and wing had become invisible.

However he roared and spat flame, nothing burned. No one heard him. When he tried biting ankles to draw Broomshanks's attention, his jaws closed without causing harm. Beyond simply vanished, he was also in limbo, unable to make himself known to cry foul, or warn that an imp had fixed a plaguing curse on a wizard's familiar.

Tired of dodging furniture, dust cloths, and wet mops, Taffire crouched, curled up on a rafter, fuming over his horrid predicament. No one noticed the brimstone smell of his breath. His angry sparks scoured no holes in the carpet. All day Broomshanks cleaned, beat the blankets, and scrubbed pots, while the Wizard bungled most of his spells, not having a faithful finder at hand to track down his mislaid ingredients.

Worse, after sundown, the imp came back. It had wheedled a djinn to avenge its blistered tail, and since Taffire had tired himself sulking, the burgling pair clapped his sleeping form into a sack, along with a spell book most enviously coveted by the imp's master. Tied up and bagged, the runt wyvern was dragged along with the loot through the crack in the earth to the Netherworld. There, he found himself locked in a windowless cell with a half-dozen captive ghosts.

The imp flaunted his singed rump and laughed, while the djinn remarked with smug glee that the unredeemed shades at least had the substance of smoke, and were the more likely to win their release.

Taffire settled his chin on crossed talons, dejected enough to think that he might be abandoned to rot for eternity.

And so he may have, except for the smallest of truths: that imps are not neat, and that djinns possess execrable manners as unwanted visitors. The former, unwisely, had spat in contempt on the wizard's rug. Its brute-fisted henchman also left marks where its claws had gouged open the sash on the window frame. Broomshanks noticed these offensive details as she completed her cleaning.

"Look here," she snapped, her nose wrinkled over the sulfurous gob on the carpet. The same brimstone reek wafted off the scraped wood and the splinters raked up in her dustpan. "I think we've had an intruder from hell. Supposing that volume of spells that's gone missing wasn't ever mislaid?"

The Wizard bestirred himself from his armchair. He scratched his white head, frowned over his stained rug, then examined the marks carved into his casement molding. Outside he discovered some ripped fronds of ivy, then the muddy footprints the thieving culprits had tromped through the rows in his garden.

"Dear me," he told Broomshanks. "I fear you're right."

Since his finder was missing, he sat down forthwith, and set about conjuring remedies.

Later that day the stolen book sprouted legs. It clapped itself shut, stumped about on the desk where the imp's master stacked his ill-gotten goods, with the black grimoires kept at hand for quick reference. The book blundered a bit, dodging skulls used as candlesticks, until, being eyeless, it tripped and fell in a heap on the floor. The imp heard the noise, but reacted too late. It pounced once, missed, and banged its head on a chair strut. While it lay moaning, the terrified spell book took to its heels and scuttled into the shadows.

For all of the lore written down in its pages, the book could not think for itself. Since it held no power to enact transformations, or escape from the deeps of the Netherworld, it crept into a cranny and cowered while the imp's horned master flew into a rage.

Lest fur should fly, and impish heads roll, the djinn originally charged with the theft was called onto the devil's carpet. There it squirmed and sweated through desperate excuses, until Taffire could be collected and collared in chain, and hauled from the cell in the dungeon.

The djinn presented the runt wyvern to its overlord and bowed, its chinless jaw scraping the rug. "An invisible gift, Master, with a proven talent for finding the Wizard's mislaid belongings. Taffire here can be made to recover that strayed book of spellcraft in no time."

"No chance of that!" Taffire denounced, tart. "I can't find an earthly *thing* in this state. The book you've misplaced won't see me, or hear me, or come when it's called, as long as I'm witched into limbo."

The imp howled with laughter, caught a glare from its master, then snapped straight in poker-faced terror. It unbound its punitive spellcraft, then sneered, "Wretched, undersize spitfire! Cower at once and mind your new keeper."

Since the Lord of the Netherworld was massive and cruel, and more unfortunately, flameproof, Taffire clamped his teeth, curbed his rebellious spirit, and folded his wing vanes in studied reproof. "You've scared that book, badly. It might be days before it calms down! If you want me to find it, I must be alone to coax it to speak, or come out."

"Until midnight, then," boomed the Prince of All Evil. "You'll be granted that time, and no more. Have that errant book back in my hands, or be thrown into the pits for amusement. My ravening, tormented demons will relish the favor of tearing your carcass into a morsel!"

With that, imp and djinn were whisked off with a bang, gone along with their horned master's departing thunderclap. As promised, Taffire was left on his own to chase down the Wizard's book.

First things first: the runt wyvern inspected his glittering scales. When he found them undamaged, he snuffed out a candle and ate one of the skulls, as its manic grin suggested it might be spying. No other fare to be scrounged in hell's dungeon suited a carnivore's fancy. Taffire burped, settled back, and picked a splinter of bone from his teeth. Then, his golden eyes slitted, he snapped, "No games! Crawl out now, since I know where you're hiding."

The book huffed from its nook, wedged under a gargoyle. "Fetch me out yourself." The legs it had grown on the desktop were gone, since the Wizard's spells of command always dissolved after sundown. "Then if you're kind, you will burn me before letting my knowledge fall into bad hands."

"I won't risk any flames," Taffire said, miffed. The snack just consumed had not eased his pique. Neither did he wish to become the ripped meal for a horde of starved demons. A puckish runt wyvern with limited wits saw no pleasant way out of his fix. As fires made smoke and caused troublesome notice, Taffire seized on the easiest remedy. He decided to eat the book's pages.

"You can't be serious!" the book squeaked.

Its protest proved useless. Taffire stalked it, then hooked it out of its hidey-hole with small but needle-sharp talons. Confronted next by an agile forked tongue, still flicking crushed bits of bone from a gleaming array of white teeth, the book reasoned, "How can the Wizard recover his property if my pages are chewed into shreds and digested?"

Taffire looked disgruntled. His busy tongue paused between polishing fangs. He didn't relish the thought that a spell of recovery might be invoked to empty his stomach. The wyvern belched up the sour aftertaste of candle wax and skull; the very idea caused severe indigestion. After all, the book was a friend, sheltered under the Wizard's protection.

"Have you got any better suggestion?" the wyvern inquired at length.

Since the book could not access the lore in its pages, it sighed. "I have not. But let's limit the damage. Suppose you consume only the worst spells? Hide nothing more than the secrets that break the strictures of common sense."

Taffire snorted a tendril of steam. "I don't know common sense from a skull with a smirk! I find lost things. It's up to the wise to maintain their guard to defend them."

"What is wisdom?" the book asked, ruffling its pages. "Can such as we even fathom the concept?"

Taffire blinked. He considered his tail. Wistfully apprehensive, he admired the shine on his scales that winked every color of the rainbow. As he was loathe to damage their shimmering beauty, he lamented, "Wisdom is knowing how not to cause hurt." Case in point, he added, "It's scarcely a guess that the Netherworld's master won't care. In this place, your rare pages will never be used to help anyone else escape suffering." Far less, Taffire realized, a misfortunate runt wyvern about to be thrown to the desperate hunger that fed off itself in the pits.

Morose, the book was inclined to agree. It feared for its own future prospects. Therefore it yielded its most perilous knowledge for Taffire to chew up and swallow.

The wyvern ate the supreme spell for provoking ill fortune, and another for destroying self-confidence. Dauntless he downed a cantrip to wreak havoc, then another, to bring longstanding alliances to ruin. These were followed by dozens of recipes for subtle poisons. Then another page, blackened with fingerprints, and another, too worn with handling not to be suspect for its rows of uncanny blank lines. Taffire ripped through more passages scrawled in a tongue only scholars remembered. The text surely cataloged distress and harm; at least the torn parchment went down like cold wind. Its nasty bitterness coated his tongue like stranded frogs baked to glue in hot sunlight.

The spell Taffire gobbled to chase *that* ugliness down was the same curse of invisibility the thieving imp had purloined to thwart him.

Disaster was immediate. Taffire vanished. Since this time the page from the book was to blame, the spell's countermeasure became lost into limbo along with the shreds in his belly.

Taffire gagged. Choked cross-eyed, he blew smoke and retched until he hawked up a stuck shred of parchment. The enchantment relented, perhaps, just a fraction. The wyvern wrinkled his snout, appalled by the stink of enchantment left on his breath. Invisible he remained, but not quite in limbo: the repeat fumes from his unsavory meal formed a noxious cloud, which distressed the locked chain on his neck. The steel trembled, and then started writhing. Animate metal sprouted black scales. The cuff that circled Taffire's throat transformed into a snake's head, which spat out its mouthful of spiked wyvern ruff and hissed like an overwrought steam kettle. Its ruckus continued as the rest of the links succumbed to the strayed bit of sorcery. The indignant length unwound itself next, until a fully enchanted serpent slithered onto the carpet.

"Oh dear," moaned the book, left open and mangled and cowering on the desktop. "You've let a bad fragment of spellcraft escape. The backlash is bound to be dangerous."

Taffire did not answer. Or if he did, nothing else in the

Netherworld heard him. Even the spying collection of skulls kept their changelessly toothful expressions.

The snake flicked its tongue, gave a last, annoyed hiss, then meandered away and coiled itself up for a torpid rest in a cranny. There it subsided back into its original state: a dropped snarl of chain that no longer contained the botched form of the Wizard's prized finder.

"Taffire," the book quavered. "Surely you're still here? You'd better have a clever idea to rescue us from oblivion."

No sound from the wyvern. Nothing but look-alike leers from the skulls, whose candle flames guttered and smoked. The book languished, abandoned to hopeless dread, until a rattle arose from the door lock. The hapless tome flipped itself shut in a panic as the panel groaned on its hinges.

"Taffire?" it whispered.

Nothing answered. Instead the door blasted open to an ear splitting squeal of iron hinges. A djinn with a murderous glower stalked in and yelled with distempered impatience, "Where's that slinking wyvern, and how did it manage to slip through my magical collar and chain?"

As the book had no answer, the djinn began poking in corners. Its thick muscles bulged as it heaved aside the array of grotesquely carved furnishings. Varnish chips flew from rough handling. Dust billowed in clouds.

The djinn's steady curses almost obscured a reptilian sneeze from the shadows. The explosion was followed by a half-strangled belch and a whiff like the breeze off a compost heap.

The djinn snarled, surprised, a stone vase and a lamp stand clamped in arrested clawed fists. "What in the Netherworld's deeps is that *smell*?" It ditched the vase and swiped the lamp shade to and fro in a furious effort to disperse the creeping stench.

The object grazed against something unseen. A wyvern scale shot out of thin air and fell, opalescently winking.

"Wretched Wyrm!" The djinn pounced. Its punitive grip trapped something living and squeezed, but too late. The gaseous spell shred had energized.

The hapless djinn became a fat frog that hopped about, whining for kisses.

Its invisible quarry chose not to take pause. A sharp breeze whiffled past. The stunned book found itself snatched from the desk, then hauled off toward the gaping doorway.

"Taffire!" it gasped, urgent, "you can't think you'll walk out of the devil's own dungeon with nobody else being the wiser!"

Already the rumble of pounding feet descended the stairwell beyond. Taffire chose to bolt upward, regardless. His invisible claws scrabbled over worn stone as he leaped the steps three at a stride. As the book did not share the masking spell's cover, it subsided, resigned to its fate. The end, when it came, was not going to be pretty. Five djinns and two imps sprinted downward to take them, shoving and falling all over themselves to be first to recover the prisoners.

No wyvern's mad dash could slip through the legs of such vengeful brutes, sent to collar him. Except the disparate sorceries in the runt creature's belly now curdled from the exertion. Taffire hiccupped. More ejected wisps of spellcraft emerged, recombined, and transposed to inflict random mayhem. The book recognized two clauses for ruin, then a forceful phrase to seed misdirection. The result made the masonry walls groan and twist with the rumbles that presaged an earthquake. Solid walls sprouted multiple spiraling corridors with the contorted dead-ends of a maze.

Taffire ducked left, while the imps and the pack of bloodthirsty djinn scattered howling and got themselves lost.

"This shouldn't be happening," the book said, distressed. "Such spells shouldn't mix. Anything could go wrong! Terrible befoulments and distortions of nature, and we're beyond reach of the Wizard's knowledge of counter spells."

Taffire wheezed, breathless, and hiccupped again. Nausea twisted him double. The book pinched in his claws bemoaned its distress, while the indiscriminate stew of downed spells brewed up more griping havoc in the wyvern's belly.

"Dear me, perhaps we should have left out the recipes for subtle poisoning. Taffire, please! If you're going to be sick, it would be for the best if you tried to heave your guts quietly."

The runt wyvern thumped the book down in the passage. Sparks of agony shot from his nostrils. His pitiful groans could not help but attract the next horde of spiteful enemies. Perhaps worse than the threat of the bottomless pit, the belches and burps of draconian indigestion unleashed still more dastardly chains of invention.

The teeth-gnashing djinn, hand-picked for ferocity, broke off their snarling pursuit. Their gravel voices burst into a soulful lament, with a warbling counterpoint screeched by the imps quavering in two-part disharmony. The book winced. Apparently the embarrassing bits of a lover's charm had entangled with an incantation aligned for ill fortune.

"This isn't funny," it insisted, upset, while the maze bounced with echoes of mangling noise that were sure to have punitive consequences. "This is the *Netherworld*! Strict rules against singing are going to fetch the horned prince down here in a temper!"

Taffire stirred. Grumbling under his fiery breath, he scooped up the book, spread his vaned wings, and tried flying.

Invisible but for the petrified book, the runt wyvern sailed up the misshapen stairwell. He twisted and soared and shortly emerged through a vent in a volcanic mountain. Below spread a lake filled with boiling magma. The heat was oppressive. Taffire battled his dyspeptic vertigo. Wrenched by sharp winds and bedeviled by updrafts, he floundered, forced into an unbalanced landing. The book stayed unscathed, clutched tight as the wyvern tumbled, tail over snout, bundled up in his own furled wing leather.

He uncurled, a bit scraped, for the most part undamaged, except for the bit of catastrophe spell shaken loose by the jolt upon impact. Taffire burped. A sealed conjury hissed between his gaped teeth. Shortly a tempest formed overhead. Icy gusts lashed the sulfurous airs of the Netherworld, then whipped up black clouds and a downpour. Steam and fog intermingled. The lava lake froze, and the balefires that harrowed the suffering damned extinguished to sopped ash and cinders.

Which gift of mercy was not going to please the cruel streak of the Netherworld's master. Through the pounding roar of the downpour, cheering and prayers soon replaced the unending chorus of screaming. The wild celebration of dancing and joy all but rivaled the paean that greeted the dawn of creation.

"Run!" snapped the book. "If we don't get away, or find someplace to hide, we'll be destroyed, or else buried until we're wiped out of remembered existence!"

Taffire scrambled erect upon unsteady haunches. No longer invisible but tinged sickly green, he recovered the panicky book. Harried by a whipped blizzard of snowflakes, he gathered his stumbling balance to flee.

Too late: the horned prince himself had arrived to

redress his disrupted regime. He snatched for the book,
tore it free of tight claws, then seized the cringing
wyvern. "You!" he bellowed through glistening bared
fangs. "Just look at the damage you've caused me! The
work of eternity, wrecked in a day! Hell's cooling off,
and all my trapped souls are happy enough to find ec-
stasy! If they keep such good spirits, they're bound to re-
pent! Then a legion of angels will invade my domain to
answer their pleas for forgiveness."

Taffire grunted, dangled by his scruff. His belly
churned and a leaked snip of bane spell raised a pustule
on the horny red fist that imprisoned him.

"Damn you both to perdition!" The devil stared, in-
candescent with shock at the blemish that upset his van-
ity. He did not loose his grip, but hastened his promise to
hurl the offenders into the bottomless pit.

"We're lost," sniveled the book. "It's all your fault,
Taffire!" With all its dangerous pages torn out, it had no
more worth than a commonplace herbal. "Spells that
should be secret are unleashed in hell and our miserable
lives will end in torment for the sake of your lamebrained
misjudgment."

Taffire had no hopeful remedy to offer, beyond changing his form to a rat. Perhaps as a rodent afflicted with
mange, he might spoil the appetite of the pit's demons.
Yet the strategy backfired, as his load of ingested pages
could not fit in a tinier stomach. Poised at the cavernous
lip of the pit, about to be cast to oblivion, he spewed. A
shredded stew of parchment and bile splashed over the
devil's furred shins and cleft hooves.

The Lord of the Netherworld absorbed the raw dregs
of six dozen forms of ill practice. Bone, flesh, and mus-
cle dissolved to raw slime, and dropped him at a loss on
his fundament. His bellow of fury shattered rocks and
cracked chains, and sprung the locks on tight barriers and

fences. Djinn and wardens were bowled over, and in the stampede, more of the damned escaped. While the Master scrabbled back from the pit to evade the vicious teeth of his own demons, Taffire, the book, and the splashed detritus of puked spells were released in a heap on the brink.

The jarring fall knocked the wind out of Taffire. Nauseous, rat-shaped, he coughed and disgorged the last spell morsel wedged in his gullet. A spitball of parchment, mottled with ink, shot into the bottomless pit. The slavering creatures imprisoned below trampled to snap up the offering. They fought, piled up, and wrestled each other to be first to devour the gobbet. The encounter changed several of them into pixies. The rest were left at a glassy-eyed loss, grazing blooms off an outbreak of daisies.

"Hellfire itself!" screamed the Prince of All Darkness. "*Just look at this mess!* You've despoiled my foul reputation!"

While his imps sang hosannas, and his torturers grinned, transfixed by the sight of their navels, he dragged his footless frame up to the book and flipped through its mangled pages. "Counter spells, now!" he shouted, enraged. "You'll restore my preferred state of chaos. Or else—"

"Or else what?" said the book. "All your werewolves and beasts, your vampires and djinn have succumbed to abnormal behavior. As you see, the runt wyvern was most indiscriminate. He devoured the remedies along with the spells, and nobody else but the wise have the knowledge to unscramble the contents."

The Lord of the Netherworld blasphemed aloud. He ranted with impotent fury. Taffire watched, in the shape of a rat, while the book, in smug tones, decreed the best chance of recovery lay with the Wizard.

"You'll need his learned help," it added, succinct,

"before your lava lakes harden to granite and start sprouting mosses."

The Lord of the Netherworld howled in vain. He pounded his infected fist. The tantrum did nothing but burst the tight boil. Splashed by an eruption of baneful pus, he watched, dismayed, as the enchanted corruption spread an itching rash down to his crotch. Now fearful his crippled state could get worse, he shot out a hand and snagged the rat's tail in clawed fingers.

"You misbegotten little pest!" The devil dangled his catch upside down and bellowed his ultimatum. "Fetch your Wizard down here to clean up your loose ends and restore the blight on my record!"

"Done!" Taffire said, and recovered enough spite to land a twisting nip on the knuckles that pinned him.

He dropped free, while his finder's summons was allowed to ring out and slice past the gates of the Netherworld. The result called the Wizard in a shower of flame straight into the heart of disaster.

The old man blinked once, stared about with bright interest, then chuckled with helpless glee. "Once in a blue moon, or when hell freezes over . . . a lot of bad bargains have come due, today. What else could go wrong in your kingdom?"

"It's your doing!" the luckless devil lashed back. "Your unruly belongings put me in this fix! I demand compensation! A full accounting for all redeemed souls, and a record of debt to square the damage to my satisfaction."

"For lost goods?" The Wizard snorted, unsympathetic. "Finder's keepers. If you're seeking for order to sort out the book's counter spells, I teach only qualified apprentices. The ones I take on must be caring and trustworthy and proven to be of good character." He glanced down his nose, poised a moment in thought. "I'll consider, if you have a candidate."

The Lord of the Netherworld glared back at a loss. "*Here?* I'm a tyrant! My subjects thrive upon fear, hate, and ruin, and my legions serve for their addictive lust to inflict cruelty. The djinn are rank liars, and no imp alive volunteers for obedience!"

The Wizard raised his eyebrows, alive with amusement. "In that case," he concluded, "you're screwed!"

He retrieved his defaced book, shoved the rat in his pocket, and walked away bursting with laughter.

IS THIS REAL ENOUGH

Lisanne Norman

Long time gamer and role-player, as well as historical reenactor, Lisanne finds real-life experiences very useful in her writing. Recently she relocated to the U.S.A., and is currently working on the eighth book in her Sholan Alliance series, called *Shades of Gray* from DAW Books.

"For Robin and Maria, the real Tekkel and Zenithia."

AZIEL STOOD, HANDS ON hips, looking at the pair of charred shoes twenty yards away. "That's it?" he demanded, a faint plume of smoke curling upward from each nostril. "That's the best those damned mages have? Last night's supper put up more of a fight!"

"It's only been ten years, Master," whined the small hunched figure at his side. "Not even a generation since the last one tried to bind you. Needs time till one emerges as leader among them."

"Leader?" snorted Aziel. "That wasn't a leader! Lately

they send thieves and adventurers through the veil to steal and spy on us," he said in disgust, stepping over the chalk circle that surrounded them and walking toward to the smaller one in the middle of the cavern floor. "He didn't even know my name! Standards are falling when this is the best that Sondherst can send against me!"

"He got the circles right, Master." The servant limped hastily past him, anxious to reach the distant markings first. "See, two lines with the runes written between them," he said frantically, trying to improve his master's temper. Lurching down onto his haunches, Twilby pointed to where the inner chalk ring had been scuffed open and one still-smoldering shoe lay on its side.

"And broke it when he saw me begin to materialize in my true form!" snapped Aziel. "What kind of mage is that? He Summoned me, yet he didn't even know my name or my form!" Stopping beside Twilby, he peered down at the arcane symbols. He needed to know which summoning spell the mage had used for that was the key to returning to his own world. The glow cast by the horn lantern the late mage had brought with him illuminated the writing just enough for him to read it. Frowning, he studied the chalk symbols, but the writing was erratic and smudged, especially where the circle had been broken. A glint of metal caught his eye briefly; he dismissed it, knowing it was only the molten remains of the amulet the mage had brought with him in the hope of binding him to it.

After a moment or two he became aware that Twilby had stopped poking nervously at the shoe and was now flicking it around with an outstretched claw tip so the vacant top was facing him.

He aimed a kick at his minion, his boot connecting hard with the other's loincloth-covered rump. Twilby shrieked in pain and went sprawling on his side, the charred shoe forgotten as he clutched at his rear end, massaging the stump of a tail that protruded from his grubby rags.

"Sometimes you disgust even me," snarled Aziel. "You'd eat anything, wouldn't you? You're vermin, not fit to be allowed out of the yard!" It had been his ill-fortune to be chastising one of his lesser drudges when he'd been Summoned to this realm.

"Only looking, Master," Twilby whimpered, wiping his streaming eyes on his forearm as he scrambled farther from his master. "Looking isn't eating. Sondherst flesh is tasty. Don't get it often. Usually you give me leftovers."

"That isn't leftovers," snapped Aziel, sending the offending shoe into a dark corner with another swipe of his foot. "It's carrion! Have you forgotten where we are? The other side of the damned dimensional veil, that's where! He may have had companions with him."

Twilby stopped whining and peered fearfully around the dim cavern before scuttling hurriedly back to Aziel's side.

"Companions, like me, Master? What we do?" he whispered, pawing at the Demon Lord's robe.

With a snort of distaste, Aziel flicked his clothing aside and, lifting his other hand, held it before him. A faint golden glow began to materialize in his palm. As it solidified, it rose upward, forming a small ball of light that intensified, pushing the shadows back to the farthest reaches of the chamber.

The hollowed-out cavern was natural, and not as large as he'd first thought—the roof was a mere thirty feet above him. Scanning the walls, he saw the carved steps almost immediately.

Leaving the globe of light hanging in midair, he strode over toward them. "Follow me," he ordered. "And not a sound!"

He took the stairs three at a time, glad that the late

mage's inept Summoning hadn't forced him to complete
the change from the humanoid form he'd assumed earlier
in the day. In a cavern this size, to be his own natural
shape would have been, to say the least, inconvenient.
Thankfully, no matter what his outward form, he lost
none of his abilities. Enhanced normal senses, plus his in-
nate awareness of and ability to use magic were all that
stood between his kind and the predatory Sondherstian
mages' desire for power.

The steps spiraled steeply to his left. Ahead he could
see a crack of light, like that at the bottom of an ill-fitting
door. Slowing down, he took the remaining steps one at a
time, head turning this way, then that as he checked the
air for any other scents. All that lingered was the stale
smell of the mage he'd vaporized. Placing his back to the
rock face, he reached for the latch on the rough wooden
door, lifting it gently before easing the door open.

Lit only by flickering candles, the interior of the room
was dim and slightly hazy, the air redolent with the stink
of stale sweat and cheap tallow. He wrinkled his nose
with distaste. The smell was offensive to one as discern-
ing as him. Pushing the door wider, he eased himself cautiously inside.

The room was empty. Small and cramped, as well as
noisesome, only one door led out of it. On his left, a small
window, hidden behind a rickety shutter, was the cause of
the guttering candles. In front of him stood a table,
scratched and dull with age, its surface cluttered with
books and papers; behind it, a chair, its padding so
threadbare the original color was no longer discernable.
As he stepped farther into the room and looked behind
him, he saw a similarly ancient sofa bearing a rumpled
thin rug and almost thinner pillow. These comprised the
mage's meager furnishings.

Almost empty bookshelves lined the remainder of the

room save for where a grate of cold ashes stood, its fire obviously a distant memory. Only half a dozen tattered ancient books remained, stacked haphazardly against each other, except for the one on the desk. Sniffing again, he detected the aroma of magic from it: it would have to wait. Despite the lack of other scents, he needed to know that he was safe first.

"Curious," murmured Aziel as he walked silently across the stained wooden floor to the exit door. Living in such obvious poverty was unusual for a mage, and a hedge-wizard wouldn't have the power or knowledge, let alone the skills, to summon a Demon Lord, even if he possessed a grimoire such as the one on the desk. But what would a hedge-wizard, or a mage, be doing living in a dank cave backing onto a mountain cavern? Hedge-wizards were itinerants, earning their living by traveling the roads from village to village and performing what amounted to tricks. A very few actually had the ability to use real magic, and then only because they were the illegitimate and unacknowledged sons of real mages.

Putting his ear to the door, he listened, sniffed, then opened it cautiously. A dark and empty corridor stretched ahead for some fifteen feet, ending this time at a stout door, obviously the main entrance.

"Twilby, go check out the rest of this place," he ordered, losing interest and shutting the door. "There's another couple of rooms off the corridor out there." Whatever the history of its late occupant, he was in no danger now—the mage, if mage he had been—had obviously lived alone.

Returning to the desk, he slid behind it, lowering his muscular frame into the ancient chair, remembering before he did to adjust his weight. Pulling the book closer, he studied the open pages.

"Is dangerous, Master," whined Twilby from where he

still hesitated in the doorway from the cavern. "Cannot defend myself if anyone there! Change me, Master. Make me more than I am."

Aziel looked up at the pathetic figure of the drudge. "You want to be more than you are?" he asked softly, his rugged features creasing in thought, as his piercing red eyes scanned the deformed scrawny frame. "Be very careful what you ask for, Twilby. I may just give you it." The drudge's petulant voice was beginning to grate.

"Afraid, Master. Not strong like you. Not able to change self into form better for intimidating others."

Aziel raised his hand, pointed at Twilby, and muttered a short phrase in his own guttural language. A faint glow surrounded the servant, then his body appeared to stretch before suddenly shrinking.

Twilby's mouth opened in a soundless shriek of terror and pain as a mass of sharp hairy bristles forced themselves through the surface of his skin, growing longer and longer before finally softening and lying flat against his now elongated back. The stubby tail lengthened, acquiring a life of its own as it whipped from side to side in panic. His features, not comely to begin with, were forced outward into a muzzle as long whiskers sprouted from either side of his tiny nose.

The transformation complete, the rat collapsed squealing to the ground, sides heaving in terror as it gasped for breath.

Indifferent to the other's suffering, Aziel had turned his attention back to the book. "Go. You have a shape to strike fear into the hearts of others, one more suited to your nature, just as you requested."

The grimoire was open at an invocation spell, one meant to call and bind one of the lesser demons. So how had this—magic user—managed to summon him, Lord of the Eight Realms, Aziel wondered? What part of the ritual had the hedge-wizard changed?

He pushed the book aside. He'd no need of it now, he already knew the reverse spell. What he did need were the dratted mage's notes. Without knowing the runes, he couldn't return through the veil. Surely he'd scribbled them on some piece of parchment to take down to the cavern. Unless, in killing the mage, he'd destroyed the only record of them? Aziel sighed, his breath turning the edges of the open pages brown. Noticing the faint curl of smoke, he shut the book hastily with a thump.

Methodically, he began to search through the pile of papers on the desk, examining each one in the hope it was what he needed. It wasn't as simple as just substituting a more advanced spell, he needed a list of the actual runes and their positions relevant to each other within the two lines of the circle.

Frustrated he yanked open the top drawer, then stopped, gazing down at the small crystal orb within. Now this was a find, and almost worth the aggravation that the Summoning had caused him. But just what was a Seeing Crystal doing in the midst of such obvious poverty?

A Summoning meant that there was a task to be done, one that required more power and magical ability than the mage had possessed. What would someone as poor as this mage obviously was want done so badly that he'd risk summoning any demon?

Aziel picked up the crystal and held it in the palm of his hand. Not a large one, to be sure, only some four inches in diameter, but it was large enough for anyone with very shallow pockets. Then he noticed what lay below it—a letter.

Lifting it from the drawer, one-handedly he flicked it open. The faded ink made the words difficult to read. Obviously it wasn't new, but to be placed under the crystal it had to be a letter of some significance. Sweeping the scattered papers onto the floor, he put the globe down carefully in the center of the desk. Spreading the letter out, he began to study it.

It took him several minutes to decipher the crabbed writing. It was from The Acquirers and Facilitators Guild in Eldaglast, asking the wizard, named, he discovered, Banray, to help them locate their next Guild Master. The fee offered was an amount that was guaranteed to tempt one so poor to risk everything—but nowhere near what a competent mage would cost.

He frowned, then the corners of his mouth began to lift slightly. So they were looking to replace the leader he'd slain several months ago, were they? More fools they for being so cheap that they hired an inept hedge-wizard.

A tiny squeak made him look up sharply. Twilby had returned and was sitting up on his haunches not far from the desk.

The drudge's voice was thin and high pitched in his rat body. "Master, the place is empty."

Aziel nodded and returned to his perusal of the letter.

"Writing on the other side," said Twilby nervously.

"What?" Aziel turned the letter over. There, hastily scribbled on the back, was a rough diagram of both chalk circles—complete with runes. He had the means to get home—and a means to relieve his boredom.

With a gesture toward his rat-shaped minion, he turned his attention back to the crystal. "Come here. I have need of you."

A minute later, still whimpering with the pain of the second transformation, Twilby was crouched at his side.

"Show me the most unlikely successor for the Guild," he commanded of the crystal, cupping it in both hands and staring into its depths. "I will ensure that he shall be their leader!"

He watched the swirling shapes solidify into a scene, then Aziel's mouth widened into what, for him, approximated a smile, secure in the knowledge that no one could have dreamed that across the gulf of space, a mind as immeasurably old and devious as his regarded them with curious eyes, and slowly and surely drew his plans.

HELL'S BARROW

"Buffs!" yelled Hurga from his position to the rear of the small group of warriors. "Now, or ye'll have to let the Cleric heal ye!"

"I hear you!" said Tekkel, cranking his arm back to deliver a powered blow with his long-bladed knife at the animated mage's corpse. As he did, three arrows, in rapid succession, whistled between him and Davon, narrowly missing his right ear, adding to the dozen or so already embedded in the wight's flesh. "Doing my best, but this bastard just won't go down!" He was already toiling, having taken several small injuries as they'd fought their way through to the main chamber.

"Watch it, Jinna!" Davon snarled, glaring back at the small female standing beside Hurga. "We don't need friendly fire."

The zombie uttered yet another howl of rage and pain as it lurched toward Tekkel, its dead skeletal hands groping and slashing at him. He dove to one side, barely avoiding the razor-sharp poisoned claws.

"Mirri, stun-shoot him, in the name of the gods!" he yelled, doing a neat forward roll and coming up behind the monster. He took a moment to glance around the rest of his party. "Zenithia, back off! You're a Damage Dealer, you can't take damage! Use a spell!"

"But I like hitting them and making them bleed."
Zenithia smiled sweetly. "Spells are so . . . impersonal."

"Just do it, before—"

She let out a low cry of pain as the zombie's left hand
managed to scratch her arm. It was only a glancing blow,
but it was enough.

Almost instantly he heard the sounds of the rest of the
group charging up their weapons' special attacks.

Shannar's arrows arched overhead, most of them spent
as they were brushed aside by the wight.

"Back, sister!" yelled Mirri, letting off another fusil-
lade of arrows that thudded into their target with dull
thumps. The animated corpse of the dead mage Tallus
staggered briefly, then froze as if rooted to the spot.

"I'm ending this now," muttered Tekkel, throwing
aside his shield and pulling his second dagger. Powering
up their special abilities, he flung himself at the zombie,
knives flashing as he sacrificed accuracy and personal
protection to double the damage with his Assassin skills.

With a low growl of anger, Zenithia's sword began
rapidly sketching arcane symbols in the air, then she
began to cast, her body straightening and standing on tiptoe as she uttered the guttural words of power.

"Heal yourself," Tekkel ordered, continuing to hack
away at the unmoving decaying corpse. Thank the Gods of
Sondherst that Mirri's stun attack had worked, but time was
running out for Zenithia. His senses strained to the limit, he
heard Davon began to mutter a prayer to his diety and
silently thanked the Gods the Cleric was with them.

He glanced up at Zenithia again, seeing her beginning
to pale as the poison took hold. "Zen, heal yourself!" he
yelled, once again slashing at the exposed zombie's back.
"Davon! Cure her, dammit!"

Bits of decaying flesh were breaking off now, scatter-
ing in all directions around him as Zenithia completed her

incantation. A ball of fire suddenly materialized in front of her, hovered there for a moment before streaking across the few feet that separated her from the wight. It hit with a dull thwump, seeming to light the creature up momentarily from within, then flames erupted from it and he had to jump back to avoid being scorched himself.

"How dare he hit *me,* one of the Gray Brotherhood," she snarled, gathering her energy to cast again.

As Davon's final words rang out, a bolt of lightning flashed down from the Barrow's ceiling and struck the already blazing corpse. Galvanized into a parody of life again, it jerked like a puppet on strings as the flames became a raging inferno, then as three more of Mirri's arrows hit it, abruptly the flames went out and it collapsed in a smoking pile at Tekkel's feet.

Zenithia staggered, falling to her knees as Davon turned toward her and began praying again.

"I said *cure* her, Davon," Tekkel snarled, leaping over the corpse to run to the wounded elf's side. "There was no need for you to attack! We were on top of it then, dammit! Have you any antidotes left, Zen?" he demanded, catching hold of her as she swayed and would have fallen to the ground.

Davon ignored him, continuing to chant and draw holy symbols in the air. A golden nimbus began to gather around him.

"Ran out of them," muttered Zenithia, her voice so quiet his long ears instinctively twitched forward and he had to bend his head to hers to hear her.

"Tekkel, catch!" Hurga called out.

From the corner of his eye, Tekkel saw a flicker of green as a phial twisted through the air toward him. Reaching up, he caught it, instantly putting it in his mouth and grasping the cork in his teeth even as he braced himself to take the full weight of the almost unconscious dying elf woman. Davon's cure would be too late: he had to stop the poison now.

He was aware of Hurga's heavy footsteps running toward them, and the dwarf beginning to chant his own healing spell as the cork came suddenly free. Spitting it out, he hauled Zenithia around until her head sagged back against his arm. The acrid taste of the zombie antivenom on his lips made him shudder as he forced her pale ones apart and poured the noxious brew into her mouth. He held her close and still when she began to cough and push the phial away. Hurga's silver healing glow bathed her in its light for several seconds, then faded. Thanks to him, her color now began to slowly improve: her gray skin was regaining some of the normal blue tint, but there was still an unhealthy green cast to it.

"Drink it, Zen," he insisted, caching her hands in his free one and forcing the phial to her lips again. "Dammit, Davon! How many times do I have to tell you I need you to monitor the party's health?"

"Not my fault my Turn Undead failed," the other muttered angrily. "She was too close, she endangered herself!"

"We knew you couldn't turn this mob before we came," snapped Mirri, running over to join them, an arrow sill nocked on his bow and now aimed at the Cleric. "You risked my sister's life! That was a Boss, an Undead Mage. It was agreed you'd be primary healer and only fight when needed!"

Zenithia struggled to push Tekkel aside as another coughing fit overtook her. Twisting to avoid the edge of the sword she still grasped tightly, he relaxed his hold slightly but remained supporting her as the green of the poison slowly drained from her skin.

"Mirri, put that bow down now. Zen's going to be

okay." He locked eyes with the other elf until Mirri had lowered his bow and settled the arrow back in the quiver.

Davon had finished his prayer, and as he sketched the final segment of the holy symbol in the air, the glow around him began to shift, moving toward where Tekkel and Zenithia sat. The white light surrounded them both, bathing them in a sensation of warmth and well-being. Now he could see her complexion begin to return to its normal healthy shade of blue-gray. The glow faded, leaving him feeling energized again and his few wounds also healed.

"I'm well now," she said, taking a deep breath and pulling free of his hold completely.

Suppressing his desire to hold on to her, he sat back on his heels and picked up his knives. This was the closest he'd been to her yet, and slim though she might be, he'd almost felt the gentle curves that lurked beneath the showy half-revealing costume that passed for a female Gray Elf Battle Mage's armor. She was usually not as cold toward him as she was today, though. . . .

He pushed the rogue thoughts of her aside and turned to look at the dwarf, now standing, flanked by their archers beside them, guarding them against further danger.

"Thanks, Hurga. Davon, you neglected your responsibilities. You were almost too late," he said coldly, then turned back to Zenithia.

"He's right, though," he said, cursing himself for having to agree with the temperamental Cleric. "You took risks too, put us all in danger. We need to fight as a team to succeed."

"I told you when I joined that I was used to fighting only with my brother," she said, her tone cool as she got to her feet. "It takes time to . . . accept that others will do their job as well as we do. And then they let us down. I will never rely on Davon again."

"Don't be so damned arrogant," said Davon, taking a step toward her, his hand griping the shaft of his mace until his knuckles showed white.

"Don't threaten my sister," spat Mirri, suddenly lashing out at the Cleric with his knife.

Davon grunted in pain, his weapon hand opening by itself and dropping the mace to the ground with a loud clatter. He looked disbelievingly at the blood running down his knuckles.

"Stop right now," Tekkel commanded angrily, getting to his feet and stepping between the two males. Anger lent him the strength to push even the heavier human back. "I'll have no in-Clan fighting! You know the rules, abide by them. Both Davon and Zenithia were in the wrong for acting independently instead of as agreed. Take this fight to the arena if you must, but not here in Hell's Barrow when the zombies will return shortly!"

He stared at Davon until the large human slowly nodded, then turned to Mirri, the other Assassin.

Slim, and with the same blue-gray skin tones as he had, the white-haired elf before him had a sullen look on his face. It was easy now he stood beside his sister to see that they were twins. He frowned briefly, mind going off at a tangent, wondering why the slimness of their common race seemed more androgynous in them than it did in him. There was a definite femininity about them both that he, his black hair shot with highlights of dark purple, lacked.

Mirri's pale gaze slid away from his and he shrugged. "As you wish, but I'm still watching you, Human."

"Tekkel's right, lads, this is no time or place to be arguin'. Did ye get the token we came for, Tekkel?"

With a start, he remembered why they'd come here

and checked his inventory. "Yes, I got it, Hurga," he said with relief as he saw the parchment.

"Then let's leave this charnel house," said Jinna. "Where to now, Boss?"

"Who's using the portal scroll this time?" asked Shannar, checking over his arrows.

Tekkel relaxed a little and smiled despite himself. With Jinna, the young goblin lass, and Shannar, one of the light-skinned Forest Elves, he knew where he was. Longest-standing members of his Clan, they were always dependable, just like Hurga and Meare. . . .

"Where's Meare?" he asked, looking around the dimly lit main chamber of the Barrow.

"Doing what thieves usually do," grinned Jinna, slinging her short bow over her shoulder. "Turning over the corpses for loot."

"Meare! Get your thievin' ass over here!" yelled Hurga, picking up Tekkel's discarded shield and handing it back to him. " 'Less you want to be left here alone. . . .' "

"I'm here," said Meare, stepping out of the shadows. "Told you I'd been practicing my sneak skills," he grinned, tossing his head to throw an unruly lock of blond hair out of his eyes.

"Well, sneak a portal scroll out of your backpack," said Jinna, digging him in the thigh with her elbow. "It's your turn to use it."

"Ouch! You watch it, half-pint!" he said, rubbing his leg and glaring at the diminutive grinning sprite. "Your elbows are sharp! Where to, Boss?"

"The Witch's Cave in the Dendess Mountains. I need to give her this scroll and get the key into Iskahar Castle." He lengthened the shield's strap and slung it over his back.

A tingle ran down his spine as he felt a familiar rush of energy course through him. Around him, the world took on a faint bluish tinge. "Hurga, hold the buffs for now, please. We could all do with a short break at the Witch's Cave before going on."

"Good idea," agreed the dwarf. "I'm a mite peckish mysel' and could be doin' with a snack and a drink."

"Fifteen-minute break, then," Tekkel agreed. "We'll be safe in the Witch's Cave."

"And what does this gain you?" asked Zenithia as they waited for Meare to dig out his scroll.

He cast her a surprised glance. "I explained it to you when we met up yesterday. It's a quest to advance myself as your Clan Leader, and gain us the castle at Iskahar."

She stood silently, her face still, as if lost in thought.

Meare activated the scroll, calling up the portal. The air in front of him seemed to twist and bend, refracting the flickering lights cast by the guttering torches that lined the walls of the chamber. A low moaning, like that of a beast in agony, began, building in pitch as an oval glowing rip formed in the very fabric of their world. The pitch of the wind from the void through which they had to travel rose, sounding now like a banshee in full voice.

"That noise always sends shivers of fear through me," said Meare.

Jinna laughed, reaching up to take hold of the young light-skinned elf's hand where it lay clenched against the side of his thigh.

"Never fear, my brave boy! I, Jinna, the courageous goblin archer, will protect you!" she chuckled.

Meare snorted and looked down at her, but didn't remove his hand from hers. "Yeah, right. You and your empty quiver!"

"Mock me not, Elfling! All fear my potent arrow spells!"

"Pity you were out of arrows then!" he laughed.

"It's the multishots. They use 'em up at a fierce rate."

"I've plenty spare arrows, Jinna," said Shannar, hold-

ing out a large bundle toward her. "Got these from the Or-
cish archers I've been hunting these past few days."

"Thank you, Brother," she said, taking them from him
with her free hand and stuffing them into her empty
quiver. "Appreciate that."

Zenithia stirred, her brows meeting in a frown as she
regarded Tekkel. "Ah, yes. I remember now. We get benefits from owning a castle—when you kill the Lord."

"He'll kill the Lord, never fear, lass," said Hurga. "We
do it this way, like a Clan of Assassins should—through
stealth, not numbers."

"Aye, the other Clans may have more numbers than us,
but we beat them all in stealth," said Meare.

"I don't like this way of doing it," said Davon. "We
should do it face to face, in daylight, not use the shadows
and dark paths of magic to achieve our goal."

"Then time you be changin' your God, laddie," said
Hurga gruffly, stepping up to the portal. "You been with
us long enough to know how we work."

"And face the penalties? Easy for you to say. Your
magic doesn't come directly from your diety," Davon
snarled, pushing him aside to step through the portal first.

His departure left an ugly silence, during which the
others all glanced at each other, then at Tekkel.

He sighed. "Yeah, I know. I gotta do something about
him soon."

"Not soon, today, Tekkel," said Jinna seriously as she
and Meare stepped toward the portal. "He's gotten worse
since Zenithia and Mirri joined."

Tekkel chose to reply privately to the goblin woman.
"We need him, he's a useful member of Cabal."

*"He was . . . till our other Gray Elves joined. No one
person is more important than our Clan. Your words,
Tekkel."*

"I'll speak to him after I complete the quest," he promised.

"So what are these benefits to the Cabal Clan?" Zenithia asked as they waited for the other Clan members to enter the portal. As was customary, Tekkel would be last through and would see that the portal was sealed behind them.

"Well, we'll own the castle. That means while we hold it, we have access to the special rooms within it. A larger storehouse for a start, to store Clan goods in, and a crafting room that allows all of us the ability to put materials together to make personalized and more powerful weapons and armor."

"That sounds a fair reward for such a bold deed as we pursue," she said, smiling gently at him. "Do we all have the skills of the dwarves with metal and gems, and the goblins with their armor?"

He nodded, suddenly aware of the warmth of her body against his. "Um . . . yes," he said, trying to pull his scattered thoughts back to her question. She was leaning against him, and as he took on board yet another of her sudden mood changes, he began looking around for her brother while wondering if he dared risk putting an arm around her.

She laughed, the sound light and pleasant. "My brother's already gone before us. We're the last. Shall we go through this portal together, Tekkel?" she asked, taking hold of his arm.

"Yes indeed," he replied, risking placing his hand over hers as he led the way.

Taking the headset off and laying it carefully on the desk, Robin sat back in his chair with a sigh. On his computer screen the waterfall outside the Witch's Cave formed an almost romantic backdrop, and Tekkel and

Zenithia were still standing close, his hand clasped over hers as she held on to his arm. Around them the rest of his Clan sat or stood while their players took advantage of the break.

Again he wondered what her real name was. Unlike the others, she and her brother—if he was her brother— steadfastly refused to give any details about their real lives or identities. He knew as much about them now as when they had approached him in Iskahar market six weeks ago. Since then she had by turns captivated and infuriated him as he'd gotten to know her.

Her features were different from those of the other Gray Elfin women who were available. Hers were softer, more delicate, but like the odd touches in her kit that personalized it, and the odd spell that acted just that tad differently, it didn't surprise him. He knew that some of the longest playing members on the server had gotten special bonuses from the Heroes of the Legacy game company for their efforts over the long months of Beta testing the game.

The phone ringing broke into his thoughts and with another sigh, he reached out to pick it up. He wished she would stop blowing hot and cold on him, then. . . .

"Tekkel, it's Davon. We need to talk."

Resolutely he twisted his chair away from the screen and gave his full attention to the call. "Yes, we do, Davon. What's gotten into you this past few weeks? You've stopped pulling your weight and become undependable, man. I need the old Davon back, the one who was a cornerstone of the Clan."

"Since the two elves joined, you've taken me off offensive duties and turned me into nothing more than a healer. I'm sick to death of it, Tekkel!"

"What do you mean? Yes, you're our main healer, but you are still one of our main fighters, you know that. . . ."

"Bullshit! When was the last time you let me fight? I'm sick of playing nursemaid to the Clan."

"You fight every time we go out, Davon."

"If you call that fighting, yes, but I don't!"

"You aren't a pure Fighter Class, you're a Healer, and a Holy Warrior. You're supposed to stand back and Bless the party, Heal them and Turn the Undead as well as fight off anything that comes too close to the other weaker party members. We all have our place in the Clan, our speciality roles. . . ."

"Yeah, well I'm fed up with mine. It's gotten worse since you recruited those two, as I said. We needed more heavy fighters, I told you that at the time! You shouldn't have . . ."

Inwardly Robin groaned and glanced at the clock, checking the time. He wanted to be back before Zenithia just in case she decided to change her mind and move away from him. He zoned out, his mind returning to the elf woman as he half listened to yet another of Davon's rants. They'd been becoming too frequent of late. Jinna had done well to remind him that in his own words, no one was more important than the overall good of the Clan. Davon was beginning to outlive his usefulness.

"Well?" said Davon, raising his voice.

Realizing an answer was expected, he tried to work out what it was. "I realize where you're coming from, Davon," he said, taking a long shot, "but I refuse to re-cruit any more people. The whole ethos behind our Clan is that it should remain small." He tried to keep his tone reasonable. "We want the best, not just anyone."

"Are you even listening to me, Tekkel?"

Robin winced. Over the phone, Davon's voice was even more high pitched than it was in the game.

"Of course I am!" Another glance at the clock—ten minutes left.

"I finished talking about recruiting five minutes ago! I'm talking about me being the Witch's sacrifice."

He sat up with a start. That he hadn't heard him say. "Not possible, Davon. We need you to heal the sacrifice. They face real character death unless they can be kept alive until I finish my quest. They'll die of the plague she gives them without someone with your skills to keep them alive." He searched his mind for something that would persuade the Cleric to drop his request. "You're vital to the quest in that role."

"You can get outside help for that. We know enough people."

"I don't want outside help, neither do the rest of the Clan, and we don't have time to find someone. We're completing the quest now."

"I told you, I'm sick of doing all the healing and babysitting! I want to feel I am really contributing something for a change."

"We're running out of time, Davon. I need you as the main healer—only your divine healing spells can save the sacrifice, I made that plain last night at the Clan meeting. If you didn't want to be involved in this, you should have said so at the time. Now we both have to get back to the game. I'll see you there."

"Zenithia can heal too—if she uses a potion of Blessing, her heals will be the same as mine."

"I need her with me. We'll need to fight off any guards we come across once we step through the Witch's portal into the castle. She's a damage dealing class, unlike you."

"Just because you've got the hots for her. . . ."

"Don't go there, Davon," said Robin coldly. "Just do your job and we'll talk about this again tomorrow."

"I find them intimidating. They're up to no good, you know. They aren't real Cabal material, Tekkel. I've been watching them for weeks now."

"Dammit, Davon, this is just a game! It isn't the real world! Get a grip, man!" He slammed the phone down angrily, not caring if he upset Davon to the point where the other logged out of the game and left them to fend for themselves. If he did, at least they'd all get some peace!

He glanced at the clock. Three minutes left, just enough time to grab a bag of pretzels to munch on while they completed the rest of the quest.

When he put on the headset, then eased his hands into the gaming gloves, he was once more immersed in the world of Sondherst. Designed for Legacy of Heroes, it surrounded him with the sounds and smells of the world, and relayed feedback from his character, and the others he interacted with, allowing him the sensation of touch. Though the avatars they each used to represent their characters might be fairly stock ones, for those with this interface, they and their world really came alive: even their facial expressions and gestures mirrored those of the players, creating a rich virtual world almost indistinguishable from the real one.

He returned to find Zenithia still leaning against him, in the crook of his arm. Around him, the others were still seated, and there was none of the usual banter going on in their Clan chatting area. He was obviously the first one to return.

"*Hi, I'm back*," he said to her, using the private chat channel.

"*Welcome back*," she said, her tone somehow making the ritual words sound more personal.

"*Is Mirri really your brother?*" he blurted out. "*Or is he . . . someone special in your life?*" She'd always avoided this issue, but he really had to know because he was already getting too involved with her. If Mirri was her partner, he had to step back from her now, before it was too late.

The look she gave him was one of gentle amusement. "*So intense,*" she murmured. "*I like that in Elfin kind, and in my men. Fear not, my dark one, Mirri is indeed my twin brother.*"

He felt an easing of tension, and a sudden quickening of his heartbeat. "*Do you play in the same room? Can he hear us talking?*"

"*He's stepped out of the room for now,*" she said, turning to look at him. "*Do you have something to say you'd rather he didn't hear, perhaps?*"

"*No . . . Yes.*"

He was floundering now, and he knew it. It had been so long since he'd dated anyone, not since his disastrous relationship with Anna in fact. It was because of her he'd gotten involved in this game, seeing in it a world that held less pain than the one he woke up to each morning. Until recently, that was.

"*Then you should hurry, dark one. Your Clan mates are beginning to return, and soon so will my twin.*"

He gathered his scattered thoughts, and his courage, and plunged in. "*I'd like you to be my partner,*" he said. "*Not just here, but in RL too.*"

There was a pause before she replied. "*In Real Life? I wonder what that is. There are so many realities,*" she murmured, then seemed to give herself a little shake. "*You want us to meet? What if the reality of me is not what you expect?*"

"*I don't care,*" he said. "*I know what you're like as a person, that's all that matters to me.*"

She put her hands on his arms and looked up into his eyes, her expression thoughtful. "*Are you proposing a betrothal between us? Will you accept my reality, no matter what?*"

He hesitated, wondering if he was ready for such a commitment with a woman he'd not yet met in the flesh. Also some sixth sense was shouting a warning to him. Sensing her beginning to turn away, he ruthlessly suppressed it and in a rush said, *"Yes! I will!"*

"Back," said Jinna in their Clan chat. "Who else is here? That you, Tekkel?"

"Welcome back, Jinna. Yeah, I'm here."

"Thanks. I see Zenithia is back. You two look rather cozy right now. Welcome back to you both. Not disturbing you, am I?" There was an amused tone to her voice.

"Not really. Just discussing something."

"Ah, Clan business," she nodded, putting a knowing finger to the side of her button nose. "I understand. She's very quiet. Lag?"

"Back," said Shannar.

"Me, too," said Meare.

"Welcome back," he murmured, watching Zenithia, wondering why she hadn't replied to him. "I don't think she's lagging. I haven't noticed any delays from her till now."

"Ah, nothin' like a full belly and a drink ta make a dwarf feel good," said Hurga as he got to his feet.

Still watching her, he added his welcome to those of the others.

"You had no right!" he heard her say in a low, almost feral hiss. "Burn it! MT," Zenithia added, moving closer to him. *"Come with me a moment,"* she whispered, then stepped back to draw him toward the waterfall that hid the opening of the cave.

He accompanied her, letting himself be diverted from wondering what was happening between her and her brother.

The roaring of the water drowned out the chatter from

the others as they stood on the edge of the fall, a faint mist of water dampening their faces and hair.

"What's wrong?" he asked, concerned.

"Nothing. Was only my brother returning. When this is over, tell me again that you'll share my world, my night creature," she whispered. *"If you do, then I'll be your partner."*

He raised her hand to his lips. *"With pleasure,"* he murmured as he gently pressed his lips to her cool skin. *"You're the moonlight in my life, Zenithia."*

A smile lit her features. *"And you have the ability still to astonish me, my dark one."*

"We must return to the others," he said, leading her reluctantly back to the group. There would be time for them later, when this quest was over.

"Anyone seen Davon?" asked Shannar suddenly. "Has he logged out?"

"I'm with the Witch," said Davon. "Hurga, you better come heal me. I'm the sacrifice."

Tekkel cursed under his breath. "I should have known better than to trust you! You've left me without a healer for the rest of the quest, dammit!"

"You can use your elf maiden," said Davon. "She has a Battle Healing spell. I know you'd rather have her along than me."

"What the hell do you mean by that?" he demanded.

"That I can see the writing on the wall, Tekkel. I won't let you use me anymore, won't let you relegate me to being just a healer. Hurga, my health is failing. If I die, then so does your precious Tekkel."

"Aye, well you can damned well wait on us now," said Hurga, readying himself to cast. "Ye'll be needin' my buffs now more than ever, Tekkel. Who's goin' with ye?"

"Dammit, Davon, this is only a game you know! It's not real! There's no need to get so worked up about it," said Tekkel angrily. "We each do what's needed for the good of the Clan!"

"It's real to me, Tekkel! I've invested several months of my time to this game!"

"Get a life," snorted Jinna.

Tekkel lowered his voice and turned to the goblin woman. "My apologies, Jinna. I appreciate you volunteering to be the sacrifice, but I'd as soon not risk losing you if anything goes wrong. Maybe this will work out for the best. Zerk me, Hurga," he said as the different glows of Hurga's ability enhancements surrounded him briefly, one by one.

"Ye sure, lad?" Hurga asked. "Berserk Rage is a risky buff for one as you. You can't take the damage."

"I know, but we have less time than we thought to do this without you. Zenithia, can you handle healing as well as using your spells?"

"I can, but I'll run low on magic power."

"Just do what you can, please. We'll have to rely fully on stealth to succeed now. There's only Mirri and I who are close combat fighters."

Mirri stirred and got to his feet. "So what's the problem? You don't need more than us two to succeed."

"You got twenty minutes, lad. Then the buffs'll fade and ye'll have to rely on your own special abilities alone. When I think o' what that Cleric is puttin' at risk just ta satisfy his own ambitions . . . Ye face character death if ye fail!"

Tekkel reached out to squeeze the dwarf's shoulder. "Peace, my friend," he said quietly. "I won't fail. How can I? I have my loyal kin with me."

Hurga looked up at him, understanding, and smiling slowly. "Aye, that ye have."

"Do your best to keep him alive. I'll not let it be said we didn't try."

Hurga nodded.

"I'll go talk to the Witch while you buff the others. Join me when you're done," he said, looking around the ring of grim faces.

"That double-dealing human scumbag . . ." began Meare. "Never have guessed we were harboring a viper like him!"

"Save it for later," said Tekkel over his shoulder, striding off into the cave. "There will be an accounting for this, you hear me, Davon?"

The witch had teleported them into the heart of Iskahar Castle; it was now up to them to reach the Lord's library, where he was closeted with his three advisers, and kill them all. Then Tekkel's Clan Cabal would not only own the castle, but he'd have advanced another level as a Leader and Assassin and get the corresponding extra skills.

Now they stood outside the library door.

"Jinna, what arrows do you have with you?"

"I've one smoke, and a couple of fire and water left," the young archer replied. "Don't want to use the fire ones in a library, though; won't do the books much good."

"Forget them. That's the last thing on my mind."

"Your health is low, Boss," said Shannar. "Too low to carry on."

"You—we—need Hurga with us!" exclaimed Jinna.

He nodded, his thoughts elsewhere as he ran through the battle plan they'd formed, then his possible options now Davon had screwed everything up.

"You still have several options," said Mirri, uncannily following his thoughts. "Success of your quest doesn't depend on keeping the sacrifice alive, does it? Sometimes a sacrifice is just that."

Tekkel looked at the Gray Elf leaning nonchalantly against the wall, paring his nails with the tip of his long-bladed knife. "It's a game, Mirri, and he's still kin, despite what he did." He'd thought exactly the same himself, but was damned if he was going to admit it.

"None of us are very healthy," said Zenithia sitting down where she stood. "I need to regen my magic powers or I won't be able to heal us and fight. I can Gate Hurga here. Tell him to leave the human with a pile of healing potions and join us."

"We still have ten minutes left. We'll rest for two now," he said, sitting down beside her. "We'll take health potions. You should all have enough."

"You're letting one human jeopardize us all!" hissed Mirri, slamming his knife into its scabbard then sliding down the wall into a sitting position with a catlike grace Tekkel envied.

"Peace, Mirri," said Shannar. "You're taking this too seriously. Only Tekkel and Davon face character death, not us. Sure, we'll lose some of our expertise if we die, but not that much."

Lightning fast, Mirri leaned forward and grasped his sister by the hand, letting loose a stream of what was obviously angry invective even thought the language itself was lyrical.

As Tekkel instinctively strained to understand them, Zenithia answered in kind, pulling herself free with an effort that caused her to overbalance into him. As he grabbed hold of her and braced himself, he caught a couple of phrases he did understand.

"Hey, guys, chill out," said Jinna, stepping deftly between them and Mirri. "I'm as angry as the next person, but . . . Tekkel's right, it is only a game."

Mirri sat back, and Zenithia used Tekkel's shoulder to steady herself as she got abruptly to her feet and stood over him. "I am ready now. Time is wasting."

"Hold on," he said, scrambling to his feet. "What were

you two talking about? Who is this one you're looking for?"

"Nothing for you to concern yourself with, Elfling," Zenithia said condescendingly in one of her characteristic mood swings.

Confused, Tekkel still caught the tiny byplay between brother and sister as Mirri leaned forward again, mouth open, and Zenithia raised her hand slightly in a negative gesture.

"The plan, Tekkel."

"We go with the aoe spells, you especially, Zenithia. Area ones will hopefully affect Lord Iskahar *and* his three guards. Your Poison cloud will chip away at their health as we do more damage. My Shadow should slow them all down too, making it more difficult for them to see us."

"Then let's get moving," said Zenithia.

"Meare, use your lock-picking skills on the door," Tekkel ordered.

A dull crash, followed by the sound of something spherical rolling across a wooden floor brought Aziel out of his after-dinner nap.

"What?" he muttered, raising his head and blinking. His sensitive ears picked up the low squeal of terror and the scuttling of bare feet on floorboards from the next room as someone ran after the object.

Now fully awake, Aziel focused all his attention on the probable culprit. "Twilby!" he roared. "What havoc have you caused now?" Then he knew. "My Seeing Crystal!"

Leaping to his feet, wings spread at half height to give him balance, Aziel crossed his sleeping chamber in three bounds.

"Not me, Master! Crystal began glowing then leaped to floor!" the drudge whined as the dragon mage's gallop was brought to an abrupt end when his shoulders crashed into the door frame.

To the sound of ominous creaks and groans, a shower of plaster and a few solid chunks of ceiling and wall debris rained down on Aziel.

He snarled, his long neck snaking through the doorway, tongue extended, nostrils quivering and leaking small tendrils of smoke as he sought his servant. Turning sideways, he reached into the room with one huge clawed hand and grasped hold of the squealing drudge.

"What did you do to my Crystal?" he roared, pulling Twilby into his sleeping chamber and holding him aloft.

"Nothing, Master!"he shrieked, grasping hold of the huge claws in terror. "I did nothing! It jumped off the table!"

"You lie!" Aziel snarled, shaking the drudge violently.

"No! I swear!"

Still snarling and hissing in anger, Aziel lowered his hand to the ground, then backed up a few paces and, tail scything angrily across the scarred wooden floor, muttered the incantation that changed him into human form.

Moments later he had Twilby firmly by the ear and was dragging him into his study. "Fetch my Crystal!" he ordered, tossing the drudge away from him.

Twilby went sprawling across the floor to collide with the side of a tall press. Scrambling to his hands and knees, he reached under it to draw out the object in question.

"Here, Master," he said, crabbing his way back to Aziel's side, the crystal held up in one sooty, ash-covered hand.

Aziel snatched it from him, rubbing it against the sleeve of his robe as he strode over to his desk to examine it.

"It's not glowing now," he said, gesturing toward the large oil lamp on his desk. As it flared to life, he sat down at his desk, remembering to adjust his weight to human normal as he heard the chair start to crack under him.

"Was when I saw it."

Aziel grunted, his hands cupping the crystal as he ran them gently over the surface feeling for any blemishes. He stopped, passing his fingertips lightly over one point, then leaned closer to the light to look at the surface there.

"It's chipped," he snarled, glaring over his shoulder at the drudge hunkered down in the corner farthest from him. It was only the tiniest of slivers that was missing; with any luck, it would still function properly.

Twilby began to gibber incoherently.

"Get out! You're disturbing me," Aziel said, losing interest in him as a faint glow began to form in the center of the crystal globe. "Ah, the Guildsfolk. I see they have found their new leader. . . ."

Tekkel's emergency plan had fallen apart the moment they entered the library and found Iskahar's minions waiting for them behind the bookcases that bisected the room.

"ADD, dammit! Skellie incoming! They've changed the whole encounter!" snarled Shannar, backing into the nearest corner and dropping his bow for the long Ranger's knife as a skeleton warrior suddenly materialized in front of him.

"Jinna, support him," Tekkel snapped, leaping forward with Mirri to engage the strongest of the three guards. "Use Stealth skills, Meare!" He spared a glance at Zenithia, making sure she was standing far enough back from the main attack.

Next he knew, everyone but him had moved and he was staggering, trying to get his balance, because Mirri had hit him.

"You got stunned," the elf said as Tekkel recovered,

then spun around to face the guard again, lashing out at him with a Poisoned Blade attack.

"Thanks," he muttered, closing in on their mutual target. "Zen, Sleep the other two! We can't fight more than one at a time!"

"I'm trying, but he's got too high a resistance. If I attack them, I'll draw their aggro on me."

"Shannar, get your ass out of that corner and Root them!" he yelled, wincing in pain as he was hit yet again from behind. The feedback from his game enhancements was getting a mite too realistic; that blow had actually hurt.

"On my way," Shannar called as the skeleton uttered a thin cry and disintegrated.

Tekkel launched a flurry of blows, complementing those Mirri was doing, then, as the guard keeled over, rounded on the one who had been doing him the most damage. A pair of knives flew past him to embed themselves in the chest of the third guard.

"Meare, same target! Support us."

"Sorry, Boss, thought I was. Very crowded in there."

"Tell me," he muttered as the third guard began to pound on his back. "Shannar, any time now would be good!"

A bolt of energy zapped past him, making their opponent stagger back. Almost before the spell had dissipated, Zen's next one went off, surrounding the guard in a casing of ice for a few seconds. From behind him, he caught the flash of Shannar's Root spell going off.

He nodded, pleased. "Good, Shannar. Nice casting speed there, Zen."

Tearing his attention out of the game, he looked at the monitor screen to check how the rest of the Clan were doing. Shannar was back with Jinna and using his bow, the two of them forming a bodyguard for Zen—and she was casting her spells almost without pause.

Checking her interface on the Party list, he saw her Magic power was dropping rapidly, but that was to be expected. On his and Mirri's right flank, Meare had placed himself against the corner of a bookcase and was throwing volleys of his knives.

A flash of pain suddenly lanced through him and he'd barely time to glance at the clock before it dragged him back into the game.

This time he really did gasp and clutch his side as his avatar was brought to its knees. What the hell was happening? This was not part of the game. . . .

"You left the fight," hissed Mirri as he slashed at the remaining guard. "Foolish! He injured you."

"Checking the time," he said, pushing himself up unsteadily to his feet, trying keep his mind focused on the encounter. "Five minutes left!"

"He leads them too well," snarled Aziel, the hand holding the crystal clenching until long talons began to replace his fingers. "I wanted a fool, not a warrior!"

With a gesture and brief incantation, the scene in the globe began to form on the top of his desk.

"Time for more direct action. . . ."

"ADD, three incoming from behind us!" Meare yelled out. "Undead Knights!"

As one, Tekkel and Mirri sidestepped, forcing their opponent around so they could see the new assailants.

"Zen, all of you, move! Fire protection buffs!" he yelled.

"Shit! This is all wrong! What the hell's happening?" demanded Meare, reaching for his sword.

"Deal with it," snapped Tekkel, powering up another

Poison attack as Mirri let off one of his Wounding ones. "Time for that later."

Zenithia, flanked by Jinna and Shannar, and casting as she ran, headed past them to take up a position farther into the room.

"Undead Knights? And too many, Zen," Tekkel heard Mirri say quietly as Zenithia finished buffing him and began on her brother.

"I know," Zen snapped back tartly. "Just do your job . . . brother."

To Tekkel, it sounded like Miri's low voice cracked slightly, taking on a higher pitch. Then, uttering a sound like a low snarl, Mirri flicked a small bolt of energy out to zap her: the elf woman stopped dead, frozen to the spot.

"Stop fighting each other!" Tekkel ordered. "Time's running out!"

As Zenithia began to move again, a pulsating circle of fire surrounded the lead Knight. Muttering the incantation to drain health from him, Tekkel instinctively winced, then braced himself as the fire flared upward before suddenly exploding outward in circles toward them. It hurt, by all the gods of Sondherst, it *really* hurt, despite Zen's buffs! Even as he gasped, a sudden icy wave swept through him, cooling then banishing the pain so he could think again. Around him he heard the others' exclamations of pain and disbelief.

"Fight! I will keep you all safe!" Zenithia called.

Still shaking, Tekkel shifted his grip on his knives. He needed to warn Zen of something, but his thoughts were still scattered. The first Knight was nearly upon them and the other two were beginning to cast their fire spells. As he readied himself, he heard Zen and Mirri exchanging a few terse words in their own language.

Calling on his weapons' special abilities, he met the Knight with raised blades as two of Meare's water arrows, one swiftly followed by the other, arced over him to hit the casters.

We need them rooted and slept now, he thought.

As he darted inside the Knight's defense, blocking with one knife and slashing with the other, he saw their fire spell gutter and die. Then Zen's Sleep and Shannar's Root hit them.

Seconds later Mirri was beside him, drawing the Knight's attack.

He backed off, checking the party health—all were low, too low, and Zen was almost out of Magic. "Potions everyone!" he yelled, leaping back in to attack again. This had to be finished fast.

"I'm out," yelled Shannar.

"Me, too," said Jinna, the tremor in her voice audible. "This is getting scary, Tekkel. I don't like it."

An ear-piercing shriek sounded from behind him. He didn't need to look to know it was Zenithia. "Iskahar!" He'd meant to warn her to watch out for the Castle Lord!

"It's Aziel!" she screamed.

Aziel? Who the hell was Aziel? He swung round, heart pounding, to see Zenithia held, a knife to her throat, by Lord Iskahar.

Beside him, Mirri let out a string of what he assumed were oaths, then stopped and in a voice altered beyond recognition, uttered one word.

"What the hell—" began Meare, taking cover behind the nearest bookcase.

"Portal, Meare," Tekkel snapped, sizing up the situation, ignoring the thought that this could not be happening. "Hurga, I need you here now," he said quietly, risking a glance back at the Knight. He stood motionless, as if frozen to the spot.

"On my way." Hurga said.

"You can't," he heard Davon say. "I'll die."

"Then come," said Hurga.

"Let my sister go, Aziel," Mirri ordered, stepping forward. "You have no business here."

"I want him," said Aziel, raising a long thin hand and pointing at Tekkel. "Give me the human and your sister is free."

"No!" hissed Zenithia, struggling in his grasp. "He cannot be trusted—" Her words were cut off abruptly as the Lord tightened the arm across her throat.

Mirri's out-thrust arm pushed him back as he stepped forward. "No," said the elf unequivocally. "He's ours."

"Dammit, Mirri," he began.

"Wait," hissed Mirri, holding him back again. "You're not our Leader yet! I brought friends!"

There wasn't time to be confused as a motley crew of beings, including Hurga and Davon, suddenly materialized around them.

Aziel began to laugh, the sound deep and echoing as if it came from the very bowels of the earth.

Tekkel watched in horror as the features of the avatar altered, the hair turning black as midnight, the skin darkening to a tanned hue, the eyes . . . Oh gods, those eyes! He groaned, shutting his own, but the huge red orbs with their vertical yellow slits continued to grow larger and larger in his mind's eye. Then his courage reasserted itself and he opened his own again, seeing this time, not just a man, but underlying it the form of something else, something that had no right existing in the world of Legacy of Heroes.

"This isn't real, it can't be," he heard himself mutter as he stared at the red dragon mage. Around him, the eight newcomers—four elves, three dwarves, and a being he took to be a half orc—moved forward to surround him and Mirri. Grim faced, with battered and stained armor, they were very different from the avatars he and the others used.

"You vermin really think you can withstand me?" laughed Aziel, moving his grip till his large hand encircled Zenithia's neck and his knife was in his other hand. "Gate in as many as you wish, elf, they'll meet the same fate as last time!"

"Let the Elf Maiden go!" Davon demanded in ringing tones as, sword and shield held ready, he stepped forward. "Pick your fight with equals, not women, you coward!"

"No, Davon," Tekkel said as all eyes focused on the Cleric. "This isn't the time for melodrama!"

Davon ignored him, stepping closer to Aziel and Zenithia as Mirri let his arm drop to pull his second blade.

Aziel cocked his head to one side and regarded him with obvious amusement. "You want to die now, Manling?"

Aziel's attention now off him, Tekkel moved slowly behind Mirri and his friends, triggered his Shadow spell, then using the last of his Haste and Speed potions, pulled out his bow. Then he stepped forward again, his eyes never leaving Davon and Aziel, watching and waiting for the opportunity he knew must come. This time his mind was made up that he would sacrifice the Cleric for Zen.

"Fight me, man to man, or do you prefer to hide behind a woman," Davon taunted.

"You bore me, Manling," said Aziel, flicking his knife toward the Cleric and raising his eyes to the rest of them.

As the knife tumbled end over tip, almost in slow motion, toward Davon, Tekkel began his run toward Aziel. Triggering Powered multishots, he let off two volleys of arrows before dropping the bow and reaching for his knives again.

"Be ready!" he whispered, toggling the private channel between him and Zenithia as he leaped high and spun around in a Poison Blade attack, hitting first the Dragon Lord, then Zenithia with the pommel of his other blade as he somersaulted over the mage's head. Coming down behind him, he twisted around, landing in a crouch. Pushing himself to his feet, he triggered his Backstab ability, checking that Zenithia had collapsed in Aziel's grip before once more launching himself at the mage's back.

Aziel dropped the dead weight that his captive had become. Ignoring the four arrows sticking out of his limbs, he began a half turn to meet him, calling out an incantation to reanimate the Death Knights again.

The chime signifying a Party death sounded loud in Tekkel's ears as he jumped over Zen, and began lashing out at Aziel, forcing the other to take a couple of steps back.

With a roar of anger, the mage began to cast, but not before Tekkel was surrounded by Hurga's healing light—and the glow from other buffs as the newcomer mages worked to protect him.

"Davon?" he heard Jinna call. "Davon! You okay?"

Lightning streaked from Aziel's hands toward him, only to rebound and hit the mage.

"Forget him, Jinna!" Shannar was saying. "Get the Knights!"

He pressed forward again, this time doing more damage to Aziel who began to back off, chanting.

Arrows flew past him, hitting the mage, breaking his concentration as Mirri and his friends came rushing past him.

Mirri stopped briefly beside him. "Dammit, that hurt, Tekkel! Take my sister and back off. Leave this to us. You don't yet know Aziel as we do."

"What?" Tekkel demanded, staring at him.

The elf's face split in a brief grin. "Get my sister. It was me you hit, in her avatar, not her. She's waiting." Then he was gone, racing after his companions.

"Well, my Dark One," said a voice he knew well at his elbow. "Are you ready?"

"Ready?" he echoed. "Ready for what? This is a game, it can't be real." A thousand and one questions were racing around inside his head right now.

"To come with me," she said, stepping closer. Snapping her fingers, her staff disappeared and a portal began to open, one unlike any he'd ever seen before. Reality bent, making the room seem to melt slightly around the edges of the glowing slit that formed in front of them. Wind sighed and moaned through it as flares of colored lightning sparked from one side to the other.

"We need to get you away from Aziel, to our realm," she said, reaching out to encircle his waist with her arms. "I thank you for your gallant attempt to save me, even though it was Mirri playing my poor Battle Mage at the time, not me."

"Mirri?" Suddenly her mood swings made sense. "You two, you kept switching avatars on me," he said accusingly, even as he put one arm round her. Another thought struck him and he felt the blood rise to his face.

She laughed gently, pressing herself close against him until he could smell the scent of her hair and feel the ample curves he knew were there despite her slim avatar.

"Tell me again you want to share my world, Tekkel," she whispered.

"My Clan," he said, pushing her back. "This battle . . . you. None of it's real."

"You still here?" he heard Mirri shout. "Burn it, Zen, take our new Leader home then we can *all* leave!"

"You heard my brother. We all go. Will you come

now?" she asked again, gently pulling him toward the portal.

He laughed uncertainly. There was too much that couldn't be explained about this quest, but there had to be a rational one. "Sure, I'll go along with your role-playing, Zen. Just don't expect me to believe in it too much."

"Tekkel, Davon's gone," said Jinna, stopping beside them. "I can't raise him at all. And his avatar . . . It's all mangled, and the game doesn't do that to us or the mobs we kill!"

"Davon?" he called out, looking round for the Cleric's corpse. He saw it lying a few feet from them, just as Jinna had described.

"He's dead," said Mirri, running up to where they stood on the edges of the portal. "And so will we be if we don't leave now!" He gave them both a hefty shove.

Tekkel felt himself falling and grabbed hold of Zenithia as everything suddenly went dark and an icy coldness spread through him.

"What the hell's happening?" he tried to say, but his words were torn from him and shredded by the bitter wind that swirled them violently about.

He felt her hand touch his neck, pull his head down to hers, then her breath warm against his ear.

"Is this real enough for you?" she asked before her lips sought his in a kiss as deep and intimate as he'd been wishing for.

Forgotten was the bitter cold of the portal, as was any thought of what was real. The kiss seemed to last forever until suddenly, with a jolt, he felt solid ground under his feet again.

He heard someone cough, then say in a voice that sounded suspiciously like it was trying not to laugh, "Welcome to Eldaglast, Clan Leader Tekkel, and welcome back, Zenithia."

Blinking like an owl, Tekkel lifted his head and squinted over the top of Zen's, seeing an elf bowing at them, realizing with acute embarrassment that he and Zen were still locked in an embrace—and that he didn't care. He looked around the large sunlit room at the small gathering of assorted elves, dwarves, and other races he couldn't readily identify as the rest of his gaming clan, then Mirri and his companions, began to wink into existence.

"This is your new home," said Zenithia, stepping back a little and talking him by the hand. "Welcome to Eldaglast's Guild of Acquirers and Facilitators."

"Better known as the Assassins and Thieves Guild," said Mirri, walking smartly over to the speaker. "Merrik, Aziel was there. We caused him some grief, and likely he'll be smarting for a while, but he'll be back. Send up the healers, then set guards for now. Oh and some food would be good—we're all starving."

Still in a daze of disbelief, he heard a small shriek then a diminutive pixie ran up to him, grabbing at his armored leg and shaking it—just as Jinna used to do.

"Tekkel! Oh my Godfathers! You're a Gray Elf! A real Gray Elf!" said Jinna. "And I'm . . ."

"A pixie," said Mirri, stripping off his mailed gloves and handing them to one of the nonfighters. "The goblins of your game don't exist here."

Startled, he looked down at himself, saw the pale gray-blue skin of his hand where it rested in Zenithia's one of the same color. He looked up, seeing not the slim almost ethereal female avatar he was used to, but an elfin woman of flesh and blood, and generous curves under the skimpy clothes she wore.

"Well am I real enough for you now?" she asked, arching a pale eyebrow at him as she pulled him to her side with a proprietary gesture. "I promise I won't let my twin change places with me again."

"He'd better not," said Tekkel, finding his voice at last as he slipped his arm around her waist.

Tanya Huff

The Finest in Fantasy

SING THE FOUR QUARTERS   0-88677-628-7
FIFTH QUARTER   0-88677-651-1
NO QUARTER   0-88677-698-8
THE QUARTERED SEA   0-88677-839-5

The Keeper's Chronicles
SUMMON THE KEEPER   0-88677-784-4
THE SECOND SUMMONING   0-88677-975-8
LONG HOT SUMMONING   0-7564-0136-4

Omnibus Editions:
WIZARD OF THE GROVE   0-88677-819-0
(Child of the Grove & The Last Wizard)
OF DARKNESS, LIGHT & FIRE   0-7564-0038-4
(Gate of Darkness, Circle of Light & The Fire's Stone)

To Order Call: 1-800-788-6262

DAW 21

Kristen Britain

GREEN RIDER

As Karigan G'ladheon, on the run from school, makes her way through the deep forest, a galloping horse plunges out of the brush, its rider impaled by two black arrows. With his dying breath, he tells her he is a Green Rider, one of the king's special messengers. Giving her his green coat with its symbolic brooch of office, he makes Karigan swear to deliver the message he was carrying. Pursued by unknown assassins, following a path only the horse seems to know, Karigan finds herself thrust into in a world of danger and complex magic....   0-88677-858-1

FIRST RIDER'S CALL

With evil forces once again at large in the kingdom and with the messenger service depleted and weakened, can Karigan reach through the walls of time to get help from the First Rider, a woman dead for a millennium?   0-7564-0209-3

To Order Call: 1-800-788-6262

TAD
WILLIAMS

TAILCHASER'S SONG

"Williams' fantasy, in the tradion of WATERSHIP DOWN, captures the nuances and delights of feline behavior in a story that should appeal to both fantasy and cat lovers. Readers will lose their hearts to Tailchaser and his companions."
—*Library Journal*

"TAILCHASER'S SONG is more than just an absorbing adventure, more than just a fanciful tale of cat lore. It is a story of self-discovery…Fritti faces challenges—responsibility, loyalty, and loss—that are universal. His is the story of growing up, of accepting change, of coming of age."
—*Seventeen*

"A wonderfully exciting quest fantasy. Fantasy fans are sure to be enthralled by this remarkable book." —*Booklist*

0-88677-953-7

To Order Call: 1-800-788-6262